BLOOD SACRAMENTS

Edited by Todd Gregory

Rough Trade

Blood Sacraments

Visit us at www.boldstrokesbooks.com

BLOOD
SACRAMENTS

Edited by

Todd Gregory

A Division of Bold Strokes Books

2010

BLOOD SACRAMENTS

ISBN 10: 1-60282-1-909
ISBN 13: 978-1-60282-1-903

THIS TRADE PAPERBACK ORIGINAL IS PUBLISHED BY
BOLD STROKES BOOKS, INC.
P.O. BOX 249
VALLEY FALLS, NY 12185

FIRST EDITION: NOVEMBER 2010

CREDITS
EDITOR: TODD GREGORY
PRODUCTION DESIGN: STACIA SEAMAN
COVER DESIGN BY SHERI (GRAPHICARTIST2020@HOTMAIL.COM)

CONTENTS

BLACK SAMBUCA
JEFF MANN

I.

I sense him before I see him. He radiates power the way a glacier exudes cold or a woodstove heat. There, that broad-shouldered silhouette, that gleam of pale hair and skin beneath a leafy canopy of vines, on the edge of Piazza Viminale. Ristorante Strega, says the sign. He's sitting back in the quiet shadow of a remote corner—as my kind tend to—watching happy humans as they feast *al fresco* on aromatic Roman food and wine in the warm summer night. When a shapely waitress bustles over to seat me, all I have to do is murmur his name and she escorts me to his table. A man well known in Rome, it appears.

He rises, smiling down at me, and shakes my hand. Though, like me, he appears to be in his mid-thirties, I know he's much, much older than I. He's several inches taller too, easily six and a half feet, and more mightily built. "*Buona sera*, Derek Maclaine," he says. His grip is strong, very strong. It makes me want to wince. Already he's reminding me of my position. He is the lord here, and I the supplicant. Not only is he older and stronger, but this is his territory. I am a mere tourist.

My centuries in the American South have made my manners immaculate, despite the displeasure I'm feeling at being the less powerful in our exchange. I meet his blue-fire gaze, then drop my eyes. "I much appreciate this audience, Mr. Colonna," I say.

"Call me Marcus," he says, still gripping my hand, then turns to the hovering waitress and orders for us both. "My guest will have Romana Black, and I my usual." Off she goes to the bright lights of the bar, leaving a hint of jasmine in her wake.

"She wears that scent for me." Marcus turns to me, face shifting from an expression both stern and impassive into a barely perceptible smile and then back again. "Welcome to Rome, Derek Maclaine," he murmurs, giving my hand another painful squeeze before releasing me and taking his seat. "Sit," he says, and I do. The man was once a Roman senator. He's accustomed to swift obedience. And in order for me to get what I want, I suppose I too must obey him.

As handsome as he is, my obedience might be more pleasure than pain. "Thank you, Marcus," I say, studying the high forehead, sharp cheekbones, and shoulder-length ash-blond hair. His lips are red and full, his chin cleft, with the shadow of a goatee about his mouth. "It's mighty fine to be in your great city at last."

"Isn't she luscious?" Marcus says, voice smooth as rose petal yet embroidered with a growl. "*Roma*, yes. But our waitress too. *Bella, bella.* Her breasts and hips...She is, as you Americans say, my type. Her name is Nigella. One night I will have her. But why rush?"

I smile. "I hadn't noticed, sir, but yes, she is beautiful." I can't recall when I last called another man "sir." Before I was changed, back in 1730? No, there was that Russian lord in St. Petersburg...and that Greek in Santorini, and, of course, the Scottish warrior who turned me.

"Ah, yes. You are a sodomite. Which will make your payment easier on us both, I suppose. I myself enjoy both the sexes, as lovers, slaves, and prey. What is your type, Derek Maclaine? And do you have a lover?"

"Yes, sir, I do. A human one, back in West Virginia. His name is Matt. He's my type. One of my types. Shorter than I, burly, hairy, with a bushy beard. A country boy. From the mountains, like me. What we in America call a butch bottom. We've been together for almost a decade."

"What is his age?" Marcus says. The waitress arrives, placing a slender glass of yellow liquid before Marcus, a similar glass filled with black liquid before me. "*Grazie*, Nigella," Marcus says, voice soft. She smiles and departs.

"Matt is forty-one, sir."

"He is your boy, yes?" A lock of yellow hair falls over Marcus's brow; he brushes it back, takes a sip, rests his elbow on the table, takes his stubbly chin in his hand and rubs it.

"Yes, sir, though not my slave. He's too—as we say in the mountains—too hard-headed and ornery for that." I want to say, *You are almost as beautiful as he*, but I suspect, powerful as Marcus is, he can read my thoughts and can already feel my desire and the way that submitting to him both shames and arouses me.

"And is he graying yet?" Marcus takes another sip. I can smell the heavy scents of sugar and lemon.

"Yes, sir. His temples are streaked with silver. His beard is as well, and the hair on his breast. He is so handsome, so ripe, a man in the fullness of his years, but…"

Marcus shakes his head. "Yes," he sighs. "*Trista*. I did that for centuries. Loved mortals. Now…not so often. Will you turn him?"

"No, sir. I don't think so. I don't know."

"Well, your other types?"

"Ah, Jesus lookalikes!" I laugh. "I like to ravish Christs. Slender boys with shaggy dark hair and beards. They make fine sacrifices. Occasionally, as understanding as Matt is of my feeding needs, they make him jealous. I do tend to dote on men such as they. Sometimes, when Matt's away on business, I kidnap one for my amusement and keep him for a few days."

"And have you had one of our Roman Christs yet?" His blue eyes flicker over me. Hunger is there in his glance, deep and fierce.

"No, sir, not yet. As you recall from our correspondence, this is my first visit to Rome. I only arrived last night, and I was told not to feed until…"

Marcus's foot nudges my boot beneath the table. "Very good. Yes. It is well that you obey. I can tell from the gray in your hair that you need to feed. Soon, I promise. Meanwhile, please sample your liqueur. That is black *liquore di Sambuca*, which, according to the bottle, 'captures the spirit and allure of the Roman night,' a sweet, dark night such as this one in which we meet, Scotsman." Another faint smile flickers around his lips. With the ball of his thumb, he rubs the tip of his right incisor: quick flash, sharp, white, anticipatory. "And tell me if tall blond dominant Roman aristocrats meet your fancy."

Undead for centuries, yet I can still blush. No reason to lie. Old and experienced as he is, he could tell if I did. "Not normally, sir. I tend toward dark-haired men. But there are exceptions. You are indeed not what I expected of a Roman." I take a sip—more sugar, the odor of anise.

"Yes, most of us are much darker than I. During my human days, my friends teased me for my fairness. They said that a warrior from

Germania had infiltrated my mother's bed. During my days with the army, my men called me *Aquila Aurea*, the golden eagle. Many of them loved me. My lovers called me *Splendidus*. From what I can sense, you might agree with them." The faint smile goes broad only for a second before returning to that intense gaze, that impassive expression. "You will be my lover tonight, Derek? My boy? You will pay the price we agreed upon? In return I will share my city with you whenever you please."

My face is on fire. I can only drop my eyes, sip my liqueur, and nod. The Sambuca is as rich, sweet, and thick as old blood, strong blood.

"Do you like it? The liqueur?"

"Yes, sir, I do. In future, when I drink it, I will certainly think of you. And you, sir? What is your type?" I lift my glass, stare into its blackness, then put it down. *Stop fiddling, Derek. Stop being such a bashful flirt.*

"Ah, in men? Many, many kinds. Men both sleek like me and rough like you. Both young men and mature men. Both humans and vampires. Tonight, I want a man who is wild and proud and in need of discipline. I want a man accustomed to being in control to submit to me, to feed my strength. Have you ever known a man like that?" Marcus chuckles. "One whose manhood might be tempered and refined by submission?"

"Yes, sir." It's all I can do not to stammer. "I love those men too. It's just that it's been so long since I myself—"

"Relax, boy. We shall have a fine night on the Palatine Hill, there among the ruins of the Caesars. I will care for you well. I will not harm you…much. And you will be the stronger for it. I must admit, you are surprisingly handsome and well-mannered for a mountain barbarian."

I look up and laugh. His blue eyes probe me. I can feel his thoughts rummaging through my head, turning over the mental stones of memory and motivation.

"Oh yes, a barbarian," says Marcus. "You Scotsman were certainly trouble. Hadrian had to build that long wall against Caledonia."

"Yes, sir. And you all never conquered us." As subdued as my customary pride must be this night, I can't help but remind him. "We Scots were about the only folks whose asses you couldn't whip."

Anger flashes in his eyes for a split second. Then he nods, another smile flickering over his stony features. "Not worth the trouble. Those thistle-sharp mountains? Those scruffy clans in their dirty tartans? Though you do present yourself well tonight." He leans forward, his glance roaming over my black jeans, black T-shirt, black cowboy boots, and the thorny tattoos on my left forearm. "You are a fine specimen of a…redneck? That is the expression?"

"My boots give it away, I guess. And my ink?" I can't help but grin. I must indeed look like a well-dressed hillbilly compared to him. An observer would find us an odd combination. On top of the tattoos and the informal attire, my hair is long and black, pulled back in a ponytail, and my goatee's like a biker's, long and bushy enough to braid. I most likely resemble a Hell's Angel trying to look nice but not quite pulling it off. Marcus, on the other hand, is the picture of a wealthy, pampered European, with his white silk shirt, beige linen pants, expensive watch, golden neck chain, and designer leather dress shoes. Scottish highlander in my human years, Appalachian for most of my vampire existence, I can't hide my rough edges even when I try. Especially from a gaze as steady and searching as his.

"And your beard betrays you, *paganus*, *rusticus*. You look like a Confederate general. You remind me of Enkidu. In need of taming, I think."

"Enkidu? In the Sumerian *Epic of Gilgamesh*, right? The hairy wild man who came down from the mountains to be the comrade and lover of the great hero Gilgamesh."

"You are better educated than I expected. That is correct. Let me see your bare chest, please, my mountain redneck, my Appalachian Enkidu."

My cock hardens beneath the table. I'd forgotten how exciting it is to be told what to do by a man much stronger than I.

"Here?" I say, half turning toward the tables of diners.

"I own Rome. I do what I please. Tonight you will do what I please. Just a glimpse."

Blushing, I pull my T-shirt up to my neck, baring my belly and chest.

Marcus takes a long, low breath, staring at my exposed torso. "Just as I imagined. Hairy as a savage. As an animal in need of a rider. Finish your drink, boy, and I will give you a tour of the Palatine. I will break you. I will make your chill skin sweat."

II.

The ruins are fluted gray in the moonlight. Under flat-topped cypresses, upon the crest of the Palatine Hill, we explore the remains of imperial palaces long abandoned, strong with the scent of pines and, this late at night, closed to tourists. Rubble now, once the homes of Augustus, Tiberius, Septimus Severus, Domitian. The fragments of columns, arcades, fountains, even a small stadium. Below us, modern Rome steams in the night, the lights of traffic pouring along its streets like phosphorescent lemmings.

"Did you know any of them? The Caesars?" I stroke a clump of oleander bloom. It is silent here, save for the distant noises of traffic and the cheeping of summer insects in the bushes and trees about us. Moonbeams slant over Marcus's white face as he moves closer to me.

"A few. Caligula raped me. He was assassinated long before I could take my revenge. I was turned in the reign of Claudius." Marcus looks down at the ruined rocks of the Forum, illuminated by searchlights for the benefit of tourists, and toward the monumental buildings atop the Capitoline Hill. "Take off your shirt."

I pull the garment over my head. Marcus takes it, laying it carefully on a jagged chunk of marble he first brushes off with the side of his hand. He turns to me now, resting his hands on my shoulders. "So you have come to Rome to pay your respects?"

I gaze up at him, trying not to tremble. "Yes, sir."

"To the Caesars or to me?"

"Both." It is hard to meet his gaze, yet impossible to look away. My victims must feel the same when I entrance them. "In all my centuries, I have never come to Rome. It is more beautiful than I ever imagined. I would like your permission to linger here, and to return when I please."

"And you are ready to pay the price? For a nest in my realm? For the freedom to feed here? This is, I sense, a price you are unaccustomed to."

"I am unaccustomed, but I am ready," I say. "Sir."

Marcus nods. Moonlight gleams off his teeth, a true smile, wide with triumph. His fingers find my chest, stroking the thick fur there. I wrap my arms around his waist, bow my head, and lean against him. He tugs at my nipples, then the rims of hair around them, then the tangled bush of my beard.

"Strip," murmurs Marcus. He gives me a gentle shove backward. "And unbind your hair."

Boots first, then jeans, then the leather cord in my ponytail, discarded one by one in dry grass. Entirely naked, vulnerable, I stand before him, in warm Roman breezes, in the scent of wildflowers, in moonlight. I stare down at my exposed body, at my inked and muscled arms, at my hairy belly and chest, my hairy legs, trying to see myself as he sees me. It has been many, many years since I have submitted to another vampire, or felt undead lust raking me with such sharp zeal. Marcus's eyes are gleaming, the blue gone a fiery red. "Shaggy brute," he whispers, tousling the long hair framing my face, rifling my belly fur, patting the face of the Horned God inked into my left arm, the barbed-wire band inked into my right. "Tattooed like your feral ancestors, those mad Celts. The antlered god of the Gauls, I see. God of beasts and mountains, yes? A hirsute, hard-cocked Dionysus. Apropos. My deity is Mithras. You will show him homage later."

From his back pocket, Marcus fetches something gleaming. "A surprise," he says, holding it before me. I can feel it already, the shining power that can make my head swim and my muscles grow feeble. Silver. He's brandishing a pair of leather-lined silver handcuffs. Open and ready to use.

I step back, unsure. "Sir? You never mentioned this. I never agreed—"

Marcus outflanks me in a split second, faster than I can further react. Again the difference in our powers gives me some sense of how outmatched my human victims must feel. He pulls my wrists behind me before I know he's there. But rather than subdue me further, rather than locking the cuffs, he simply stops. I stand there, trembling. A blunt hardness that must be his erection bumps my back. It seems that subduing me is exciting him as much as being subdued is exciting me.

"Trust me, barbarian. I will make this sweet. I will make you enjoy this." Marcus sniffs me and noisily licks his lips. "Ah, you are sweating now. You stink. You smell like mud and grass and woodland. You smell like the Gallic prisoners I used to take in Mamertine Prison, only yards from here. Your hair"—he takes a strand in his teeth and pulls—"and your unruly beard remind me of them." He nips the skin over my spine.

I can feel his chin's scratchy stubble. "Dirty and wild…forest scum, so proud at first before they were chained and raped and broken. Warriors become slaves…they sobbed and shook beneath me. They lay in the prison's straw and dung and wrapped their mighty arms about my feet and begged me for release. Will you sob for me?"

"No," I say, teeth gritted. "I'm no slave."

"But you will submit?"

"Yes."

"You might sob yet. We shall see." The cuff snaps over my right wrist, painfully tight. The leather saves me from that terrible burn, but the poisonous silver's near enough to cause my knees to buckle. I would drop to the ground, but Marcus wraps an arm around my neck and heaves me upright. His knuckles graze my ass cheeks before the cuffs lock just as tightly about my other wrist. He releases me; groaning despite myself, hands firmly secured behind me, I sink to my knees and fall on my side in the grass. The silver weakness shudders through me, nauseating.

Marcus nudges my chin with his elegant shoe. Then he steps back, toes off each shoe, and strips, very slowly, laying each article of clothing in the grass with such care you'd think the fabric was fragile as glass. I roll with discomfort onto my cuffed hands to watch as his muscular body, as hard and perfectly defined as a gymnast's, is revealed. Entirely naked, he stands over me, astride my waist. His body is pale, smooth, gleaming like the face of the moon, a study in Carrara marble, with a dusting of gold. "I was quite the athlete when I died," he says, running hands over his curved pectorals, big brown nipples, and ridged stomach before taking his fur-clouded cock in hand. It lengthens rapidly in his grasp, escaping its skin-sheath. It is intimidatingly huge. The head glistens, slick and knobby, moonlit pommel of a sword. I am, I suspect, soon going to be hurting bad.

By now I'm hard as well. "I can see your appreciation, boy." Laughing, Marcus presses a bare foot against my cock. "Stiff with shame, I see. I know men like you. I know them and I love them. There is a secret slave, very frightened yet very hungry, inside that coarse Scots warrior, is there not? Something tender, submissive, shy? A boy eager to suffer, to endure, to be enveloped and devoured and rocked like a child?"

I shake my head, but my denial has no power. There's my body's unarguably honest answer, beneath Marcus's foot, hard between my thighs. He presses down, and I gasp.

"Not much fight in you with those cuffs, highlander?" He presses harder.

"No, sir. Silver saps my strength almost entirely. How did you—?"

"Handle silver without consequence? After my first thousand years it lost its power over me. Now it barely makes me tingle." He lifts his foot from my crotch only to press his sole against my mouth. "Lick, boy. Let Caledonia at last give Rome her due."

I run my tongue over his foot. Hard as embossed steel. Smooth and taut as the skin of ripe fruit. He nudges me onto my side. I moan as he pushes his big toe into my mouth.

"Suck, barbarian."

I do. I suck, lick, nibble. More toes join the first, my mouth crammed full. He tastes like metal and wind. I stretch my jaw, taking him in further.

Abruptly he pulls his foot from my face and steps back.

"Get up here, wild one, my Enkidu. It's time to show your fealty."

With effort I rise to my knees, and, kneeling, shuffle over to him. I've hardly opened my mouth before his bulky cock's thrust inside me to the hilt, balls pressed into my beard. His hands grip my long hair, holding my head still while he rides my face. My throat expands, contracts. I choke and slobber. My gorge rises; I force it back. He pounds my mouth steadily, his pre-cum streaking my tongue with salt. Drool drips off my chin. I try to bring subtle techniques into play, try to lick the head, run my tongue up and down the shaft, but to no avail. Marcus wants nothing but a hole, a deep one. He batters the back of my throat the way Hebridean oceans batter sea cliffs, unceasing, inexhaustible.

Just when I think the savage throat-beating I'm getting will soon ensure me a white mouthful of foam, Marcus lifts me by the arms, spins me, and throws me onto my belly in the grass. He's on top of me a split second after I hit the ground, one hand on the back of my neck, shoving my face against the earth, another wrapped around my chest. "Ah, yes. This is what you came to Rome for, is it not?" he whispers in my ear, his cock bumping my buttocks. "I enter you, you enter my kingdom? Yes? Yes?"

"Yes," I groan. Heat-dead grasses scrape my face; Roman earth dusts my lips. I grit my teeth, readying myself for the pain.

But Marcus is taking his time. His lips brush my ear. "How long, barbarian? How long since you were taken this way?" Beneath me, his fingers trap a nipple. His nails begin to dig.

"Sir, my lover Matt sometimes…we switch. We even…we have silver cuffs at home."

"Ah, so you bottom occasionally? Then this will not be as grand a trauma as I'd imagined? A pity. How long since another vampire took you then?"

"Half a century, sir. In Santorini."

"Yes? The blood is strong there. Older even than mine." Marcus's hand leaves my neck, positioning his cock against my tightness. "You want this, do you not?"

Again, I know better than to lie. "Yes, sir. I don't want to want it, but I do."

"Beg me, my hirsute captive," Marcus sighs. "Beg me to take you."

I hesitate only for a second. That long-submerged part of me is rising, eager. "Please, sir. Please, Marcus. Take me…" I arch my ass, rub it against him, brush his hard belly with my bound hands. "I can't fight you. I'm too weak. I'm your captive, sir. Do what you please."

"And so I shall." He slips down my body. His fingers play over my ass, tugging on the cheek and cleft hair, and then his hands clutch my hips and his teeth sink into my right buttock.

"Huhhhh," I gasp into the grass. His lips clamp down, sealing the sudden wound, sucking hard. I can feel my strength receding further, the silver-weakness mingling now with blood loss.

The suction stops. Liquid smeared between my ass cheeks. Lubrication of my own blood. I grunt as his finger enters me. I buck back onto his hand. Another finger slides inside. "Open. Open for Rome," Marcus whispers. His muscled weight, like a great sculpture, settles atop me, his cockhead pressing against me, his arm wrapped around my torso.

"Be easy, highlander. I will care for you well."

I nod, trying to will myself open. His cockhead replaces his fingers, easing inside. Damn, so thick. Pain spasms through me, forcing out a whimper.

"Easy, boy." To my surprise, Marcus does not simply shove it in and rape me, as the earlier mouth-pounding suggested that he might. Instead, to my relief, he moves the head in and out in short strokes. He pulls out, adds more bloody lube, pushes the head in again. More shallow strokes, till the pain at last recedes and he can sense my readiness. Then, very slowly, with surprising gentleness, he slides entirely inside, filling me completely. More waves of pain; I give a loud, deep moan. Marcus's hand grips my jaw, palm pressed tightly over my mouth.

"Quiet now, boy. There, there. Yes." Cocking his hips, he moves slowly in and out, in and out. I moan inside his muffling grip. "Ruffian. Lovely, smelly, hairy Scot. I will use you now, mountain man, will I not? Beg me to use you. Do you not want to be used? Used hard?"

He pulls out, resting his cockhead against my entrance. The sudden emptiness is an ache.

"Use me, sir. Hard, please, sir. I can take it." Muttering into his hand, I flex my ass cheeks, grinding back against him.

"So reluctant to be ridden, now so eager to be used? If you insist." Marcus thrusts, quick and hard, shoving his entire length up inside me. I wince, gasping against the tight gag of his hand. A steady pounding begins. Cuffed, silver-weak, I lie there entirely helpless, impaled by bliss, deep grunts—"Huhh, huhhhh, huhhhh, huhh!"—forced out of me by the rhythmic hammering of his hips. Marcus's growl is as steady as my grunts are staccato.

He's off me before I know it. Again I'm aching and empty. Not for long, I sense. Seizing my bushy goatee, Marcus drags me across the grass to a broken column lying on the ground. He heaves me across it, bends me over. My face and knees are sunk in dead grass, my ass cocked in the air. He fang-nips both cheeks, spreads them, roughly shoves up inside me and begins pummeling me anew.

I've no sooner started a new series of rapturous, stuffed-full-to-the-brim grunts than his right hand's again clamped over my mouth. His left hand finds my left pec. He manhandles the thick flesh, tugs painfully at the chest pelt. "A better angle, is it not?" Marcus pants into my tangled hair. "And a small price for all of Rome?"

What ecstasy it is to be completely vulnerable and completely owned, thoroughly plowed. I had almost forgotten. Nodding, I close my eyes, spread my thighs, push back onto him, and grip him from inside, as if I were squeezing the handle of a sword. "Ah, yes. Very nice. You are skilled for a dirty savage," Marcus says, increasing the speed of his thrusts. "You have learned well beneath my predecessors."

Smiling beneath his palm, I squeeze and relax, squeeze and relax. He rides for a bit, sighing with delight, letting the sweat build up between us, before he says, "I will hurt you now, boy. Yes?" Marcus pants into my ear. "You are ready to suffer for me? I may mark you?"

I grunt an affirmation, nodding against his firm grip. Immediately his fingernails sink deep into my nipple. I clench my teeth as he brings blood, twists and tugs the tiny nub of flesh, cuts deeper still.

Keeping one hand over my mouth, with the other he rakes my torso, my nipples, and my back with his sharp fingernails, leaving long, deep wounds. Blood wells up, trickling into my chest hair, down my spine. "And now, I think..." He shifts the position of his loins just a fraction, pulls back, shoves forward hard. My eyes roll, my fangs gnash my tongue, my own blood tinges my mouth.

"Here, I think, is the bodily seat of your submission, yes? This spot here?" Marcus chuckles. "Am I right, forest trash? Wild one so sweetly tamed?"

Yes, deep inside me he has found what few men have ever found, the point that makes me shake with the greatest pleasure. I go wild, bucking and writhing in his arms, crying out against his hand, trying to pull him into me even deeper. Giving my chest one last savage clawing, he locks his arm around my head and sinks his teeth into my neck.

The sucking begins—an irresistible gravity, a riptide more and more intense—hard and steady to match the pounding below. Within a minute, I'm immobile, sprawled limply across the column that once bore the weight of an empire, rocking helplessly inside his thrusts. I hear him hissing against my split skin, feel him stiffening atop me, pumping my depths. Then Marcus's bloody hands grip my shoulders, his fangs slip from my flesh. He gives a shout, a final thrust, gushes into me, and collapses.

Blood tickles my neck. The column's marble is cold against my belly; my master's weight is great upon my back; my hole's a throbbing circlet of fire. The grass before my eyes smears, a brittle gold. That grades to red, then unbroken black.

I wake cradled in his lap. He is rocking me in his arms, gazing down at me, blond hair curtaining his face. Again that faint smile. He bends over me, caressing the blood-ooze claw trails his nails cut into my chest. I try to embrace him, only to find myself still weak, still cuffed. His lips meet mine. I can smell and taste my own blood in his kiss.

"You will be scarred for a time," Marcus says. "My nails leave welts even undead bodies have difficulty healing." He runs a finger along my chest, daubs up some blood, laps it off. "But you are even more beautiful scarred, no? And these scars will mark you as mine during your stay in Rome."

From the seat of a ruined altar, he rises, holding me in his arms. "The temple of Cybele once," he says, wistfully. "You should have seen it as it was." Enervate, I lean against him, wrists throbbing in the tight cuffs. Birds are singing somewhere. "Almost dawn, yes," he says, carrying me through aromas of pine, crunching of needles, then beneath an arch and down a long underground tunnel. "You may use this nest in future, if you please," Marcus says. He shifts me with ease from his arms to his shoulder, then edges aside a flat rock. Here, a grave large enough for the both of us. He lowers me gently onto my side, climbs in after me, pulls the rock in over us. "I have hidden our clothes nearby. We will spend the day together here, my bound barbarian," Marcus says, gripping my cuffed hands and pulling me against him. We kiss, lengthily and deeply, before he presses his hairless chest against my mouth and says, "I can feel your famine. Drink, boy."

"Thank you, sir," I whisper. "Gladly." My tongue finds his nipple. I tease it into hardness, then slip my fangs into him. He sighs, running his fingers through my hair and along the gashes on my back. His semen oozes from my ass and trickles down my inner thigh. The sun must be nearing dawn, for sudden drowsiness washes over me. I fall asleep suckling Marcus's breast, feeling the old blood glow and shimmer inside.

III.

"We should have killed them all. What trouble those beasts have caused."

Marcus and I are strolling through what remains of the Colosseum. He's dressed in a dove-gray suit, crimson tie, and leather loafers, I in camo pants, black work boots, and a black tank top that allows Marcus to savor the sight of both my tattoos and my fresh scars. At his request, my hair's unbound. It's approaching midnight of our second night together. The great broken bowl of the stadium is empty of tourists. We walk along the corridors, under the barrel vaults, and take seats where emperors once did. Only a few feral cats are our companions tonight, and the moon, nearly full. Before us is the cross erected by a long-dead pope to commemorate the Christians who died here.

"Are they as troublesome in your land, my highlander? The Christians?"

"Oh, fuck yes!" I snarl. "They're a plague. They run through my mountains like a virus. They befoul the air!"

Marcus wraps an arm around me. "You are passionate about this, I see."

I flush and nod. "I do hate them. The hard-core kind, at least. They've caused me and mine much grief. Still, forgive the language, sir. We 'forest trash,' as I believe you called me during that fine pounding… I'm still a little sore, by the way. Not that I'm complaining." I rub my butt and grin. "We forest trash do tend to be dirty-mouthed. I don't mean to be vulgar. I suspect a sophisticated man like you is used to fairer-spoken friends."

Marcus pulls me against him. I lean my head against his chest. It is a great relief, to relinquish strength and control for a change. "But you *are* vulgar. And I love it. I grow weary of refinement sometimes. Yes, we should have fattened our lions more efficiently. And speaking of flashing fangs and vigorous devouring, are you ready for your gift? You took little blood from me before you slept; your hair and goatee are still silvery. It's time to remedy that."

"Yes, I'm ready. What have you been up to?" Marcus has shown me several sights tonight—the Forum, the Capitoline, the Arch of Constantine—but before that tour, he'd left me silver-cuffed for several hours in our Palatine tomb while he "attended to business."

"Come with me." Marcus rises and takes my hand. "It's five minutes from here, down Via San Giovanni de Laterano."

Leaving the ancient stadium, we make our way past well-lit cafés, noisy, fragrant restaurants. We hold hands, the sleek aristocrat and the undead redneck. God help the homophobic human who might object. But we meet with no objections, just a few stares, and soon we are swathed in shadow again, slipping down a narrow street and then inside the colonnaded courtyard of a church.

"San Clemente," Marcus says, pulling open the broad wooden door and ushering me inside. "I worship here."

"A Christian church?"

"No, no. Come, come." Marcus takes my hand. He's moving fast through the dimness, leading me past columns, mosaics, and choir screens—Christian irrelevancies—then through a swinging door and down broad stone steps. Here is a lower floor. I can make out bare stone walls, a distant flicker of candlelight; I can smell earth and human sweat, hear a faint, very human moaning. "Here?" I say. My fangs throb and lengthen.

"Not yet, young one, eager one. First you must pay homage."

Down another flight of steps, a deeper level yet. The sound of rushing water.

"Beneath the floor. The Cloaca Maxima, ancient Rome's sewer. That is what you hear." Marcus pulls me down a corridor to a doorway in the rough wall. "Here, here is where we need to be. The Mythraeum." Behind a locked grate is a low-ceilinged cave, a white marble altar flanked by stone benches. Marcus fetches a key from his pocket; the padlock snaps open; we enter the shrine.

"The Lord Mithras. He is the god of soldiers." Marcus runs his hands along the low reliefs. "Here, see, he sacrifices the bull. He cuts its great throat. And here, here are the dog and serpent. They drink the blood." He grips my shoulder. "On your knees, *rusticus*."

I do what I'm told, kneeling beside him. Closing his eyes, Marcus mouths a few words I can't make out. Bowing my head, I give thanks to this foreign warrior god—for the splendid man by my side, for his beauty, ruthlessness, and strength, for his marble-white, marble-hard muscles, for his sharp golden desire.

Marcus tugs my beard. I jerk with surprise, then rise. His arms enwrap me, hugging me hard. "The god gives his approval. Now for your gift."

Back along the corridor and up one flight of steps. "This was a fourth-century church," says Marcus. "It also makes a fine feast hall for my coven." There's a distant sound of sobbing. We follow it, turning several corners before coming into the low nave. I stare down the rows of double columns and flickering candelabra, to the stone canopy of the baldacchino at the far end, the high rectangular altar beneath it, and, most especially, what lies atop that altar. I growl deep in my throat. I run my tongue over my fangs.

"You are pleased? You said you doted on Christs."

"Oh, fuck. Oh, yes!" My lip curls up; I snuffle the rich air, heavy with terror and sweat.

Bound belly-down upon the altar is a young man. He's naked. His limbs are spread, wrists and ankles shackled and chained to the posts of the canopy. He stares at us with black, long-lashed eyes before breaking into soft fear-sobs again.

I cross the yards between us in a heartbeat. I wrap my fingers in his long black hair and pull his head back. Thick chain has been threaded between his teeth twice and padlocked behind his head, filling his mouth, muffling his cries. I study his handsome face, his tear-stained, half-crazed eyes. His weeping grows more violent still. He squints against his tears, then, unable to hold my gaze, clenches his eyes shut.

"His name is Francesco," Marcus says, somewhere behind me. "He's twenty-one. He speaks English fairly well. He lives with his old mother in the ghetto south of Rome. He uses his good looks to hustle tourists on the Spanish Steps. No one will miss him save her. He is yours now. To drain, enslave, keep, or kill."

The mention of murder evokes in Francesco a fresh bout of sobs, a few weak words his gag makes unintelligible. His white teeth grit the chain. He thrashes in his bonds. The steel links rattle and clink.

"*Aiuto. Per favore.* He's crying for help. So delicious." Marcus stands beside me now, fingering the spit-shiny chain between our prisoner's plump lips. "The boy's half starved. But he gave us a fierce fight, like a wild animal. Rather than damage him badly, we drugged him. He's been kept bound down here for hours, watched over by some helpful minions of mine. He has little strength left. So he will do?"

"Ohhhh, yes," I hiss. "He's fucking *fine*. Thank you, Marcus!"

Francesco's face is thin, with prominent cheekbones and an aquiline nose. His shoulder-length hair is ink-black, as is his neatly trimmed goatee. He's very lean, rib-staves and hipbones ridging dirty skin. He's shiny with sweat; he smells of the street, of urine and long hot days without a bath. Other than the whiteness of his buttocks, his skin's an olive hue. Here and there are bruises, the result, I'm guessing, of the struggles he put up during his capture. I circle him now, stroking his long, thickly hairy legs, the muscles' straining definition. I caress the wet hair-nests of his armpits, the hair dusting his belly and chest. When I touch his buttocks, hard curves covered with fine black fur, he starts and shudders, shakes his head violently, cries out more chain-hampered words I can't make out. His fear's a liqueur, black and sweet. I laugh low, running a fingertip along his ass crack. So moist, so warm, so aromatic.

"Oh, yes, he can guess what's coming next. Do what you please, barbarian. Use him as I used you." Marcus fetches two glasses and a bottle from the floor. Black Sambuca again. He pours out the liqueur, hands me a glass, clicks his glass against mine. I take a sip, lick the sugary anise off my lips, rest the glass on the corner of the altar, and strip.

I am naked now. Marcus brushes his fingers across my chest, along my arm. "White scars amid such black, black fur. Black tattoos against such white, white skin. Snow and coal. Comets streaking the darkness. The white wake of waves across the Mediterranean at midnight…" He sounds almost reverent, his eyes gone vague. "Ah, I am a bad poet. My apologies. But I am very glad you came to Rome, Derek Maclaine." He steps back, face again an ivory mask. "I may watch, may I not?"

"Yes, sir. I'd relish that." I leap up beside Francesco and stretch out. His face is pressed against the altar. I cup his bearded chin in my hand, turning his face toward me.

"Oh, you are so *fucking* beautiful," I sigh. "I am going to take you now, little Jesus. I am going to fuck you up the ass. Do you understand?" I smile, showing my fangs.

Francesco gives a sharp gasp. Francesco stares. Francesco pants with panic around his mouthful of chain. Drool wells through the links, dribbling onto my hand.

"I'm guessing you've been ass-fucked before? What with those eager clients on the Spanish Steps all salivating for your sweet favors?"

My prisoner continues to stare and pant, speechless. Customary behavior at the first sight of fangs.

"You'll answer me if you know what's good for you. I like my slaves mannerly."

"Uh-huh," Francesco grunts, nodding.

"If you obey, you'll survive. If you struggle, you'll die. And if you give me enough pleasure, I might decide to own you, to keep you around. You understand? I need a slave here in Rome, to watch over me and my new home. If I own you, I will care for you. And your worries will be over. You will live long and prosper."

Francesco nods. More warm drool, clear as water, drips onto my hand.

Fetching my glass, I slip down to kneel between my captive's widespread thighs. Across the pale curves and fuzzy crevice of his ass, I drip Sambuca. I can hear Marcus's chuckle as I spread Francesco's cheeks and begin a deep nuzzling.

IV.

Francesco limps beside me through the old neighborhood of Vecchia Roma, over bumpy cobblestones, past pink and cream stucco walls. His stride's stiff, a little less than graceful. With good reason. Last night, after entering him as gently as Marcus entered me, I rode Francesco long and hard, on and off, for hours, wanting our first time to last. As I pounded him, I drank his delicious blood till he fainted. I sipped Sambuca with Marcus till my captive came to. I beat his brown back and white buttocks with my belt, leaving bruises and welts, before climbing upon him, embracing him, entering him, drinking from him again. Francesco pleasured me with his ass, with his street-taught skills, coaxing cum from me time after time. He obeyed me in everything, didn't struggle or shout, was entirely acquiescent, limp with blood loss as dawn approached. We unchained him then, carried him to a secret crypt near the Mythraeum. We bound his hands and feet with rope. We tenderly gagged him with Marcus's silk tie. Marcus stripped, and the three of us lay together. Francesco spent the day between us, paralyzed and entranced, curled against the naked dead.

Tonight he is clearly hurting. But a slave is the last to complain. By now he bears a chain I have locked around his neck. By now he bears the marks of my teeth, on his buttocks, on his shoulders and neck. By now he is entirely my thrall.

This is the address. As Marcus promised, the medieval tower is in fine shape. I unlock the door, tugging Francesco after me by his collar.

Together we ascend the winding stairs. At the top is a thick wooden door, and, behind that, the snug apartment. It is furnished beautifully, a mix of both antique and modern furnishings. And its little kitchen table is heaped with steaming food.

"Oh, *Signore!*" Francesco's belly growls. "May I?"

"Wine first." I nod to the sideboard. Beside a bowl of red roses, Marcus has left a bottle of red wine, another of black Sambuca, and several glasses. Francesco jumps to it, opening the wine and pouring out a glass. He looks up expectantly.

"Take off your clothes."

Francesco hurriedly shucks off his dirty garments. Again the arch of an expectant black eyebrow.

"Yes," I say, running a finger down the line of hair bisecting his flat belly. "You may eat. From a plate on the floor."

Not a second's hesitation. In a flash my handsome little Jesus has fetched a plate from the cupboard and is holding it out. He's positively salivating, staring first at me, then at the heaped table. I study his nakedness for a moment, his olive skin, his midnight-black pubic bush, his limp, uncut cock. This one will prove precious, I can already tell. And sweet Matt, back home, is going to love him. Matt's going to have the boy's legs in the air so damn fast. I can't wait to show Matt around Rome.

"How long since you last ate?" I sip the wine. It's very fine: cobwebs and blackberries. Of course. Aristocrats like Marcus always have superb taste.

"Three days, *Signore.*" His mouth quivers.

"Poor boy. Let me." With utensils on the sideboard, I dole it out: bucatini all'Amatriciana, eggplant Parmagiana, roast pork with potatoes, spaghetti carbonara, Caprese salad, focaccia. I place the full plate on the floor and pull out a chair. Francesco drops onto his elbows and knees, crawls over, and begins gobbling. I prop a booted foot upon his back and sip the last of my wine, taking joy in his joy. When he's finished his first plate, I pile him up another. He hunches over it, shaggy black hair falling over his face, slurping and chewing with abandon.

Patting his prettily propped black-fuzzed ass, I leave him there to fill his belly while I indulge in a little exploration. Here are the big bedroom, the guest room, the study, and the secret panel where Marcus said it would be, behind which I will spend the days. And here, in the entrance hall, is an envelope I'd missed before, one addressed to me. I tear it open and read the note.

Enkidu, my handsome one, my wild forest trash, my musky butch bottom. Here is your new home. I hope it meets your needs. The rent is steep: your blood, your body, and your submission, whenever you are in Rome. I do not think you will mind paying such a fee. I hope your little Jesus enjoys his feast. Savor your Sambuca. You said it would cause you to think of me. I hope that is so. I am leaving Roma for a week, for business meetings in Berlin. Meet me at the Pantheon two weeks from tonight. There is a vampire bar near there that serves an excellent blood orange gelato. Mithras bless you. Marcus.

"*Signore*? I am done." It's Francesco, crawling down the hall on his hands and knees. His goatee and red lips gleam with grease. I lift him to his feet, kiss him, lick the oil from his mouth, and lead him into the kitchen. "Fetch me a glass of Sambuca," I say, and he does. "Follow me," I say, hooking a finger under his chain collar and leading him out onto the balcony. I sit back in a lounge chair; my thrall sits cross-legged at my feet.

"Tomorrow we will move your mother into better housing. You'd like that?"

"Oh, *Signore*..." Francesco's eyes glitter wetly. He puts his face in his hands, then scoots over, wraps his arms around my legs, and rests his head in my lap. "*Grazie, grazie.*"

I take a sip of Sambuca, looking out over the lights of Rome, the far, lit façade of Castel Sant'Angelo, the dome of Sant'Andrea della Valle. I stroke my slave's black hair. "Ain't you something fine? Hungry little savior. Furry little street whore." I pull him up onto my lap, then push my thumb between his teeth. He licks it, then closes his mouth around it and gently begins to suck. I rock him as Marcus rocked me on the Palatine.

"Tomorrow, while I sleep, you'll take money and stock the shelves with all your favorite foods and wines. Buy yourself some handsome clothes as well. And some limoncello for when Marcus visits. He's fond of it, I think."

"Sì, Signore," Francesco murmurs around my thumb. His mouth is tight, wet, and hot.

"This is the reward of submission," I say, taking another sip of liqueur. "For both you and I." The moon's glow edges the eastern horizon. It will be full tonight, soon to shower the old quarter with pearl-white light. "When I'm done with this glass, I'm taking you inside. I'm going to tape your pretty mouth shut and tie you belly-down to that big bed and prop your hairy ass on pillows and fuck you till you bleed and come inside you and lap the blood from your luscious, hair-fringed hole and drink from your neck till you pass out. I'm going to keep you bound and tape-gagged till dawn. I'm going to hold you close all night. Would you like that, my sweet little Jesus?"

Francesco nods, sucking harder, with all the intensity of the newborn. He suckles me and I rock him. Soon, just as it did in the time of the Caesars, in the time of the half-mad mercenary Renaissance popes and the fully mad Mussolini, the moon will rise, over the Colosseum, the Palatine, the Forum, over this renovated tower, older even than I. Bathed in summer moonlight, I will think of the few men I've loved. Once a century, that's all I can endure. Angus McCormick, my first and thoroughly inescapable passion, who was stabbed to death, murdered by hateful Christians, on the Isle of Mull in 1730, the night I was turned. Mark Carden, my bushy-bearded Rebel soldier, who was shot through the head in the Battle of Chickamauga in 1863. Gerard McGraw, who bled to death in the trenches of Belgium in 1945. Matt Taylor, this century's spouse, who has many blessed years left, who waits for me in the mountains of home.

And now, I think, Marcus Colonna, who flies tonight to Berlin. I have never loved a Top before. Perhaps he will comfort me in a few decades, when my sweet Matthew dies, when I find myself alone on Mount Storm, my West Virginia retreat, face streaked with tears, sorrow the color of Zinfandel, while snow drifts outside, sculpted by the mountain winds. Perhaps Marcus and I will preside while hillfolk neighbors bring in comfort food: potato salad, fried chicken, deviled eggs, macaroni and cheese, cherry pie, banana pudding. We'll lift glasses of black Sambuca to all the brief beauties we have reluctantly and irresistibly loved. Perhaps together we will tend Matt's grave. Stubborn, cussed, and handsome as Matt is, I will probably plant purple thistles atop his ashes.

Well, that will be years yet. There it is now, the full moon, the disk of bruised bone. It rises over the eastern hills, the silhouettes of buildings. Ah, *shit*. I wipe tears off my unshaven cheeks. Pulling my thumb from my thrall's fervent mouth, I rise, lifting him into my arms. "Time you were crucified," I snarl. Turning my back on all of history, I carry him inside.

KELLS
JAY LYGON

Used to be, I lived for glimpses of Kells in the hallway at school. He was the guy who swapped dirty jokes with the coach at soccer practice while the rest of us ran drills. Even if he sat out most of the game, he always took credit for our wins. No one ever called him on it. Somehow, he had us convinced that he was the star of the team.

After practice, Kells sauntered naked through the locker room, dick bouncing, smooth white ass flexing with each step. Confident fucker. I admired that. I lusted after his big pink nipples; jerked off to fantasies of his muscled thighs.

I was the opposite of him. I had to work my ass off to stay on the varsity team. Being part Japanese, I was so short that I was easily overlooked, so I was surprised when I heard Kells tell the coach to substitute me into an important game.

"Kobi knows how to take out their striker without getting caught," I heard him whisper as he trotted near the coach on the sideline. "We won't get to state finals if we lose today. Put Kobi in."

Sure, he wouldn't risk being thrown out of the game, but I was expendable, and I was okay with that. I was small, quick, and vicious, but looked innocent enough to pull it off. Even the referee didn't want to believe I'd tackled cleats up on purpose.

Kells didn't thank me, but he knew I was the reason we made it to the state finals. I hoped that meant he'd choose me to be his roommate at the hotel. The whole bus ride to the game, I thought about us sharing a double bed, and how our arms might touch or our legs might get tangled together during the night. It wasn't even about sex. I just wanted to be with him. Of course he roomed with his friends instead.

The night before the game, leg cramps kept me awake. So I eased past our snoring chaperone to walk them off. Gasping at the pangs shooting up my calves, I limped down the hallway. When I reached the far end of the hall near the ice machine, a door jerked open. Flinching, I expected someone to shout at me for waking them. Instead, it was Kells, with a towel wrapped low around his waist. A creepy, pale lady stood behind him.

"Gimme change for the machine," he said to her.

I froze. I'd seen him naked a million times in the locker room, but somehow it was different with the white towel riding low on his hips. The smell of sex clung to him. There were big, red bruises on his neck. That wasn't his room. He wasn't supposed to be awake, or in that room with that woman. For some reason, I felt betrayed, but damn, I was so fucking turned on that it must have showed on my face.

When Kells turned and saw me, he looked in my eyes. Suddenly, he knew my biggest secret. He laughed that stupid, dopey laugh of his, even dopier because he was wasted. "Oh man." His giggles shredded me.

The lady wrapped a white hand around his throat and yanked him back. As she reached around Kells to shut the door, she looked at me with dead eyes.

My life was over. I knew it. Kells would tell the world that I had it bad for him. I slammed my fist into the wall beside the ice machine, and then again, and again, and again until the pain cleared my head. I realized I had to save my punches for the fights that were going to come. The last month of school was going to be hell.

Imagine my relief the next day when Kells missed the team bus. He didn't make it to the game either. He had us so convinced that we couldn't survive without him that we were barely in the first half of the game. Somehow we came back to life, though, and won.

Later, when the cops asked us who had seen Kells last, I let someone else pretend they had. I never mentioned the woman. Believe me when I say that it never occurred to me that he could be in real trouble. He was Kells, the chosen one, the golden child. He'd turn up eventually with some wild tale that left us crazy with envy.

So a week after that, days before graduation, it seemed fated when I ran into him. It was late. I took the shortcut through the deserted business park, the kind of place where body shops and printers worked. It gave me the creeps when I sensed someone lurking nearby, so I walked faster. When Kells slithered out of a shadow, I was surprised but relieved.

His jeans and T-shirt were smeared with dried dirt. "Hey! Want-ta-knob-me," he called out.

Shit. The fag jokes were starting already. "People are looking for you," I mumbled.

"Fuck 'em."

I almost asked, "Where'd you go?" but I didn't want him to think that it mattered to me. By sunrise, everyone in school would know without a doubt that I was queer, so I kept walking. Knowing that he'd betray me, my cock still wanted him; my brain was a little more wary.

"Wanna suck it?"

That stopped me. Rather than look at him, I stared down at the metallic rainbow of an oil slick floating on top of a shit-brown puddle. Chunks of the asphalt road crumbled at my feet. Blocks away, cars rushed across the bridges, fleeing because the sun was down and somehow that made the city more dangerous.

"You know you want it." He moved faster than I expected and suddenly he was wagging his limp dick at me. His giggle was high-pitched and his eyes were glazed as if he were on something. "I'll let you have my cock if you let me have some of your blood."

As strange as it sounds, even though I realized right away what he'd become, I wasn't scared of him. I should have been scared of me, because I wanted him so bad that I didn't even think about running away. Instead, I got on my knees. Kells smelled funky, like stale sex and earth. It almost made me gag. I'd never given a blow job before I gulped Kells's limp dick into my mouth. When I fantasized about him in my sweat-drenched bed, he always had a hard-on for me, but in reality, his dick only moved when I pushed it around my mouth with my tongue. Still, as the blond curls of his pubes mashed against my nose and I smelled that boy funk on him, it nearly made me shoot in my jeans.

After half an hour of fruitless licking and stroking, he smacked me, sending me flying. "What kind of faggot can't give head?" he shouted.

When I rose from the ground, blood trickled out of my nose. I wiped away the gush with the back of my hand. He stared at me the way he did in my wet dreams.

"I'm thirsty, Kobi," Kells whined. Suddenly his old confident self, he flashed his white teeth at me. I was a goner. "Now it's my turn. Come here."

There's no explaining why I went to him. He draped his arm over my shoulder, pushed aside my hair, and gnawed at my neck. My feet went cold first, then my hands. I was freezing and his hands were colder. I shivered. Lights flashed in the darkness behind my eyelids. My hands were prickly numb but I tried to wrap one around his neck in an embrace.

Kells made growling sounds as he chewed the tendons of my neck and God help me, it got me stone hard. My brain went foggy, and then light, and then it hurt, and the lights flashed faster behind my eyes and I wanted to groan but couldn't. My tongue felt too big and the little blood I had left was froth. I opened my eyes. Kell's head was so close, bent over me. I wanted to say "I love you," but couldn't, and later was glad I didn't, but my heart pounded loud in my hollow chest while emotions overwhelmed me.

I tried to stroke his sun-kissed skin but couldn't lift my arm. Man he was hot, so damn perfect in every way, and I was close enough to kiss him. Close. My lips brushed his hair. Oh fuck, his eyelashes teased my throat. Even with my eyes open, lights flickered and flashed behind them. My brain was drowning in death. I saw black and oblivion. Oh God—Kells. My balls squeezed and warm jizz bathed my cock.

When I woke, I was in a drawer in the morgue. Kells didn't come for me. He probably thought I was dead, but he should have known I'd survived. After all, he did too.

It took me about three days to find him. He was still hanging around the business park. He didn't look surprised or upset or even happy to see me, but he let me tag along with him. All night, he went on about his lair, so when dawn came, I followed him down into the culverts under the city that were used to drain rainwater into the bay. He had a place set up in a side channel that was blocked off, but calling it a lair was a bit dramatic.

Later that week, Kells found a coffin to sleep in even though he didn't need it. It's not as if we died during the day like I thought we would. It was more like being a nocturnal animal that stayed in a state of semi-slumber, although I figured out quickly that the part about sunlight was mostly true.

He kept dragging weird shit home until our hidden apartment began to look like the set of a low-budget horror flick. He could spend hours drifting his hand through the flame of one of the many candles he kept burning, but couldn't seem to rouse himself for anything fun. I couldn't talk him into moonlit soccer games, movies, or even dancing at clubs. Worse, he started dressing in velvet and shirts with lacy collars—and he called me the faggot?

The only time he wanted to go out was when we got the thirst and went up to street level to find prey. With all that athletic skill, he couldn't manage hunting without fucking it up.

Impatient with him one night, I left him lurking in the parking lot of a grocery store. My path took me to a deserted boulevard. Broken brown glass and discarded cigarette butts were pushed into drifts along the uneven pavement. I kicked a can a couple feet ahead of me across the sidewalk. Occasionally, I'd send the can hurtling against the metal grates covering windows and shop doors. As they rattled, I lifted my arms in victory and shouted "Gooooooooal!"

While I was doing my victory dance, a piece-of-shit car made a U-turn and paced along behind me. I glanced over my shoulder at the driver. He had a hairy face and lips that were too wet. Security lights sent strange gold halos reflecting off his eyes, like a wolf or something, but I was no lamb. He opened the door. I got in. A couple blocks later, I was face-down in his crotch. His dick was huge. It was my first time going down on a real hard-on. What got me off was the smell of his blood under his skin, so I shoved his flabby thighs apart and pierced him with my teeth. His screams brought Kells running.

After that, Kells didn't even bother to hunt for himself. As the months passed, I was going out more on my own, so I was a little surprised when he started following me. He whined the whole time, but I tried to keep it friendly, as if he were invited along.

"Let's go dancing. I know a club I can get into." I couldn't get enough of the heat and the pounding of human hearts. Sweat-slicked boys grinding to techno drove me nearly mad with bloodlust, but it was so beautiful, that kind of pain. I rarely fed on the dancers, though. I only wanted to be with them, feel their bodies writhing near mine, listen to the surge of blood, smell their arousal, taste their skin. Killing those boys would be like murdering fireflies.

"I told you, I don't like those fag bars."

I punctured my tongue with my fangs. One day soon, it would be bitter words instead of bitter blood in my mouth. "I know a place that's straight. DJ sucks, though. You want a girl?"

Kells spat. To my knowledge, he'd never been able to get it up after his death. He always blamed me, of course, but I would have been able to smell his cum on the girls he lured into the cars I stole for him. They weren't able to get him off either.

As dull as it was, that was my life. Then the cops decided to push the sex trade into a new neighborhood, seeing as how all these upstanding citizens were turning up dead with their pants around their ankles on our streets. I shadowed the other rent boys—the breathers, I called them—at their new hangouts, but I wasn't comfortable off my turf.

The first night in the new territory, I picked a corner near a board shop. Ignoring the men who cruised me, I stood illuminated in neon pink and stared at the snowboards and gear displayed in the window. It made me sad to think of the shit I'd never get to do now that I was dead. Even if I could get the money together and figure out how to travel though, Kells would ruin it for me somehow.

The big dude who managed the store opened the door and asked me to trick in front of someone else's place until they closed for the night, but he said it in a nice, gruff kind of way, so I moved on. Every night, after the shop closed, I went back to press my nose against the glass and figure out which skateboard I'd buy when I got some money together, until some guy would pull to the curb and call me over to his car.

Hunting wasn't as glamorous as you'd think. Really, they came to me. I had eternal youth, the kind that called like a siren's song to the lowlifes. They seemed to assume that because I was part Asian, I would be easy to smack around. A couple of real scummy guys even tried to kill me. Weird as it seemed, I got off on that. Nothing was better than whisky breath covering my face or an ashtray tongue licking the inside of my mouth. I loved cars that stank of day-old burgers and floorboards that were carpeted in fast food trash. I jonesed for whip-skinny white weasels, those mean motherfuckers with greasy hair and fuzzy tattoos who pursed their pale, thin lips while they decided that I was young enough for them. I needed the hurt they dished out, because it made it easier to believe they were the monsters.

Yeah, I was jaded as hell. At the top of the food chain, there wasn't much to be had in the way of thrills. I'd even started exposing my hands and feet to pinpricks of sunlight to create sun tattoos. At first they were more like prison tats, small and crude, simple shit like teardrops. After a while, I got into designs like the henna stuff women from India put on their hands. I had to work the older, smaller scars into the bigger designs, but I liked the effect. It hurt like hell, of course, but I had to push the limits of my existence to keep from going insane from the monotony.

Yet some part of me stayed tender for Kells, or at least the version of Kells I had a crush on. The real Kells was beginning to get on my nerves. I avoided him more and more, but I guess he was afraid his meal ticket would disappear, so suddenly he decided we were best buddies and followed me up into the city. He wanted to grab a car and cruise.

"I want something cool, Kobi. No shitty Hondas." He shoved at my back. "Get me something fast and I'll let you suck my cock." That was always the bribe. When he wanted something, he whipped out his dick.

Mist glinted in the security lights like static in the air. Water trickled down my neck, soaking the T-shirt I'd lifted from some place in the mall. The clothes I died in went out of fashion a couple years back and I had to have the right look to bait my traps.

"The BMW will do." Kells nodded at a white car slowly prowling near us.

Anyone who regularly paid for sex knew the trade had moved three miles away, so the guy in the BMW was new to it. It would make it easier for me to pick him up, though. No competition from the breathers.

I was about to step out into the light when the hair went stiff at the nape of my neck. Crouching suddenly, I fought the low rumbling at the back of my throat. My keen sense of smell caught something out of place. My head whipped around as I searched the metal gates of the closed shops on the boulevard.

"Only a 300, man. Cheap-ass bastard. At least it's a convertible." Kells sneered at the make of the car as he whisked water droplets off his velvet cloak.

"Something is here," I warned Kells in a barely audible voice, not even daring to move my lips. "Something." I smelled musk and earth and death.

Kells pushed me out of our shadow. Since I couldn't be bothered with a kill right then, I gave the BMW driver a look that made him shit, or come. Either way, he was done for the night. He gunned the engine and sped past us.

"Ah fuck it!" Kells screamed at me.

I scanned the roofs. Something was lingering on the edge of perception. I took a step toward the alleyway but Kells clamped his hand on my arm. My skin stopped prickling, but electricity washed through me. I felt on edge like I hadn't in a long time.

"I want that car, Kobi."

I yanked away from Kells's pale hand. "Get it yourself."

Lately, I hadn't felt like putting up with his shit. Lately, I made trouble over sharing my kills. Lately, I figured I had outgrown him and those stupid velvet costumes.

The BMW driver actually stopped at the sign at the end of the block. What a good citizen. So law abiding. His red brake lights reflected as red smears on the wet asphalt.

"Kobi," Kells whined, dragging my name out. "I'm thirsty."

In that moment, I knew I was over Kells. I couldn't remember the last time I ached for his friendship, his approval, his body, his limp cock. He had me numb with familiarity.

Something moved in the dark near us. "I have business to take care of," I told him.

"You fucking faggot." He ran down the street, black cape flapping behind him.

Figuring all eyes were on the idiot in dress-up, I sank back into shadow and moved noiselessly to the business park off the boulevard. Whatever the something I sensed was, it seemed to be back that way.

The hunt was on. Me versus the mystery. I climbed to the roofs and outran drops of rain, exhilarated at the rush. My sensitive ears listened for clues, but all I heard was Kells's clumsy technique: brakes applied hard, safety glass punched, a man screaming.

Raising my nose into the air, I sought the elusive scent. Past the print shop, I caught a whiff. Sliding down the red bricks, I went back to street level, where I caught another, stronger nose full. Cautiously moved toward it, stopped, stepped back, squatted down, and waited. I slid my gaze right to left, fearing a trap. Crawling forward, I listened.

Avoiding the open, I slunk against the brick walls until I reached the metal back door of a wheelchair repair shop. A fresh, large, wet oval stain covered the lower half. The scent was thick there, almost a fog of male presence.

He marked in my territory.

Black fury settled on my brain. Even Kells wouldn't dare spray in my hunting grounds. Not that Kells would understand what that was about. He thought he was fucking Lestat; I knew we were more animalistic than that.

I pressed against the door, my upper lip curling back so that I could pull the stranger's flavor over my tongue. It wasn't enough. I had to know who violated my turf. My hands clenched into tight fists. Extending my tongue, I licked the door, tasting him.

He coated my mouth, made me wild. I wanted to rip out his fucking throat! I wanted to taste him fresh. I dragged my lips from the top of the stain down a long, solitary path, and kissed the drop that still hung at the end of the line. His piss burned the tip of my tongue.

I whipped out my dick and covered his mark with mine, spraying higher and wider. The challenge grated raw on my temper.

One thing I'd learned over the years was that blind anger led me into trouble. I figured I needed to cool down a bit before I went after the fool who dared challenge me, so I went to see how Kells was doing with his kill. It was bound to be good for a laugh.

The BMW sat just past the stop sign. Toxic clouds of exhaust puffed from the end of the tailpipe. The passenger door of the white car hung like a broken wing and the ragtop was ripped open. The body in the gutter was a mangled mess. Leave it to Kells to fuck up a simple snatch and suck.

Reaching into the car, I flicked the key, killing the engine. Vowing it was my last time to clean up after Kells, I had to force the man's head to his knees until something finally cracked and his body fit into the small trunk.

"I have him," a male voice caressed my ear. I whipped around. "Your blond bitch."

I laughed at the implied threat. "Keep him."

"Dude, that's not how the game is played. I don't want him either."

Kells grunted as he was thrown against a Dumpster. Before he dragged his sorry ass off the ground, we were in motion, the intruder and I. My route hugged cluttered, dark spaces. Every lightbulb I saw, I broke. From the sounds I heard, he did the same.

He was good, but so was I. We drew near and pulled back, our game of tag expanding out of the business park and onto the streets I called mine. At first I was pissed off at him, but then I realized I was having fun the first time since I turned. Passing stores that were protected behind iron gates, I stole toward the bridge. At an intersection, I caught a glimpse of my prey. He faced the wrong way. He wasn't that tall, but his legs were so lanky that he gave the impression of height. Probably pure Japanese. His hair was bleached and spiked. I couldn't help myself. I laughed. He spun, but too late.

The sound of his chuckle ran down my chest and to my groin. That caught me by surprise. I hadn't felt horny in a long time. Suddenly my night was alive. I wrung mist out of my hair. Probing above my gums with my tongue, I searched for remnants of his flavor in my mouth.

He darted up a cinder-block wall; I ran at top speed for the freeway. Between impounded cars in a lockup, I caught him again, that time brushing against his shoulder before moving past.

"Does that make me It?" His voice carried on private vampire frequencies.

"It makes you slow." On my next pass I swept his feet out from under him. Muscle strained against muscle as we fell together and wrestled for control. I ground against his thigh. He didn't fight it.

"Follow me," I ordered. Without checking to see if he did, I headed for the bridge.

Traffic sped across the bridge. Tires hissed over the damp pavement. Above the bridge, on each tower, a red light shone. At that height, the mist tightened into fog.

Scrambling over razor wire, I climbed the open ironwork of the trestle until the concrete bed of the road was above my head. Birds, startled by my arrival, took flight into the dark. I went there a lot, but I never showed it to Kells. In the dark, the details of the city faded. All that was left were the lights, the smell of the distant ocean, and the sound of the wind.

The new vampire grinned at me before swinging his lean legs over the girder. A small scratch of beard showed at the tip of his pointed chin.

"Kobi," I offered my name.

"I know." He grinned again. Sleek, hard muscled, he was something beautiful. "Lee."

Since my chats the past couple years were limited to tricks and Kells, I'd lost the knack for conversation. I gnawed at the rough skin around my thumbnail as we sat there. I needed something to do with my hands.

He pushed up his T-shirt and pinched his nipple in a slow roll. Even in the dark, I could see his muscled stomach and wanted to touch it.

"Watched you hunt over on Osage," Lee told me. "Saw you working it."

Suddenly, I was wary. I never knew I was watched. It seemed I should have sensed it. It never occurred to me that I'd been hunting in someone's territory. I braced for trouble.

"First time I saw you though was in a club. You were dancing on the edge of the floor, eyes closed, lost in the music. I was going to try to pick you up, but I got close and realized you were like me. So I followed you. Watched. You're incredible. That blond idiot you hunt with is a disgrace, though. Sloppy. No stealth."

"Kells? Yeah, he's kind of a loser." That slipped out before I could stop it, but once it was said, I knew that was how I felt.

Lee's head tilted back when he laughed, showing his throat. The urge to lunge at him almost swept me away. I curled my fingers under the steel girder to hold back.

"Then why do you hang out with him?" He gave me a sideways glance.

I shrugged. "Habit." That was the best explanation I had.

"Cool sun tats." Lee nodded at the burn marks on my hands. "Never seen anyone who could stand to do that twice, much less make designs."

I glanced at my hands even though I already knew what was there.

Lee raised his chin again and showed me his neck. I lanced my palms with my fingernails to make myself hold still because I was ready to knock him down and sink my teeth deep. I didn't understand that rush of lust. Necks never turned me on before.

When I didn't react outwardly, his eyebrows furrowed. My silence seemed to make him nervous. All the earlier bravado was gone. Lee lowered his gaze but sneaked glances at me and seemed to wait for me to do something.

Slow, I was so slow to catch on, but I didn't know any other vampires besides Kells, and Kells didn't go out of his way to turn me on. When Lee bared his neck to me the third time, I quickly pressed the flats of my teeth to his skin. It felt good, hot. My stomach muscles clenched in that good kind of way.

Lee's eyes went dreamy. "You're the greatest hunter I've ever seen." His voice vibrated against my teeth. "How you play with them. You let those guys think they have you, and then suddenly, you have them, and they never even see it coming. You should see the look on their faces when you feed. Ah, so cool, like they're having the best, longest orgasm of their life. No fear, just ecstasy. And then they start screaming; only they can't make a sound because you've destroyed their throat. Totally lethal."

It wasn't like that. I let them have me. I liked locking my heels behind their necks as they banged into my hole. The warmth of their come in my ass was as close as I got to life.

"It's so cool that you're ridding the world of the creeps."

Oh yeah, I was some kind of hero. There was no crusade; I hunted what came to me.

Lee leaned into my teeth. "Have you ever had vamp blood? No? Dude, you don't know what you're missing. Go ahead."

I'd never even thought of biting Kells. I pulled back, not sure how I should do it.

Lee was hurt that I refused him. Not wanting to see that look on his face, I took his hand and brought the palm to my lips. His eyes widened. Suddenly, I knew how Kells saw me that night in the hotel. That terrible hurt, that aching hunger, the exposure. I never expected to see someone look at me like that, especially not someone as hot as Lee.

"I've seen lots of hunters. You're the best. I know you're tight with that other guy, but we could do some stuff together, mess around. It'd be fun."

"What kind of stuff?"

"I've seen you at the board shop. I know a deserted swimming pool we can skate in. Have you tried it since you turned? Nothing like it. It's like gravity doesn't exist. Or we could go out dancing. I noticed that Kells doesn't go to the clubs with you."

I could smell Lee's hard-on, that whiff of man and lust. His finger sliced open easily under my sharp teeth. His mouth opened as I worked my lips across it and drew it into my mouth.

His blood oozed thick as cum over my tongue. His flavor blew me away. There was no drug like it. It felt like that moment when my balls tightened and every muscle in my body coiled behind my hard-on. I sucked deeper, pushing my tongue into the slit of skin. He shuddered and so did I, like jizz was ready to explode out my dick.

"See? I told you. There's nothing like vamp blood." His free hand yanked his cock out of his pants. It curved up toward his belly, slender from base to head, but long. Thick veins bulged under his taut, gold skin. Like me, he wasn't hairy.

"Stroke it," I whispered.

Seeing his hand work his shaft was killer. He rubbed the palm over his head and then ran a feathery grip up and down so fast it was almost a blur even to my eyes. I spat on it for him, and his hand jerked quick near the head with a firmer grip.

I milked blood up his arm so that I could take more. The little taste was barely enough. Stars danced behind my eyes. The hot, thick blood coated my mouth. Oh fuck, that was great.

Lee groaned. His hand fell away from his cock.

Grasping his jaw, I glared at him. "Don't ever fucking mark in my territory again or I'll bring you real-death."

"I'm sorry. I just wanted to get your attention. I promise..."

God, he took me so seriously! I licked my blood off his teeth. We shared it back and forth until the coppery flavor filled both our mouths.

"Yeah, like that." He sighed.

I shoved back his head and forced my fangs into his throat. It was like sinking my dick into a hot mouth. A spasm chased through his body. He came in warm gushes over my hand as I pumped his dick for him.

The lights flickering on the edge of my vision and the warmth under my skin built until I didn't think I could take it anymore, but I didn't want it to stop. My thirst was never so sated, and yet couldn't be quenched. Lee touched my arm. I drew deep from him. He tasted like dark kisses and sweat and feverish sex. Voices murmured in my ears, the sounds of men fucking. Every nerve tingled, and for that brief moment, I was alive again. A bubble of feeling welled inside me. My muscles clenched and then— There were no words for the mouth orgasm that charged through my body.

I pulled out of Lee's throat. His eyelashes fluttered as he moaned. "Did I take too much?" I asked, suddenly afraid for him because he seemed fragile, like a human. My kills looked like that in the moment before their life ended.

"Holy fuck. I haven't edged like that since I was turned."

Lee was so light and frail in my arms. I touched his face, not afraid to be tender with him because he knew what I was and wanted me anyway. "Will you real-death if we don't get you more blood?"

"I don't know."

"Shit." I wasn't sure what to do, so I hooked my hands under his pits and dragged him off the girder. I was panting by the time I dragged him up to the road. Headlights blinded me as we staggered down the bridge. People hit their horns, but kept driving. If one of them would have stopped, I would have snatched them and let Lee feed, but they were speeding by too fast and I didn't want to drop him in the middle of the road. Hell, I would have been happy to see a cop.

By the time we reached my territory, Lee was really messed up. I was so screwed. I finally found a guy that would be cool to hang with, and I fucking drained him.

He scratched his arm. "I need to feed, bad."

We sank to the sidewalk. I rubbed my face along Lee's, leaving scent trails on his skin. Dragging my tongue across his throat, I bathed his wound. He smiled and snuggled against my chest. I was younger, I was smaller, I was nothing, and he worshipped me. He was worth a thousand Kells, or at least worth trading for the one I was stuck with.

Fuck if that didn't seem like a really hot idea.

"Will you be okay if I leave you here for a couple minutes?"

Lee nodded as his eyes slid close.

"I swear I'll be back really fast. Stay awake."

"There's no traffic this time of night. Besides, who would stop for two teenage boys in this part of town?" He wrapped his arms around his stomach and rocked. "Damn, that hurts."

I knelt in front of him and held his face in my hands. "Trust me, I can get someone for you. Just hang on till I get back, okay?"

"The corpse in the BMW? I can't feed off him if he's already dead."

"Him? Hell no. I got something better, someone who owes me about a thousand pints of blood. So feel free to drain him." When Lee opened his eyes, I smirked. "Kells."

He ran his tongue over his fangs and nodded, smiling. "Kells."

BLOODLETTING
TODD GREGORY

The damp air was thick with the scent of blood.

It had been days since I had last fed, and the desire was gnawing at my insides. I stood up, and my eyes focused on a young man walking a bicycle in front of the cathedral. He was talking on a cell phone, his face animated and agitated. He was wearing a T-shirt that read *Who Dat Say They Gonna Beat Dem Saints?* and a pair of ratty old paint-spattered jeans cut off at the knees. There was a tattoo of Tweety Bird on his right calf, and another indistinguishable one on his left forearm. His hair was dark, combed to a peak in the center of his head, and his face was flushed. He stopped walking, his voice getting louder and louder as his face got darker.

I could smell his blood. I could almost hear his beating heart.

I could see the pulsing vein in his neck, beckoning me forward.

The sun was setting, and the lights around Jackson Square were starting to come on. The tarot card readers were folding up their tables, ready to disappear into the night. The band playing in front of the cathedral was putting their instruments away. The artists who hung their work on the iron fence around the park were long gone, as were the living statues. The square, so teeming with life just a short hour earlier, was emptying of people, and the setting sun was taking the warmth with it as it slowly disappeared in the west. The cold breeze coming from the river ruffled my hair a bit as I watched the young man with the bicycle. He started wheeling the bicycle forward again, still talking on the phone. He reached the concrete ramp leading up to Chartres Street. He stopped just as he reached the street, and I focused my hearing as he became more agitated. *What do you want me to say? You're just being a bitch, and anything I say you're just going to turn around on me.*

I felt the burning inside.

Desire was turning into need.

I knew it was best to satisfy the desire before it became need. I could feel the knots of pain from deprivation forming behind each of my temples and knew it was almost too late. I shouldn't have let it go this long, but I wanted to test my limits, see how long I could put off the hunger. I'd been taught to feed daily, which would keep the hunger under control and keep me out of danger.

Need was dangerous. Need led a vampire to take risks he wouldn't take ordinarily. And risks could lead to exposure, to a painful death.

The first lesson I'd learned was to always satiate the hunger while it was still desire, to never *ever* let it become need.

I had waited too long.

He started walking again, and I began following him, focusing on the curve of his buttocks in his jeans. The T-shirt was a little too small, riding up on his back so I could see the dimples in his lower back just above the swell of his ass. He was a little more slender than I liked, but it didn't matter since I wasn't going to fuck him. I was just going to pierce his neck for a moment and drink from his veins until the desire faded and I returned to my normal state.

You haven't been normal in over two years, a voice whispered inside my head.

I ignored it as always.

He crossed St. Ann Street and continued on his way up Chartres, still talking on the phone, completely oblivious to everything and everyone around him. There weren't many people about on Chartres Street as darkness continued to fall on the Quarter. I felt power surging through my body with each step I took. The darkness is the vampire's friend, making us even more powerful, stronger. My eyes adjusted to the darkness. At first the clarity of my night vision always caught me off guard, but now I was used to it. I started walking faster, figuring I could catch up to him and pull him into one of the many shadowed doorways. Anyone passing by would assume we were simply enjoying a public display of affection—and the groans of pleasure he would emit as I drained off some of his blood would give further proof to the lie.

The blood scent was so strong I could almost taste it, the need rising in me, and I knew I had to catch him soon—

"Cord?"

I froze, stopped walking.

"My God, it *is* you." A hand grabbed my arm from behind and spun me around. "I—I thought you were *dead*, man."

"Let me go." I growled, the need beginning to push everything else out of my mind, and I was dangerously close to losing control.

"No way, man!" My old roommate from Beta Kappa, Jared Holcomb, was smiling at me. His entire face lit up with the smile the way it always had. His thick blond hair was longer than I remembered it being, and his muscles were thicker, stronger. He was wearing a tight pair of low-rise jeans and a tight blue shirt that hugged his torso. "Where have you been? My God…I'm so glad to see you!"

Always feed before the desire becomes need, my maker, Jean-Paul, had lectured me, over and over again. *When it becomes need, you cannot control yourself and you will take risks you usually don't, you put yourself at risk.*

It was too late.

I grabbed Jared with both hands and pulled him into an unlit doorway, wrapping my arms around him and pressing my body up against his. He made a shocked noise, squirming a bit before I sank my teeth into his neck and drank.

I could feel my cock hardening. I could feel his hardening against mine as he began to moan as the delicious warm blood filled my mouth from the little wounds I'd made, as his precious life force entered my body.

I pulled my head back, wiping at my mouth, gasping.

Jared remained leaning against the door, his breath coming in shallow gulps. His eyes were half-closed, and blood was dribbling down his neck from the holes I'd left in his throat. I took a few steps back and checked the street. There was no one nearby, no one closer than Jackson Square a half-block away.

"Fuck," I muttered under my breath. I'd gotten lucky. I shook my head, furious at myself. What if he hadn't been alone? What if someone had come walking along at just the right moment, or a police car had come around the corner at St. Ann just as I grabbed him?

When desire becomes need, a vampire forgets everything but the blood. He makes mistakes, takes risks he shouldn't—and frequently gets caught. It must never become need, else you risk everything. Most vampires are caught—and killed—when they've gone too long without feeding. Don't let that happen to you.

I must have been crazy to let it go so long—especially when there were always people about in the Quarter to feed on. What had I been thinking?

You weren't thinking, that's the problem, I scolded myself. *Seeing how long you could go? That's madness, and a one-way ticket to death.*

I shook my head again, then pricked my right index finger with one of my teeth and rubbed my blood over the two little holes the way Jean-Paul had shown me.

The holes didn't close the way they usually did.

I stared at the wounds. It couldn't be. They *always* healed.

I could feel the panic rising in me as I rubbed more of my blood over the punctures. I heard myself muttering "come on, come on, come on" over and over again, but the wounds weren't healing the way they were supposed to. Instead, Jared's blood continued to seep slowly out through them, dribbling down his neck and staining his shirt. The pale blue was turning dark just below the collar, where the running blood came into contact with the tightly fitting cotton. His nipples were erect, and all of his weight was leaning back against the wall. His eyes opened a little wider yet were still half-closed. Other than the bleeding neck, his eyes looked like so many others who drank more than they should in the Quarter. They weren't focused and looked a little cloudy to me. "What"—he swallowed, his throat working, the Adam's apple bobbing up and down— "wha—happen? Cord? I feel—I feel funny."

I couldn't just leave him there, with his neck bleeding and his shirt getting darker with wetness every passing second. Something was wrong, something was seriously wrong, and I had to get away as quickly as I could, but I couldn't just leave him there.

Modern society might not believe in vampires, but when the police found him—and he would certainly wind up in the hands of the police—they might not go for the notion of a vampire attack, but I couldn't take the risk he would remember seeing me and mention me to the cops.

And since Cord Logan had died in a fire two years earlier on Lundi Gras, that was a can of worms best left unopened.

I put his left arm around my shoulders and placed his head down on my neck. At least the wounds were hidden that way, and in the growing darkness maybe no one would notice the bloody shirt. "Come on, buddy, you need to walk with me," I whispered to him.

His head tilted back for a moment and his face lit up with a crazy grin. "Cord, buddy. I knew you weren't dead. I tole them all you weren't dead."

"Come on, it's just a couple of blocks." I smiled into his eyes, willing him to start walking. "Use me for support if you can't stand up."

"Okay, buddy," he replied, and started walking. Most of his weight was on me, and had I been a mortal, we probably would have both fallen to the ground. But I was no longer mortal, and while I had not matured into my full strength as a vampire—Jean-Paul said it would take another fifty or so mortal years for that to happen—I was still stronger than I'd been when I was a twenty-year-old college student. We shuffled our way past the Presbytere, no one really paying any attention to us. It was a common sight in the Quarter—Jared looked like another young man who'd had too much to drink and needed to be helped back to his hotel. We turned and headed down the alley between the Presbytere and the Cathedral. The alley was empty and silent other than our footsteps against the stone. Even though I was stronger, I was still having trouble drawing breath by the time we reached Royal Street. We headed up Orleans, past the crowds on Bourbon and the dancing hand grenade in front of Tropical Isle, and before I knew it we were climbing the steps of Jean-Paul's house. I put the key in the lock and helped him inside, setting him down on the couch.

As I turned to shut and lock the front door I stared at the little cottage across the street. It was still in the process of being rebuilt after the fire. It was there that Jean-Paul had rescued me from the witch Sebastian, and brought my dying body back across the street to his house. It was on that very couch where Jared now lay that Jean-Paul had opened the vein in his arm and had me drink his blood, the blood that transformed me into what I am now, no longer human. I shut the door and drew the curtains shut, flipping the light switch. The overhead chandelier came to life, casting strange shadows into every corner.

I knelt down beside Jared. His eyes were now fully closed and his breathing was shallow. His skin felt cold, and I pressed my fingers against his wrist. His heart was beating, but not strongly. The wounds on his neck had stopped bleeding but still were open and angry. I put my hand up to my mouth in order to open another wound in a finger but stopped.

Think about it, Cord, you must be doing something wrong. You've done this before a thousand times and it always, always works.

But as much as I thought about it, hard as I tried to remember, there was nothing else I could remember doing differently I wasn't doing now. It was very simple—you merely opened a wound and rubbed some of your own blood over the mortal's wounds. Within seconds, those wounds would close just as your own would. I shook my head and punctured my thumb.

I pressed my thumb over his wounds, rubbed gently, and pulled my thumb away. Even as the wound in my own thumb closed, the wounds in Jared's neck remained clearly visible.

I took a deep breath and tried not to panic.

Jared opened his eyes again and smiled weakly. "Cord, buddy. I knew you weren't dead." He reached up with a cool hand and touched the side of my face. "I just knew. Everyone said you were dead, they had a funeral and everything, but I knew." His face clouded with confusion. "But how...I don't understand..."

"Shh," I whispered, my mind racing as I tried to figure out what to do.

This was precisely why Jean-Paul had forbidden me to return to New Orleans. He was right again, as usual. *Yes, I know you're not from there, but you do know people who are, and they all think you're dead. You cannot risk going back there. What are you going to do if one of them sees you? How are you going to explain being alive? There is no explanation, Cord, and you will have to kill them.*

And even though Jared had been one of my best friends, one of my fraternity brothers, I knew if Jean-Paul knew what was happening, he would order me to kill Jared. Kill him and make sure the body was never found.

If you don't kill him, you risk exposing yourself. And everyone else in the vampire world—is that what you want, Cord? To prove to them vampires DO exist? They would hunt us all down and kill us. It's either him or us, Cord. You know what you have to do.

"I feel funny," Jared said, shifting around on the couch and his eyes opened even further. They weren't as glassy and unfocused as they had been earlier; that was a step in the right direction.

Maybe he would recover normally.

I placed my fingers back on his wrist. His pulse felt stronger.

The wounds on his neck were scabbing over.

That's a step in the right direction, but it's still not normal. My blood should have healed the damned things! What's wrong? Maybe Jared is somehow different than other humans?

But that doesn't make any sense.

"Kiss me," Jared whispered, smiling at me.

"What?" I stared at him. "You can't be serious."

"I want you," he whispered. His lips spread in a smile. "I've always wanted you, Cord. Always."

I gulped. In the three years at Ole Miss I'd known Jared, I'd never once gotten the slightest inkling he was gay, or even the least bit curious. We'd pledged together, shared a room at the house, and been as close as brothers. Jared was the only person in the house I'd come out to—and he'd been supportive, even going with me to Memphis to a gay bar. It had been Jared's idea to come stay with his parents for Mardi Gras, and he'd helped me break away from the other fraternity brothers who'd also come down so I could go to the gay bars. Neither of us had any way of knowing the trip would result in my becoming a vampire—well, Jared just thought I'd been killed, burned to death in the fire. I'd always been attracted to Jared, but never considered acting on it—no matter how drunk or high either one of us might have been.

And it was very tempting.

"Jared—"

"I mean it." He licked his lips. "I was too much of a coward to ever do anything. That time we went to the bar in Memphis…I wanted to kiss you that night. It broke my heart when you died, Cord. And now you're alive. I'm not going to miss this chance. I've been sorry ever since you died I never had the courage to do anything with you." He smiled again. "But now you aren't dead." He reached out and touched my hair. "Somehow, I knew you weren't. I knew that wasn't you in that house."

Tears filled my eyes. Oh, how I'd longed to hear those words from him! How I'd longed to kiss him, to put my arms around him, to put my mouth on his cock, to let him fill me up with his. But this didn't feel right somehow, it was wrong, like somehow my biting him and sucking his blood had done this to him—was making him think and react in a way that wasn't natural to him.

But his wounds hadn't healed. That wasn't natural, either.

He leaned up and kissed me.

It felt like an electrical current ran through my body.

Not even kissing Jean-Paul had felt like this.

I felt my cock growing hard inside my jeans, and as Jared's tongue slipped between my lips and inside my mouth, I could see in my head that he was getting hard too. I reached down and caressed the thick hardness beneath the denim, and he moaned, never removing his tongue from inside my mouth. He stroked my chest, pulling and tweaking at my erect and sensitive nipples, and I pushed him back down on the couch, climbing on top of him, our hips beginning to move back and forth as we ground our crotches into each other.

I pulled my mouth away from his lips. He smiled up at me. "I love you, Cord," he breathed, "I always have."

Jean-Paul never said that to me.

I wanted to believe him.

But still, in spite of how badly I wanted him, the animalistic need driving me, I couldn't shake the sense that something, somehow, was not right about this.

His hands came up, caressing my hardness through my pants, and my desire pushed all other thoughts out of my mind.

I reached down and undid my pants, freeing my cock. He smiled up at me and licked his thumb. He started running it over the head of my cock.

"Ooooooh," I moaned.

I pushed my pants down as he kept rubbing away. Unable to stand it anymore, I grabbed the front of his pants and pulled, the riveted buttons holding his fly closed popping and flying away. I got to my knees and yanked his pants down, freeing his long, beautiful cock. As I yanked I heard the denim tearing and once they were free I tossed them aside like torn rags. I reached for the bottle of lube and squirted it onto his erection.

"I want to be inside you," he breathed as I mounted him, spreading my butt cheeks and lowering myself on top of his cock.

The pressure against my anus was sharp and painful, then my muscles relaxed and I slid down, feeling his urgency filling me. I gasped and moaned as I continued to slide, settling down onto him when I felt his thick balls pressing against my cheeks.

His entire body began to tremble, his eyes closing partway as I started moving up and down. He tried to push up into me as I went upward, but I held his hips down with my hands. He struggled against my strength at first, to no avail. I was much stronger than he—he had no idea how strong, nor did I want him to find out. I was still not completely used to how much power my muscles now contained, and I was afraid if we started struggling I might accidentally hurt him.

"Your ass is amazing," he whispered, tugging on my nipples and sending electricity through my body. "It feels so good, please don't stop."

I smiled. The pleasure was so intense I couldn't stop had I wanted to. I reached down and stroked his chest, and his entire body convulsed, bucking upward. The thrusts were strong, intense, and it felt as though I was being split in two.

I cried out, my head going back as he continued driving up into me. My entire mind was consumed with the pleasure from his cock, which felt as though it were burning inside me. No one had ever fucked me this way, not Jean-Paul, not any of the others in our little fraternity of vampires. The passion, the power—my eyes began to lose focus, and everything in front of me seemed to be seared with white, and I was vaguely aware that he was forcing me backward, never stopping with the thrusting, not once relenting, and the pleasure, my God, the pleasure, and I was on my back and he was on top of me, and in the mirror behind him I could see his powerful back, the fleur-de-lis tattoo on his right shoulder blade, his beautiful round white ass clenching and unclenching as he drove into me, as though he were trying to get his cock so deep inside me it might never come out, and I wanted him inside me, I wanted to feel his entire body consumed inside of mine, and the thrusting and driving to never stop...

And his lips were at my throat, moving from the base of my chin to the hollow where my neck met my chest, his tongue darting out and dancing against my skin.

And it went on, the pleasure building inside me until I could barely stand it any longer—

And his head went back and he screamed as his body went rigid, and I could feel him squirting inside me, his body convulsing and racking with the pleasure with each spurt—

And my own splashed out of me, raining onto my chest and my face and into my hair.

He convulsed a few more times, then collapsed on top of me, his energy spent.

I lay there panting for a moment or two, enjoying his weight and warmth on top of me.

His breathing shallowed and became even, and I gently pushed him aside, feeling his softening penis slide out of me. I slid out and gently rolled him over onto his back, staring at his beauty as he lay there in the soft glow of moonlight coming through the stained glass just above the front door of the house.

Blood still oozed from the wounds on his neck.

I grabbed a towel and wiped myself off, then spit onto my fingers. I rubbed them over the wounds, but again, the wounds did not close.

I don't understand, it has always worked, what is wrong, what is so different about this time that the wounds will not close?

He started murmuring in his sleep, tossing a bit on the couch.

I walked over to the front windows and opened the red velvet curtains a bit, looking at the house across the street—the house where I'd almost died, a victim of the desires of the mixed-race witch, Sebastian, and his thirst to combine the power of the vampire with his own witchcraft. I closed my eyes and remembered being tied to the bed while Sebastian violated my body and went through the mysterious ritual I had not understood until Jean-Paul and the others had come to my rescue. I remembered the feeling of dying, of my body going cold as Jean-Paul wrapped me in a blanket and carried me out of the house and back across the street, and the metallic taste of his blood as he fed me in order to save me.

I tried to remember if my own initial wounds from him had closed that first night he had fed from me, that night when I'd run into him and his friends at Oz while the madness of Carnival raged in the streets of the French Quarter.

Perhaps I took too much from him. Maybe that's why the wounds wouldn't heal. Jean-Paul and the others always warned me about taking too much—but they never said why.

I started to turn away from the window when something flickered in one of the windows across the street. I spun my head back, but whatever it was, was no longer there.

Now you're imagining things. There's no one there, the house isn't habitable yet.

Jared moaned in his sleep, and I walked back over to the couch. I knelt down beside him and marveled again at just how beautiful he was.

I'd always had a bit of a crush on him back at the fraternity house, but he was straight—he'd made that very clear to me.

Then why did he—it doesn't make any sense. Was it the connection forged when I took his blood? His life force? There's so much you still don't know about all of this, Jean-Paul was right, you should have stayed in Palm Springs with him and the others.

I reached over and stroked his brow. He shifted again, and his eyes opened. I recoiled—they were no longer blue, but rather brown.

He smiled at me. "Sebastian does not rest, Cord."

My hand froze on his forehead. "You don't know that, Jared, you couldn't possibly know that." *How does he even know about Sebastian in the first place? And what is wrong with his eyes?*

His eyes closed and he moaned. When they reopened, they were clearly blue. I must have imagined what I'd seen. Besides, it didn't make any sense. Eyes couldn't change color like that, could they?

"I don't feel so good," he barely whispered as I started stroking his forehead again. "What—what have you done to me, Cord?" He shifted again on the couch. "So cold, so very very cold."

I allowed my other hand to come up and press on the jugular vein in his throat. The heartbeat was weak and faint.

I've killed him.

I felt tears rising in my eyes.

I raised my wrist to my mouth and bit into the artery there. As my own blood began to flow over my skin, I lowered my wrist to his mouth.

I heard Jean-Paul's voice in my head. *You are too young to this life to create another such as ourselves. Your heart isn't strong enough yet, so you must never ever try to turn a human until such time as I tell you that you can.*

But he would die unless…

"Drink," I whispered, parting his lips and allowing my blood to run onto his tongue.

Jared's eyes opened at the first taste of my blood, and color began to return to his cheeks. He closed his mouth around the holes in my wrist and began to suckle.

I closed my eyes and allowed my head to fall backward.

Whatever the risks, I had to take them.

AGAPIOS ISLAND
S.A. GARCIA

How fast must I run to defeat my flagging nerve? How to assure not halting before I plunged off the seaside cliff and soared into the endless Aegean sky? How to ensure I arrived at my ultimate end?

Damn that screaming seagull! It needed to shut up. The sent-from-Hell bird couldn't comprehend how I concentrated on serious matters like the ratio of proper leg acceleration in regard to dying. I considered tossing my wineglass skyward but my numb fingers denied completing the simple motion. Instead I sucked down another mouthful and carefully poured a fresh glassful from the nearly empty bottle. When I settled into my Agapios island empire, my concerned housekeeper Korina offered me what she called superior Greek medicine via various rare Greek wines. The former nurse hoped I grooved on the wine instead of depending on nasty modern drugs or illegal concoctions. Hmm. What a sweet, well-intentioned woman. Enough wine provided me the proper mental kick. This strong, silky Robola definitely enchanted my tastebuds. What a surprise, it was atypical and expensive, just like me. Ha.

Still, this selfish man needed to apologize. When Korina brought me a healthy salad, I snapped like a turtle, told her to leave me alone, told her to stop fussing, stop caring about me! What a discourteous jackass. Mental note: apologize to Korina before she laced my food with baby laxative. No, the concerned woman would never resort to such petty cruelty. Instead I should apologize out of remorse. Good, my corroded soul still felt remorse. Something shining winked under the soul shit.

Korina usually lived in the main villa but I wanted my space. Making her walk across the island from her ancient family home to tend me felt rude, but I needed to be alone. I think the caring woman understood my problem. Or at least my selfish soul hoped she understood.

Damn. Late-afternoon humidity crept over stony Agapios in sopping reams. The ancient olive trees spreading over the island did not wilt, unlike the wild poppies coloring the sun-washed landscape. Their drooping petals felt as conquered as their owner. The annoyance forced uncomfortable warmth against my flesh but my muscles felt too limp to move my languid body from my poolside lounge chair back into my villa's cooler confines. Wait, I occupied no mere lounge chair—no way, this chair was my throne, yeah, my reclining throne, where for the past month this wasted king of what little he surveyed sprawled and watched the sunny days march along without him.

My typical day began by greeting life in the early afternoon, when the harsh island sun grew demanding enough to conquer the burgundy drapes. A few fresh figs, dates, or ruby pomegranate seeds offered me energy. Fragrant chilled mint tea prodded my awareness. Granted, I could hold court anywhere on my private island, but this umbrella-shaded spot suited my fickle whims. My wine awaited me on the gleaming teak table, the pool's sky-hued water mocked my continued inactivity, and the black cliffs, they a mere twenty-odd meters away from my throne, constantly murmured their seductive death promise to me. Jagged, volcanic-hued teeth awaited my final plunge.

Captivating. So captivating.

My wandering mind calculated death and the exact speed ratio for plunging off my inviting cliff launch. I'd never follow through with the final act. Let's face it, what was the point? Knowing my luck I'd drop from the edge, bounce off a sharp outcrop, and hit the small beach area expensively maintained face first. Did my tremendous exertion kill me? No. I knew my spine splintered in exactly all the wrong places. After my effort I knew something mechanical forced my body and mind to endure an even more dismally shattered life.

My mind saw the video. I never enjoyed seeing my face shatter. Nasty.

Fuck it, what was the bloody point? Better to sprawl and rot like an abandoned grape left on the vine. A rejected, unsuitable-for-wine grape. Instead of shattering I'd simply decline into slime. The lazy act suited me.

My high-strung Bjorn definitely comprehended the important death point. My dramatic Dane understood how to die, yes sir, he understood the concept to the final limit. Urgh, I hated the memory, yet if I pulled back the protective mental veil, I saw my physically glorious yet mentally damaged man standing before me, naked, mmm, he owning a perfect thick dick that always supplied me superior interior pleasure. Yeah, push harder, remember alllll the sick details.

What a thrill.

Talk about a tragic day, ha, after partying all night I staggered home comforted in dawn's misty wrap. My feet carried me up stairs. I stood in vague heroin-induced amusement watching the unfolding scenario. A play I never purchased a ticket to unfolded in my bedroom. The first and only act featured Bjorn hoarsely accusing me of being a fucking unfaithful whore and a self-centered prick. Grand venom. Although blasted out of my mind, I remembered him accusing me of engineering everything rotten in recent British history, except Diana's death, then he, employing baroque passion, slit his throat with a glass shard fetched from my broken Art Deco mirror. My amusement quickly turned black.

All right, fine, of course I was a fucking unfaithful whore but dear Bjorn was a fucking drama queen, plus his endless blood ruined my priceless sixteenth-century Turkish carpet. My inconsiderate lover transformed our, excuse me, my, my, my expensive bedroom floor into a gruesome abattoir.

What a selfish, unthinking bastard. How dare Bjorn act so noble and accusing toward me? Prick. Nasty, accusing prick. How dare he leave me?

How dare he check out in such marvelous passion!

My heart captured a bizarre beat. Definitely abnormal. So what. At least it still beat.

The breeze tickled my sweating flesh. I swore lost souls rode the sea-tainted draft. Pathetic brooding tossed a wet net over my soul. My aching body shifted against my padded throne. Mmm, I missed my wild actor, yeah, imagine, I missed Bjorn enough to try joining him. Unfortunately my deliberate heroin overdose created an unexpected heart attack minutes before I reached my London town house. Splat, down I dropped into the dense Saturday crowd swarming in front of

Harrods, my helpless body mere steps away from my waiting limo. At least no one stomped on my face, but the timing defined sucky luck. I mean come on, I shot up in a Harrods bathroom intent on dying during the drive home to Regent's Park. How sad, planning my own death swerved beyond my skill. What good was I? Withdrawal and a blasted heart, yes, what an ugly combination.

Damn it, why did seagulls sound so bloody annoying? My lips managed a pathetic hiss. I lifted my left arm and lazily flapped my numb hand against the uncaring sky. Wow, Steady Stewie, the dynamic gesture told them who was the real boss here. I showed the flying shit machines who ruled da island. Big whooping deal. In congratulation for my heroic effort I sipped more wine.

Once sweet death courted me, I couldn't erase thinking about my tempestuous Bjorn. We represented damaged love at its finest, ha, two emotional vampires ripping and tearing at each other, but still, deep in my shallow, worthless soul, I loved my wild stage actor. My very own Hamlet. What a stunner, I cheated on my handsome Dane, but Bjorn knew I was a true blue slut. Remember, I cheated on Andy to seduce my Bjorn. Did I swear everlasting fidelity to Bjorn? Not quite. Hmm, did a clichéd till death do us part line prevent the nasty, thick blood gushing from my lover's sturdy neck? Too late for such regrets. Before that wretched afternoon I never felt so much blood taint my flesh. I literally enjoyed one helluva blood bath. Just call me Bloody Boy Barlow.

Ah. Fuck. Ouch. The sharp twinge infecting my chest demanded serious medical attention, so logically I ignored the swelling pain and consumed more delicious wine. Okay, fine, firing my nurse and throwing out my arsenal of colorful pills defined impulsive, stupid, and willful, yes, my wonderful triumvirate, but not bright. After all, modern meds offered me an easy exit. Trouble was my twisted mind thought overdosing on prescription meds sounded too easy. Such nonsense equaled kiddie play! Come on, ripping your throat open with a jagged mirror bit, yeah, now that act told the world you possessed stellar cojones. You owned clichéd big brass balls. You were da bleeding to death man. The ruin my carpet man. The destroy my life man.

Not fair, not fair, not fair. There, I said it three times, third time's the charm. I conquered the pain swelling inside my chest, right?

No.

Ahh. Another sharp pain drifted through my chest. Damn,

suddenly the distant sea sounded too loud. I gasped for breath. Shit, I just fucking didn't care about my damaged heart; instead I urged the faulty organ into a ruinous last act. No worries about that happy event since my concerned Uncle Samuel, the faithful family watchdog, would send a new nurse by, hmm, I predicted no later than later tonight. Overprotective Samuel would helicopter a nurse in from the mainland pronto since, after I fired David yesterday, I spitefully ignored my uncle's furious calls. Yeah, fine, the old man meant well, but I didn't want a nurse nagging me on how I conducted myself. I didn't want advanced meds coated with silly warning labels advising not to operate heavy machinery or drink while ingesting said drug.

Yeah, imagining me rolling around the island in a bulldozer, blasted out of my fucking skull offered a giggle fit. Classic. Wine dribbled streams down my chest.

No, now I wanted to die. I wanted to flee life's ugly pain and stress.

No one understood the simple concept. Come on, please, life frustrated me. After all, experiencing life required a set of complicated rules no one ever bothered explaining to this poor little rich boy. My parents never possessed the time for me since drinking themselves to death ranked far above caring for their weird, introverted son. Well, their plane crash when I was ten hastened their demise and ended any chance for parental revelation. My tolerant relatives passed me around but no one knew what to do with the freaky bad seed. When my hormones hit, I tried experiencing what I imagined life to be via frequent sexcapades. Ingesting interesting concoctions or dancing strung-out and naked around Picadilly Circus soothed my soul. Imagine, the authorities frowned on my life-affirming stunts. Wicked spoilsports.

Mmm, this particular bottle of wine tasted more seductive than usual. Ouch, when I set the glass down on the table, my completely numb fingers spasmed hard against the smooth glass. Nothing to feel alarmed about, right?

No, I didn't want to enter rehab again. I didn't want to talk to endless, bland-faced morons with lofty initials messily trailing after their stilted names. Those assholes knew nothing about life, ha, all they understood was control and self-denial. Well fuck it deep into the dirt, I wouldn't be denied.

The burning pain in my chest advanced and determinedly

launched. Fresh pain blossomed into my right arm. Of course I never felt my previous attack; someone felt too wrecked to understand what happened in his gasping-for-life body.

Shit. More wine always helped, right? I reached for my glass. My helpless fingers twitched against the cool surface and sent salvation flooding across the wooden table. I glared at the liquid sparkling in the late-afternoon sun. I gasped in abrupt, excruciating agony. Fuck, what happened in my chest, why did it hurt so damned fucking bad, anddd... ahhhh...wait, shouldn't I feel happy at this event, I wanted this event to happen so much but it hurt like denied love, it ahh, noo, it huurth, ahh, burned, burned, burrrnnnned...

Searing glints speared into my eyes, blinded me, wiped away the unsympathetic world, the sky, the sun...I...I...

❖

What the hell?

I quickly blinked into the final magenta-kissed sunset and wondered what happened to me. Wow. How odd, I felt completely fine. No pain, no depression, no nothing negative, well, okay, whatever, bothered my mind or body. Why did I feel healthy?

Instead of moving I sat and monitored my body. My mind told me I felt better than I had in, admit it, years. Somehow I sensed before now I never felt this contented. What happened to me? My confused stare traveled over my long torso, yeah, my body looked the same: lean, smooth and pampered. I loved how my sleek flesh hid the festering soul rot merrily eating away at me. This wealthy boy did not accept a collapsed junkie body.

The sun dipped down until dark golden light filled the world, the glow surging burnished and bold against low purple clouds until it vanished. Dazzling. The sight humbled me. Wine, yes, I poured out a mouthful and sipped. It tasted sublime.

What? Did I hear singing? The somehow confident sound soared up from the cliff edge and drifted into my hearing. I sat up in my throne and angrily shook my head. All right, I didn't fancy someone trespassing on my private island. I rose from my chair and almost staggered; whee, I hadn't moved so fast in ages. My bare feet guided me to the cliff's edge, then I peered down. Suddenly trespassing didn't sound so bad, no, not when the trespasser looked like a lusty prototype for a Greek god.

I stared in total admiration. Although the light waned, my eyes focused without hesitation.

A tall, black-haired man, his lean hips lovingly encased in a tight, cherry red swimsuit, strolled along the surf's muttering edge. He cheerfully released a rollicking song into the sultry air. The brash tune sounded like something echoing from Greek pirate ship. Who was he? Well hell, no one halted me from asking, right? I waved my right arm and called down. "Haaalllo!"

My muscular songbird halted and peered up at me. He anxiously waved back.

My next words sounded perfectly logical. "Care to come up for a visit?"

White teeth, so bright against his tanned flesh, appeared in a dazzling grin, then the man waved again and walked toward the steep flight of narrow stone steps leading toward me. I walked to where the stairs met the cliff's eroded top and almost fell on my Speedo-clad ass. How did the man ascend the stairs so quickly? My singer's haste didn't upset me since now my searching eyes confirmed what I thought, whoa, the man was an utter prize. If I viewed this enticing physical specimen in a London club, I would have walked right up, dropped to my knees, and declared my undying lust for him. My singer defined cliché: tall, dark and handsome in the masculine flesh. Firm, proud pecs jutted toward me below broad shoulders caressed by tousled hair. His piercing dark eyes, fuck, passionate eyes that saw everything and understood the world, tenderly gazed at me.

A man who understood life stood before me. His intensely knowing eyes told me the truth. This man had experienced something equal to my own sorrow but he somehow had defeated the damage. I instantly wanted to know how.

My inner slut also wanted his cock rammed deep inside me. No question about the act. I wanted this man. I needed this man.

We stared at each other until the man inclined his heroic head toward me and offered me a riveting smile. "You must be the new owner."

"Yeah, that I am. Stewart Barlow." As I held out my hand in greeting, I left off my 17th Earl of Portentous Puff and Stuff identity.

The high-and-mighty bit always sounded so bloody egotistical. Yeah, fat lot of good the creaky old family title did me, right?

My hand slid into a firm, callused grip and let it be squeezed in greeting. "Athan Nikephoros at your service." His divinely rich gaze traveled past my shoulder and examined the villa tucked against the ancient olive grove. "So I finally see the old place. It truly is beautiful."

"Why didn't you see it before now?"

"Before today I was never invited up here. The previous owners acted reluctant about receiving unexpected guests." Athan's intense gaze snapped back to my face and assaulted my eyes. "Thank you for acting so gracious toward me."

Ha, obviously the previous owners were blind or, yeah right, not partial to burly, nearly naked, handsome Greek gods roaming on their beach. What a pair of snobs! I never knew the noble pair since I impulsively bought this island a year ago after seeing it online. I paid taxes, paid Korina, paid for maintenance, but, in my typically wasted and grandly callous manner, I never visited my expensive and supposedly haunted new toy until this month. Now I wished I'd traveled here the second I signed the deed.

My common sense tried nudging me. No. Go away. I knew this man. I knew he wished me no harm.

I knew.

Feeling inspired I gestured toward the secretive villa and offered my guest my charming smile. "Athan, would you enjoy a villa tour?"

"Yes, a tour sounds delightful." Athan held out his hand to me and smiled in complete acceptance. Fuck me, the buff boy definitely read my mind. I grasped his large hand again and turned toward the villa. The white walls beckoned in supreme beauty. Before we continued, I slowly gazed around the twilight-embraced island and shook my head in bewilderment. Amazing how even under the approaching gloaming everything truly looked brighter and sharper. Amazing how I felt so renewed, so focused. What was wrong with me? Or, confess, what was right with me?

I hoped within the next few minutes pure, wet rapture told me the truth. My hand squeezed Athan's, then we walked to the villa and continued up to my large second-floor bedroom. Instead of using the bleak electric lights I quickly lit candles. Without hesitation Athan tossed aside his snug bathing suit and revealed a potent cock. His power needed to explore my flesh. Mmm, when I removed my red Speedo, his eyes filled with sincere appreciation, then Athan extended his muscular arms toward me in a strangely religious gesture. I willingly became his supplicant and folded against his comforting yet surprisingly cool body. For some bizarre reason being cuddled by his arms felt like safety.

"Stewart, ah, beautiful one, I waited for someone like you for so long, yes, I waited for someone to release me from my exile. You need me and I need you. You need healing."

I laughed against flesh, licked, and sucked in salty majesty. My cheek rubbed against smooth chest flesh. "You sound like Korina."

"No surprise since Korina raised me from infancy on. I'm her only nephew." As his words stirred my hair, Athan's strong fingers urgently pressed into my upper arms. His fingers communicated something I wanted to understand. "My mother died giving me life. Unfortunately I didn't listen to dear Aunt Korina seriously enough, no, I didn't understand her ill-perceived quaint lessons on how this island feeds a lost soul. Instead I needed to challenge the world, so I left here at age sixteen and returned when I understood what I needed. The powerful world proved a daunting and ultimately destructive advisory."

Yeah, that sad story sounded familiar. His damaged words faded into the warm air. I drew back and gazed up into Athan's sad features. "But you're back now, right?"

A disturbingly haunted smile frightened me. Athan's low voice captured an emotion so alien to me I wanted to sob. "Yes, Stewart, I am back forever because I didn't let the island nourish me. Now I possess the chance to correct the problem. I own the chance to nourish and guide you toward ecstasy."

Despite the air's warmth and my soon-to-be lover's smooth, supple flesh connecting against mine, a despairing chill shot through my body "Athan, stop, you sound so bleak. I won't have it, no, I won't endure a handsome man acting sad while standing naked in my bedroom. Come on, Athan, if you're going to heal me, start now." I lunged up and pressed my lips against his soft fullness. My fingers slid up and teased his cheekbones.

As my body flowed against his cool strength, Athan's fingers tightened against my flesh in near painful intensity. He easily lifted me up and tossed me into the welcoming sheets. In response I angled my hips up toward him and whispered in want, need, yes, overwhelming need. This time I was the one to hold out my arms in complete welcome. "Come heal me, Athan. Nourish me back to health. Use your power in me. Heal me."

Haste did not rule my new lover's soul. Athan stood by the bed and silently gazed over every inch of my body. He knelt on the bed and ran his fingers across my flesh, the tips tracing designs and perhaps soothing words on me. Somehow his touch drove security into my mind. Athan finally slithered his muscular body against my tingling skin then we kissed for long, heady moments, our tongues dancing and darting in perfect union. Each wild kiss somehow made me feel more centered and focused. Amazing. I'd never been kissed so purposefully, so deliberately. So healingly. We bit, nibbled, attacked, but always returned to our lips creating celestial light, the glow somehow healing a million cracks festering in my damaged soul. Athan's fingers performed fresh inscriptions against my flesh, the tips tapping out messages from his soul.

I floated in the essence of sexual joy. Wait, fuck, was I crying? Absolutely. Why? Simply because of the supreme joy washing over me in powerful waves. The force reconnected me to something monumental. Someone finally taught me about life. Someone took the time to make me feel without demanding anything from me. Liberating. Incandescent.

When Athan's stiff cock, it dampened by sweat and my tears, tenderly entered my eager channel, I screamed in sheer amazement, ahh, I thrashed under him in complete adoration and offered my being to him. More, please, please, please fill my longing emptiness. My inner muscles tried sucking every ounce of juice from his thick cock. Fuck me, how could a man's primal cock feel so healing, so soothing? Magical. I arched up and adhered to Athan's muscular goodness. Nourish me? Obviously I needed serious nourishing, hmm, my flesh lapped up what Athan offered me. I couldn't gain enough of his healing powers. I didn't understand any of it, yet a primitive part of me knew everything and accepted.

When Athan gained his true rhythm, he thrust deeply into me and hit my inner point. A sudden blinding light ripped across my eyes, then an orgasm the size of understanding rippled and shook my astonished flesh. I felt like I might vibrate apart, yeah, fuck, my flesh might whirl into the air like an uncontrollable sexual tornado.

As he rested against me, Athan smiled down at me, then he swiftly kissed my tear-streaked face. The expression filling his dark, knowing eyes looked jubilant yet somehow sad. "Thank you, Stewart. Be nourished. Your nourishment completes me, heals me, saves me. Thank you. I shall protect you until you are ready to be with me."

Ready? What did he mean? My needy soul demanded knowledge yet my lips refused to ask.

"Stewart, know I will be here for you. Know and accept my power." His arms held me close. Athan nibbled my neck, then his teeth pierced my flesh. I screamed in acknowledgment. We dissolved into perfect unity, blood to blood, soul to soul, into a endless red eternity.

I willingly submitted to his need.

I willingly surrendered.

I willingly ceased to exist.

❖

"Stewart, are you all right? Stewart! Please speak to me!" A rush of Greek hammered my hearing until English resumed. "Stewart! Gods, I knew I needed to check on you earlier. I am a fool for letting you drive me away! Stewart, come back to me."

Warm, callused hands, wait, what the fuck, they felt much smaller than Athan's powerful hands, shook my limp shoulders. What? I blinked and stared into Korina's frantic face hovering above me against the deep purple sky. A lantern shed light over us. My lips opened, failed, then tried again for speech. Why was I still alive? What happened to me? "Korina, what are you doing here? Where's Athan?"

Korina's weathered face paled into ivory. Her heavily accented voice whispered in bleeding pain. "Stewart, why do you ask me about Athan?"

"Because I was just with him! Where the hell is he? We embraced in my bed and now…" Hold on. I realized I sprawled on the burnt-red brick tiles leading to the mockingly serene pool. Another two inches and I'd float in the pool's deadly water.

What had happened here? Movement felt impossible, damn, why

did every muscle in my body feel stiff as marble? Despite the pain, I willed my trembling hands to reach up and touch Korina's warm arms. "Where did Athan go? Korina, please, I'm sure you don't approve of Athan's lover but he did something for me. He nourished me. He healed me. He wanted to help me." My mind babbled, *Athan bit my neck and made me feel rapture.* Why didn't Athan kill me? Why? Why did Athan leave me here?

To my distress, Korina reared back from my tentative touch like I was the Devil himself, crossed herself, and uttered a hoarse cry. "Stewart, why do you act so wicked to me?"

What did she mean? "Korina, no, Athan spoke to me just a few minutes ago! He's tall, muscular, and graced with a Greek god's classic face. There was something so sad about him but when we made love he made me feel wonderful, he made me feel so alive! Please, Korina, he…" He left me alive. Damn him! Why did Athan leave me live? Why did he bring me back to the pool? Nothing made sense.

Korina lunged back at me and latched her capable fingers, they strong from years of labor, into my shoulder tendons. She shook my body in complete fury. "Stewart, listen to me. My gentle Athan disappeared at the foot of the stairs three years ago. My despairing nephew felt so heartbroken over his lover's suicide he didn't want to live, so he ventured from my house during a dreadful storm and let himself be swept away from the beach. After his Gregory's death, Athan returned here to die! There is no way you could have…" Korina abruptly halted her rushed words, then her wise gaze lashed into my glazed stare with manic intensity. "What did Athan say to you?"

My mind twirled in confusion. My lips, they still tasting Athan's comforting kisses, stuttered out words. "After we loved, Athan thanked me for letting him nourish me then, damn, we merged in a manner too wonderful to describe and now I'm alone again!"

My selfish words made Korina's eyes glitter with sudden tears. "You ignorant boy, you're not alone. Now I know my lost Athan passes into grace. You supplied his true chance to redeem himself. He saved you, ahh, he nourished you to save you. He felt your damaged pain."

What did I hear? I blinked in profound disbelief. Renewed confusion created pain in my head, it far minor to what happened in my decayed heart. "But if Athan is dead, then…"

"You allowed Athan to move along."

"No, this is completely insane. I refuse to hear this nonsense. Are you telling me a man who died three years ago loved me to secure his heavenly prize? No fucking way! No!" My throbbing neck told me otherwise.

Korina glared at me. "Ignorant boy! Why Athan nourished you is beyond my comprehension. You are an undeserving fool, a rich wastrel."

No fucking way part two. "Korina, look at my neck."

"What?"

My quivering fingers managed to reach my neck. My flesh felt the small puncture wounds. "Look at my neck. What do you see here? Does the bite tie in with your pretty moving along theory?"

Shocked silence filled the air until Korina gently touched the stinging area. "So it's true. My tormented Athan still haunts the island. I never believed the strange tales from the last owners, since I despised them and thought they enjoyed tormenting me but…" Korina shook her head and clutched the cross hanging at her neck. "But he is still a good man! He wants to help you!"

What? I frantically rolled my head against the hard tile. "Fine, brilliant, you tell me you know Athan still dwells here. Well guess what, I don't think he's as good as you think! Come on, fuck it, he used me, then left me just like everyone else leaves me! Why am I always left behind to feel the pain?" Damn, could I sound any more insane or selfish? A mythical vampire seduced me in a glorious dream, bit me, and now I sprawled alongside a pool wailing about right and wrong. Idiot. I tried rolling in to drown but my body acted like a lead lump.

This time Korina's intense gaze softened in sadness. "Nonsense, you sad, lost child. Think about it, young one. Athan is with you, yes, here, I believe he saved you from death. He left himself here for you to give you peace. He knows what you need and I hope you help him find happiness. There is good in you, Stewart, or else Athan would not try to save you. Hold him here." Korina stroked my skin just above my aching heart. "Now try to feel calm. When I saw you I called emergency, so a helicopter comes to take you to the Nisyros clinic. It's best they check your condition."

"I don't want to go!"

"Shh, I know, but we must act normal and cautious. I will go with you." She paused and glanced around. Her smile broke free. "Yes, Athan will be there for you."

What? How? My fuzzy mind couldn't handle this spiritual bizarreness. Yet when I concentrated, definite warmth welled in me. Suddenly life didn't feel so awkward or useless.

Athan?

A soft humming murmur flowed through me, the sensation sweet and satisfying as a song borne aloft in the glistening sea breeze.

I shut my eyes and relaxed into Korina's lovely embrace. Bats circled overhead and sang to me of future glory. Their piercing song called to me.

As if to mock my completion moment, another sharp pain crushed down on me, the force feeling like it compressed my lungs into a messy bundle of helpless twitching gore. I gasped in surprise and stared into Korina's frightened ebony eyes. I tried telling her it was all right but coherent speech staggered beyond my feeble control. Fuzzy darkness ate my vision's edge, it ripping away from me bit by bit. The world slowly died around me, wait, no, I performed the departure ritual.

But it was all right, since I wanted to die, and now I obtained my true wish. Still, it seemed fucking stupid to finally understand life only to lose it so quickly. Athan failed me, yeah, he failed me just like everyone else in my dismal life. Obviously playing the abandon Stewart game proved damned popular.

As I succumbed, I settled into the sudden darkness and floated free.

Yet as I drifted into an odd nimbus, a sensation, ahhh, it felt like powerful hands gripping me, shoved my shoulders and forced me back. The same thrilling ecstasy lashed through me and guided me backward, do not pass into death, do not give in. Do not doubt.

Apparently Athan was one detail-oriented vampire.

But why did he let me live?

❖

I awoke surrounded by bleak, ancient machinery and deadly white walls. No. Fuck no! Needles attached to tubes threaded into my left arm. Numbers detailing my health pulsed on a mobile bed side unit. Wrong, so wrong. I needed to escape back to Agapios. The urgency attacked me. Escape! My trembling fingers finally pushed the call button.

A young nurse entered and smiled in greeting. She managed to look comforting, frightened and sincere. What an accomplished actress. "Lord Barlow, how do you feel?"

Like I wanted to escape from this medicinal hell, but instead I managed a faint smile. "Much better, thank you."

"Unfortunately you suffered another stroke, a minor one, but you need to be monitored for any further problems. The doctor will help you make arrangements on where you wish to recover; we're too small to help you in case of, well, something more serious."

How I managed not to scream eluded me. My voice uttered polite words. "I see." Yes, I understood I needed to escape before Samuel heard about my stroke and trapped me in yet another hospital hell far away from here. I needed to remain close to my special island. I needed to remain close to Athan's power.

I needed Athan to heal me. He needed to heal me into eternity. After he healed me, we would make Agapios our undying home. The island wanted us there. Agapios fed on love and we would supply the demand.

The nurse cocked her head toward the door. A few black curls shifted against her graceful neck. So pretty. "Your aunt Korina and cousin Athan want to see you. The poor woman is beside herself with grief so we allowed her to stay although it's almost morning. Can I send her in?"

Thrilled joy coursed through my itching skin. "Yes, please, send my dear Aunt and Cousin in for a visit."

The nurse left, then Korina edged around the door. My glorious Athan hovered at her shoulder. His marvelous eyes conveyed his joy to me.

They both smiled in anticipation. Korina stepped forward. Her rough hand stroked my cheek. "You returned my Athan to me. Bless you."

My drug-clouded mind tried to understand. "How?"

Athan sighed in remorse. "I feared my dear aunt's rejection but she understands me. I should have come to her and let her know my situation. I feel shamed to underestimate her love. She will protect us, Stewart." He stared into my eyes. "Will you let me heal you?"

"Please. Please tell me what I need to do."

His adoring smile conquered me. "You need to live until you understand life. You need to use your fortune to nourish others. One day after a final, defining moonrise, we shall connect in everlasting paradise, a paradise anchored on our amazing island. Do you understand? If you willfully plunge off that calling cliff, you will end up like me, waiting for someone to invite us into their life. I won't be able to save you. If you kill yourself, you sentence us both to wander the island because Agapios refuses to reward those who deny life. This island owns strict rules. Do you accept the rules?" Athan stroked my hair. "A little longer, then we embrace eternity together. Can you be patient?"

I nodded in eager obedience. "For our eternity, yes. I will tell my relatives to leave me alone. Korina shall care for me and keep me safe."

"I vow to keep the world away from Agapios." Korina's skilled fingers began removing the needles from my flesh. "Now we need to escape."

Athan's cool lips brushed my cheek. "Ready to come home, Stewart?"

I was.

Forever.

THREE
'NATHAN BURGOINE

I prefer hunting at the bar since they banned cigarettes. The scent of prey, so easily lost in the blue haze, has made a delightful return. I might not have noticed him, were there still those clouds of smoke. The pleasure of forcing a deep breath into my chest—a trick it took me a good while to learn—allows me to fill myself with the musk of the men around me.

An earthy scent with a slight trace of smoke of a different sort curled in my nose. I closed my eyes, took another lungful of air to make sure, then released it. I hadn't been mistaken.

Nothing ruins a good hunt like a demon. If the demon in particular is Anders, I count myself lucky to have only one night ruined. We have history, if rivalry can be considered history.

Nevertheless, seeing Anders's broad shoulders, generous biceps, and thick wavy black hair, I allowed myself to enjoy the sight. The incubus had his back to me, but it was still a good view. As usual, he was wearing a sleeveless black shirt and a pair of faded blue jeans.

I hesitated, the moment stretching. He had not seen me; I could still leave. I stood motionless, considering. I did not want to give up the night, not so early.

Anders sensed me, and turned enough to make eye contact. He offered me a mocking wave. I raised my own hand, an insincere smile on my face.

It shouldn't have surprised me to see Anders. The whole of the supernatural world is busy on the three nights of the full moon. The covens practice, the packs run, the demons worship, and the vampires gather.

We few who walk alone are safe these three nights. Safe enough to hunt on our own. I'd been caught by another vampire once before, and did not relish the thought of repeating it. Made and abandoned, I am a slave to the will of nearly all other vampires—if they told me to step into the sun, if only for their own amusement, their will would force me to act. These three nights were all I had to call my own, and I was loath to give up even one of them.

Still, I wavered. To share a hunting ground with Anders? It didn't bear thought. But to leave merely because he was present? That credited him with entirely too much influence.

No, I decided, and strode toward the demon.

"Anders." I smiled and slid my arm around his waist possessively. The young blond he'd been speaking with blinked, as though coming out of a daydream.

Anders flashed me a fake smile. "Luc. You look pale."

My French Canadian heritage balances my sunless complexion, but likely Anders was just trying to raise my ire. I smiled.

"Too much sun is bad for the skin," I said, then noted his darkly tanned arms with a notable arch of one eyebrow. "Though you positively reek of health." I tugged him toward me and leaned against him. He wrapped his muscular arms around my waist and squeezed. His grasp had enough strength to be uncomfortable.

"It's been too long," he said.

"You only say that when you're trying to pick up cheap little blond things," I said. The cheap little blond thing glared at me. "You know I don't mind you fucking around, as long as you still come home to me in the morning."

"Asshole," the blond said, and pushed past us to return to the dance floor.

"*Dommage,*" I said, and pouted at Anders. "That hurt my feelings."

Anders let go of me roughly. "I suppose that's vengeance for last month?"

I blinked, the picture of innocence. "Last month?"

Anders smirked. His face is one of angles, chiseled and strong. His brow is perhaps deeper than I would prefer, but he certainly exudes masculinity in a traditional—if overpowering—way. That he is shunned by his own kind I have always thought had as much to do with jealousy as anything else.

"The redhead?" he reminded me.

I knew what he meant, of course. Last month I'd had a red-haired young man completely ensnared in my glamour, all but begging me to take him home. Before I'd managed to have so much as a sip from my date, he'd vanished. Anders had "bumped into" the redhead in the bathroom and taken him home instead. He claimed he'd had no idea, which was about as likely as either of us showing up for Sunday Mass.

"Are you going to chase away all my choices?" Anders asked when I didn't respond.

I shook my head. "No. *Détente* will do."

Anders frowned. "What?"

I sighed—a carefully studied trick for one who does not breathe. "A truce."

Anders offered his hand. I took it. When we shook, he squeezed just short of breaking bones.

❖

As with Anders, I smelled my prey before I saw him. He was out of my line of sight, and he smelled of simple things: soap, and sweat, and also something less tangible but far more alluring. There was an innocence in the air. A scent not unlike vanilla, or the air moments before lightning strikes. Something new.

It is the new—or even the false new of the rarely encountered—that stops me from giving up. Three nights a month is not much, and means dozens more hiding, drinking mostly from vermin and avoiding the notice of the other vampires.

A trace of the scent returned, stirred in the air. Fresh. Clean.

I walked slowly, turning my head, and kept my eyes sharp. The bar was dim, but no trouble for my night eyes. I traced the air, following the currents around the lower level of the bar, where people stood around tables with too few seats, played pool, and tried not to let on that they watched each other.

My prey was at a back corner table, on one of the rare chairs, and alone. He was not tall, though his wide shoulders saved him from seeming small. He was clean-shaven, with dark brown hair and eyes that matched, behind a pair of black-rimmed glasses that were both slightly out of date and style. Unlike the rest of the crowd—who all seemed to have been told the uniform of the night was monochromes of black and white only—he wore a plain pair of tan pants and a pale orange V-neck shirt that left an inch below the hollow of his throat exposed. A simple silver chain, from which hung a small orange crystal of some sort, brushed his throat when he took a sip of his drink.

Seeing the stone touch his neck was all it took; I wanted him. Almost unbidden, I felt my glamour wash over my skin.

The crowd around me shifted perceptibly, and I smiled. My glamour is particularly strong, a rare gift from my broken lineage, and the men around me were caught unawares. They looked at me from the corners of their eyes, lost the train of their conversations, or openly stared, whichever was closest to their preference and how naturally open their minds were to such influence. I made eye contact with Anders's cheap young blond thing, the sort I myself might take on my first night, quickly and with a more animal pleasure. The boy had to lean back against the wall for a moment, blinking at me.

Perfect.

I watched my prey a moment longer, and seeing his glass—I could smell tonic water, and gin—was nearly empty, stepped to the bar and ordered a replacement. The shirtless, muscular bartender, who I could tell worked here for the money and had no interest in men, poured me the drink and handed it over with a shaking hand. I smiled and passed him a ten dollar bill, letting my fingertip trace his palm as he took the money. A flush crept up the man's neck, his arousal and confusion palpable.

Perhaps I would have him tomorrow night. I do love a challenge.

Tonight, though, was for the prey in the corner.

I brought him the drink, the glamour cool on my flesh. I put the drink on the table, and he flicked his gaze upward at me, startled.

"Oh," he said, and took me in.

"Your glass was almost empty," I said, letting a little bit of my French accent come through. I leaned against the tall table, half facing him. My glamour spread like frost, taking my appearance and casting the most favorable qualities to his attention. If he preferred a strong man, he would see the hard planes of my chest; if he was a kisser, he would see the line of my lips, or the cut of my jaw; if he secretly wished to be debased, my height would catch his attention, and he would imagine himself kneeling before me, taking me in his mouth.

Behind his glasses, his brown eyes blinked, once. "Thanks," he said simply. "Listen, could you do me a favor and watch my seat for a second?"

The smile froze on my lips. *"Quoi?"*

"I just need to make a run to the bathroom, and I don't want to lose my spot."

I forced myself to nod, and he hopped from the high stool and slid past me. He was nearly a head shorter than me, and as he passed, he looked up, and I willed my glamour at him.

He blinked and touched his forehead, blushing only slightly. "Uh-oh. Maybe I should skip the other G and T." There was only the faintest hastening of his heartbeat.

Then my prey was gone, heading for the bathroom.

I gripped the table so tightly with one hand I heard the wood crack.

With my glamour still alight on my skin, I asked the two men sitting at the table beside me if I might have one of their chairs. They both wanted to be the one to do me the favor, and I ended up with three chairs at the table. When my prey returned, I had regained my composure. He seemed surprised at the extra chairs, but sat across from me readily enough.

"Thanks," he said, not quite meeting my gaze. "Sorry to just run off like that."

I willed my glamour to its strongest, and my prey looked up, a slight flicker in his eyes, and swallowed once.

"I'm Curtis," he said, extending his hand.

I took it, holding it strong enough to assert a kind of dominance, and said, "Luc."

He bobbed his head, smiled, and picked up the glass. "Thank you for the drink, Luc." His heartbeat did a small skip.

I was starting to realize that he was not immune to my glamour—something so rare I could barely believe it possible—but extremely resistant. He obviously had a strong will belied by his disarming nature. As he took a drink, his Adam's apple bobbed, the orange stone flicked on the chain around his neck, and I wanted him all the more. The skin above the line of his shirt was smooth and tanned.

Carnelian, I thought, placing the gemstone at last. I lifted my eyes from this throat.

"So how is it you're on your own?" I asked.

Curtis winced. "Sad story," he said. "Which I refuse to tell since I'll come off pathetic if I do."

I raised an eyebrow. "I doubt that."

"It's my birthday," Curtis said. "I didn't want to be at home alone on my birthday." He held up a hand to the air between us and hunched his shoulders as if bracing for an impact. "Go on, say it. Pathetic."

I leaned forward, took his wrist in my hand, and said, "Not pathetic."

He looked at my fingers on his wrist, and relaxed. "Thanks."

"How old are you?" I asked.

He laughed, and swallowed some of his gin and tonic. "Oh sure, kick a guy while he's down. I'm twenty-one." He flicked his free hand to check his watch, showing no signs of being upset that I still had his other hand in my grasp. "Or I will be in about three hours." He looked up slyly. "Why? How old are you?"

"Older than you," I answered dryly. I'd been twenty-five when I was changed. I wasn't twenty-five anymore. I didn't often think of how long I had been hiding, scratching out an existence poured into three days of every month.

"Wiser?" he asked, and I forced myself to smile. I could feel the pulse in his wrist, and started stroking the line of his arm with my fingers. He smiled, glancing down at the table.

"In some things, I'm sure."

"Ah," Curtis said. A blush colored his neck, and I felt my fangs tighten in my mouth, as well as my flesh hardening.

I let go of his hand completely and leaned forward. "Blushing suits you."

"Ah," he repeated, and the heat of his skin increased. He took a gulp of his drink, setting the glass down empty. "You're...uh..." He seemed to lose his train of thought, then frowned at the table. "Hey, you don't have a drink. It's my turn."

"No." I shook my head. "It's your birthday. I'll get them."

"Okay," my prey said cheerfully. "But I've already had more than I usually drink in a month. Can I just have a ginger ale this time?"

"Absolutely." I rose, and leaning forward, cupped one hand quickly behind the back of his neck and pulled him in and kissed him. He had the flavor of tonic, and that otherness I couldn't place, but was happy to taste. When I pulled back, his eyes were half lidded. My fangs twitched.

"I'll be right back," I said.

He nodded, mute. Strong willed or not, I would have him.

The bar was growing busier, and louder. It took a little longer to clear the throng at the bar the second time, but the bare-chested bartender nodded to me and yelled, "Another G and T?" as soon as he saw me. I shook my head.

"Ginger ale, and a red wine," I said back, and let myself enjoy the broadness of his chest and the drops of sweat that were forming as the pace of the bar increased. When I took the drinks from him, I loosed my glamour again, and he shivered visibly. The patrons to either side of me turned to watch, transfixed.

"I'll be back for you tomorrow," I murmured. He watched my lips, but frowned.

"What?" he yelled.

"Thank you for my order." I smiled, and lifted the drinks. I turned back to my prey.

He wasn't alone anymore.

❖

"Anders," I said brightly, sliding into my seat and nodding at the demon who now sat to the left of my prey.

"Oh," Curtis said. "You two know each other?"

"Old friends," I said, placing the ginger ale on the table. Curtis bobbed his head in thanks.

"We've known each other a long time," Anders agreed. Then, with a wicked smile my way, he added, "Long enough to know Luc here hates to dance. You wanna dance?" As the demon spoke, I felt the heat of his own influence—raw flames of lust to my cool glamour—ignite in the demon's eyes. He met Curtis's gaze, and I could feel the demon pour all he had into the influence.

"Oh," Curtis said. "No thank you. I'm not very good."

Anders actually leaned back, a look of genuine surprise on his face. I had to struggle not to laugh out loud. He glanced at me, frowning. I twitched one eyebrow. Curtis didn't seem to notice.

"Actually," Curtis said, "I'm not sure really why I'm here."

"It's your birthday," I reminded him.

"Happy birthday," Anders said, in a deep rumbling voice, squeezing one of Curtis's shoulders and making eye contact again. Curtis blinked once, but showed the same resistance to Anders's influence as he had to mine.

"Thanks," Curtis said, and took another sip of his ginger ale.

"Any birthday wishes?" I asked.

Curtis took a deep breath, and his eyes lost focus. "Not to be alone," he said, then seemed to come back to himself. He raised his glass, and I joined him with my wine, but before he clinked, he noticed Anders had no drink.

"Wait," he said. "Bad luck to toast without a glass. What are you drinking?"

Anders smiled. "Canadian."

Curtis hopped up and touched both our shoulders as he passed. "Don't go anywhere." He left for the bar.

"What happened to the truce?" I asked.

"I didn't know you were with him," Anders growled, looking past me at my prey. He licked his lips. "He's putting off a scent you wouldn't believe."

"I would, actually," I said dryly. "What's it to be, then? I can ruin your chances, and you can ruin mine. What's the point?"

His chest tightened and his biceps flexed. "I want him," he said simply.

I nodded. "I understand the allure. Surely there's someone else's soul here you'd like to draw?"

He mimicked my accent. "Surely there's another neck you want to suck?" The demon's eyes were hard, his lips turned in a grim smile. He wasn't going to let my prey go. Neither was I. There was no solution, short of cutting Curtis in half, which wouldn't please either of us. I opened my mouth to say so, then thought about it a second time. No, we couldn't divide Curtis in half, but...

I felt my lips curl, and my fangs extended.

Anders saw it. "What?" he asked.

"You don't want his blood," I pointed out. "And I don't want his essence."

Anders nodded, impatient, then froze. The same look crossed his face that I'm sure was on mine.

"He is remarkably resistant to glamour," I said. "But if we worked together?"

Anders lips curled into something more predatory, but before he could say anything, Curtis returned and handed him a Canadian. My prey sat again and raised his ginger ale.

"To not being alone," Curtis said.

Our glasses clinked.

"Speaking of that," Anders said, and leaned forward to whisper in Curtis's ear.

❖

Our prey's home surprised me. I'd expected an apartment, not a stately home with a view of the river, which threw its price range somewhere into the half-million range. It was done in a deep red brick, had a beautifully tended lawn, and the only name on the carved wooden mailbox was *Curtis Baird.*

He lived here alone. I'd been half expecting to need to glamour a roommate or two.

Curtis unlocked the door and stepped inside. He turned to see that neither Anders nor I had entered.

This was sometimes tricky.

"Are you going to ask us in?" Anders said boldly, leaning against the door frame, one arm above his head. His sleeveless shirt rose an inch, revealing a stripe of tanned flesh dusted with dark hair. I forced myself not to roll my eyes. Demons have a reputation for subtlety. I have never quite figured out what went wrong with Anders.

"Sorry," Curtis said, and blushed again in that delightful way. "I've never actually done this…uh, I mean…" He turned redder still. "Come on in, both of you."

Like a rush of cool air, the barriers of residency, one of the oldest magical conceits of this world, opened to us. I smiled and stepped through the door.

"Lovely home," I said, and once again raised the estimation of my prey. The entrance hall was done in Venetian plaster, offset with two dark wood chairs and a small table. Fresh-cut lavender was displayed in an earthenware vase on the table. The room smelled welcoming.

Curtis flashed his nervous smile, glancing at the lavender. "Inherited. My parents..." His voice trailed off. "I'm an orphan." This last came out sharper, and something in his voice made me look at him again. The orange crystal at his throat drew my gaze to his neck, and any deeper thoughts I might have had were lost in the thought of taking him.

"It's a nice house," Anders said, then walked over to Curtis. The demon hooked one finger into the V of Curtis's shirt and tugged the young man toward him until their foreheads touched. "But where's the bedroom?"

I took Anders's shoulders and pulled him back a step. Sliding my hands over his thick chest, I put my chin on his shoulders and smiled.

"Don't mind him," I said, locking eyes with Curtis and rubbing my hands up and down Anders's biceps. "He doesn't mean to rush."

Curtis turned even redder—the poor man looked sunstroked—but he kept my gaze.

"It's okay," he said quietly. "The bedroom is upstairs."

Our prey led the way.

❖

Curtis stood to the side of the bed, arms behind his back, watching us look at his bedroom. Like the rest of his house, Curtis's room was tidy and understated. His bed was king-sized and covered in a simple blanket and sheet set in deep greens. Matching bedside tables done in a dark wood sat to either side, and bookcases lined either wall. Anders dismissed the bookcases, but smiled at the king-sized bed. I took a moment to trace my finger across the spines of the books. Many were texts on languages and art. On the opposite wall from the bed sat a chair and writing table, a few papers and what appeared to be a calligraphy set on its surface. Curtis, it seemed, was a cultured young man.

"Very nice," I said.

"Thank you," Curtis said. His voice wavered slightly. The poor young man was nervous. I took air into my lungs, and could smell the faintest touch of fear from him.

Delightful.

Anders stepped toward Curtis. Curtis shifted to the left and said, "Do either of you mind if I light some candles?"

Anders chuckled and shook his head. I nodded assent. Curtis took a small lighter from the writing desk and lit a candle there, one on each bookcase, and then two more that sat one each on the bedside tables. They were all simple white tapers, and they lit the room gently when he snapped off the lights.

"Come here," I said to him. Curtis stepped over, and I took his shoulders in my hands, facing him. "Relax."

He breathed out a shaky sigh. "Sorry. I've never…uh…had…"

"Two men who want to make you feel wonderful?" I offered.

He nodded.

I turned him around and wrapped my arms around his waist. I put my lips to his ear and whispered, "See how Anders is looking at you?"

Anders stepped forward, face-to-face with our prey. I felt Curtis shaking, but he nodded.

"That's what you do to us, Curtis," I said. I pressed myself against him, ensuring he could feel my hardness against the small of his back.

Anders leaned in and kissed Curtis. Curtis's hands went up to Anders's chest, and I flicked my tongue at Curtis's ear.

"Nice, yes?" I said.

Curtis broke the kiss, and nodded. "Yes."

Anders grinned. "My favorite word." He took Curtis's glasses, folded them, and placed them on the closest bedside table. Then the demon hooked one finger into the V of Curtis's shirt again, and tugged gently. I slid my hands along Curtis's waist, and between us, Anders and I tugged the shirt off over Curtis's head. Curtis took a sharp breath when my hands, likely cooler than he expected, slid along his smooth stomach.

Anders dropped the orange shirt and then pulled his own shirt off in a slow, calculated motion that made his biceps flex and the lined muscles of his stomach ripple beneath the dark hair that covered them. I could feel Curtis's pulse increase, and pressed my lips to the beat on his neck while he watched the demon's shirt join his own on the floor.

Anders pressed himself against Curtis and reached around him to tug at my shirt. I released Curtis's waist and raised my arms. When my shirt was off, Anders kissed Curtis again, deeper, and more forcefully, pressing his thick hairy chest against the young man while I kissed and teased Curtis's neck. My hands roamed downward, and my fingers caught the waist of Curtis's khakis.

Curtis shivered, and Anders moaned into the young man's mouth. The kiss broke, and Anders slid a hand between Curtis's legs, cupping his cock and balls through the khakis.

"See? It's all good." The demon smiled.

Curtis turned his head, and I kissed him, sliding my tongue into his mouth while I moved my hands across the front of his pants. Anders's fingers traced up from Curtis's stomach to his nipples, which he gently pinched. Curtis groaned into my mouth, and I undid his belt.

Anders dipped to Curtis's neck and sucked while I loosened Curtis's button and zipper. The demon took Curtis's mouth to his own again while I slid slowly down, kissing the back of Curtis's neck, between his shoulders, and the curve of his spine. When I tugged the khakis off his slender hips, his whole body shivered, and I kissed the small of his back. After he stepped out of his pants awkwardly, I curled my fingers into the waistband of his boxers and slid them down slowly, letting my tongue trace the slight downy hair that slid between his cheeks.

Curtis moaned again, and Anders broke the kiss with a chuckle, then sank to his knees and took Curtis's cock into his mouth.

Curtis gasped.

I smiled and pressed my tongue between Curtis's firm cheeks. While Anders surrounded the young man's cock with his hot mouth, my cooler tongue flicked at Curtis's hole.

"Oh God," Curtis said. His hands gripped tight in Anders's dark curled hair. His back arched, and I gripped his thighs, my fingers lacing with Anders's.

Anders let Curtis's cock out of his mouth, and rose again. Curtis fumbled with the button and zipper of Anders's jeans, distracted by my darting tongue, and Anders stepped out of his jeans—he was going commando, of course—and his thick, uncut cock rose, already stiff. Curtis reached out, not hesitant any longer, and took Anders's cock in one hand.

"Mmm," Anders murmured. He leaned into Curtis's ear. "Put it in your mouth," he whispered.

As Curtis sank to his knees, I rose and undid my belt, stepping out of pants and underwear both. I stepped around Curtis to stand beside

Anders, my own cock hard before me. Anders put an arm around me and tugged me in for a brief but forceful kiss as Curtis began to lick at the hooded tip of his cock.

"This," Anders growled in my ear, "is my kind of truce."

I laughed, then felt warmth on my cock as Curtis released Anders's cock and took mine into his mouth. I leaned my head back, enjoying the heat of the young man's mouth and the motion of his tongue as he pressed and massaged the underside of my dick.

"Bed," Anders said, and reached down and pulled Curtis to his feet. He all but pushed Curtis onto the bed, where he fell backward with a little laugh. Anders climbed over him, and I slid onto the bed beside the two. The demon ground his crotch into Curtis's and covered his mouth with a rough, possessive kiss. When they broke, I slid closer and kissed Curtis myself, gentler, but keeping my eyes open, locked on his. Curtis shivered as my tongue explored his mouth while Anders pressed his strong hairy body against him.

Anders slid to the other side of Curtis, and while I kissed the young man, Anders slid down the bed, taking his turn at the young man's lovely ass. The demon's tongue was hotter than mine, and I felt Curtis jerk as Anders began licking.

I reversed my position and took Curtis's cock into my mouth. I felt him take mine into his. I took him deeply into my mouth, until I could feel hair against my nose and chin, and he groaned around my cock. There were benefits to needing no breath. I took the length of him into my throat and felt the strong pulse in his thigh against my cheek. My fangs quivered, and I had to pull back or I would have bitten him. As his cock slid from my mouth, I saw that Anders had replaced his tongue with a finger and was gentling himself into Curtis's warmth.

He met my gaze and winked. I smiled, showing some fang. Anders's eyes had darkened, barely noticeable in the glow of the five candles. They would soon blacken completely, and he wouldn't be able to control himself much longer after that. I could already see a slight distortion in the air, like heat over concrete, as the incubus began to draw lightly on our prey's very essence.

I shifted again, letting my cock come free from Curtis's mouth, and once again lay face-to-face with the young man.

"Anders wants to fuck you now," I said, and licked at his neck and ear. The scent of the young man, fresh and clean, was driving me closer to the edge. My cock was rigid, and my fangs were slipping further from my gums.

"Yes," Curtis hissed, and Anders needed no more than that. Anders rolled onto his back, thick cock standing at attention, unsheathed from its foreskin. Curtis reached past me, into the bedside table, and tugged the drawer open with a jerk. Removing a condom and lube, he rolled onto his other side and tore the package open, then rolled the condom onto Anders's throbbing cock. Anders put his arms behind his neck, flexing chest and biceps, and smiled at Curtis, eyelids low.

Curtis's whole body shivered. I slid behind him, pressing my cock against his thigh. "Lie down on me," I said, and gently took his shoulders, drawing him on top of me, our cocks touching, his warm chest against mine. I kissed him again and felt Anders work some of the lube into Curtis.

The weight of Anders pressed against us a moment later, and Curtis pulled out of our kiss to crane his neck back. His eyes were closed, and his neck was right before my face, veins protruding. The orange crystal Curtis wore on his neck winked in the candlelight, dangling between us. I felt my fangs extend completely.

Curtis flinched as Anders pushed into him, and Anders whispered into the young man's ear. "Good, that's good...Relax...Good boy."

Curtis winced once, then twice, then nodded. "Okay. God... Okay."

I leaned up, and licked the young man's neck. His cock throbbed against mine.

Anders pulled back, then moved forward again, sinking deeper into Curtis. Curtis groaned, and Anders let out a long, low, growl. "Fuck..." The demon breathed the word, guttural.

Curtis pushed back toward Anders, wanting more of him, and slid his cock against mine. The friction was fantastic, and I dug my fingers into the young man's ass, pulling his cheeks apart for Anders while Anders braced his thick arms beside us.

The demon met my gaze over Curtis's shoulder. My lips were pressed against the young man's neck. Anders's eyes were a midnight black. He nodded.

I winked.

Anders began to fuck Curtis in earnest, with thrusts that ground the young man into me and made him yelp and writhe in pleasure. I nibbled, licked, and sucked at his neck, feeling the hot pulse beneath my tongue. A little longer. I needed to wait just a little longer...

Curtis braced himself between us, his hands fisted in the sheets, and when I felt his orgasm arrive and the first hot jet of his cum spattered between our stomachs, Anders roared, and I sank my teeth into his neck.

"Necto!" Curtis yelled.

Even as the hot salty taste of his blood filled my mouth, I realized something was wrong. I felt my own release, my own explosion joining his, and could feel Anders jerking above us both as he came inside the young man. I arched my back as I hit my peak, swallowed one delicious mouthful of the young man's blood—it was so potent, so charged with life!—and then felt numbing coils of magic wrap around my limbs and hold me still.

Anders's low groan let me know I was not alone. My teeth retracted, and Curtis heaved himself hard to one side, toppling Anders over to the other side of the bed. Curtis yelped as Anders's cock slipped free, and put a hand to the puncture wounds on his neck that I had made.

"Wow," he said, then winced at his neck. Curtis closed his eyes and ran a finger over the wound.

"Curatio," he murmured, and the twin punctures scabbed before my eyes.

"Mage." I forced the word through lips mostly numb and immobile. I was bound. It was a good spell, a strong one. Too late, things I should have noticed made sense. Curtis's strong will, not affected by our glamour—a protection spell? The five candles—points of the pentagram centered around the bed, ready to bind a vampire and an incubus. His scent and his blood—overflowing with life. Even the necklace he wore—a carnelian, a crystal that made its wearer more alluring. It was all magic.

Curtis nodded. "Yes." He knelt between Anders and me, regarding us.

"Release me," Anders said, fury fueling his voice through the binding.

"Not yet, not till you hear me out," Curtis said, and raised one hand.

Anders's snarl was not particularly agreeable, but Curtis continued anyway.

"You're a vampire," Curtis said to me, then turned to Anders, "and you're a demon. Incubus, I think. You're both alone, otherwise you'd be with your fellows." He paused, looking at me. "I'm guessing your maker didn't intend to make you, and didn't present you to the others." He looked at Anders. "And incubi are supposed to seduce women, so they probably just threw you out on principle."

Both Anders and I went silent. Curtis looked down, sadness in his eyes.

The last piece clicked into place.

"Orphan," I managed to say. Curtis was a wizard born not to the magical families that ruled from the shadows. Orphans just happened, young men and women not raised to know magic was a real force.

"The magic came when I was seventeen," Curtis confirmed. "The other wizards showed up when I was eighteen. I had no idea what I was doing, what the rules were, none of it."

"They killed your family," I guessed. The more upset he became, the looser the binding. My lips tingled.

Curtis nodded. "Orphaned in both senses of the word. I'm not allowed to practice magic unless I find a family willing to adopt me." Anger flared in his eyes. "As though I would go to them after they killed my parents."

Anders shifted slightly. The binding was weakening. I felt my fingers twitch.

Curtis looked up. "The rules. I didn't know the rules. But I've learned them since, and do you know what rules we all have in common?"

"Vengeance?" Anders suggested, fury still writhing in his voice.

Curtis glanced at the powerful demon, then shook his head. "No. I understand if you want to just kill me. The binding won't last forever. But I'm talking about the law of three."

I frowned. "That which you do comes back by three?" My feet moved. I needed to keep our prey talking. If I could free myself...

Curtis blinked at me, then shook his head. "No, not the rule of three, the law of three. I'm not surprised you don't know it." He leaned forward, placing his left hand on my chest, his right on Anders's. "Three wizards make a family. Three vampires make a coterie. Three demons make a clan. Three of us—*of any of us*—is enough to be protected under their own laws."

"So?" Anders snapped. "You're not a demon, I'm not a vampire, and he's not a wizard." He managed to lift one arm from the bed, muscles straining across his chest and shoulder, but then fell back against the duvet again.

"Doesn't matter," Curtis said, speaking quicker now. His hands had started moving in slow circles on our skin. "If the three of us form a group, it's the same thing. We're three. *Three.* Not one, not alone. Think about it." Curtis turned to me, voice racing. "If you're part of a coterie, the other vampires can't force you. Their dominance won't work. You wouldn't have to hide. No more hunting three nights of the month and living off rats and dogs and cats or whatever." He looked at Anders. "You wouldn't have to deny yourself most of the time. You wouldn't be prey to the other clans, their own laws would bind them from slaughtering you just as a diversion. You could fuck all month, sate yourself on souls, stay strong." Curtis smiled wryly. "Strong enough to beat a basic binding, if you had enough." He leaned back, removing his hands.

Anders fell silent. He turned his head to look at me, eyes black with need.

I looked back, the binding loose enough now to let me tilt my own head. My fangs slid free.

"Either way," Curtis said. "I'm done. I'm exhausted. I can't have the magic and not use it, it's killing me. And I can't find another way out of this. So I'm going to release the binding. If you want to, tear my throat out, fuck me senseless…I don't care anymore."

Curtis snapped his fingers and released the spell.

❖

"Two gin and tonics," I ordered.

The bartender turned, met my gaze, and shivered. He was shirtless again, and just as intriguing. I let my glamour cross the air between us like an autumn breeze. He nodded. "Two G and T's." It took him a moment to move, then he seemed to come back to himself and poured the two drinks, trying not to be obvious about glancing my way from the corner of his eyes. His confusion was palpable, the scent of arousal a delight in the air I pulled into my lungs.

I smiled as he handed me the drinks, and paid with a generous tip.

He nodded and tucked the change into the front pocket of his jeans. He watched me walk away, carrying the drinks.

Anders and Curtis sat at the small table—our table—and took the glasses.

"You're not having anything?" Anders asked.

"I think he's having the bartender," Curtis said. I winked at him.

We waited, tense. It was not a full moon. In the past month, we'd done everything we'd needed to do, according to Curtis's research. I'd shared blood with them. Curtis had taken us through a magical rite. We'd spent a very athletic evening "bonding" with Anders as well—no surprise that incubus demons joined with sex. If Curtis was right, we'd know soon enough. If he was wrong…

Well.

"One of your kind," Curtis said, glancing over my shoulder at the entrance. His glasses—which I'd since learned he ensorcelled to help him spot those of us who were less or more than human—glinted in the dim lights of the bar.

It was a vampire I knew, and when he realized who I was, his lip curled in distaste. He walked straight to the table, confident and full of a mean amusement. I couldn't remember his name—not surprising, since I tried so hard to hide from the other vampires—but I knew he was a member of the largest coterie in the city. He was tall, and blond, and lean.

And angry.

"This place is mine," he said, without preamble. "Leave. Now." I felt the will of his coterie flex from him, swarm against my skin, demanding my obeisance…

…and dissipate.

"Non," I breathed. I smiled, and let my fangs show. "We're staying right here." Then, feeling a rush of pure freedom, I added, "You leave."

Something happened. Curtis gasped, Anders grunted, and I felt my own will slam into the blond vampire.

He stumbled back a single step, a stunned look on his face. He opened his mouth, shivering, but said nothing.

I met the blond vampire's gaze again, and this time, actively called upon my will. It gathered quickly, snapping into place with a force I couldn't believe. This wasn't just vampire. Nor was it just demonic, or magical. It was *more*. I leaned forward. I felt my will build, a pressure between my eyes that was almost painful, and then repeated myself.

"Leave." My will struck out like a thing alive.

The blond vampire nearly tripped over himself scrambling back, and didn't stop once he reached the other end of the bar. He was nearly running by the time he pushed through the doors and into the street.

Curtis stared at the door, his mouth open slightly.

"I'd call that a success," I offered mildly.

Curtis turned to me, mouth still slack. Anders grinned and raised his glass.

"To not being alone," the demon toasted. Curtis laughed and raised his own.

"If you'll excuse me, gentlemen," I said, looking back at the bar. The bartender blushed and looked away. "I need to go see about my drink."

Under the Full Moon
Charles P. Tautvid

It was advertised as a "Leather and Levi" bar but a strict dress code was never enforced. Muscled boys in tight tanks and jeans, cigar-smoking shirtless bears, tourists in shorts and sandals, aging queens in satin shirts, stern slaves in harnesses and leather-brimmed caps and even the occasional painted peacock in blond wig and sequined gown pushed and pawed their way around the dimly lit space. The only light came from the glow of small red lamps that hung from the ceiling along with several flat screens depicting naked men in compromising positions performing uncompromising acts.

Shadowed in the smoky haze from the lamps and screens, Reid squeezed between a toned, smooth ab and a fat, hairy one and approached the bar. The bar was a large black-wood square 'round which patrons could cruise, checking out the men straddling stools or those positioned in various poses against the walls. Nearly shouting to be heard above the blaring music and cacophony of conversation, Reid ordered a beer and, with bottle in hand, circled the bar sliding past sweating bodies till he reached the back door. Leaving the din behind the door, Reid stepped into the quieter outside patio.

The patio was warm in the tepid Fort Lauderdale air and almost as smoky and stuffy with the Saturday night crowd. Enclosed by an eight-foot-high wooden fence, the patio was long and narrow with an additional bar, wooden benches and even a pillory for the occasional public flogging. In the far corner by the door was a small set of bleachers. It was here that Reid liked to sit and observe the people and proceedings. As luck would have it, there was an available spot.

Plopping into the spot, Reid gulped his beer and gazed up at the midnight sky. The black sky was dotted with few stars but the not-quite-full moon was visibly bright. Recalling an astronomy lesson of lost youth, he knitted his brow. "Now, what's the phase before the full moon called? Waxing...Waxing...Oh, yeah...Waxing gibbous!" Pleased with himself, he returned his gaze to the patio and watched the parade go by.

Passing directly in front of him, Reid spotted a shirtless old goat undoubtedly in his late sixties. Long strands of white hair lay plastered over a bald spot while a small tuft of curly gray hair drooped wilting between wrinkled breasts. With a lascivious leer, the withered lecher slid his fingers across the well-defined, hairless, bare chest of a handsome young stud leaning against the fence. Like the waxing moon above, the young man appeared to emit an ethereal glow, affecting a seemingly otherworldly air. With a pale moonlit hand, the exquisite youth gently, but firmly and without malice, removed the elder's paw.

Observing the scene, Reid was reminded of his own sagging fifty-six-year-old body. He sighed. "Is that gonna be me someday?" As the years mounted, his middle spread, making it harder and harder for Reid to hold in his stomach. Besides the tire ringing his waist, his hair was graying and thinning and his mustache and goatee were interspersed with white hairs. What was even more discouraging was the fact that it was becoming increasingly difficult to attract younger, good-looking men. So it was to Reid's unexpected surprise to catch the strapping young hunk studying him. Reid, in timid anticipation, smiled weakly.

Seeing the smile, the sexy stranger returned a wide grin and walked over to Reid. Face-to-face, Reid felt compelled to stare deep into his eyes, eyes that seemed unnaturally dark and fathomless. Lost in those ebony orbs, Reid for a moment felt mesmerized, almost hypnotized. Then, recovering, Reid blinked and simply said, "Hi."

"Hi," mimicked the young man again, grinning broadly. In that smile, Reid noted teeth that looked dazzling white against pallid yet strangely luminescent skin. The clean-shaven cheeks were smooth and soft over classic chiseled features, and the cleft in his chin seemed to dance when he smiled. The smile was even more accentuated by the medium-length tousled raven hair that framed his face.

His face was so unnaturally striking that Reid was immediately aroused with both tingling excitement and guarded suspicions. His suspicions raced rampant through his head. "Why would this guy want me? He's obviously only in his twenties. Very good-looking. Aggressive. Not drinking anything. Must be a hustler."

As if reading Reid's mind, the alluring colt affirmed, "I know what you're thinking. I'm not a hustler."

Ignoring Reid's embarrassed, feeble laugh, the young beguiler offered his hand and introduced himself. "My name is Atan."

"Atan?" repeated Reid, not sure he had heard right.

"Yes. It's short for Atanasio."

Taking his hand, Reid was seduced by Atan's sturdy, sensual grip. "I'm Reid," he stammered.

Instead of the usual "what are you up to" line, Atanasio asked, "What does the moon tell you tonight?"

A bit baffled, Reid responded, "Well, it's not quite full, if that's what you mean."

"I watched you staring at the moon before."

"You...watched me." Reid scoffed, though only half kidding. "Now, what does a good-looking young guy like you see in an old man like me?"

"I'm not as young as I look. So I don't think like a young man." Atan paused as if for effect. "I'm really two hundred fifteen years old."

"Well, you look damn good for your age."

"It's no joke." Atan became deadly serious. "I'm a vampire."

Reid immediately thought, "Here we go. I always meet all the nuts." But he said aloud in a slightly mocking tone, "Nice to meet you, Dracula."

Without comment, Atanasio pressed closer to Reid, revealed his teeth, and produced two menacingly sharp fangs.

Startled, Reid jumped back, hitting his head on the fence behind the bleachers. His heart dropped to his stomach, fluttering madly like a caged wild bird. He quickly looked around to see if anyone else had noticed. No one had. The other patrons were preoccupied with their own comparatively pedestrian nocturnal encounters.

Retracting his fangs, Atan placed a hand on Reid's shoulder. "Sorry," he said in a calming voice. "Don't be afraid. I mean you no harm."

Reid regarded the intriguing fang-bearer with a mixture of morbid fascination and nervous excitement. Reasoning he would be safe in the crowded bar, he found himself more curious than fearful. "How?" he asked in a slightly shaky voice.

"Did I become a vampire?" Atan added.

Reid nodded intently.

"It was in St. Augustine," Atanasio explained. "I was born there in 1794 while the Spanish still held the city. You can't imagine how difficult it was growing up a 'mariposa' in such a strict Catholic environment. From the time I was fifteen, I would walk the streets late at night hoping to meet others like myself. It was rare, but the few times I did, there was so much guilt and shame and fear that I never saw them again. Then, on my twenty-third birthday, it happened."

As Atan's voice grew more passionate, Reid listened raptly engrossed in the tale of Atan's terrible transformation.

Atanasio and friends had celebrated till after midnight at the rustic home of Josef Buchanti. The small wooden dwelling had not only served as Buchanti's residence but also as a local tavern. After much draught and revelry, Atan had bid his friends farewell. Drunk with wine and desire, Atan had headed for the Plaza de la Constitución in the heart of the city.

The large rectangular plaza, carpeted with grass and landscaped with live oak trees, had derived its name from an eighteen-foot monument standing in the west end of the park. The monument, a white obelisk constructed of coquina stone, had been built in 1813 to commemorate the Spanish Constitution of 1812. So named the Plaza de la Constitución, the park had been the hub of St. Augustine's public life with its common well and marketplace. The marketplace, a long stone structure with a colonnade supporting a red tiled peak, had bordered the east end of the plaza. Facing the park's north side had been the parish church of St. Augustine, not yet a Basilica Cathedral. Overlooking the west perimeter had been the Government House. The two-story Government House, a stately mansion with masonry walls and a second-floor balcony that spanned the length of the building, had sheltered beneath its shingled gable roof the offices of the colonial ministry.

Passing by the Government House, Atan had entered the deserted plaza. Far beyond the witching hour, the public square had been veiled in a shroud of night save for the glow of the full moon. Like a lighthouse beacon, the moon had illuminated the tip of the obelisk, which cast a long deep shadow across the damp lawn. Within that black velvety silhouette, Atan had discerned the barely visible figure of a cloaked stranger. The mysterious man had waved a hand gesturing for Atan to follow.

"I remember being afraid." Atan admitted. "I sensed danger. But the liquor and the fire in my groin got the better of me. So I followed him."

With his sable cloak flapping like wings, the intriguing enticer had moved so swiftly that Atan had had to run to keep pace. Nervous sweat dampening his brow, Atan had paused by the well. Leaning against the weathered rock base of the well, he had thirstily eyed the wooden bucket that hung from the slanted Spanish moss–covered pine roof. But there had been no time for Atan to drink. His design had left the plaza. Breathing hard in the breezeless, humid air, Atan had dashed from the well to overtake the stranger. The salacious seducer had led Atan to the parish church.

Built of sand-colored stone and shingled with vermillion Spanish tiles, the face of the church had risen one hundred feet. The top of the front wall was crowned by a freestanding Mission-style façade that towered above the roof. Within arched openings of the façade, six exposed bells had hung silent in pyramid fashion. Far below the bells at ground level, five carved coquina steps led to two heavy oak doors framed by Doric columns bracing a circular arch. Perched just above the arch, the marble statue of St. Augustine faithfully guarded the entrance.

Feeling a tinge of guilt, Atan had stopped to behold the sacred figure. The saintly statue seemed to look down on him disapprovingly from its pedestal. Denying his shame, Atan had turned away in time to spy his lure slipping round the side of the church. Lust outweighing reason, he had pursued. Hidden in the shadow of that holy edifice, Atan, trembling with fear and anticipation, had approached his waiting obsession.

"Even in the dark I could tell he was very handsome. And I remember thinking I would be cursed for doing this in the shadow of God's house. But I wanted him so badly I didn't care."

Panting heavily and heart pounding, Atan had stopped directly in front of the tempter, so close that their bodies had nearly touched. The clandestine man had pulled Atan tightly into his arms and wrapped his cloak around him. In the crush of those arms, Atan had pressed against him, scared and excited at the same time.

"Then I felt his fangs pierce my neck. I tried to scream but could not. I could feel the life draining out of me. In panic, not knowing what else to do, I bit into his throat and drank. And drank. And drank till he pulled away and pushed me to the ground. I could hear his devilish laughter as he disappeared into the darkness. I lay there weak and dying. Somehow, I knew I had to get out of sight."

Determined to hide, Atan had struggled unsteadily to his feet. Feeling his way along the cold stone wall, he had staggered to the front of the parish, crawled up the steps, and pushed open the heavy door. Passing under the arch, he had entered the lofty church. The Classical-style church, adorned with several fifteen-foot stained glass windows and dark wood beams supporting a peaked ceiling, was dimly lit by candles that lined the side walls. Their dancing flames glinted on the edges of the polished pews that all faced the large crucifix that hung on the ochre-colored back wall. From the wood cross, the face of the porcelain Christ, flickering from the glimmer of candles beneath, gazed sadly upon the red and gold brocade draped altar below.

Averting his eyes, Atan had not been able to look at the crucifix. Christ, he had believed, had forsaken him. Keeping his head bowed, Atan had grabbed a candle to penetrate the gloom. Supporting himself by leaning on the pews, he had slowly stumbled forward until he reached the back of the church. Here, he had found a narrow door that led to a windowless storeroom. In the room, there had been over a dozen wine casks. Closing the door behind him, Atan had discovered several upright casks lined side by side along the rear wall. He had inspected the casks and found one that was empty. Prying open the cover, Atan, with his last remaining strength, had climbed into the vintage damp barrel. With the chill of death expelling the warmth of life, Atan had pulled the lid shut, entombing himself in that cold, sunless cavity.

"I hid unnoticed for two days. That cask became my grave. For there, I slept and I died and I was reborn. On the second night, I rose from the cask. I left the room and walked down the aisle with my back to God and to Man. I emerged from the church a new vampire, frightened and hungry and…" Realizing he might say too much, Atan abruptly ended his account. "Well, that's enough of that."

Fascinated, Reid persisted. "What about your family?"

"I never returned to my family. How could I? I hid by day and prowled by night. To my family and friends, I had vanished without a trace. Then, in 1821, when Spain sold Florida to the U.S., the Spanish left and so did my family. But I, of course, remained." Once again, he flashed that dangerously charming smile and quipped, "And here I am today. Talking to you."

"Wow, that's quite a story."

"Yes, it is, isn't it? Atan continued playfully. "It turns you on, doesn't it?"

"What!" cried Reid, taken aback. "You mean sex?"

"Yes. Even vampires have their needs."

"Yeah, sucking blood!"

"Not to kill. It's like a drug. Sucking blood during sex heightens the pleasure for both."

"Really. Pleasure? But aren't you, you know…dead?"

"Can the dead do this?" Atan ran his hand firmly along Reid's inner thigh. When Reid stiffened in apparent discomfort, Atan laughed provocatively.

Reid stopped Atan's hand from pressing further but did not remove it.

"So, you're telling me you can still have sex?" exclaimed Reid, incredulous.

"Sure. It feels good, too." Looking down at himself, he bragged, "And believe me. You wouldn't be disappointed."

At that, Reid rolled his eyes.

"Of course," he explained. "I can't get off in the human sense."

"Oh, you're human all right," retorted Reid as he pushed Atan's hand away.

"No, I'm not."

"You're pretty sure of yourself, aren't you?" countered Reid.

Atan shrugged with a conceited snicker.

"You laugh, don't you? And you sure as hell get horny. And I bet you cry, too. And get mad. And jealous. Hate…And love. That's what makes you human. Not whether you're dead, undead, immortal or whatever you are."

"Touché," conceded Atan. He leaned seductively closer to Reid and whispered, "So, do you want to sleep with a vampire?"

Once again, Reid was lured into those dark, hypnotic eyes. Drawn ever closer, he leaned forward, teetering on the edge of the bleacher as Atan's cool lips brushed his. Feeling that chill, breathless mouth, Reid started with a gasp, sat upright, and threw up his hands.

"No, I...I don't think so!" Reid stuttered. "I really should be going."

With that, Reid jumped up and headed for the door. Looking back, he caught Atan's spellbinding eyes and bewitching smile. Atanasio called to him.

"Perhaps, next time, when the moon is full." He grinned.

Reid rushed through the door, pushing and bumping his way through the crowd. As quickly as he could, he left the bar. Practically running to his car, he kept looking back over his shoulder, half expecting Atan to be following. But there was no one. Heart racing, he got into his car and in near panic inspected the backseat. It was empty. He locked the doors, started the car, turned on the headlights and sped home.

At home, Reid tossed and turned in his unlit bedroom. In the dark, he was haunted by the specter of Atan's supernatural smile and stirred by the virility of his touch. The spot where the evocative vampire had groped him tingled as if his hand had never been withdrawn. Placing his own hand over the spot, Reid drifted into a fitful sleep and dreamed.

In his dream, he was still in his own bed. Beside the bed rested a black wooden coffin. Leaning over the edge of the bed, he surveyed the casket and ran his hand along the lid. As he did, the lid was suddenly flung wide. From the open coffin, two muscular glowing arms reached out, clutching him with strong masculine hands. Caught in their powerful grip, Reid was pulled into the coffin. Within the confines of that burial box, he was held tightly. Crushed against a brawny chest, he once again faced those hypnotic eyes and that mesmerizing grin. As the grin grew wider, sharp fangs sprang from upper incisors and lustful laughter burst forth, reverberating against the sides of the narrow enclosure. The wanton laughter echoed louder and louder as the pointed incisors came closer and closer. With those fangs almost upon him, the lid of the casket snapped shut.

The closing slam of the dream coffin woke Reid with a start. Heart pounding, he hastily scanned the brightening room. Streams of early-morning sunlight revealed he was alone. Assured he was safe, he sat up in the middle of the bed still shaking. Amid the tangled sheets, he trembled panting and sweating and, to his astonishment, aroused.

Unsettled by this, he got up, walked into the bathroom, and splashed water on his face.

"Maybe the whole night was a dream," he said aloud. "It couldn't have been a vampire!"

Making a concerted effort to push the very chance of a vampire from his thoughts, Reid followed his usual Sunday ritual of household chores and preparation for those tedious Monday-morning-back-to-work blues. Still, whenever there was a lull in his routine, the haunting face of Atanasio flashed in his mind's eye and the imprint of his hand tickled his inner thigh. Beset by these tantalizing images, he passed the sunlit hours into the moonlit night.

That night, Reid once more dreamed of Atan. This time, in his dream, Reid's entire bedroom was a tomb. In the center of the tomb, surrounded by tall blood-red candles, lay Atan on a black satin shroud, naked and expectant, waiting with fangs exposed. Reid fell onto that sensuous sable cloth. At once, Atanasio rolled on top of him engulfing him like a cool consuming wave. As Atan covered Reid with the shroud and his body, the incessant harangue of the alarm clock stirred Reid. Once again, he woke trembling and aroused. Still inflamed, Reid readied for work.

Throughout the afternoon, the look and touch of Atan continued to excite him, playing in and out of his daydreams like a flickering erotic film, making it difficult to concentrate on his job. After work, Reid joined his usual Monday-night league for a few games of bowling. But even the light glinting on the white bowling pins reminded him of the pale flesh of Atan. Leaving the bowling alley, Reid returned to the bar.

The bar, with only a couple of dozen patrons circling like vultures, seemed dismal and deserted. Empty as it was, Reid met no delay buying a beer and finding a seat on the bleachers in the back patio. Sitting in his customary spot, he gulped his beer. Because he'd already had several bottles at the bowling alley, the brew buzzed his brain and blurred his vision. Through bleary eyes, he looked up at the moon. The moon was full. Still squinting at that bright hypnotic orb, Reid didn't notice Atan approach.

"Hello again."

Reid flinched, a little startled by the appearance of the sultry bloodsucker.

"Sorry." He laughed. "I didn't mean to scare you."

"No. That's all right," Reid spluttered. "How've you been?"

"Waiting for you," enticed Atan with a wildly disarming smile.

Both tense and titillated, Reid gaped mutely into Atan's enigmatic eyes. In pace with his racing pulse, Reid's breathing quickened as Atan moved closer.

Leaning into Reid, Atan enfolded him snugly in his solid arms. Held helplessly in Atan's forceful grip, Reid did not struggle. Nor did he resist when Atan pressed his cool lips over Reid's warm mouth. Atan kissed Reid long and passionately. Overwhelmed, Reid rested limply against Atan's athletic chest. Brushing his lips along Reid's skin, Atan drew his mouth near to Reid's ear.

"The moon is full tonight," he whispered seductively. "Will you come home with me?"

Kindled by that torrid combination of danger and desire, Reid could not refuse. "Yes," he agreed weakly. "Yes."

Spurred by his acquiescence, Atan pulled Reid firmly to his feet. Intoxicated with alcohol and hunger, Reid let the vampire usher him from the bar and into Reid's car. Once in the car, the aggressive sanguinarian caressed Reid's inner thigh while directing him to his house.

The one-story house stood inconspicuously at the end of a dead-end street. With its peach-painted stucco walls, lime Bahama shutters, and roof of cinnamon clay tiles, the secluded dwelling abided almost completely hidden by lush foliage. The branches of two twenty-five foot gumbo limbo trees formed a canopy over the gray slate walkway that led to the front door. The yard on both sides of the path teemed with leather fern, hibiscus, wild coffee, and arrowroot spreading rampant and wild.

Shrubs were beginning to violate the driveway where Reid parked the car by the side of the shadowy property. The murky premises were illuminated only by the warily watchful glare of the full moon. In that gloom, Reid was hardly able to see. To guide him, Atan vigorously grasped Reid's shoulders and hastened him along the walkway. Passing beneath the arch of branches that sheltered the path, Reid felt a sense of foreboding as though he was entering an ominous netherworld from which he might never return. Ignoring the dread, he allowed himself to be pushed inside the house and hustled through an unlit hallway into the back bedroom.

The bedroom, to Reid's astonishment, mirrored his dream. Like the chamber in his vision, several crimson candles seductively lighted the room. Their quivering flames created an eerie yet erotic ambience. In that seamy light, Reid observed that the windows had been blocked, transforming the room into a sealed vault. In the center of the tomb-like room, a king-sized mattress lay covered with black satiny sheets.

Easily lifting Reid with powerful arms, Atan dropped him roughly onto the bed. Caught in the surge of Atan's supernatural passion, Reid sprawled helpless, scarcely able to breathe. Like a relentless satyr, the ardent aggressor swiftly removed all of Reid's clothing. Lying naked on the luxurious cloth, Reid swelled with anxious anticipation as Atan quickly tore off his own garments. Standing nude, Atan's sinewy, toned physique glistened in the candlelight.

With shadows from the flickering flames dancing on his bare back, Atan kissed Reid's foot, then grazed his lips and the tip of his tongue along Reid's leg and inner thigh. The middle-aged mortal shuddered. As the handsome hedonist continued upward, skimming his mouth across Reid's abdomen and chest, his buff body glided over Reid like the smooth underbelly of a stingray. Reid convulsed involuntarily when Atan's mouth fully covered his and the vampire's firm figure completely covered his compliant flesh.

Panting beneath that strapping frame, Reid let out a low moan when Atan mounted him. The bloodsucker bared his fangs and bit. Reid gasped as the incisors sank deep into the tender tissue of his throat. As Atan swallowed, Reid felt his blood coursing through every artery of his body. His pulse raced beyond the human norm and his eyes glazed. All of his senses seemed to elevate, floating in that delirious realm between the physical reality of fabric and flesh and the spiritual boundaries of Heaven and Hell. It was as if every facet of his being was simultaneously climaxing in its own orgasmic ecstasy.

Exhilarated and exhausted, Reid rested completely spent beside Atan who, propped on one elbow, regarded him with a self-satisfied smirk.

"Well?" posed Atan smugly.

Before replying, Reid fingered the two tiny holes where the fangs had pierced his skin. The minute wounds were ever so slightly sore but virtually painless.

"That was the best sex I've ever had!"

Atan brushed back his hair with his free hand in a gesture of boastful vanity.

Reid paused to exhale a contented sigh.

"I guess," he continued. "I should give you my number. Maybe we can get together a—"

"No!" Atan interrupted emphatically. "I never see anyone twice."

"Why not?" demanded Reid disappointedly.

"We vampires are a solitary, territorial lot. And we live forever. I don't get involved with humans."

"It must get pretty lonely?" Reid implored.

Atan turned away.

"Nah," he remarked with wary disregard. "There's so many of you, it doesn't matter."

Reid quietly studied the now sullen vampire.

Breaking the uncomfortable silence, Atan insisted, "You'd better go now."

Reid soundlessly dressed. As he finished tying his shoes, he looked up to see Atan, still naked, standing by the door, waiting. Ogling that shimmering and inviting physique, Reid was instantly overcome with uncontrolled desire. On impulse, he strode over to Atan and wrapped his arms tightly around the vampire's irresistible torso.

Pressing against him, Atan could feel Reid's quickening heartbeat pumping its precious elixir throughout Reid's pulsating body. With supernatural senses, the immortal could smell the warm, fresh blood. The temptation was too overpowering. Extracting his fangs, he plunged them into Reid's exposed neck. With unquenchable thirst, Atan sucked in furious abandonment.

Reid tried to scream but could not. He could feel the life draining out of him. In panic, not knowing what else to do, Reid bit into Atan's throat and drank. And drank. And drank.

NEVER FOREVER
ROB ROSEN

I'd been hiking all day, over steep terrain, across beautiful countryside, seemingly alone. I suppose I got a bit turned around, lost. Not too frantic, but just enough; just enough to lose my bearings, to trip, to fall. The earth sped by, brown blurring with endless green before suddenly turning to black. Deep, dark, pitch black. Then white, a pinprick that grew and grew, nearly blinding me.

I awoke, cold, naked in a strange bed, the room massive, the moon's rays pouring in through the window. I sat up, scratched my head, felt the wound. No blood. No pain. Just cold, endless cold, infinite cold. I stood up and walked around, oddly light on my feet, my hand caressing the wood furniture, the granite countertop, hard, unyielding. I heard a floorboard creak and I froze, watching, waiting, breathing in, breathing out.

The door slowly opened. I backed an inch away, crouching down to hide my nudity. He entered, the smile on his face suddenly cast in silver light. "You're awake." The voice deep, rumbling, like a rushing river across heavy stones.

"I, um, yes, looks that way," I managed, my eyes locking on to his as he made his way inside, standing before me, dressed all in black, tall, stunning. Not like any man I'd ever seen before. "But, um, how did I get here?"

The smile widened, teeth a shocking white, eyes smoldering like cinders. "You fell, hit your head. We found you."

"We?" I asked, trying to look away. Trying and failing.

He nodded, his hand reaching out. I took it, flesh on flesh, a spark running up my spine like wildfire. Fire minus the heat. "I am Steven," he replied, helping me to my feet, effortlessly. "My brother Nathan and I found you."

I stared deeper into his eyes, the draw unworldly, mesmerizing, tantalizing. "How?" I asked, barely in a whisper. "I was out hiking up the mountain. No houses for miles. None as big as this one seems to be."

He closed the gap between us, eye to eye, lips mere centimeters apart, his hand on my shoulder now, firm, reassuring. "You lost a lot of blood." The word stretched out into a groan, my cock stirring at the sound of it, at the proximity to him. Pounding, arcing out, up.

I felt for my wound, reflexively. "No blood now, though."

Again the smile. Again the nod. In the blink of an eye, the gap closed further still, his lips on mine, soft like down, a tongue darting out, pushing inside, invading, entwining with my own, a moan escaping. His or mine, I could no longer tell. His mouth pressed flush, his strong arms encircling me, naked flesh against cool silk. He pulled away, eyes aglow. "We healed you, Eric," he whispered into my mouth, an icy exhale that invaded my lungs, ripping through my body like a tornado.

"You know my name?" I asked, my body against his, my arms around his narrow waist, my tongue gliding languidly up his neck.

"We know all there is to know," came the cryptic reply, his head tilted to the side now, alabaster skin exposed, a throbbing blue vein beneath my slithering appendage, a hunger manifested, multiplied, monstrous.

"I lost too much blood," I stated, suddenly aware of what had happened, that knowledge, and only that, suddenly present inside my head.

"Too much to survive," he purred, pulling me in, my teeth at once jagged, razor sharp, piercing his flesh in a glorious instant, the taste of blood all consuming as he flowed inside me, a raging river of life. The moan repeated, both of us this time, his eyelids fluttering as I fed, sucking, suckling.

Sated, for the time being, I retracted my fangs, pulling away, slightly, just slightly. "I feel you," I told him, a temporary calm welling up. "Inside of me, I mean."

He reached over, his hand upon my cheek, a soft caress. "Yes, Eric. In one way, yes."

I stared into his eyes, an endless depth of need and want clearly evident. "In one way?"

He smiled, his cape falling to the floor, the black shirt unbuttoned, yanked out from black slacks, parted open to reveal white flesh, nearly translucent, perfect as polished marble, nipples rigid, just as white, just as perfect. An ancient statue now animate. "Would you like to see the other way?"

I nodded, the hunger returning, ravenous. "Show me, Steven." I lay on the bed, my cock ramrod straight, thick now with his blood.

The shirt joined the cape on the wooden floor, his torso fully revealed, completely unmarred, a smattering of ebony hair trailing down between finely chiseled pecs. All muscle and sinew. White, so very white. He inched in toward the bed, his hand deftly unbuttoning his slacks, his boots kicked off. He bent down, sliding off his black leggings before yanking down his pants, leaving him in red briefs, a devilish twist to his wardrobe that sent my grin northward.

I sat back up and cupped his crotch in my hand, feeling him pulse beneath the material that I eagerly and swiftly pulled down and off, his cock springing out, thick and veined, the wide head slick, leaking salty jizz, the acrid aroma wafting up my nostrils. I engulfed him whole, the length and width of him filling my mouth as he shoved his way inside my throat, sending a happy gagging tear cascading down my cheek.

"Yes," he moaned, his fangs exposed, long, saber-like.

I stared up at him while I sucked him off, his face handsome, chiseled, unearthly. His body much the same, even more so. I popped him out of my mouth, unable to wait a moment longer. "Fuck me, Steven," I pled, nearly in a whimper.

He stared down, a tender stroke across my face by long, tapered fingers, nails like miniature daggers, the pain exquisite. I leaned back, my legs up and out, ass on the edge of the bed, hole exposed, beckoning him in, hungry, ready for the onslaught. He moved up, his steely cock battering up against my portal. In an instant, a heartbeat, if I still possessed one, he was inside me, sliding his way to my farthest reaches as I sucked in my breath, ravaged by absolute ecstasy, the likes of which no mortal man could ever dare imagine.

He leaned in, his body over mine, his hand stroking my cock as he mashed his mouth into my mouth, lips splayed, tongues slithering together as one, while he fucked me slow and steady, hour after hour after glorious hour. To say it was divine would be sacrilege; saying otherwise would be the same.

"Come with me, Eric," he repeated. "Come with me."

I sensed he meant something deeper, but took it on a baser level, waiting patiently, joyously, for him to fill me with yet another of his bodily fluids. "Now," I growled, biting down on his lip, a stream of blood eddying around my aching throat as he bucked his cock inside my hole, his heavy balls banging against my rump, my prick exploding in a torrent of cum, spewing across my belly and splattering his chest, his load streaming inside my ass, as life-giving as the blood, his blood, that coursed through my veins.

He collapsed on top of me, sweat-soaked, his mouth mashing into mine, his eyes open, locked, invading my very soul while I panted beneath him, desperately trying to catch my breath, his hands running rampant across my skin, mapping out uncharted territory.

He turned me over, wrapping me in his arms, his prize, but sunrise soon approached. I sensed it was not for us to witness. He left as he'd arrived, quietly, not another word said or needed, just the smile, just those eyes on mine. I quickly shut the curtains tight, casting the room in a gloomy pall. I was asleep in seconds, a dreamless, cold, forsaken sleep, disturbed only when the moon once more made its inevitable appearance.

I sprang up to find I was no longer alone, feeling his presence before actually seeing him there.

"Hello," he said, sitting in a chair by my bed, looking much like his brother, perhaps a few years younger, white hair instead of jet black, his features a tad more severe, still just as perfect. He was naked, erect, stroking his club of a dick as he stared at me, balls rising and falling, a hunger cast menacingly across his face.

I nodded. "You must be Nathan."

He leered down at me, his teeth pearly white, sharp. "And you are Eric." He stood, taller than his brother, leaner. "Now that we have that settled, remove the sheet."

I did as he commanded, my cock now revealed, already at full mast. He spanked the shaft, sending my tool swaying, then lifted my legs, smacking my hole before his mouth dove in for a savage suck and slurp, violent where his brother was tender, yet no less intoxicating. A finger joined his tongue, two, three, all pumping away inside my ass as his free hand came crashing down on my stomach, my chest, a yank and a pull on a nipple, twisted until blissfully bruised.

My head tilted back, mouth open, fangs out, sharp, lethal, saliva dripping down as he thrust his digits in and out, in and out. He laughed as he assailed me, the sound drowned out when his mouth found mine, the fingers replaced by his massive cock, rammed in without prelude, popped out lightning fast, shoved in again, and again, and again. Pleasure and pain, pain and pleasure, interchangeable.

He moaned, loudly, his face twisted to the side now, his neck mine for the taking. I sank my teeth in deep, deeper still, his blood flowing in, his cock filling my hole, our bodies, our very souls, united in a writhing tangle atop my bed.

"Now come," he grunted, sweat dripping from his pale brow, the salt mixing with the blood, the taste like ambrosia.

He bucked a final time while I jacked my prick, both of us shooting mighty loads of cum, thick, viscous, copious amounts, the sticky mess pooling beneath my chest, dripping out of my ass, both of us moaning and groaning, shaking the very rafters above our heads.

Breaths caught, the foray continued, the black and blue welting up, only to quickly heal, his cock steely for hours on end, filling my holes with wild abandon. All this I took. All this I gave back in return. Tit for tat, spank for slap, fuck for fuck. I hated this man as much as I desired him. Hated him as much as I felt for his brother. Strange, so very strange, as if I'd known them forever, was meant to be there.

Once more the sun, the bane of our existence, loomed just beyond the horizon, ready to make an appearance I feared I'd never witness again, its warm rays never to touch my skin, never to dapple across my face. Nathan hurriedly left. I slept, falling dead away, dreamless.

This ritual continued, year in and year out, decades into my servitude. I'd awake to find one of them by my bed, never both. My life was at their disposal. Their desires, my desires. On occasion, they'd take me hunting with them. More often than not, I simply fed off them during the throes of passion. It was an odd existence, if you could call it that. Never alone, I was still lonely. Never hungry, I always hungered. Never tired, I longed to sleep, to dream once more.

I learned little of the brothers, how they came to be, though I knew that one of them had rescued me from certain death, changing me just before the last drop of essential blood seeped from my wound. I, however, was their only creation. Except for me, when they fed, they killed, slaughtered, obliterating any traces of their existence.

Still, I knew their story, and I dreaded what I knew I must do in order to alter it.

Wood was evident throughout the house. I crafted my salvation from something that would not be missed. Waking to find Steven by my bedside, I asked if I could hunt with them that evening. They never denied me my wishes, what few I had; that night was no different. No different, that is, except that everything would in fact be different come sunrise. I'd grown as strong as them over time, strong enough to know that my plan would work, must work.

I lifted the stake above my head while they fed, when they were at their most vulnerable. They stared up, blood dripping from their gaping maws, resignation more than shock on their pale faces.

"Which one of us will you kill, Eric?" Steven asked. "Which one will you kill before the other returns the favor?"

I smiled, staring into his eyes, willing my thoughts into his head. He smiled in return, his reddened teeth glinting in the moonlight as I brought the stake down, the sharpened wood piercing his chest in an instant, his lifeless body crumpling over his prey as a sudden burst of wind rushed over his brother and me. The deed was done, a new ending to their story unfolded.

A pause. We watched each other. Waiting.

"How did you know?" Nathan finally asked, rising, his normally pallid cheeks suddenly tinged with red.

"The eyes are the windows to the soul," I replied. "He could hide little from me."

Nathan nodded, solemnly, knowingly. "You loved him, didn't you?"

I pondered the question and echoed the nod. "In my own way, yes."

He moved toward me, no fear that he would be my next victim or I his. "And he loved you as well, in his own way. Which is why he changed you. I think he knew this would all happen. It is why he changed me, too, to bring me along with him through time, to make his existence less lonely. You, however, made it something more than that." He tilted his head, his eyes narrowing. "But why not kill me instead of the one you so adored?"

I touched his cheek, warmth at long last flowing through both our bodies. "One must kill the progenitor to restore the followers; and we, Nathan, have been restored, followers no longer."

Again he nodded. "And will you leave me now, Eric? Leave me as he has left us?"

I held his hand, leading him out of the forest. "No, Nathan, I will not. You are all I have left of him." I turned to face him, the smile returning yet again. "But when I dream, and oh how I long for that moment, I will see his face, see the endless abyss in his eyes, his insatiable desire for me, and I will remember him, forever and always."

Though forever, of course, had been obliterated for the three of us. It was a forever we were never to have.

THE CELTIC CONFESSIONAL
DAVEM VERNE

Insula sacra!"
  The monk's voice filled the hollow oratory.

"My holy island! Protect me from the heathens invading your shores!"

Brother Dónal remained inside the stone oratory that evening, fasting and illuminating a sacred manuscript. The shadows against the stone walls attended him and a damp draught penetrated his flesh. He fastened the rope around his habit in a restraining knot and listened to the crash of the sea against the rugged coastline outside. For hundreds of years the embattled cliffs along the West Coast had defended the island from barbarians. But tonight, the Normans were drawing near. They came by sea, as the Celts had come long ago, in the hopes of sacking Ireland.

Quickly, Brother Dónal composed a letter to the Bishop in Dublin. His pen quivered. The short, lean strokes trembled across the parchment. He was brief, outlining the situation and no further, afraid an elaborate letter would disturb the Bishop. In the stone oratory, Brother Dónal worshiped without supervision and his unorthodox practices were tolerated from afar. The Monastery knew of his proclivities; word had spread among the Brothers. His intimate knowledge of the pagan population was evidenced on the manuscript page by obscure Celtic symbols which were forbidden by the Church.

"Inishmore and the Aran Islands are conquered!" he wrote without breathing. "The barbarous Normans travel in fishing boats, surprising and attacking the mainland. Forget about me! I am already captured, enslaved by the primitive rites of these heathens! Your Grace, heed this warning. Protect Dublin!"

The pyramid-shaped oratory, which three generations of monks had built on the isolated coastline, now crumbled stone by stone with every lashing of the wind. Brother Dónal prayed for deliverance. He prayed for protection. The demonic world was strong this evening; he could sense the rapport it shared with Satan. Depraved souls and the Devil's tireless legions were occupying the land, bringing with them all manifestation of evil. In his anxiety, he thought he heard the sound of copper helmets in the distance and the clank of iron swords marching towards his chamber. *The Normans are coming!* But it was only the rain striking the iron crosses in the cemetery...

For a moment, his heart weakened and Dónal felt his soul slip by. He closed his eyes and begged for mercy from the pagan gods. In betrayal of his true faith, he implored the vulgar servants to watch over him. Surely they knew the countryside better than the Saints; surely they had means to quell the oncoming storm. Alone and in their dark company, Dónal entertained a host of tragic endings for Ireland, such as enslavement by the Norman lords or blood sacrifices in nearby villages. The offences to Irish body and soul would only be the start of the Devil's perdition!

Suddenly, the cemetery gate opened and a fist assaulted his door.

A trembling voice shouted, loud and hysterical, calling his name.

"Dónal! Dónal!"

Brother Dónal recognized it not. Quickly, he covered his manuscript, fearing it might be a Norman invader seeking to pillage his sanctuary, or worse, another cleric who wouldn't approve of his obscene illustrations. In his manuscript, Dónal had generously populated the borders with stout Celtic characters instead of the Saints. The hairy male figures danced amidst the Gaelic letters with erect phalluses and red buttocks. If the beacons of the Church saw his lewd artistry, they'd strip him of his habit and cast him into the dungeon with the unconverted knaves, rapists and rogues who would gladly defile a renegade monk through the night!

Dónal pondered this torture and he rather fancied it, so he opened the door wide.

"Brother Dónal, help me!"

Young Fionn, a village farmer, glowed in the moonlight like a Celtic deity. His long hair draped his forehead and his luminous eyes gazed at Dónal with a pleading expression. Brother Dónal stood back, alarmed at the sudden appearance of the youth. Many farmers visited the monk during the day, bearing crops for his meal or performing small repairs outside the oratory. But never had one appeared this late, at the very hour the sun fell down.

"What purpose brings you here, my son?"

In the youth's frightened face, Brother Dónal perceived a millennium of rural Irishmen, rugged and homely but loyal to their country. For ten generations, Fionn's clan had struggled to protect the West Coast of Ireland from hostile invaders, and many had died for the cause. Tonight, in the footsteps of Fionn, their steadfast spirits marched towards the present to seek Brother Dónal and warn him of the impending attack.

"Do you have word of the Normans?" Dónal asked in a pressing breath. His eyes glanced at Fionn's bulging pockets, which concealed some rural elements: a squash and two potatoes, modest sustenance for the monk's dinner. "What do you hide in your trousers, boy?"

"Brother Dónal, I've sinned!"

The farm youth opened his palms and bowed his head. A whimper escaped his lips. Under quick inspection, Dónal saw the stains upon Fionn's hands. It wasn't blood or dirt or splintered wood from a farmer's tool; instead, thick streaks of robust semen lined his hands, slowly drying. The fluid stuck to his palms and bore the impression of a virile erection. Fionn dripped more beads of cum from his fingertips and they speckled the black stones at his feet, mocking the house of prayer. Shame covered Fionn's face and he turned from the Brother.

Dónal shook his head. He prayed silently for salvation while eyeing the farm boy's sweaty buttocks. They were moist and firm, partially exposed from the recent charge up the hill. Dónal knew what had occurred as clearly as if he had witnessed it himself. The impending night had frightened poor Fionn. A multitude of temptations had visited him in the field. Serpents, sinners, and probably a Succubus! The dark enticements menaced the boy with charms and kisses until he was forced to obey their sorcery. Unveiling his manhood above the virgin soil, they rushed through his body and boiled the semen in his loins to such a steamy ingredient that it fired from his member in creamy heaps.

"Come in here!" Dónal ordered, glancing into the night. "Let's clean that up."

This wasn't the first time young Fionn had fallen from grace. The traps set by the pagan spirits often found him a willing prey. On many a stormy midnight, Fionn's farm in the lowlands was besieged by the souls of unburied chieftains, warriors, and blood-spirits. They elicited mischief in the sheep, uprooted vegetables in the garden, and whispered libidinous thoughts into young ears. Weekly Fionn sought the sanctuary, bearing filthy hands or clutching an incorrigibly erect penis; and Brother Dónal would summon original ways to forgive Fionn's sins, like a sponge bath around his loins or a towel dipped in goat's milk and applied tightly to the offensive member.

He forgave Fionn, for in his heart Dónal knew that the boy was as innocent as the earth upon which he labored. It was the other villagers, those unrepentant Elders, who were at fault. Every winter, the Elders performed heretical ceremonies intended to conjure the ancient spirits and expurgate Ireland of barbarians. The superstitious sacraments by the old-timers only roused the Celtic spirits to wander the desolate lowlands, hungry for a sacrifice. And when invaders were in want and the spirits grew bored, they persuaded chaste youths like Fionn that his manseed was theirs, by ancestral law, and demanded proof of his filial loyalty. As sunlight beat upon his face and warmed his round flanks, they induced him to litter the broken ground with his Irish cum. Fionn obeyed, masturbating upon the stones day and night until he was weary and withered. He ignored Brother Dónal's warning about sensual temptation and once more spoiled the earth with the seeds of his race.

Dónal bolted the door and sat the young man on his stool. He kneeled into Fionn's lap, shaking his head solemnly, and scrubbed the coarse hands with an unused rag. Farmer cum dries thick, so it was very hard to peel off. But the monk assumed his duty with humility, rubbing each finger, curling them to the palm and massaging the knuckles. Fionn's hands grew bright red like the figures in Dónal's manuscript. And his cheeks blushed like polished apples when Dónal found more cum starching his cuff.

"When will you learn to distinguish cum from communion?" Dónal asked.

"I don't know, Brother," Fionn confessed. "But when it starts growing, I need to pick it up like a plough and work it until it breaks!"

Rolling up a sleeve, Dónal eyed Fionn's forearm. Blond hairs covered his limb and sprouted from his armpit. Dónal frowned and kept his thoughts private. Irish youths rarely inherit such soft, light fur. Fionn was clearly a bastard child, his mother the victim of a Nordic raid twenty years prior. There were many such bastards farming the land, begotten by aroused Norsemen who traveled as troubadours in disguise or pretended to be lost in this infertile land while they secretly scouted villages in anticipation of attack. They played their tin whistles in the ear and bosom of any farmer's wife and planted their oppressive seed too deep to uproot. Dónal could hear Fionn's mother cry out and her clit twitch as the fake troubadour startled her with the size of his jangling flute!

"Brother Dónal!" Fionn cried. "It's growing again!"

Fionn exhibited no self-control. He let his woollen trousers drop to his boots and spread his thighs. Between them, his swollen cock rose from a flurry of blond hairs and dominated his waist like a flesh-pink altar.

"Put that away, Satan!"

"I can't! It's too late!"

By the size of the member, Dónal understood at once what afflicted Fionn. A field fiend! The malevolent spirit of a peasant or vagabond who had died by the impaling kick of a donkey or ass! It had locked itself inside Fionn's body, probably when the boy was pissing or squatting too low to the earth. It possessed him through that rear orifice and encouraged wild, animal cravings in his gut. Fionn's manhood grew engorged, filling with all the unruly lusts of the fallen spirit. His wide thighs extended farther, supporting a boner that loomed in the air, claiming the center of the oratory and mocking the sacred vessels that Dónal so highly revered.

Fionn clutched his cock.

His face grew red.

He began jerking wildly.

"Let go of that abomination!" Dónal warned.

Fionn clasped his hands behind his back, wrenching and squirming on the edge of the stool. The hand job in the field was not enough. Fionn's cock perched on his lap like a billowy gargoyle and demanded deliverance of its own device, in a sanctified hole that secretly desired damnation. The sacred oratory was inimical to the phallus as it slithered about Fionn's lap, seething with cursed juices, and sensing the penitent Brother.

"*Insula sacra!*" Brother Dónal gasped.

The possessed penis hissed.

"Fiendish spectre abiding in this boy, I cast you out!"

The sneering serpent fluttered its golden scales burning irreverently in the candlelight. When it saw Dónal, it shrieked. Its pink head pierced the atmosphere. It began blandishing scorching ejaculations at the Brother, contaminating his robe.

Dónal hid behind his hood as he was assaulted with cum. He reached for a weapon, his manuscript pen or book of prayers. But these instruments had not prepared him for the lewd testament. How do you observe prayer with a provoked peter?

Rocking upon his knees and chanting a verse, Dónal recalled his novitiate days at the Monastery, where he was routinely chastened for being too radical a monk. He once solicited the Abbot for extracurricular favors, such as inviting celebrity clergymen to the cloister or hosting Gaelic saga readings in the cellar. His attempted worldliness may have perturbed his Order, but they never conceived he would one day hear the confessions of a man's loins or presumed he would endure such a carnal covenant. There were no passages in *The Book of Kells* instructing a shepherd on taming this sort of sheep. Perhaps in the Egyptian *Book of the Dead*?

At once, the repressed energies in the oratory convulsed. The diabolical dick sought a virgin to impregnate. With each fiery discharge, Fionn's seed perverted the century of prayer that protected the oratory. Following the path of a thousand martyrs, Dónal stood alone; no sermon could shield him. Dodging the dick-eye but covered in cum, Dónal's own unspeakable cravings awoke from the prison of his vows.

Not long ago, in Dublin, he had seen the cock of a cleric slip out of hiding in broad daylight to fuck a whore in the alley beside the chapel. Dónal had witnessed the accursed assault firsthand and secretly desired it for himself. He wished he had been that insatiable harlot, wearing her cheap amulets and receiving the cleric's charity in his own gaping asshole. The forbidden vision haunted him, preying upon his days, until he begged the Bishop to be sent away, far away, to the barren cliffs of the West Coast where he could purify his soul from all temptation.

Now, lifting his hood, he was arrested by spiritual agony. The sight of Fionn's muscular appendage invited him. He witnessed drops of semen capture in Fionn's navel, daring the holy man to taste and drink it with his dry lips. Dónal would be damned if he cocksucked the youth and received this unsaved pollution! But the beautiful bastard boy had interrupted his prayers with courageous fervency. Did he know the Normans were advancing? Had the villagers spread the news? Perhaps this was a test before the Norman conquest? A message must be sent to Dublin!

"Cleanse me, Brother!" Fionn moaned, thrashing his legs about the stool.

The hot semen boiling in his testicles bubbled for release. Fionn pulled his balls apart with a helpless hand. He glanced at the Brother and jiggled his nuts. His gesture delayed the frenzy of cum from escaping too soon before it could be blessed.

With sudden bedevilment, Dónal dove unto Fionn's thick crotch, rejecting the chastity of his Order for the nutrients of Today. He swallowed the pleasures of the male flesh as they exploded in full bloom before him. The naked contour of the young man's thighs met his hands as he plunged his mouth atop the swollen genitals. He sucked the two bastard balls between his lips and showered each cum-sealed chalice with delicate kisses, biting the nuts in order to rupture the seed. Then he worshiped with gross display the altar of manhood, which stood as full and luminous as the concupiscent characters in his manuscript pages. Irish cock! Farmer cock! The holy vessel of man! Dónal surprised his heathen lover as he unashamedly growled for joy.

Then Dónal froze, his lips lathered, staring at Fionn. He must not continue. He must not risk damnation. Atop the roughened ballsac, glistening with Dónal's blessing, stood the shrine of Succubus, the Devil's own scythe, an unrepentant dick coveting its first blow job! After years of denial, the vessel of all mortal foil towered before him, Fionn's hard penis, bouncing to be blown. Fionn moaned as Dónal dove deeper to chew each aching testicle, frightened to finish the ultimate task. With coarse palms, Fionn buried the Brother's face into his golden pubes in order for the monk to savour the sticky sweat of his plough.

And Dónal fell in that moment. He fell farther than the parchment on which he blasphemed. He swallowed Fionn's penis and worshipped its length as dearly as he made love to his relics on many a lonely night. He squeezed it in his hand; he jerked it from base to head; he smeared his lips with the yielded pre-cum. Fionn's barbaric club responded, beating Dónal's face and purging a preliminary load across his brow. The dick-eye glowered menacingly and sought complete entrance into Dónal's throat.

Hastily, Dónal cocksucked his young parishioner before the gods could intervene. The candlelight scarcely observed the deed, keeping the despicable dinner hidden. Dónal's jaw locked around the pulsing prick and blew it repeatedly. So long and ripe! So pink and fleshy! This bastard's flute was clearly the instrument of devilry, sent to earth to condemn Dónal. And the cum-lust Dónal was experiencing, the heightened obedience to his new master, seduced him utterly. He immersed himself in his bodily reward, ignoring the odious noises exhaling from his lover's chest.

Young Fionn gripped the stool and humped Dónal's lips. The innocence of his arrival had degenerated. He began to speak cruelly, face-fucking the man while spitting insults at the monk. An ancient Celtic dialect, known only to field fiends and exhumed spirits, echoed through the oratory as Fionn blasted a tirade of obscenities, exorcising the confessional of its sacred precepts.

"You depraved swine!" Fionn called. "You monastic snake! My father says you are an emasculated goat, prostituting your beliefs on the farthest coasts of Ireland because you are unfit to breed! Don't you remember that your father was a man? He ravished that whore you call mother so she could produce a coin-earning son, not a salacious saint! He should have tossed his only child on a spike rather than see him grow up to be the male-sucking pig you are now, ally only to a farmer's anus!"

"No, it's not true!" Dónal cried, as he sucked harder.

"You are a poisonous potato! You lie in the earth with the worms, baking in this unclean oratory. By the glow of your candles you abide, blistering with all your spoils, when I should grease that candle and shove it up your butt!"

Dónal suffered greatly then. Not by Fionn's sentiments, which he could barely hear at this point, but by the massive hard-on pounding vehemently in his throat. The youth was severely aroused, past his previous anxiety, and dominating the monk's mouth with a succession of charging thrusts. Each cum-fueled stab impaled Dónal until he could no longer breathe.

"Suck it like a Succubus!"

Fionn's prick did not adhere to the natural principles of a healthy youth. It curled and uncurled, now pink, now red, thrashing repeatedly between Dónal's lips, which were dry from years of exaltation. Then it untangled into a fork and Fionn cock-fed the parched mounds as if he were gorging the baker's daughter, fattening the monk with his bodily beliefs, his uncivilized faiths, and lording over tongue and throat with a prick that fumed of all the appetites of an overcharged farmer.

"Your mouth gasps for meat!" Fionn growled, laying his hands on Dónal's head. He urged Dónal to deep-throat the immoral feast. "Since you suffer, let me confess my sins in your backside. Let me canonize you on the ground in the filth where you belong."

The moaning monk gulped the loosened seed that escaped Fionn's prick. He begged Fionn to wait, strangling each testicle to unload its miracles. Fionn pushed him down upon the stony earth, where Dónal writhed in mute agony, his teeth gnashing at the vacancy in his mouth. He had hoped for all of Fionn's fuck-fluid, to hear another string of abuses while finally digesting the delights of rural male cum. But Fionn stood over him, spanking and jerking his tremendous plough.

"You let me in, you horrible hypocrite!" Fionn barked. He kicked the thick layers of Dónal's robe. "Servant of St. Succubus! Brother of St. Snake! You've shown me your fangs. Now take off the shroud that conceals your impotent loin and let me reform your pinching hole!"

"No!" Dónal shrieked, untying his robe.

Dónal struggled beneath Fionn's trampling boots, quickly removing his long-flowing habit to reveal a lean body, white as a ghost and celebrating its decadent vigil with a hard-on pointed directly at Fionn.

The boy scowled, fitting a boot on Dónal's crotch.

"Turn around! This time you won't leave your anointments in the forest where you spy on our poor! You'll spill it upon your own foul bed!"

Fionn stroked his stake and stepped out of his boots as Dónal prostrated himself face-down on the damp earth. Dónal knew he was assuming an unholy position between men, yet he did not dispute it nor intervene to oppose it. Like a groveling dog, he waited for his master to lie on top of him. He spread his ass cheeks with his fingers and widened his hole with a long, dark fingernail.

Fionn crawled on top of the monk and drove his weapon between their hips. He rode the space between them for a while, warming Dónal's tight virgin void. Then he impaled the Brother violently, straight into his opening.

Dónal squealed wretchedly. His face burrowed into the stony ground. Their bodies became one as the barbaric farmer hammered his cock into the monk's butt. Dónal squirmed under the desperate plunges. His rear resisted at first, vaulting upwards into the air, then surrendered as Fionn persevered, mercilessly submerging his pagan organ into the bowels of the clergyman.

Terrestrial howls accompanied their grind; voices from the sea smashed against the bleak cliffs outside the oratory. The Celtic fiend possessing Fionn despised the authority of the Cloth and preferred the bright flow of blood. This primitive soul was the antecedent to the enlightened demons that centuries later would walk the streets of Dublin. It invaded the monk through Fionn, riding the holy man aggressively, hearing his cries of lost chastity before drawing his blood.

As the insatiable screw raged on, Dónal lay defeated in a pile of clerical cum, his own production. Casting menacing curses into his ear, Fionn broke the sacred seal and poured his peasant load into the ecclesiastical orifice. Fionn bit Dónal's ear and snapped his jaws wildly while successive loads descended into Dónal's asshole, soiling the future saint for all eternity. No din of metal was heard, no hoarse shout of Norman invasion. Only the profound murmur from between the monk's legs as two spirits collided and Fionn came.

Then, while their bodies struggled in rapture, Fionn's teeth bit the monk on the nape of his neck and tore an opening. Dark blood of the spine emerged and Fionn licked it. They became blood brothers then, Young Fionn and Brother Dónal. An eternal door had been opened to the Celtic gods; henceforth, their spirits were welcome to enter and exit as they pleased, occupying Dónal and assuming his body to fulfill their appetites. Fionn had one, a marked opening beneath his right ear. The baker's daughter had sucked his neck one night after he fucked her on the cliff. She had bestowed the Celtic charm onto him; and now Fionn bestowed one upon the monk.

Satisfied and strong, Fionn threw his clothes on, a glint of triumph on his brow. The oratory door banged in the wind as Fionn escaped to the lowlands. The youth had liberated the oratory of its prayerful properties; and through the swinging door, the dead chieftains from the cemetery entered under the guise of a salty breeze and paraded about the oratory, laughing at the monk. They would never again be barred from this soil and found dark corners to wait and watch.

After an hour or more of tears and shame, the monk lifted his head from the loose ground. He weighed his soul in his stained hands and found it wholly corrupted. He had been fooled. The innocence of a young farmer had seduced him and he had surrendered to a Celtic blood-spirit. Or to put it more simply, he made love to a horny youth.

Dónal sat up, wrecked. His only real weapon lay between his legs like a rinsed rag. He looked around his monastic stronghold, the oratory walls, the domed ceiling, the shelves of manuscripts, and the candle extinguished by his own renegade breath, and everything disgusted him. They were the trappings of honorable employment and nothing more. Worse, he was bleeding, no longer from his spirit, now from his neck.

"Where are the Normans?" he cried. "Why haven't they invaded?"

They might have protected him from the assault. Or better yet, they might have killed him, hammered a spike through his heart and saved him from the blood feast.

But the Normans were in the East, landing on Banginbun. The West Coast was too isolated for conquest by boat, but not by male ravishing. The barren parcel surrounding the oratory was the only battlefield this night, Dónal's battlefield, and he had fallen into its abyss. Tonight, he had rejected his pious beliefs in favor of Celtic cum—half-Nordic cum!—and his faith had been consumed. At last, the avenging ancients had sent a deliverer, Fionn the Cocker, and indoctrinated Dónal into their unearthly order.

As he sat on his stool, Dónal had nothing to pray for, nothing at all, except the fleeting hope that Fionn would return the next day and resume the rituals of his ancient tribe. With palms steeped in semen and pagan blood coursing through his prick, Fionn would feign elaborate tears and the monk would yield. Dónal would administer to Fionn like before, wipe the young farmer's cum-soaked hands, and exclaim his universal love for the handsome youth. He would offer his blood at the sacrificial opening and patiently await another Celtic confession.

LONG IN THE TOOTH
NATHAN SIMS

Did you see the finish on that coffin?" Victor scoffed. "Frankly, I've had outhouses with better craftsmanship."

"That's what you get for letting your attorneys plan everything," Trevor replied. "If you'd let John do it as he asked—"

"No thank you. John would have had a horse-drawn carriage, a twenty-one gun salute, and a national day of mourning if I'd left it to him."

The funeral service was at an end, and the two men were tucked away safely in the backseat of the limousine heading out of the city and back toward Victor's estate in Potomac.

"And you would have complained about that just like you're complaining over a silly box," Trevor said. His words were dry and cracked, like wind whipped through the desert. The old man resembled no more than a dried husk, susceptible to the first breeze that blew his way.

By contrast Victor looked like a fresh bloom, fragrant and lovely. "Silly box?" Trevor's oldest friend asked. "*A silly box,* is that what you call it? Well, I'll be sure to use the same mortuary when it's your turn."

"No thank you," Trevor grimaced, "that place was a dive. Did you hear the canned music they had piped through the speakers?"

"Mmm-hmm, that's what I thought," Victor said triumphantly, patting his friend's wrinkled hand. Its paper-thin skin barely covered the brittle bones beneath. Trevor noted with embarrassment the liver spots and other signs of age he lugged about like so much excess baggage these days. He cast an envious glance at Victor's reborn hand. It had been so many years since he'd known the feel of fresh, unscarred skin wrapped tight against muscle and bone he could barely remember how it felt.

"You know," Victor said as he watched tendons dance their way up his arm, "I think Celeste might have the right idea here."

"Victor, placing Celeste with the words 'right idea' in the same sentence has only ever led to disaster. What ever possessed you to turn that woman in the first place I'll never know."

"Say what you will about her—and Lord knows I've said it all—I can understand why she kills herself at the first sign of a wrinkle."

"Please! Using our gifts as a form of plastic surgery is so plebian."

"I don't know. This feeling can be quite addicting."

Trevor hated to admit that Victor (and by proxy Celeste) was right. He always loved that time of life when everything was new and full of promise, when, like unscarred flesh, there were no mistakes yet, only a lifetime of opportunities.

"Well, you haven't told me yet what you think," Victor said, interrupting his musings.

"Think of what?"

"You know perfectly well what! How do I look?"

"You're quite handsome."

"Quite handsome? *Quite handsome?* That's all you have to say?"

"Victor, you look exactly as you have after all your other rebirths. What do you want me to say?" There was no recrimination in Trevor's voice. After nearly two hundred and fifty years of friendship, it was impossible to take Victor's railings seriously.

"That I'm beautiful. That I'm as handsome as I've ever been. That you want to rip this Fioravanti suit off my body and ravish me here and now."

"Victor, the days of you wishing me to do anything to your body ended three lifetimes ago."

"That doesn't mean you couldn't at least want to," Victor said. He turned a pouting look out the window to watch River Road pass by smoothly on the other side.

Trevor shook his head and sighed. He hated getting dragged into these petty squabbles with Victor. He'd learned to avoid them as best he could. Yet like the prodigal son returning home, he always found himself returning to these well-trod paths in the midst of some superficial debate. He wasn't even certain why he was being stubborn about the matter. It would be quite easy to give Victor the accolades he craved and to mean every word of it.

His friend never looked better than when he was fresh-born: his luxurious black hair offset by those rich blue eyes; his sharp cheekbones cut into a face sweeping down to a chiseled chin; and that lithe, compact body housing such potency. A lifetime of memories came flooding back—of doing exactly what Victor had suggested and ripping his expensive suit off to find the pleasures hidden beneath. Trevor shifted awkwardly in the limousine's leather seat as recollections of their mutual, mounting blood lust caused more than just his fangs to grow.

No, complimenting Victor on his appearance would be as simple as acknowledging the sun was setting. Yet try as he might, he didn't have the taste for that particular game. Not today. Instead, he attempted another tactic to soften his friend's mood.

"So, regrets or resolutions?"

It was a tradition each time one of them closed another volume in their long life. Trevor wasn't sure if any others of their kind ever played at this, but it had always fascinated the two of them: to take a step back from their previous life and gauge their mistakes as well as their victories; to see the whole of a new life, rich with possibilities, spreading out before them; and to find the courage to take the first wobbly, tentative steps into that new life. It was always a heady time— heady and a bit disconcerting—well, for Trevor at any rate. Victor always seemed to adjust more readily to the idea.

"Oh, well, definitely no more stock market or hedge funds," Victor said, instantly warming to his favorite subject: himself. "I'll pay someone else to do that this time, thank you. I think I want to do something with my hands," he said. Trevor watched him admire his long, manicured fingers. "I was thinking maybe a surgeon."

"Victor, you always say you're going to be a surgeon."

"That's because I always want to be one."

"And what, pray tell, would happen the first time the thirst hits you during the middle of an operation, and you decide to bend over for a little nip from your patient? It might raise a few eyebrows."

"Well, after three hundred years I should hope I have more self-discipline than that."

"True, you'll just saunter down to the blood bank for a little pick-me-up after surgery, where you'll only end up ruining that three-hundred-year streak of anonymity."

"Fine, then, perhaps I'll be an attorney."

"Aren't most court proceedings held during daylight hours?"

"Why do you always feel it necessary to dash my dreams?"

"Why do you always feel it necessary to put me in this position?"

"Because you're nothing but a damned realist."

"And you're nothing but a hopeless dreamer."

"Fine! Then maybe I'll just enjoy the fortune I've spent the last five lifetimes amassing. Maybe I'll jet off to the Riviera and revel in the life of a playboy. Or maybe that's too impractical, too?"

"I have no complaints. I only wonder what John might make of it."

"Oh, John," Victor sighed, his tone instantly softening. "The poor boy—this has all been so traumatic for him."

"The first time always is," Trevor agreed.

"You know, he actually wanted to go to the mausoleum to see me off, the dear." Victor smiled, dabbing at his eyes with a handkerchief.

Trevor wasn't sure he would use the word *dear* to describe Victor's most recent partner. However, he could say with certainty: "He's going to want to join you quickly now."

"Mmm-hmm, he's already mentioned several ways he might hasten his demise."

"Already?"

"Well, he's so young—only ninety-three. You remember what you were like at that age."

"I remember how terrified I was the first time I died."

Victor took Trevor's hand and leaned over, kissing him on his weathered cheek, and said, "You cried like a baby. And there I was beside you, telling you everything would be all right."

"And it was. I went to sleep and when I woke up I was young again."

"Young and beautiful."

Trevor smiled at Victor's tender lie and patted his friend in appreciation.

In response Victor slapped Trevor a stinging blow across his knuckles.

"What was that for?"

"That's how you compliment someone!" Victor snapped. "Not 'you're quite handsome'!"

Trevor grinned. "Victor, you know I've never laid eyes on anyone more ravishing than you—not in four lifetimes. From the moment I saw you standing on the docks in the firelight chucking those crates of tea into the harbor, I never wanted anyone more."

Victor clutched Trevor's aged hands and nodded. He turned to look out the window and said quietly, "Well, it wouldn't hurt for you to say it once in a while."

Trevor chuckled and cast a glance out the window as well, watching the world slip by the darkened glass. The memorial service had been scheduled for near dusk, making it safe for Victor, Trevor, and John to attend. They needn't have worried, though. The weather had been more than accommodating as thick storm clouds spent the day blocking out the sun.

He looked back at his friend and chided him. "And don't think I didn't notice how deftly you diverted the subject from John."

Victor sighed at his latest lover's name. "John is wonderful. He's all I could ever ask for. Gentle."

"Always attentive," Trevor offered. He supposed it sounded better than *clingy* or *possessive* would have.

"Handsome as hell. The first time I saw those green eyes—ugh!"

"And that laugh of his."

Both Victor and Trevor were silent for a time.

And then: "How are you planning on breaking it off?"

"I haven't decided yet." Victor stretched, spreading his legs out as far as they would go. "He really is a dear and I do love him—"

"But you need your space."

"Precisely!" Victor said, tapping the older man's knee for emphasis. "There's so much for me to discover. I just need to be unencumbered for a time—to breathe freely and on my own. I need to—"

"To spread your wings and fly?" Trevor asked with a glint in his eye.

"Oh, well, if you're going to be maudlin about it, Ms. Midler, then yes. That's precisely what I need. I need space."

"Just do me a favor. Pull the bandage quickly this time. Don't alienate him until he's so frustrated he storms away and won't speak to you for a hundred years."

"I would never—"

"Celeste?"

"Well, how would you have dealt with that impossible woman?"

"Archibald?"

"One lifetime with my dreary, old sire was more than enough, thank you very much."

"Gilbert?" The name was past Trevor's lips before he could stop himself. It hung in the air between the two of them like a bomb reaching its final second of life. Trevor saw Victor bristle but moved on quickly before his friend had a chance to respond. "And me."

"No!" Victor said emphatically. "No, my oldest and dearest friend, never you."

"How quickly you forget."

"Forget what?"

"You fled to Europe to be rid of me! You never even told me you were leaving. I just woke up one night to find you gone. I didn't hear a word from you for over fifty years. By the time I saw you again Grant was in the White House!"

"Well, you just said it should be quick."

"Use your words, you silly old man."

"And say what? That it's over? That I need to move on? That a lifetime with him was heaven, but now I need to wallow in hell for a time? Please, spare me a poet's ramblings."

"That you can't commit to any one person for more than a few decades—"

"I can so commit!"

"Really? Can you?" Trevor studied a defiant Victor for a moment as the limousine pulled through the iron gates and onto the estate that had been Victor's home for the past hundred and fifty years. Finally, Trevor said, "Victor, my dear, I am a member of a very elite club. Perhaps you've heard of it. We call ourselves 'Victor's Formers,' and very shortly now we'll be inducting a new member."

Victor opened his mouth and shut it again. It opened a second time but no words came out. He made a final attempt and then withered in his seat. "I really am a miserable old letch, aren't I?"

"Now, don't start that."

"No, it's true. I promise someone an eternity of bliss but give them only a handful of years."

"Well, I wouldn't exactly call all of them blissful."

"No, I can't even provide that, can I?"

"Your eye does tend to wander a bit."

"I'm hopeless."

"Now, now."

"No, it's true. I should just ban myself from the human race." Trevor saw a light dawn in Victor's eyes. "That's my resolution—no contact with humans this go-around. I'm taking myself off the market."

"Mmm-hmm."

"You think I'm joking, but I'm not. No trysts. No affairs."

"Mmm-hmm."

"No promises of eternity. No youngling to turn and then train."

"Mmm-hmm."

"You don't think I can do it, but I can. I'll have none of it this time. Oh, what are you waiting for, Trevor? Hurry with this life, won't you? Take a page from Celeste's book and be done with it. And once you're reborn we'll travel the world together—you and I. Separate, alone, above all the twaddle of day-to-day life, beyond the affairs of man or beast. We'll take our rightful place near the realms of the gods and look down on the rigors of daily life, thanking the heavens we're no longer caught up in this sorry existence of humanity. Promise me, Trevor, promise me we'll do that very thing. What do you say?"

The idea was a tempting one. Victor painted a lovely picture, and as Trevor studied the other man's eyes, he believed his friend meant what he said. He believed Victor might truly change. He believed that perhaps it wasn't too late to travel a path different from the one he was on now—one with Victor at his side. As the limousine pulled to a stop in front of the house—a vast thing of brick and stone and columns—Trevor took Victor's hand and said, "Victor, if you truly mean it, then ye—"

"Hello, what do we have here?" Victor interrupted, his attention drawn to something outside the limousine.

Trevor turned to find a young woman standing on the broad steps leading up to the house's entrance. She wore an elegant black dress that mingled well with the rich shade of her skin. Her hair was pulled back at her neck and a row of white teeth revealed themselves in a smile as she walked down the steps toward the limousine, a black leather binder held tight against her chest.

The driver opened the door and Victor stepped out.

"Mr. Crowley, my name is Scarlet Harvey." Trevor watched Victor warm instantly to the young woman's British accent. "I'm from Ackerman and Stern, your grandfather's attorneys. I'm so sorry for your loss."

"I appreciate that," Victor said as he clasped the delicate hand she offered in both of his. "Thank you so much for delaying the ceremony until my flight arrived from Europe. I just had to be in attendance. The old man meant the world to me, you see."

"Certainly. I trust everything went smoothly at the funeral home."

"Do I have you to thank for that?"

"Yes, I hope everything met with your satisfaction."

"It was beautiful. In particular, I appreciated the tasteful selection of coffin."

"I'm delighted to hear that," she said, offering him another smile. "Now, I know it's a terrible time, but there are a few papers here I need you to sign."

"Not at all. Let's retire to the library, where you can show me precisely what it is you need," Victor said as he led Scarlet Harvey up the stairs into the house.

The driver leaned in and extended a hand to the elderly gentleman. "Is there anything you need, Mr. Whitworth?"

Trevor ignored the hand and with surprising agility climbed from the limousine's backseat and headed toward the house. As an afterthought he turned to the driver and said, "Actually, there is something you can do, Michael. If you have an ounce of chivalry left in your body, find it. It looks like someone's going to be in need of a good saving tonight."

❖

Soon after Victor and Trevor made it home, the storm clouds delivered on their promise. Through a bank of French doors leading out onto the walled veranda, white curtains of rain fell on an amazing display of lightning. Great streaks of electricity connected earth and sky, and the heavens' appreciation could be heard in the booming applause immediately after. However, nature's display was nothing compared to the show going on inside the house.

Papers signed, Victor and Scarlet Harvey were pocketed away on one of the several richly upholstered sofas scattered about the spacious wood-paneled living room. A fire crackled on the other side of a stone hearth just a few feet from where they sat, driving away any chill the late spring storm might cause. Although nothing untoward was yet happening, Trevor had seen Victor on the hunt too many times to doubt that his impetuous friend was well on his way to choosing another companion to turn.

From his vantage point in a deep-set leather chair on the far side of the room, Trevor swallowed the acid taste of bitterness on his tongue. He watched as Victor leaned over to whisper something in Scarlet Harvey's ear and she laid her head back to laugh. And in that moment the new path he had imagined might be available to him vanished before he'd even taken his first step.

He chided himself for believing the resolutions his friend had made not fifteen minutes before in the backseat of the limousine. Victor was Victor, and there was no hope of changing that. Why would Trevor even try? He didn't have an answer to that one and was grateful for the bright bolt of lightning that drew his attention away from the matter altogether.

The flash of electricity made him wonder if lightning might have the same impact on his flesh as fire, one of the few forms of death that could truly end his long life. A morbid thought, to be sure, but what could one expect with another death looming so close at hand? He wondered how it might feel, that wave of electricity coursing through his body—one final moment of intensity before the nothingness of death.

Of course knowing Trevor's luck, nothing so fantastic would happen. If he stepped out the glass doors and into the lightning storm, more likely than not, he would only catch cold, develop pneumonia, and die a slow and miserable death before being reborn.

And then what? Trevor asked himself. *What are your regrets and resolutions this turn around the dance floor?* He scratched an itch between two knuckles on his weathered hand and chuckled to himself. *Many, too many regrets to count*, he answered. *And many, too many resolutions to make.*

Some were the same vintage promises he'd made and broken repeatedly over his various lifetimes. They sat like well-aged bottles of wine in the cellar of his soul, dusted off now and then, but never opened and permitted to breathe. Meanwhile, other resolutions were fresh and crisp like the spring leaves filling the budding trees just outside, waiting to flourish and grow.

As quickly as the resolutions came to mind, the regrets followed after. He shivered more from the memories than the drafty room he sat in as he recalled the mistakes he'd made in this life and catalogued them away with the ones from his previous lifetimes.

One in particular hung heavy on his soul: *Gilbert stood outside his window, calling for him, begging him to answer. Trevor never even acknowledged the man's pleading. He would never forget how he felt the next night when Victor came to him frantic, telling him that Gilbert had taken his own life.*

Never again, he swore to himself as he remembered each of his regrets vividly.

"Wine, sir?" A young waiter stood at his elbow, a tray of glasses filled with deep red liquid balanced on his palm. Trevor smiled at the young man and accepted a glass. As the waiter looked on, he tipped it to his lips and sipped. Trevor recognized the wine as one of Victor's favorites.

"Very good, thank you," he said, and the young man smiled and walked away.

Now there's a resolution for you, Trevor old-boy. He grinned to himself and watched the waiter cross the room to where Victor sat in hushed conversation with Scarlet. They both accepted glasses of wine before the waiter returned to the bar with his tray.

He appreciated the look of the young man—Scandinavian in appearance with slightly rounded cheeks, a square jaw, and small, dark eyes. Dark hair, rather than blond, topped his head—a testament to generations in the melting pot of America. And when the waiter had smiled at Trevor, he noticed a single dimple in his left cheek. He watched the young man lean over the bar to say something to the bartender. Trevor couldn't help but enjoy the way his tuxedo pants clung tightly to the fine curve of his rear end.

Trevor cast a glance toward Victor and found his friend staring at him, a wolfish grin on his face. He lifted his glass in toast, then drank deeply. Trevor looked away, embarrassed his furtive glances had been observed.

He knew he shouldn't be ashamed of looking. Victor certainly never was—no matter what his age. Of course, Victor held no doubts about his appearance and how to use it to full advantage. Likewise, Trevor had no doubts about his own appearance and the limitations it set in his path.

Even if he were fresh-born right now sitting in this chair, the waiter still wouldn't have given him a second glance (if he were so inclined). He knew that not even his preternatural powers could improve the average looks with which he'd been born. Certainly nothing to match the fine features of Victor, or John, or especially Gilbert before he abruptly ended his own life. No, for Trevor there would be only a small pocket of time when he would age into his looks and for a few, brief years might turn an eye or warrant a smile of appreciation. However, that would be closer to forty-four rather than the twenty-four he would reawaken as once reborn.

He wondered for the millionth time what had attracted Victor to him originally. What had caused him to be drawn to his tall, lumbering form and bland (nearly oafish) features? What had made Victor decide that this twenty-four-year-old was worth turning and spending a lifetime staring at? Frankly, in two hundred years Trevor had never had the nerve to ask.

He took another sip, enjoying the subtle flavors of the wine as it traveled past his tongue and down his gullet. Experience told him to revel in the flavor now; it wouldn't be nearly so pleasant coming back up. Naturally, his body couldn't absorb the liquid and so, like any food he ingested, it would only sit in his stomach until he expelled it back the way it had come. Not the most pleasant element of his long life. Still, if he expected to enjoy any of the flavors that food offered, it was either that or let the food fester in his stomach and rot.

The room's thick wooden doors opened wide and Trevor's musings were interrupted by the entrance of the party who had braved the storm to attend the interment. Trevor grinned, imagining what they would say if they ever realized they'd gotten soaked watching sandbags be entombed.

It was a rather large crowd filled with business associates that Victor had amassed in his previous life. Several others prided themselves on being called "friends of the family" (no doubt hoping that friendship would translate into a spot in the old man's will). The party was headed up by Victor's most recent lover, John, who walked briskly into the room despite his ninety-plus years. He spotted Trevor first thing and made straight for him.

"Trevor, good to see you made it back all right."

"You as well, John. I hope the storm didn't make a shamble of things."

"Not at all. It held off until near the end. It was rather a beautiful moment, I must say." Trevor stifled a groan as he noticed the glimmer of a tear in the other man's green eyes. Of all his options, how had Victor ever chosen this fop? "The priest had some moving things to say, and I also added a few additional thoughts of my own. Just then the clouds erupted, as if heaven itself mourned his passing. It really was quite lovely. I only wish…I wish Victor had been there. Where is he?" he asked, dabbing at his eyes and soldiering on. "I must see him. I must see my dear, sweet boy. Where is he, Trevor?"

"John," Trevor said, avoiding a glance at the couple in front of the fireplace, "perhaps you should go upstairs for a rest. This has been a trying day for you."

"I don't need to rest. I need my precious boy," John replied as he scanned the room and found his lover seated on the couch with Scarlet, oblivious to the recently arrived mourners. John's puffy eyes narrowed. The wrinkles lining his face twisted into a scowl, and he said, "That bitch."

As annoying as John might be, Trevor couldn't help but feel sorry for the man. He knew firsthand how difficult it was to watch a lifelong relationship dissolve in the arms of Victor's newest acquisition. "Now, John, don't be hasty. She has no idea of the matters at play here."

John glanced at Trevor, then back at the young couple secreted away on the couch in front of the fire and growled, "Who said I was talking about her?" and then stormed across the room to confront his lover.

As John approached, Victor looked up in surprise, "Uhhhhncle John, I didn't know you were back from the mausoleum."

"Yes, I am."

"So soon!"

"Too soon, it would seem."

"Not at all." Victor smiled, rising from the couch. "You must be tired. Why don't we take you upstairs?" He tucked his hand around the man's elbow and tried to steer him toward the door, but John would have none of it.

He reeled to face Victor. "How dare you. You're not even…your *grandfather's* not even buried an hour and here you sit in his house on his sofa with this…this floozy making a mockery of yourself…of him…of me! You should be ashamed!"

Trevor glanced about the silent room. All eyes were turned toward the scene playing out before the fireplace.

Scarlet rose from the couch and grabbed her leather binder, saying, "Perhaps I should…"

"Yes, perhaps you should," John spat at the girl, full of venom.

"No," Victor said, surprising Trevor with his even tone. "Scarlet, stay. Uncle John, you and I need to talk. Now."

As John was guided from the room, his tirade could be heard on the other side of the living room's closed doors and up the stairway that traveled to their suite of rooms on the second floor. Once the noise had faded and the room was once again silent, all eyes turned back to Scarlet Harvey.

The young lady valiantly met the gaze of several of the mourners for a moment before an eyebrow rose and she smiled, saying, "Having a lovely time, are we? Wonderful." She turned and stalked toward the open door of Victor's private library, shutting it soundly behind her.

The group stood silent a moment longer before twitters of conversation sprang up across the room. Soon a general ruckus was in motion as everyone began discussing the scene they had just witnessed. Not Trevor, though. He sat resolutely silent, thinking that perhaps Victor had taken his suggestion of pulling the bandage off quickly a bit too literally.

The conversations were only beginning to build to full volume when the living room's double doors opened wide and in walked a vixen dressed in black. Her blonde hair was done up in a tumble of impossibilities that dangled down in curls around ears ringed in large, bejeweled hoops. The hem of her small black dress seemed only scant inches below a bodice that swept her breasts up toward the ceiling in a dazzling display. Long legs hosed in fishnet stockings stretched toward the floor, ending in stiletto heals that generously offered the petite woman several inches on her normal height. She sauntered into the room on the arm of a man that modeled perfection and (Trevor hated to admit) would have put Victor and John and even Gilbert to shame. They stopped in the center of the room as conversation died and every eye turned in shock at the woman's lack of decorum.

"What?" the vixen very nearly purred. "You look as if someone just died."

Trevor rose quickly from his chair and rushed to meet the woman and her escort. He extended his arms in greeting and kissed her on both cheeks saying, "Celeste, so good to see you."

"Trevor, darling! Sorry I couldn't make the funeral. Our flight out of Milan was delayed."

"I'm sure Victor will understand," Trevor said as he guided Celeste and her companion toward the series of French doors and away from the scandalized crowd.

"Ah, Victor. Where is the darling cherub?" And from the acid in her tone, Trevor guessed Celeste was sincere with neither the *darling* nor the *cherub*.

"He's upstairs talking with John."

"Already? My, my, he isn't wasting a minute this go-around, is he? With me it was a year, and with you dear, sweet Trevor, it was what, at least three months?"

Trevor returned her icy grin. No matter that nearly a century had passed since the woman had fallen from Victor's favor, she had never forgiven Trevor for their sire's seemingly limitless affections. And not for the first time Trevor rued the fact that of all their sire's past loves, he alone was the one abiding constant in Victor's long life.

"It's nothing like that," he said, swallowing his pride. "John made a scene, and Victor took him up to their room to lie down."

"Poor John, he has no idea what's about to happen to him, does he?" Celeste sighed. "But you'll be there to help him through, won't you, good and ever-faithful Trevor. You'll nurse him through the pain and the heartbreak just as you did me—oh wait, that's right." Her lips pressed tightly together in a smile that promised venom as she said, "You didn't."

"Trevor, a whore for my funeral? You shouldn't have," a voice behind him said. Trevor turned to find Victor joining the small group.

"Victor!" Celeste gushed. "Why, I wouldn't have expected to see you looking so vibrant, what with your death and all."

"Rumors of my demise have been greatly exaggerated," he joked, taking her hand and kissing it. "What are you doing here, Celeste?"

"Well, I couldn't let one of my sire's rebirths go by without stopping in to honor it, now could I?"

"How sweet, seeing as how I've missed, how many of yours is it now?" Victor asked. "It's so hard to keep track these days."

"Seven, but what's a couple of deaths between friends?"

"Indeed," Victor said, grinning.

"How's John?" Trevor asked, diverting the conversation to more civil topics.

"He's upstairs," Victor said, eyeing the Adonis on Celeste's arm. "He's resting."

"Lying sprawled on the bed, no doubt," Celeste volunteered, "ready for you to cut out his heart and tear it in two."

"Celeste, I think perhaps—" Trevor said, attempting to intervene.

"Oh no, my dear," Victor replied, "I only crush the hearts of those I never loved."

Trevor tried again. "Victor, let's not do—"

"You? Love someone?" Celeste laughed. "Victor, you say the most adorable things."

"Enough! Both of you," Trevor snapped. "Not with company present."

"Quite right, quite right," Victor agreed, eyeing the crowd filling the room, and then, "Speaking of company, Celeste, you haven't yet introduced us to your latest toy."

"How rude of me." She beamed, turning toward her escort. "This is Jean-Claude."

"Jean-Claude." Victor offered a hand in greeting. "Nice of you to come."

"Jean-Claude hasn't licked English yet," Celeste explained, taking Victor's hand and lowering it back to his side, "just like he won't learn to lick you."

"Celeste, I'm hurt you would even think—" Victor's words were cut off by a scream coming from behind the library's closed doors. It was punctuated by the sound of shattering glass from across the room.

Trevor's eye was caught by a streak of movement crossing the room as the young waiter raced toward the library. He kicked the door open to reveal Scarlet pressed against the room's large mahogany desk with John on top of her, lathered fangs at her throat.

"Hey!" the waiter shouted. John looked up just as the young man flung his empty tray. The metal disk went swirling through the air to lodge deep in the man's throat.

Gasps escaped the crowd. The small cluster standing by the French doors looked on in horror as their centuries-old secret was revealed. The waiter reached behind the library's door and produced a sword.

"Where the hell did that come from?" Victor asked.

The young man leapt onto the desk. As John yanked the tray from the bloody gash in his throat, the waiter replaced it with a swipe of his sword that severed head from body.

The waiter hopped from the desk and turned to a frozen Scarlet Harvey, the headless body tumbling to the floor at her feet.

"Are you all right?" he asked.

The woman's eyes were wide and vacant as she watched blood pour from the corpse's open neck and pool onto the room's thick carpet.

"Are you all right?" the young man asked again more forcefully, shaking her.

"What was that thing?" she asked, never taking her eyes of the body.

"Questions later, run now!" he ordered, shoving her out the library doors back into the study.

Their movement broke the spell over the room, and the crowd erupted in screams of panic as they ran for any exit they could find. Some ran out the study's doors and through the front hall to their cars parked in the driveway beyond. Others raced for the French doors and into the night. They could be seen wading their way across the estate's soaked lawns as the rain continued to pour down on them.

Within a moment the chaos had ended and the room stood empty but for the waiter and the remaining members of Victor's blood-clan.

"You bastard." Victor's words sliced through the silence of the room, quiet and deadly. "You dare come into my home and slaughter my family? I'll kill you where you stand, you coward. I'll skin you alive and wear your flesh as a trophy."

"It's you, isn't it?" The words were Trevor's. He watched the young man standing before the fireplace slowly spinning the hilt of his sword in his grip.

"It's me," the waiter agreed.

"It's who?" Victor spat. "Who is this gnat that I'm going to crush?"

"Victor, it's him," Trevor explained, "the hunter that's been cleaning up the city, ridding it of the werewolves and the goblins, the ogres and the other trash."

Victor smiled. "So now you've come to the burbs? Lucky us."

The waiter shrugged and said, "Figure you look hard enough, you can find trash anywhere."

Movement out of the corner of his eye caught Trevor's attention. While the others had the waiter's focus, Jean-Claude saw his opening. He leapt, fangs and claws at the ready. He swiped at the man with his jagged nails but missed. By the time his hand passed by the other man's face, four severed fingers were tumbling to the ground. Jean-Claude lifted the stump that had been his right hand. Blood gushed from where fingers had been. Too late Jean-Claude looked back at the man as the sword plunged through his chest. It pierced his heart and blossomed out his back in a spray of crimson.

The body slid off the length of the waiter's sword and crumpled to the floor. The swordsman shook his head and said, "Damn, but I hate killing the pretty ones."

"Jean-Claude!" Celeste howled, racing toward the waiter. She was brought up short as the point of his sword pressed against the flesh of her bosom.

At the other end of his sword, the waiter smiled that twist of a smile. It revealed the single dimple in his cheek that Trevor had been so enamored of just moments before. He said, "Do your worst, blood rat."

A brief moment's reflection and Celeste turned and retreated toward the front hall. The swordsman grabbed a small marble statue from the mantel and threw it at her. It connected with her skull as she passed through the doorway. Her head jerked to the right and slammed into the door frame.

Stunned, but still on her feet, Celeste shook her head as the man advanced on her, his sword extended. Without warning, she batted the sword away. He tried to recover, but she leapt on him, her teeth at his throat and her claws digging deep into his back. Losing his balance, the man tumbled over the arm of the chair Trevor had been seated in. It skidded out from under him, and he slammed hard into the stone floor of the room, his sword slipping from his grasp.

The waiter tried to shove Celeste off but she held on tight. Instead the two combatants rolled so that she was on the floor while he straddled her. He tried to pull away, but her claws ripped through his tuxedo shirt and shredded the flesh of his back as they rolled again. He slammed the palm of his fist under Celeste's jaw to keep her fangs at bay while he reached for his sword. It lay several feet away next to the chair's leg.

Trevor felt Victor move to intervene, but he placed a hand on his chest to stop him.

"But it's Celeste," Victor said.

"Precisely," Trevor agreed.

"We have to help her," Victor said, trying to push past the hand restraining him.

Trevor cast him a sideways glance and smiled, asking, "Do we? Really?"

Victor looked to his friend and then back to the woman. Trevor could see a lifetime of arguments and regrets play across Victor's face as he watched Celeste struggle with the man. A grin crept across Victor's face and he finally said, "No, I don't suppose we do."

Trevor shared a smile with his sire and turned back just in time to see the waiter rip free one of the large hoops dangling from Celeste's earlobes. A spray of blood trailed in its wake. He plunged the earring down into Celeste's eye. It ruptured the cornea and passed through the squishy gelatin to dig into the socket.

Celeste screamed in agony, releasing the man and groping at her face. He jumped up and ran for his sword, turning back just as Celeste raced after him, the earring still dangling from the center of her eye. He leapt onto the chair's seat and made several slashes that landed deep cuts across Celeste's face, driving her away.

"My face! My face!" she screamed, covering her mangled features. "My beautiful face!"

"Trust me," the man said, drawing his sword back for the killing stroke, "it wasn't all that beautiful to begin with."

Celeste opened her mouth in a snarling hiss and the man rammed the weapon deep into her mouth and on up toward her brain. It caught on the top of her skull, and he jammed harder till it cracked through the bone and ruptured her head. Grey matter dribbled out the hole, catching on her blonde curls before landing with an indelicate *plop* on the floor.

Placing a foot on the body's shoulder, the swordsman pulled the blade from the woman's skull and wiped the blood and goop of her brains onto her dress. Trevor could see the man was in no hurry. Neither were he and Victor, for that matter. They stood quietly before the French doors like hunters ready to spring, or prey ready to bolt—both knew better than to reveal which.

A flash of lightning on the lawn was answered by a rumble of thunder from the clouds.

"Who *are* you?" Victor asked the man standing amid his fallen family.

"My name's Dyson, and you," the waiter answered, pointing his sword at him, "are Victor Goodman Crowley, three hundred and twelve years old."

"Three hundred and six!"

"Give or take." Dyson grinned and that single dimple reappeared in his cheek. "You're freshly reborn which, if memory serves, is when you're at your weakest." He continued to speak as he walked slowly across the room toward the two men, his sword en garde.

"How do you know all of this?" Trevor asked.

"It's my job to know," Dyson said, then added, "Mr. Whitworth, age two hundred and sixty."

It was Trevor's turn to smile and say, "Give or take."

Victor watched their interaction, then sighed. "Oh, Trevor, you always did have the worst taste in men."

"Shut up, Victor."

"Well, it's true. Even now when he's killed John and Celeste and that French fellow, here you are flirting with him—another of your round-faced retards from the Midwest. You're pathetic."

"And what about you?" Trevor retorted. "Not five minutes after promising me a life in the heavens you're diddling some secretary at your own funeral."

"Legal assistant," Victor corrected. "She's working nights toward her law degree."

"Oh well, with that pedigree, I can't imagine why you haven't turned her already."

"You are an elitist snob."

"And you are a vile whoremonger, sticking it in wherever you can."

"Would you two shut the fuck up!" Dyson said, standing just a few feet from them.

"Excuse me, young man, I will remind you you're in my home," Victor reprimanded.

"Dude! This is why I hate you guys," Dyson said. "Always bitching. Always caught up in your own little dramas, thinking the whole world revolves around you, thinking everyone's got the time to just sit by while you yammer on and on and on."

"Speaking of yammering on," Victor said, rolling his eyes.

"You traipse around, seducing people just to drink their blood then leave them for dead. Don't you feel anything? Remorse? Regret? Is there an ounce of humanity left inside you? Of all of the fairies—and I mean all of them: elves, ogres, werewolves, dwarves, goblins, every last one—your kind are the most disgusting, heartless creatures I've ever met."

"Oh, and what of you, Mr. Dyson?" Victor asked. "All of twenty-three? Twenty-four? Who are you to judge us? What regrets do you have in your *long* life? What would you change if given the chance? Let's just find out."

Victor's eyes turned to slits as he grasped his friend's hand. Trevor's mind reeled for a moment as he joined Victor in invading Dyson's brain. A flurry of images opened to him…

…A woman dying as her heart is pierced while Dyson looks on helplessly…

…A young man walking into a bedroom with a broad grin on his face and a joke on his tongue, only to find Dyson lying in the arms of another boy, the grin quickly vanishing from the young man's face…

…Dyson reaching out for a brown-robed figure as it leaps through a portal into another world. Dyson screaming out a name. The brown-robed figure never looking back, only running on into the woods on the other side of the portal and vanishing from sight…

…A man losing his grip on a cliff's face and slipping to his death as Dyson stands by doing nothing…

…Thousands of bodies dead and dying beneath the water's surface as Dyson is unable to stop it…

"Get out of my head!" Dyson screamed, staggering backward. Trevor felt a wave of dizziness as the connection broke.

"What was that?" Victor asked, impressed. "Well, well, it looks like our young friend here has more than a few regrets of his own."

"I said, get out of my head!" Dyson screamed, lunging at Victor, his sword at the ready.

Instantly, Victor pivoted to the side and grabbed Dyson's sword arm, propelling him through one of the unopened French doors and out into the night storm. The young man tumbled through, shattering glass and landing sprawled across the patio's slick stones. His sword skittered out of his grasp and down the steps, clattering onto the stone path crossing the lawn.

Victor readied to step through the glass and follow him out onto the veranda, but Trevor laid a hand on his arm and said, "He's right, you know. You are fresh-born. You're at your weakest. Let me."

"He just killed John," Victor replied. "He invaded my home and ruined my funeral. Do you really imagine I'd allow anyone else this pleasure?"

Trevor released his arm and watched Victor leap through the shattered doorway and out into the downpour. "No," he said as an afterthought. "No, I really don't."

Trevor looked on as Victor grabbed the young man by the collar of his shirt and lifted him off the ground, landing a fist in his gut that sent him flying backward. Dyson smacked against one of the stone columns encircling the veranda and rebounded off it, landing with a thud on the floor.

"Well, this is exhilarating," Victor said as he crossed to his opponent and yanked him back to his feet. "The estate hasn't seen a row like this before."

Dyson struggled to regain his breath saying, "Well…we are…a full-service…catering company."

"I'll keep that in mind for my next event." Victor smiled at the young man, and with as little effort as if he were throwing a pillow, he tossed him off the veranda and out into the yard.

Dyson landed and slid several feet through the slush of the lawn. While he struggled back to his feet, Victor stepped down the stairs and picked up the other man's fallen weapon. "Not so tough without your sword, are you, Mr. Dyson?"

"Yeah," Dyson groaned, "these fair fights are a real bitch."

The young man wiped the mud from his face as he fought to regain his footing, but before he could steady himself Victor backhanded him with a blow that sent him flying several feet into the air. Dyson came back to earth hard, knocking the air from his lungs.

Victor strolled over to him, sloshing through the puddles, with the sword resting on his shoulder. "Well, Mr. Dyson, I hate to cut this short, but really I'm going to have one hell of a time salvaging these shoes."

"Yeah, I've got plans tonight, too," the young man said, trying to rise to his knees. His body gave way, and he crumpled back down with a splash.

"Normally, I'd relish drinking your blood, but really, severing your head with your own sword seems much more fitting an end, don't you agree?"

If the waiter had an opinion on the matter, his words were lost in the jumbled heap of his body on the ground.

Victor laid his head back, the rain slapping his face and soaking into his hair. He spread his arms wide, the sword extended in his right hand, and shouted, "Oh, Mr. Dyson, wouldn't you agree this is quite the poetic end?"

He raised the sword, ready for the kill. But before he could land it, a streak of lightning connected with the blade and sent a jolt of electricity through him. His body locked in a perverse, jittering dance before crumpling to the ground.

Dyson slowly rose to his feet as his opponent lay moaning on the grass. He retrieved his sword from where Victor had dropped it and yanked the other man's head up by a hand-full of his long, dark hair and said, "Personally, I never liked poetry." The blade sliced through the air and connected with Victor's throat, severing it. Dyson let the head fall to the earth with a splash and said to no one in particular, "I always thought it was for fags."

After a moment Trevor waded out onto the lawn to where the young man stood over the body of his fallen friend. Finally he said, "Huh." And then, "So lightning won't kill us after all."

"Guess not," Dyson agreed, "but it sure came in handy."

Trevor looked up from Victor's body and studied the assassin.

"Forgive me. I assumed I was getting a petite blonde—stereotypes and all."

"I get that a lot," Dyson said, wiping away the stream of blood continuing to trickle from his mouth.

"I left the details of the matter to my associate, you see."

"No worries. Has the money been transferred to my account?"

"Already done," Scarlet Harvey said as she joined the two men on the lawn.

"There she is," Trevor said, applauding. "A most impressive performance."

Scarlet laughed and took a bow before sharing her umbrella with Trevor and snaking her hand around his arm.

"I especially thought the scream was quite lifelike," Trevor offered.

"Well, I should say so, what with John's fangs at my throat."

"That was a bit unexpected, but a useful entrance for our friend here." Trevor said. "Did he sign the papers?"

Scarlet gripped the leather satchel to her chest. "Congratulations, Trevor Whitworth. You are now the sole beneficiary to Victor Goodman Crowley's estate and all his holdings."

A phone chimed from Dyson's pocket. He pulled it out and read the name that appeared.

"Your boyfriend?" Trevor asked.

Dyson smiled. "I said I had plans tonight."

"Well, you shouldn't keep him waiting," Trevor suggested.

"He'll be all right," Dyson said, pocketing the phone.

"Love is a fickle thing, Mr. Dyson," Trevor said, glancing to the woman on his arm. He gripped her small, dark hand in his own. "It never comes as you expect it to, and it can leave just as quickly. You should never take it for granted."

"And when it leaves, you what?" Dyson asked. "Kill everyone left behind?"

Trevor looked at Victor's body lying dead on the lawn. He watched the blood pool onto the grass, the rain diluting it before it vanished into the earth. It seemed that with that blood a lifetime of regrets washed away. Finally, he said, "My resolution for my next life: a fresh start."

Dyson snickered as the rain continued to fall. "Fresh starts don't have to come with a body count."

"In my experience I've found you can't escape your past if it can still show up unexpectedly for a visit."

"Maybe so," Dyson said, "but it seems to me you'll never escape your past as long as you keep making it your future." He glanced at the woman entwined on his arm.

Trevor turned to Scarlet. She stood studying the decapitated body. There was a look of excitement in her eyes that made him nervous. It reminded him of something, of someone. Before he could ask himself who, Scarlet glanced at him and grinned, tightening her grip on his arm. He smiled in return and patted her hand, pushing his worries far away.

Dyson watched the silent exchange and said, "Yeah, but what do I know?"

The sound of distant sirens drew their attention.

"Guess that's my cue," the young man said, wiping the last of the blood from his sword onto Victor's expensive suit.

"If you head down the lawn, you'll find I unlocked the back gate," Scarlet volunteered.

Dyson nodded. "You sure do think of everything."

"She's indispensable, really." Trevor smiled proudly at Scarlet.

Dyson turned to leave. He looked back at the mismatched couple standing beneath the umbrella and said, "Well, good luck—with that fresh start and all."

Trevor and Scarlet watched him go as the sound of sirens competed with the patter of rain hitting their umbrella.

"We should go back inside, my love," Scarlet said. "The police will be here any minute, and we need to be ready to greet them." Trevor allowed himself to be steered back toward the house as he heard her say, "Soon enough we'll be able to leave here and start our new life. Together."

"Yes," Trevor said. "Yes, I suppose we will."

"What will it be like?" Scarlet asked as they approached the steps leading back into the house.

"What will what be like?"

"When you turn me." She laughed, gently slapping his aged and wrinkled hand. "Tell me what it will be like to be young and beautiful forever."

"I told you you won't be young and beautiful forever. You'll still age. Just look at me."

"Not me," she said emphatically. "The first sign of a wrinkle and I'll chuck it all—on to my next life." She laughed giddily and laid her head on his shoulder.

As he took the stone path back to the house, he realized who she reminded him of. Suddenly he felt very tired. He consoled himself with a comforting thought: if need be, he could always hire the young Mr. Dyson again.

THE PROVIDER
KYLE STONE

I'm not a pimp!" cried Bryce. "I'm a provider. A care-giver."
"You're trying to make me dependent on you!" Galen shouted.
"I need the taste of the streets!"

"They're trash, can't you see? They sell themselves for a fix!"

"And you don't? Who are you that you should presume to judge!"

"I'm only trying to save you from kids like Zane."

"Be silent!" Galen's voice exploded against the shadowed walls.
The tall narrow windows shook behind the velvet drapes.

Bryce stood his ground. He had seen the mindless anger, the
searing rage, many times. He knew what it meant. "I have kept you
from becoming an animal," he said softly.

Galen smiled, in control again. "So you like to think. If it gives
you pleasure, go ahead."

Pleasure. The word, spoken by Galen's pale blood-starved lips,
seemed stripped of meaning, an empty word with no associations.

Galen slumped back in the ornate chair, a pale hand curved over
each armrest. The blast of anger had drained him. His head was bent, the
soft blond hair falling over his forehead. The nape of his neck gleamed
ivory in the dim light.

Bryce knew this creature was incapable of love, but the knowledge
made no difference. His fanatical devotion burned strong and hot as
ever. At times, he knew that Galen hated him. At times when he was
needed. Like now. But Bryce still clung to one fact. Galen needed him.
And every now and then, he would have to acknowledge this.

Galen raised his head and stared across the dim room, lit by the
soft oil lamps he insisted on. His green eyes glowed dully. His face
looked gaunt, the pallid skin stretched tight over the high cheekbones.

Bryce looked away. He couldn't stand to see the one he loved suffer, but he must. It was all he had.

"Come closer, Bryce. I'm weak. You know when I'm weak." The voice was a whisper on the air, more like a subtle suggestion than words. "How can you turn away from me now? You know what to do."

Bryce nodded. Even after the fights, his pain, he knew he would open his shirt and kneel in front of Galen, between his long legs. Because only then, while Galen sucked his life blood from the plastic tube inserted over his heart, would he allow Bryce to touch him.

Bryce opened his shirt and knelt. He gathered Galen into his arms, guiding the pale head to his chest. He winced as he felt the hot dry lips touch his skin, felt the first strong pull. For a moment, he swayed and had to steady himself. Then his hand went to Galen's bent head, his fingers straying through the fine spun-gold hair. He could almost feel the strengthening pulse at the temples, under his fingertips. *Because of me*, he thought. *I am his life.* But his elation was brief. He knew anyone could perform this task. Others had before him. If he wasn't careful, others would again. He bent his head and touched the silky hair with his lips.

With a shuddering sigh, Galen pulled away, as always forcing himself to stop well before he had slaked his thirst. He laid his head back against the carved oak. Waiting. Allowing Bryce his one act of intimacy.

Bryce slid to the floor. As he undid the buttoned fly, he forced all thoughts out of his head. He, too, was hungry, with a thirst that would never be satisfied. The damp earthy smell made his senses reel as he opened his mouth to his lover's cool white flesh.

All too soon, it was over.

"We're little better than cannibals," Galen said with a lazy smile. He wiped a trickle of blood from the corner of his mouth with one finger. "We feed off each other."

"You are surprisingly whimsical sometimes," remarked Bryce, buttoning up his shirt. As always, he felt slightly sick after submitting to Galen. It was a delayed reaction that hit when he stood up. He made his way carefully to the table and helped himself to wine.

Galen stretched, lifting his arms to the ceiling, arching his back, twisting slightly at the hips with sensual grace. Already color had seeped back into his cheeks, staining the fine skin like crushed strawberries. The green eyes sparkled, a fire that gave no heat. "Get your jacket. It's time for you to go out."

"I told you—go yourself. You don't need me."

"I know." Galen was enjoying himself. It was as if the shouting and the intimacy had never taken place. They both knew that Bryce was powerless, now, helpless to stop what would happen next.

"Galen, I'm not going."

"Aren't you my 'provider'? My 'care-giver'? You said so yourself just a few minutes ago." He smiled, the green eyes taunting, cold as ice, slicing into his soul.

Bryce sighed. "How many?"

"Three would be nice. See what you can do." Galen turned away, his mind already moving on to the designs he would sketch for the eighteenth-century movie that was his current project. It amused him to reproduce on stage the clothes he and his friends had worn in the long-vanished days of his youth. It amused him still more when he was praised for the historical accuracy of his designs.

Bryce watched him leave the room, listened to his light step going up the stairs. He glanced at his watch. All the strength and purpose seemed to have drained out of him. From far off in the bay, the low wail of the fog horn echoed his despair. Outside, the cool dampness of the evening kissed his lips with salt. Long ribbons of mist swirled along the driveway, hiding the low bushes and setting the trees adrift in a sea of fog. The sickly yellow glow of the wrought iron gas lamps made little impact on the gloom. Bryce shivered as he got into the car.

When the gates of the estate slid shut behind him, Bryce slipped a CD in the player, hoping the music would soothe him. After a few moments, he switched it off. *I hate him*, he thought, giving the wheel a savage twist to the right. The big car spun out briefly, then straightened. Rain spat at the windshield. Bryce took a deep breath and headed downtown.

He was always surprised by how easy it was to pick up boys. He had never had the desire to do so for himself, and the first time he had come here for Galen had been difficult for him. But merely a mention of Galen's connection with the movies was enough to gain the interest of the most halfhearted hustler. They were all eager to win his favor. They never could, of course. Except for one. Bryce winced at the memory, the tall, wide-eyed boy with the black hair curling down his back. Zane, a name as false as the angelic smile.

The fog was thicker near the water. The great black car slid through the deserted streets, gliding slowly through the swirling mist. Tonight's hunt took longer than usual, but at last he found two. They were friends, apparently. Once the fee was settled on, Bryce discouraged conversation. He preferred to keep his distance.

When they got back to the house, he found the studio empty. Bryce led the boys down the hall to the master bedroom and knocked.

Galen flung open the door, a brocade robe draped carelessly over his slender body. He was naked underneath. "You took too long," he said. His green eyes glowed in the dimness. Over his shoulder, Bryce glimpsed the four-poster bed, a familiar tousled head, a long pale thigh. "I've made my own arrangements. Get rid of them."

Bryce thrust his foot in the space between the door and the jamb. "You promised—you swore to me you wouldn't go out. We had an agreement!"

Galen laughed. "You are a fool," he said. "You think you can contain me, my appetites, my needs? I am far beyond your feeble comprehension." He began to press the door against Bryce's foot, a steady pressure, without apparent effort on his part. "How do you think I have survived as long as I have?"

Bryce winced as the bones in his foot began to grind. Tears came to his eyes but he refused to acknowledge the pain, to back down before that pent-up malevolence. "I'm not afraid of you," he said, his voice shaking. "Do what you want. Kill me! Would that make you happy?"

"Happy? You are a bigger fool than I realized!" Galen gave the door a final excruciating squeeze.

In spite of himself, Bryce cried out in pain. "Damn you, Galen!"

"I was damned a long time ago, and you had nothing to do with it!" Galen released the pressure, kicked the mangled foot away. "Run the bath for me." He slammed the door in Bryce's face.

Bryce leaned against the wall trying to control his ragged breathing. The boys had disappeared. He could hear their steps pounding down the stairs and across the hall. The front door opened. Closed. He was alone. Except for Galen. And Zane.

He wiped his face with his sleeve. "It's over," he whispered.

But how can something be over that never really began? It was all a fantasy, spun out of his own heated imagination. He had tried, oh how he had tried to make Galen desire him, need him. How he had tried to open his veins to that hot mouth and be drained to the point of floating between their two worlds. Only by doing this could he join Galen forever, be at his side, his shadow, his lover. But Galen had always refused, forcing himself to back off time and again, keeping Bryce at a distance by inserting the tube over his heart, so they would barely touch as he fed. Over and over Bryce had brought home boys, young men, anyone whose eyes were needy, whose lips would ask no questions, whose bodies would not be missed if Galen became violent, as he did sometimes. Especially if there was no one there to stop him.

Slowly Bryce dragged himself along the hall to the huge old-fashioned bathroom. He would obey once more. But this time, there would be a difference.

He ran water into the bathtub, mounted on its graceful clawed feet. He threw in handfuls of scented beads. It was agony taking the shoe off his mangled foot. Blood oozed from the crushed toes as he peeled back the sock. He had to keep stopping, letting the pain roll over him. At last, he gently lowered himself into the warm water. He wondered idly if Galen had always been a sadist or if this had come on him centuries ago, with the Change.

The warmth was calming. The scented oils wreathed the room in heady perfume. The throbbing of his foot was almost pleasurable now. He reached out for the ivory handled straight razor on the shelf behind him. Without pausing, he drew the thin blade across first one wrist, then the other. He watched, fascinated, as his blood swirled slowly into the water. Then he grasped the tube above his heart and pulled. The unexpected pain jolted him, and for a moment he was afraid. Then the warmth swam over him again and he closed his eyes.

When he heard the door click, he opened them again. Galen was kneeling beside him, a silver goblet in one hand. The green eyes burned so brightly, Bryce blinked in pain.

"Fool," Galen remarked. He reached down and pulled the plug to let out the reddened water. "Never waste good blood." He pressed the silver goblet against Bryce's chest and watched blood ooze over the rim.

Bryce smiled as Galen's fingers touched his chest, squeezing the artery to pump the blood out faster. Then the smile faded as he became aware of another person in the room. Zane. Naked. He was very pale. Several scars stood out against the whiteness of his neck.

"Come," murmured Galen, holding out his goblet to the boy. "Drink. A token of my love."

The last clear image that Bryce's mind recorded was the picture of Zane's full lips, blood-red against the silver.

THE BONE BOX
JOSEPH BANETH ALLEN

With hands tightly clenched in the pockets of his father's old leather flight jacket, Tommy McDevitt casually walked past the 1966 red Mustang he had discovered parked and empty at the Starlite Twin Family Drive-In Theater.

Tommy's green eyes carefully surveyed the distance between the Mustang and the other cars in the parking lot of the aging theater. The pale illumination from the movie screens pushed back enough of the cool darkness for him to see the steamed windows of the cars and trucks ahead of him. Everyone was either too preoccupied with the ancient movie plots being played out on the dual screens or in other pursuits to notice a solitary nineteen-year-old boy.

He exhaled a sharp breath as he touched the Slim Jim for comfort. The Mustang was a restored beauty and would fetch enough money to allow him at least a couple months of freedom from Jacksonville's streets. He decided to take the car. Carter always gave good prices for the classics.

The Slim Jim slid easily into the window crevice.

"Smooth," he said, proud of the ease with which the first stage of the theft had gone.

A hand grabbed his upper arm and yanked him roughly away from the car. "You little punk! I'll teach you to break into my car."

A harsh blow landed on his cheek and the side of his nose. Tommy cried out in pain as he was thrown to the ground. He tried to scurry away, but a well-placed kick connected with his side, and he fell to the ground in further anguish.

Tommy rolled away from the approaching footsteps. Despite the torrent of pain screaming through his body, he managed to assume a shaky defensive position and faced, with Slim Jim in hand, his attacker.

Tommy managed a few ragged breaths as his one good eye searched for a means of escape. None was forthcoming from any of the parked cars around him. He faked a lunge. His tormentor jumped back and he took off running. He got maybe three feet before a hand clenched the crown of his auburn hair and yanked him down. He fell to his knees and desperately slashed at empty air with the Slim Jim.

A Nike connected with his stomach. He dropped the Slim Jim as he felt his insides turn inside out, and made a vain attempt to scurry away. This time the Nike hit him squarely on the side of his head. The impact caused his teeth to puncture his tongue, and falling, he tasted warm, wet blood trickling down his throat.

"It's not naptime just yet." His attacker laughed as he easily scooped up Tommy's legs in his arms. "The party has yet to begin."

Tommy feebly tried to grab anything on the ground to prevent himself from being dragged back to the Mustang. He tried screaming for help, but could only gurgle out blood and salvia. Somehow he managed to find enough strength to grab a handful of gravel and sand as he continued to be dragged forward toward the car.

"Stop and turn around, you bastard," Tommy silently prayed and readied himself for the one slim chance that might avail itself, provided he could see to aim out of his bruised and swollen eyes.

They came to a stop at the Mustang. As the pain caused his eyes to roll back, he caught sight of a patch of extreme darkness as it detached itself from a nearby row of parked cars and gracefully slid around them, effectively cutting them off from the rest of the drive-in. His attacker found his car keys and swore as he fumbled around for one that would allow him to open the door. Someone else was nearby. Tommy could sense a hidden presence lurking somewhere in the seemingly impenetrable dark. A solitary match split open the womb of night.

"Shit!" he whispered. The keys dropped from his hands and fell to the ground with a dull clatter. Tommy saw the match drop from a black leather–gloved hand as it grabbed his attacker by the neck and lifted him skyward. He closed his eyes briefly and relaxed, allowing the gravel and sand to slide out of his hand like the grains of sand in an hourglass. He would have smiled if it didn't hurt so much.

"Ready for a joyride?" Tommy heard his rescuer ask. He stiffened again as the mustang's door opened. And a feeble thought crossed his mind: "How?"

Tommy opened his eyes just in time to see his attacker being thrown into the backseat. A tall man shrouded with the night's darkness followed and the car door slammed shut. He watched as the car rocked back and forth in the violent frenzy of two lovers desperate for release and unaware a voyeur was watching.

Tommy's attacker rose up from the backseat only once. A gloved hand covered his mouth, but his eyes pleaded for mercy. From the light of the movie screen, Tommy could see the man's shirt was torn, and his chest, bloody. He was pulled down again, arms thrashing wildly, and that was the last he ever saw of him.

Tommy tried to gently ease himself up and on his feet, but failed. He fell back to the ground and bit hard on his lip to prevent himself from crying out in pain. Whoever had proven to be his savior, he didn't want to attract any attention before hiding in the nearby bushes and seeing the overall package of his savior. Tommy had begun to inch his way toward possible refuge when he heard the car door open again.

He froze. Tommy's lower lip trembled as he turned to face whoever was getting out of the Mustang. The man's fingernails seemed to retreat back into his gloves. Despite the pain, Tommy blinked to clear his cloudy eyes. The gloved hands appeared normal now. The unappraisable darkness of his shadow Tommy had at first welcomed, but now was terrified of, approached him with a dizzying speed. Before he could utter a sound of protest, his rescuer swooped down and gently lifted him from the ground like a mother would raise a newborn from a crib.

"Huusshhh. I'm just going to take you to my office, where I can get you cleaned up," he softly said, with a falsetto of reassurance. He paused long enough to savor the waves of growing helpless terror that emanated from Tommy's body. "We'll talk about repayment after I've gotten you back on your feet."

Any words of protest Tommy had died when he looked at the dark blue eyes and a devilishly handsome aristocratic face framed with an impeccably neat red beard and mustache. The embers smoldering in his eyes showed he tolerated no defiance and would be swift to deal out retribution to those who tested the limits of his patience. Tommy positioned himself in his arms so he wouldn't touch his damp clothing. Tommy was familiar with the odor of blood and bone. His lean body and clothing sang the stench proudly. A squat building rapidly came into view, and the man paused long enough to open a side door. It was almost as if he had taken one giant step forward. Tommy grew increasingly nauseous from the distinct odor of blood and the intense patch of shadow that swirled about him. A single light illuminated a long, narrow staircase. He remained silent as his savior leaped up the stairs, then paused long enough on a landing to open another door leading into a room illuminated only by the white light leaking out of two gigantic clicking movie projectors.

He set Tommy down in a worn, but comfortable wing chair, and after removing his jacket, took a step back to examine the young man. Tommy watched him through half-opened eyes.

"What a lovely sight you are," he sighed with disgust. He removed his gloves. "Might as well get started cleaning you up. I don't need you whole, but I do need you in working condition."

Tommy watched as he tossed his damp gloves onto a nearby table and with a taunting promise dancing in his eyes, licked his fingers as he approached him. Tommy shrank back against the chair, but it provided no safe haven against his rescuer's steady advance.

He paused long enough to grab Tommy's left arm. "I don't have time for you to waste in hysterics. I need to get you to the drop-off site, and time is running out."

His hot breath brushed against Tommy's cheek and ear. "Watch closely and learn to enjoy."

"No!" Tommy screamed, but his weak struggle proved useless. With a surgeon's delicate skill, the man split open a vein on Tommy's arm with his fingernail. He traced the path his fingernail had taken with his tongue. The painful throb of gushing blood immediately stopped and was replaced by a warm, pleasant tingle. Tommy sighed in release as the blaring pain from his bruises and injuries were momentarily numbed and replaced with a euphoria he desired more than escape, regardless of who offered it to him.

His still nameless rescuer released his arm and stepped back. Tommy hastily pulled back his arm and examined it. Only a thin white scar now remained. "Who are you? What are you?" he managed to say in a whisper, still savoring the fading euphoria the saliva had brought him.

"Darren Frazier." He took another step backward and bowed. "I'm the sole proprietor and projectionist of the Starlite Twin Family Drive-In Theatre."

Darren came forward again and leaned against the arms of the chair. With Tommy's face almost touching his, he smiled and displayed his razor-sharp teeth in the façade of a friendly smile.

Tommy found himself trembling from a combination of fear and desire. He wanted to run his fingers across those glistening teeth and suck out every second of intense pleasure each droplet promised. "And what use do you have for a badly battered, practically useless car thief?"

"I need you to help me find Roger, my partner," he said. "He's been taken from me."

In an unconscious gesture of frustration, he ran a tired hand through his hair and moved away from the chair. His back was to Tommy. "He was in a car wreck about a month ago and after a quick examination the rescue workers discovered his connection to me. They took Roger to a rehab center designed to break the bond between us. I want him back. I need him back."

Darren walked over to a nearby table and picked up a picture frame. He had a sorrow-filled smile as he walked back over to Tommy and handed him the photograph. "My beloved, Roger."

He turned away and Tommy felt a pang of sympathy for Darren as he studied the photograph. Tommy could see Roger's sorrowful brown eyes reflected a deep love for the person on the other side of the camera.

"Breaking people out of institutions isn't my specialty," he said. His gut instinct warned him that Darren wasn't being entirely truthful about Roger's incarceration. His only choice was to keep Darren talking and try to ferret out the truth while seeking an opportunity to escape.

"Why not get a lawyer to spring Roger from wherever he's being held?" Tommy set the picture frame down on his lap and waited patiently for a response.

"Roger is outside legal jurisdiction, and I don't know where he's being treated for his so-called malady." Darren turned back around and Tommy studied the anger that burned in his eyes.

It reminded Tommy of the anger a child would express when

being denied a favorite toy. "Your battered body will guarantee you admittance into the shelter, once I provide an additional touch or two. I'll drop you off at one of their lookout points, and once you're inside the shelter, find the address and give me a call.

"After you've called me, your obligation to me will be done and you can go on your way. And Roger will be entwined in my arms once more."

Tommy stiffened and nearly blacked out from the pain the effort had cost him. "Granted you rescued me from that son of a bitch, but I'm not the Marines, and I don't owe you any special favors."

His rich laughter, filled with an uneven mixture of bemusement and annoyance, poured into every nook and cranny of the office. Darren smiled and began advancing toward Tommy. "Your fingerprints are littered all over the Mustang."

"So?" His fear was increasing by each racing second. Tommy did his best to maintain his best poker face.

"The son-of-a-bitch is dead." Darren said it so simply. His ear-splitting smile was terrible to behold. "I tore him to shreds, and wore gloves while doing so."

"There were other witnesses," Tommy weakly protested. His heart roared in his throat. He desperately wanted to down a cold beer to soothe the speed at which his heart thundered away.

"I think it's a simple trade-off. Help me find Roger and I won't turn you over to the police for murder."

Tommy resisted the urge to make a rash dash for freedom that lay beyond the office door. He knew Darren would have probably anticipated such a desperate attempt and would be alert. Instead Tommy shifted uncomfortably in the chair as his thoughts swirled in desperation for any conceivable way out of his predicament. His wired brain could not think of a way to escape.

A damp finger caressed Tommy's swollen eye. Warm desire induced by the contact of Darren's saliva on his skin hazed his thoughts. A sigh escaped his lips as Darren's finger slowly followed the curve of his cheek down to the base of his neck.

"Please," Tommy weakly protested. "I can't think clearly."

"It's not so bad a trade-off," Darren murmured. "A couple days inside a clinic with hot meals and showers. A temporary roof over your head. I'll even throw in a finder's fee of a couple thousand dollars. It's probably all you would have gotten for the Mustang anyway.

"Oh yes, I'll even destroy the car to get rid of the incriminating evidence. Such a shame too. It's such a beauty." Darren's saliva-tipped fingers moved underneath Tommy's shirt collar, and Tommy felt himself being swallowed up by the intense pleasure he experienced as Darren's touch began arousing his nipples and other parts of his nineteen-year-old body.

"Anything." The weight of Darren's continuing advance caused the last of his faltering defenses to crumble. "I'll agree to anything for more," Tommy whispered.

Roger's picture fell to the floor, and the glass within the frame shattered, but Darren and Tommy were way past caring.

Snatches of hurried conversation and piercing flashlight beams roused Tommy from the dreamless state he had buried his numb thoughts and body in. He tried to stretch and open his eyes to identify his surroundings with a rapid visual sweep, and met with limited success. Sharp objects impeded his hands from exploring, and his still swollen eyes would only open wide enough to let woefully thin slivers of moonlight in. It was the smell of rotting vegetables and meat that identified his surroundings. Darren had caused Tommy to soar to heights of ecstasy he had never experienced in his few brief sexual encounters with guys and girls, but had read about in the soft-porn romance novels he occasionally lifted from bookstores; and then he had abandoned him in the pick-up site for the sanitarium—a garbage Dumpster.

"Josh, in here," someone shouted. A wandering beam from a flashlight snared Tommy's eyes and he raised an unsteady arm to block the powerful light. "I think we found ourselves another one of the companions!

"Hang on, honey, I'm coming in," he told Tommy. Paper, cans, and glass crackled and crunched under the weight of the person who jumped into the Dumpster. Tommy tried to avoid him by inching into a corner, but a cardboard box blocked his retreat. He whimpered as each crunch of garbage brought the stranger closer. He wanted to continue the spell Darren's deft hands, tongue, and teeth had forged on his body.

Rough knuckles caressed Tommy's cheek in a gesture of reassurance. "I need to check you out before I move you out of here," his rescuer told him. He gently eased Tommy's head aside to expose his neck. "Get the kit ready, Josh!" His voice was a bittersweet mixture of disgust and pity. "He got his taste of juice within the last hour or two, I'd say."

Callused fingers probed his neck. "Holy shit, Josh. It was his first taste. He's still fresh!"

He picked Tommy up from the refuse and carried him over to the open Dumpster door. He was transferred over to Josh's waiting arms and placed on a ready gurney. "It's going to hurt a little, but I need to get some fluids in you," Josh told him.

Tommy watched in silence as he swabbed his arm down with an alcohol wipe. Josh searched for a plump vein on Tommy's arm and found one right away. "Now, this might hurt for a moment, but afterward you won't feel a thing."

Tommy tried to bolt from the gurney as Josh prepped an intravenous needle, but with the patient skill of a seasoned veteran he held him down and placed his arms and legs in restraining straps. "Now hold real still so you won't get hurt," Josh cautioned him.

"No! Leave me alone. I want Darren!" Tommy screamed as the needle pierced his arm and entered the readied vein. He screamed again as he felt his blood boil from the fluid the intravenous bag was pumping into his ravaged body. Tommy's screams died as he sank into oblivion.

❖

Brilliant daylight flooding in through open window blinds jolted Tommy awake.

He was in a hospital room. His skin felt raw, as if someone had scrubbed him down with a wire brush. He raised a hand and ran it through his dirty blond hair. It had been washed and cut short. His beard stubble had also been freshly shaved away.

"Ah, good afternoon, sleepyhead! I was going over your records, brief as they are, so I didn't see you wake up. Feeling a bit hungry? I'll call up a plate from the cafeteria, and while we're waiting for it to arrive, I can get some information on you for our records."

Tommy turned to face the chubby man who was speaking to him. The desire to leave the hospital room and be with Darren again fueled the claustrophobia growing within him, but Tommy remembered why he was there and what he must do in order to gain his freedom and another taste of Darren.

"I need to make a phone call," Tommy said. "I have to let my boyfriend know I'm all right. Can you give me the address for here? I know he'll pick me up right away."

The chubby man smiled sadly and shook his head. "I'm sorry, hon, I can't do that. If we're lucky, you'll soon be free from any influence he has over you. You're lucky. You managed to come to us only after one taste of juice. Drying out should be easier for you than it has been for our past patients."

Tommy carefully propped himself up on the bed and quickly studied the man who sat patiently waiting for the expected next round of pleas and shrill threats. Past experience with escapes from youth detention centers and runaway shelters had taught him not to volunteer worthless bits of personal data so quickly. It was always best to let the goody-two-shoes social workers think each soul-wrenching revelation resulted from hard won trust. Tommy would only cast suspicion on himself if he immediately played ball.

Despite the warmhearted, fatherly appearance of the man, Tommy suspected he would know a line of crap when he heard one.

"Will I get something to eat if I tell you my name?"

"Provided it's a proper introduction. I'm Chris Newsome. I was one of the very first patients here. Now I'm director of patient admissions."

"I'm Tommy McDevitt. When can I leave?"

"I'll be honest with you, Tommy. We have never treated anyone who had just one taste of juice. You're going to be a challenge for us."

"I'm rather a hungry challenge right now," Tommy said. He slowly lay back on the bed.

"One chicken dinner coming right up," Chris said. "Afterward, if you're feeling up to it, perhaps you would like to take a walk around the clinic and acquaint yourself with the surroundings and some of the ongoing therapy sessions."

"Can I go outside for a stroll and some fresh air?"

A bemused smile graced Chris's face and momentarily erased the crow's feet that the toll of years had etched. Tommy cringed as sad eyes replaced Chris's natural good humor.

"None of us ever go outside. So few ever recover enough to function normally again. And those of us who do manage to shake free from the shackles of the juice don't risk going outside. Even a day like today, with brilliant sunshine, offers no safe harbor for us." Chris reached over and gave Tommy a gentle squeeze on the shoulder. "That's why we're so excited by your arrival. You may be the first patient from the clinic to go out into the world again.

"I'll be right back with your lunch."

Tommy watched Chris depart and reached out for the folder had left on the chair he had sat on. The effort brought on a bout of dizziness and nausea, but he fought it down.

Tommy carefully scanned through each document. All he had learned was that he had been severely dehydrated when they brought him in and was suffering from severe withdrawal psychosis brought upon from a lack of the juice. The memory of Darren's glistening teeth briefly aroused his body. Hearing footsteps approaching, Tommy quickly replaced the folder and resumed a prone position on the bed. Learning the address of the clinic and relaying it to Darren was not going to be an easy task. All the medical and personal information on him had been written down on paper that offered no written clue to his whereabouts. Tommy knew his best chance of finding the information he needed was getting into Chris's office.

Chris appeared in the doorway with a covered tray. He rolled a table over to Tommy's bed and set the tray down. "Eat up, and afterward, if you feel up to it, go exploring and meet some of the people here. There's a robe in the closet to protect you from any drafts.

"Just follow the yellow line on the floor. It leads to the community room. If you have any questions, just ask someone. Or if you want to talk about setting up a recovery program, the purple line leads to administration and my office."

"Thank you." Tommy weakly smiled. Chris beamed at him and departed.

Tommy's stomach grumbled and he lifted the lid off the tray. Tearing off a piece of chicken, he chewed slowly and thought. He decided to enjoy the meal before searching for the means to regain his freedom.

Chris had been true to his word. Tommy slowly followed the yellow line painted on the floor and found himself in a large community room filled with a variety of people ranging from his age all the way up to seventy. People waved and greeted him, and Tommy smiled and waved back, secure in the role of playing the shy newcomer to the group. He was well versed from living in group homes and with foster parents to know what was looked for and expected.

His agenda focused on bumping into a small, isolated table where a gray-haired woman was humming away as she concentrated on shaping a wire sculpture of a horse into form. Tommy "accidentally" ran into the table and knocked a few bits of scrap wire onto the floor.

"I'm so sorry," Tommy said as he picked up pieces of wire from the floor and pocketed a couple for his use.

Startled, the woman looked up. She smiled in relief when she saw Tommy had been the one responsible for the sudden shift of the table. "Oh, that's all right. You can just leave those scraps of wire on the floor. I'll pick them up later."

Tommy apologized again and departed from the community room. He followed the purple line now down a long corridor that led straight to the administration wing of the clinic. Once he located the brass nameplate that announced he had arrived at Chris's office, he knocked on the door and waited. There was no response. Tommy cautiously surveyed his surroundings. No one was around in the administration wing. He tried the door. It was locked.

Tommy removed the two strands of wire he had acquired from the sculpture table and inserted them into the keyhole. He had the door open before he had reached the silent count of five.

Once inside, Tommy closed the door and raced over to the desk. Chris had been studying a report on how long it took ambulance drivers to reach the clinic from various parts of the city. The first paragraph of the report summed up the study and listed the clinic's address. Tommy glanced over at the phone. It had a lock on it. The bottom file drawer's lock was harder to pick. Tommy's finally gave up picking it and pried it open with a pair of scissors. It contained Chris's wallet and inside that, a cell phone. Tommy flipped open the cell phone and got an immediate dial tone. The numbers Darren etched into his memory easily came forth and as he waited patiently for him to pick up, Tommy stole a glance out of Chris's spacious picture window. The setting sun cast the sky in vibrant hues of orange and red.

On the fourth ring, Darren's answering machine picked up the call.

Tommy waited impatiently for the message to finish, and once the beep sounded, he poured forth the information with a triumphant rush until Chris walked in with a man he recognized. The man in the photograph Darren had showed him and cried over. Roger.

Tommy quickly slammed down the receiver.

"So you called Darren," Chris said. There was no recrimination in his calm voice. "Meet Roger, his battered partner. He arrived about a month ago with the same medical technician who found you."

Chris brought Roger farther inside and shut the door.

"Show Tommy."

Roger hesitated. Horrific shame and embarrassment danced in his still haunted eyes. He clenched tightly at the collar of his shirt in a futile attempt to keep under wraps the legacy of shame his eyes showed.

"Show him," Chris said more gently this time. He reached out and lightly brushed Roger's arm with his fingers.

"It's all right. We still have some daylight left, and the blinds are closed. No outsider can see, but Tommy needs to see your scars for himself."

Roger closed his eyes as he unbuttoned his shirt. Tommy watched in nauseous fascination as the older man's blouse fell down past his shoulders and down to the floor.

Tommy could see Roger's body had been firm and beautiful once. Somehow the firmness remained despite the patchwork of thin white scars where razor sharp teeth and fingernails had traced path upon path of vicious biting and tearing.

"The pain is fleeting," Roger said. He smiled wistfully and began tracing a scar on his stomach. "Pretty soon all you live for is their drool upon your body as it numbs out the pain and replaces it with euphoria."

His finger stopped at his left pec. A firm dark nipple should have been at the ragged scar tissue where his finger rested. Roger smiled at Tommy. "Do you remember the pleasure you felt after his teeth were inside your jugular vein? Do you remember wanting more? Begging for more?"

The memory of Darren's incisors breaking into the skin of his neck flooded back to Tommy from the corner of his mind where he had buried it.

"No!" Tommy screamed. He blindly ran from the room, tears burning his eyes.

Somehow Tommy managed to maneuver through the maze of people and furniture and found the way back to his room. He ran into the small closet and curled up into a fetal position on the floor. The full memory of his time with Darren surged to the surface of his brain, and he bit deeply on his right hand to prevent himself from screaming in humiliated disgust.

Tommy knew he was no better than Roger, Chris, and all the other patients in the clinic. When Darren had slid roughly inside him, Tommy had begged him to nibble on his body again so he could savor the euphoria his drool offered. Darren had just bared his teeth in a tantalizing tease as each thrust carried his cock farther inside Tommy.

A comforting hand squeezed Tommy's shoulder in reassurance. Startled, he cried out and scrambled away in terror, only to be blocked by the closet wall. Through tear-blurred eyes, Tommy saw Chris smiling sadly at him.

"It's okay, honey," Chris said as he sat down beside Tommy and brushed his hair off his sweaty forehead.

"It's not okay," Tommy bitterly cried. "You don't understand. I told Darren the shelter's address."

The laughter in the older man's eyes stopped Tommy for a second. Then he yelled, "Damnit! Darren's coming here. He's coming for Roger!"

"Tommy, oh Tommy, you're not the first person who has been used by one of them. We've had moles before. The founders of this abuse shelter expected one or more vampires would attempt to reclaim a so-called loved one. We exist solely to break the cycle of abuse."

"But he's coming. I invited him here. I pleaded with him to come. No wall or door can prevent him from reclaiming me or Roger." His voice shrank to a shrill whisper. "I don't want him to touch me ever again."

"Tommy, listen to me carefully. The sun has set and we don't have much time left." Chris pulled him off the closet floor. "Before the founders opened the doors to this shelter, they realized that there would have to be a shelter within a shelter. Darren can't get to us in there because you haven't invited him inside there, and we won't let you. But we've got to leave now. Otherwise, no one will be safe from him."

"It's already too late. I've come back to reclaim what's rightfully mine." Darren grabbed Chris and pulled him roughly up from the floor. Tommy screamed and Chris shut his eyes at the sight of saliva dripping from Darren's sharp incisors. "Where's Roger?"

With eyes tightly shut, Chris struggled uselessly against Darren's tight hold. "Go to hell. He's safe from you!" he yelled.

"Why don't I take you to heaven instead?" His tongue traveled up the length and breadth of Chris's thick neck. Tommy watched in mute horror as Chris moaned in orgasmic pleasure and went limp in Darren's arms.

"Where's Roger?" Darren whispered in Chris's ear. "Tell me where he is and I'll give you another taste. It's been a long time, hasn't it." He tickled Chris's chin with the tip of his tongue.

Tommy regained a fragile hold on his terror and rose from the floor. "Leave him alone, you bastard." He rushed him. Darren threw Chris aside. He hit the floor with a dull thud. Darren easily caught Tommy. Two harsh blows landed across his cheeks and pain surged anew in Tommy's still bruised face.

"Tell me where Roger is, and it's happy time for everyone. Otherwise…" Darren smacked Tommy across the face again.

"Tell me." He raised his hand to strike Tommy again, but paused. "I see we have uninvited company." Darren threw Tommy down and he landed on top of Chris. The older man's body was still in the throes of orgasmic seizures brought on by Darren's saliva. Tommy scrambled off Chris and dragged the unconscious man away as Darren turned to face whoever had been bold enough to interrupt him.

An orderly armed with a crossbow stood in the doorway. He fired as Darren dropped to the floor and rolled over to him. The arrow sailed uselessly into the far wall. He knocked the crossbow out of the orderly's hand and grabbed him by the throat.

"Perhaps you have the information I need," Darren said. He dragged the squirming man into the closet and slammed the door shut.

"Chris, please wake up," Tommy pleaded in whispered tones. "We have to get to the shelter. Chris!" Tommy lightly slapped Chris's face.

Tommy froze at the sound of clothes being ripped and a scream piercing the room. He watched helplessly as the closet door shuddered against the sheer force of the violent coupling on the other side.

The closet door opened and the naked orderly stood momentarily before he dropped. Blood gushed out of a large bite from his neck and oozed down his body. His eyes were dull. He was dead before he hit the floor.

Darren emerged from the closet and wiped the fresh blood from his lips and chin with a handkerchief he pulled out of his shirt pocket. He turned his attention back to Tommy and Chris.

"No," Tommy whispered. With Chris in tow, he began to back away, but Darren walked over and grabbed him by the shoulders.

"I'm only going to ask one more time." Darren's hot breath stank of blood and his teeth scraped across Tommy's left cheek.

"Darren, take me home. I want to go home." Roger stood in the doorway. Arms outstretched, smiling.

"Later," Darren whispered to Tommy. He let go of Tommy and turned his attention fully to his partner.

"Get away from him!" Tommy screamed as he cradled Chris once more, but his words had no effect. Roger hadn't bothered to put his shirt back on. Smiling, Darren instantly went over to him. Roger smiled as he cradled Darren's face in his hands.

"Give me just one more taste before we go home," Roger pleaded.

As Darren closed his eyes and readied his teeth to strike on his neck, Roger removed a sharpened stake that had been taped to his back with electrical tape and plunged it into his back, through his heart.

Darren screamed in pain and outrage, but still managed to grab Roger. In a parody of a loving embrace sealed with a kiss, Darren pulled Roger forward and impaled him on the stake that was sticking out of his chest. "Taste me now," he managed to rasp before embedding his teeth in his neck. They fell to the floor, dead.

Tommy closed his eyes. Bitter tears flowed as he rocked Chris back and forth. "It's going to be all right," Tommy told Chris. He wasn't aware if the man heard him. "It's going to be all right. We'll go out in the sunshine together. Someday. I promise. Together."

Tommy cried hysterically, hugging Chris tightly, as more orderlies rushed in.

LIFEBLOOD
JEFFREY A. RICKER

L et's get one thing straight: I never bit Darren. I never drank from him. I never tried to turn him into one of us.

I didn't even think about it until the end.

If I'd offered, though, he would have said no, of course. I could have begged, but I think I've forgotten how to do that. I would have done anything Darren wanted. I would have walked right out into broad daylight if he'd asked me to.

Not that he would have asked me to do that. Not that it would have made any difference, either. Here are a few more things to get straight. Certain myths are true: We need blood to survive. We never age. We're hypersensitive to the sun, but I can't say I've ever seen one of us burst into flame. That's not to say it's impossible. The part about having no reflection is total bullshit. So's the part about turning into a bat, a wolf, or a mist.

Right. I wish.

I met him in a bar. Like most other people there, I was looking for something to drink. I noticed Darren, who'd already had more than a few, was leaning against the bar, alone, and looked like easy pickings. Also, from the back, the other thing I noticed about him was the four-inch rip just below the left back pocket of his jeans. That, and his lack of underwear.

I leaned against the bar next to him and ordered a round. When the bartender slid a fresh Corona in front of him, Darren turned to me with a dopey, tipsy grin and lifted the bottle in a silent toast. This was going to be easy.

❖

Drinking someone's blood without killing them is delicate, tricky, but not impossible. It's like two people pulling on opposite ends of a string. As long as you feel resistance coming from the other end, it's okay to keep going. Once you start to feel the other side start to slacken, though, you have to stop.

If you can. Like I said, it's tricky.

I make a point of trying not to kill them. Most of the time, I go for the ones who are really drunk or really strung out. (The latter can give the blood an odd flavor; it's an acquired taste.) Once, I drank from a woman three hours after she ate a lot of magic mushrooms, and even I tripped for a little bit.

Every once in a while, you find someone who gets off on it. There's one guy—I don't know his name—who won't let me drink unless I fuck him, and he makes me wait to drink until he comes. It sounds like the sort of thing I should pay for, but I think he'd be willing to pay me to do him, too (though I don't think I was the only vampire he was spreading his legs for).

The thing that's nice about that is not just the blood or the piece of ass. It's that I don't have to pretend. He knows what I am, and I don't have to pretend to care who he is beyond that exchange. All I have to do is make sure he doesn't die.

Sometimes I tell people the truth. They ask what I do for a living and I say, "I'm a vampire." Usually they laugh, come back with something like, "Yeah, right," or if they're especially creative, "So how long have you been a lawyer, then?" Telling them the truth, I've discovered, makes any necessary lie a little easier to hide. I tell them I'm in investments and omit the fact that I've been compounding interest for over a hundred years.

❖

By the time we left the bar, Darren wasn't in any shape to ask questions. Unfortunately, he wasn't in any shape to tell me where he lived, either. Normally, this wouldn't be a problem—just prop him against a wall, have a little drink, and then let him sleep it off in a bus shelter or on a park bench and wonder the next morning just how much he'd had to drink the night before.

Instead, I took him home. To my place. Which I'd never done before.

We vampires have a gravitational pull. I don't know where it comes from, but it's as basic to me as sight or smell. If I want someone near me, I just have to look at them and imagine it happening, and it will.

In Darren's case, the attraction worked in reverse. I was drawn to him. He glowed, his magnetic appeal was as massive as the sun all of a sudden, and it wasn't just the beer or the rip in his jeans or the smile. It wasn't the conversation either, because he couldn't put a subject and a verb together to save his life by the time I got him undressed and into bed.

And then I watched him sleep all night.

The next morning, when he finally woke up, I was still sitting in the chair by the bed, still watching him. I gestured toward a glass of water and a pill bottle on the nightstand.

"You probably have a headache."

He ran a hand through his hair and sat up, smiling. "I never get hangovers." He glanced under the covers. "Did we…?"

I shook my head. "You were *really* drunk."

"Oh." He looked around, maybe trying to find his clothes. I pointed to them, neatly folded on the dresser, but out of his reach.

"Would you like to get dressed?"

"Maybe in a minute. I'm embarrassed to say I don't remember your name."

"Michael."

"Well, thank you for respecting my virtue last night, Michael. Where did we meet?"

"At the Loading Zone."

"And what do you do in life as we know it?"

"I'm a vampire."

He raised an eyebrow. "Seriously?" I nodded. He leaned forward. "Let me see your teeth."

He made room for me to sit next to him on the bed. I tilted my head back a little and opened my mouth wide enough for him to see the canines. He leaned closer, then reached up toward my mouth.

"You mind?" he asked. I shrugged, and he gently grasped one

of the canines between his thumb and forefinger and gave it a little jiggle.

"Well, it's either real or some very expensive fetish dental work," he said. We were now sitting with our faces only a few inches apart, and when he lowered his hand, I felt his breath against my cheek. I had no breath for him to feel. His hand grazed my throat on the way down. Fingers skidded across the buttons of my shirt until they came to rest on my thigh.

"I guess I should thank you for respecting more than my virtue last night," he said.

I swallowed. Was this what nervousness felt like? I'd forgotten.

"Why aren't you afraid of me?" I asked.

"Because you're not going to kill me," he said. "Why are you afraid of me?"

I almost laughed. "I'm not afraid."

He smiled. "You're a very bad liar," he said, and lifted his hand to my chest.

And my heart beat.

A vampire's heart only beats after he's fed, and then only for a short time. But this time it kept beating as he pushed me backward onto the bed and crawled on top of me. This naked and perhaps still drunk man should not have had any of the control in this situation, but I was powerless beneath him as he slowly and deliberately removed my clothes, and for the next hour he made my heart beat in ways it hadn't in decades.

Blood is like a magnet. It's the most powerful force of attraction to a vampire. Like a law of physics, we must obey its pull. Darren, though, had the ability to rewrite the laws of physics. Whenever I fucked the nameless blood donor, my focus was always on the drink that came when he did. Darren made me remember what an equally strong imperative the sex drive can be. Thoughts of blood and drinking fell away from my mind as he lowered himself onto me. Thoughts disappeared, period. If I needed oxygen, I would have been breathless by the time he came.

"If it weren't for the whole blood-sucking thing," he said, rolling over onto his back, "I would highly recommend everyone get a vampire lover."

"Details, details," I said, but I could feel the hunger rising in me. There were spare units in the fridge for cases like this, but drinking cold, old blood was worse than flat soda or a tepid martini. It was more like drinking sour milk.

"Does that mean I won't see you again after this?" I asked.

The words were out before I knew I'd said them. He propped himself up on one elbow and looked at me skeptically. Skeptical is a difficult look to pull off while naked and messy, but he gave it his best shot.

"Let's leave aside the question of why I would want to see you again. Why would you want to see me?"

I turned my gaze back toward the ceiling. "I don't know, but there it is."

He hmm'd noncommittally and hoisted himself out of bed. "Do you mind if I take a shower? I might be able to think more clearly without the spunk drying on my belly."

Suddenly I was no longer at the top of the food chain. You know how tigers and lions never look like they have any fear in the world? That's what it's like for a vampire. You don't worry about something eating you when you're faster, stronger, and smarter than every other species on the menu.

At least that was how I felt until Darren zigzagged onto the list of specials. He was right that I wasn't going to kill him, but I had no idea why. He was ripe for the picking, and he wasn't afraid. I'd met others who weren't afraid, the people who gave themselves to it willingly, but underneath their bravado was always an awareness of the danger. Darren, if he felt he was in danger, never let it show. And I would have seen it. I would have smelled the slightest elevation in his adrenaline, I would have detected the slightest of flinches when I touched him.

And I couldn't keep my hands off him. I wanted to touch him as often and as much as I could. He'd barely get through the doorway before I'd start pulling at the waistband of his pants, lifting up his shirt. It wasn't even because he was beautiful, though certainly he was that. Still, the soft blond hair had a cowlick that never stayed down and his nose was crooked. He was fit, but he didn't look as if he'd just walked off a runway.

So why could I not stay away?

What we had over the next couple months was less of a relationship and more of an obsession, at least for me. I knew very little about him and his life—where he lived, what he did for a living, how old he was. If he wanted to ask me any of the standard Barbara Walters questions—how old were you when you were made, how old are you now, how did that make you *feel*—he kept them to himself. We never went out. We stayed in and fucked in just about every room of the house. He fell asleep after that and I drank a lot of bottled blood and watched him sleep.

I miss sleep sometimes. Other times, I wonder if I'm asleep right now and the only time I was awake was when Darren was alive.

❖

"Where have you been?" I asked when he finally showed up at my door. Three days had passed since I'd last seen him. He shut the door and I pulled him toward me, his answer lost in my kiss. As I slipped my hands under his shirt, my heart began to beat. The drum of it thudded in my ears, the sensation like an electric current to my chest. It was a wonder he didn't feel it, didn't hear it. I hadn't told him about this strange effect he had on me, and perhaps I should have. But it seemed like the one thing too strange that might make him realize the insanity he was in right now.

"Maybe I should give you my phone number," he said, once I finally allowed him to come up for air.

"That might be a good idea."

His hands began tracing a similar path beneath my shirt as well, and soon there was no more thought of talking and I pulled him to the floor, right there in the front hall, not for the first time.

Our routines were very physical—fuck, eat, sleep. While he showered, I had a drink, then I made him something to eat. There was actual food in my kitchen for the first time, and the meals I made him were simple. I'd never learned to cook when I was alive—it was a less enlightened time, and men weren't expected to know that sort of thing.

As he ate the steak I had made for him—it tended toward the rare side—he also told me about his recent visits to the doctor, the strange pain he'd been experiencing, the battery of tests, the biopsy, and finally the diagnosis. As timing would have it, while he relayed his death sentence, my heartbeat began to slow—after it fell to once every fifteen seconds, it was finished.

"Is there anything to be done?" I asked.

He smiled and shrugged. "You could pass the steak sauce."

That was the way he was. I was tempted to rail at him for not taking his predicament seriously, but what else could he do? And how seriously would he take criticism from someone who never had to stare into the abyss looming below him now?

I passed him the A.1. and he finished his steak. A yawn and a kiss later, he said he was exhausted and wouldn't mind going to sleep. I lay in bed next to him, my arms wrapped around him as if that could protect him from any intruder, until he finally fell asleep. Then I gently untangled myself and withdrew to the armchair at the end of the bed. For the rest of the night, I watched him sleep.

You can tell a lot about a person from the way they fall asleep. The conscious mind moves back into the shadows, and the ego loosens its grip. The changes in a person's face or a body posture are no longer an act of will, but are more a reflection of the person's true nature.

Darren was not afraid. He slept the heavy, restful slumber of someone at peace. He lay on his back and stirred very litle. His left arm was flung across the bed, while his right rested beneath his head and the pillow.

Quietly, I slid my chair closer and placed my hand in the center of his chest. I closed my eyes and listened as, in time with his breathing, my heart began beating again.

❖

For someone at peace with his fate, Darren's decline was frighteningly swift. He came to see me at home only one more time— he barely ate and went to sleep almost immediately. Taking any sort of liberties with his body would have seemed like a violation. He was on a leave of absence from work while he underwent chemo and rested at home, but he couldn't bring himself to take a leave of absence from me, he said.

When I took him in my arms, he smelled dark and earthy, as if he were already buried in the ground. In spite of that, as he fell asleep against me, his head lying on my chest, I wondered if he could hear my heart beating.

Three days later I got the call from Darren's roommate, whom I hadn't known existed before now, to tell me Darren was in the hospital.

I hate hospitals. Usually, I only go into them when I'm desperately hungry. They don't smell right. It's like opening the refrigerator door three days after everything inside has spoiled.

But my desperation to see Darren was like a hunger itself. I went.

The earthy smell I'd noticed during Darren's last visit had intensified. Walking into his room was like walking into a forest after a rain shower. I expected to see moss blanketing the floor or a tree leafing out in the corner. Instead, there was just a lot of machinery and a lot of IV tubes, and Darren at the end of them all.

He smiled when he saw me, but he didn't have the strength to lift his head from the pillow.

"See? I told you I knew you wouldn't kill me."

"You're not nearly as funny as you think you are." I sat in a chair at the bedside and took his hand. His skin felt like old paper that would crumble if I held it too tightly.

You would think that everlasting life would be liberating, right? Wrong. It's more of a burden. All of the things we carry with us in life—the disappointments, the fears, the sadness—are multiplied at the same time they are flattened. You have hundreds of years behind you and maybe thousands ahead of you, so what's to make any one missed opportunity or lost love any greater than another?

The selfish thing would have been to turn him into one of us. It's not like he was in any position to resist. But it changes you—how could it not?—in more ways than the "never get old" and "never need to go to the gym." He could come out the other side hating me just as easily as anything else.

Either way, I'd lose.

In that case, maybe letting him die was more selfish. I don't know.

"Deep thoughts?" he asked.

"The deepest."

"Any deeper than six feet is overkill." He laughed, but the sound was full of ashes. I drew his hand closer and kissed it, then held it to my chest. He slid out of my grasp and placed his palm flat against my shirt.

"Hang on…Ah, there it is." Sure enough, my heart was beating again. He smiled. "Glad I can still get you off on my deathbed."

"You knew about that?"

"Not at first. After a few times, I caught on." He laughed, or maybe coughed. It was hard to tell. "Everyone wants to make someone's heart beat a little faster, but to get it going from zero? I always knew I had mad skills."

He smiled again and I kissed him, placed my hands on his stubble-roughened cheeks, and imagined I was kissing the earth.

"Can you open the curtains?" he asked, frighteningly short of breath now, and here's how selfish I am: I didn't want to do that for him. I didn't want to get up from my seat next to his bed. Didn't want to stop touching him for fear that he would be gone when I turned around, and my heart would never beat again.

I must not be a total bastard because I did get up and open the curtains. It was a gray, overcast day. The hospital was across the street from the park, and eight floors below, the treetops were just getting touched with the flame of October color.

"Cloudy, that's too bad," he said. I returned to the chair and took his hand again. "I was hoping for sun."

"Speak for yourself."

"I was. Besides, I thought you said that thing about the sun was bunk."

"Not totally, but why take chances?"

"Because it's fun that way. You should try a few."

"I will," I said. "I promise."

I wanted to tell him something else, like I'd never forget him, or that tomorrow or the next day I'd go for a walk through the park and see if I catch fire like the trees. Instead, we sat there quietly, staring out the window, until eventually both our hearts stopped beating.

CENTURIES OF LONGING
DAMIAN SERBU

Piotr heard the telltale cadence of footfalls behind him. Too perfectly in tune with his own step, too light and quick. Once pursued, he also knew that contact was unavoidable. He rushed around the corner, off Euclid Avenue, down East Ninth Street, and toward Lake Erie. He hurried by the Rock and Roll Hall of Fame and into Voinovich Park. The stalker followed.

The glow of lights from Cleveland Browns Stadium illuminated much of the now-deserted park. The crowd roared next door. He had almost gone to the football game that night but got distracted by a news story. He always stopped everything to listen to news about the gay community, which mesmerized him. Born long before anyone could safely love another man, he marveled at this modern era and especially the way that two men could couple. He longed for such a thing himself.

He hardly had time for such contemplation, however, before a beautiful woman came out of the shadows and approached him.

"You shouldn't just run like that." She brushed a strand of her long brown hair out of her eye and smiled, allowing her fangs to descend. "I assume you know the ethic. We can't harm each other."

"Of course I know. I just wanted to be alone."

"You're not with your mate?"

"I don't have one."

She raised an eyebrow. "Such a sexy specimen, with a foreign accent no less, and you can't find someone? What about your maker? Where did she go? I'd have a hard time letting go of that muscular chest if it were me."

Piotr dreaded telling his story again, with the angst it caused him and the inevitable pity from the receiver. "Why are you so interested? Are *you* alone?"

She laughed, tossing her head back and coming toward him. She linked her arm through his elbow and turned them back toward the museum. She guided him to a nearby bench that gave them a better view of downtown but relative seclusion at the same time. The stadium crowd had started to exit, with throngs of people going in every direction.

"They must have won," she said. "The people are happy."

"It's preseason. No one cares."

"Are you a fan? How funny."

"I just like the game." He rubbed his hand on his shorts nervously, wanting this to end.

"I'll answer your question, but I demand reciprocity. I do have a mate, but we often wander alone. He stayed in Nebraska. We own a farm there and he likes to feed on wandering farm hands. But I crave the city from time to time. I'd never been to Cleveland. Could you show me around?"

"I doubt you'd like my company."

She furrowed her brow. "We could cut to the chase and go have sex. I find you adorable."

"I have to go." Piotr pushed himself off the bench and started to walk away but she seized his T-shirt from behind and pulled him back down.

"Nice muscles." She ran her hand along his back, then up his arm and grabbed his bicep. "You can't get away that easily. Where's your mate?"

"I already told you that I don't have one. I never have. I also don't talk about it." He leaned back, knowing that this would never appease her. "Don't make me prolong this. I had a maker, and I have no idea whether or not she still lives. It was a few centuries ago. She was of noble birth and accustom to taking what she wanted. I walked along the road one night when she swooped down and captured me."

He paused, not wanting to relive the events or tell the details. He could still feel the strength of his maker's arms as she wrapped them around him and ran through the night. He had no idea at the time how a woman could simply pick him up and speed away. In her castle, she wasted little time stripping him down, bathing him, and then chaining him to a bed. Moments later, two men entered, both naked. She jumped onto the bed and kissed him deeply. "Too afraid to be aroused?" She clutched his limp penis and tugged at it. "This will help." He watched in horror as fangs descended and she plunged them into his leg near his crotch.

He died then. As he drifted away, hoping at least to escape this hell, warm liquid ran down his throat and he instinctively sucked at it. Rebirth came instantly. He felt stronger and had heightened senses. He yanked the chains from the wall and sat up to see this woman, now also naked, laughing with glee. He pried the shackles off his wrists and dropped them to the floor. She got back on top of him and rubbed her crotch against his, but still he felt nothing.

"No," she snarled. "You"—she pointed at one of the men standing nearby— "test him." One of the naked men came toward Piotr, a lean youth with slight muscles, a smooth chest, and long brown hair. He leaned over and stared into Piotr's eyes, then softly ran a hand down Piotr's chest, all the way to Piotr's now rock-hard dick.

"Dispatch him," the woman said.

"Madame, that violates the ethic." The other, more mature man walked cautiously toward her. Unlike the youth, he was older, perhaps in his thirties, and more muscular.

Piotr stood paralyzed, not knowing where to run or what to do. He had the oddest sensations, because the transformation from life into death had given him a power he had never experienced before. He glanced at the chains that he had yanked from the wall and clenched his fists, just to feel the strength in his hands. He tensed his entire body and knew that he could jump clear across the room if he wanted, with almost no effort.

Yet the others seemingly had the same power, so instead Piotr remained frozen in place. They knew more about this new state than he. They could presumably kill him with ease.

"Out!" she commanded the youth with a forceful wave at the door. He bowed and rushed from the room. "He's not one of us yet. I told you not to talk about this in front of him. He doesn't need to know the ethic even exists." She charged at the other man, who stood as still as a statue as she spat in his face. "Do as I say. You're lucky I saved you. A vagabond vampire, wandering alone in these parts. I could have sent the villagers after you. And still can. Don't challenge me. Get. Rid. Of. Him."

He nodded silently, and then she left the room, slamming the door behind her.

"Are you going to kill me?" Piotr had no idea how to combat another vampire, so he resigned himself to whatever fate came his way. He had already died once that night, why not again? He had been miserable in life anyway.

"We don't have much time, so listen closely." The vampire strolled back and forth, his large penis mesmerizing Piotr despite his dangerous predicament. "She wants me to kill you, yes. But it's forbidden by the vampire ethic. I belong to a secret council that oversees all vampires to ensure that they obey it, for the protection of innocent humans and ourselves. I came here to investigate her, to build a case for execution. Trust me."

Piotr sat on the bed, naked and self-conscious. This man sat next to him, his hairy arm brushing against Piotr's leg.

"I can't explain everything now. I wish I could." The man leaned over and gripped something from under the bed. "You'll need these clothes. Most importantly, once I get you out of here, read this manuscript carefully. It explains everything you need to know to survive. It teaches you about the ethic. Run as fast as you can, and find a crypt before morning. Don't stop until you're far away. You'll survive without feeding for several days."

Piotr got up to leave, still unsure of himself, when the vampire pulled him back. Piotr landed on his lap and felt his hard penis beneath him. The man grabbed Piotr by the head and pulled him into a long, passionate kiss. They fell back on the bed, rubbing against one another as the vampire licked Piotr's nose, his cheek, and then his eyes. "I love green eyes," the vampire whispered. They kissed more deeply, then Piotr took the man's penis in his hands. Oh, how he had always wanted this! Always dreamt of lying with another man and kissing and holding and fondling one. He could not contain his excitement when the vampire returned the favor. He slid his strong fingers along Piotr's penis and tickled at his balls. In but a couple of yanks Piotr came all over their stomachs. He helped his mate climax when something crashed in the hallway, breaking their revelry.

"Out, now." The vampire lurched up, then threw the clothes at Piotr.

Piotr dressed hurriedly. The vampire handed him the manuscript and pushed him toward the window. "Trust me. You can make it. Jump to the ground and run." Piotr hesitated, his human instinct telling him not to jump from this height, at least three stories above the ground. He felt the pressure of a hand on his back and turned around. The vampire kissed him softly on the lips and shoved.

Piotr hit the ground without harming himself. He looked back up, but the vampire had disappeared. And so he ran. Ran away to Paris, then Rome, and finally to America. In all this time, he had never found a mate. Never been with another man. He had met very few vampires, either, and always chased them away, never wanting what they offered. He had lived for over a century, hoping that the vampire who had saved him would find him, might teach him how to live as a vampire who loves other men. He never came. And Piotr never found another vampire like himself.

Even in this new era, when men called themselves gay and openly courted each other in public, fear paralyzed Piotr. The manuscript had said that vampires coupled. But how? It explained how to make another vampire, but then gave a litany of rules and warnings about it. It threatened death for various transgressions if one violated these rules. A council enforced it, but Piotr had never met anyone from this council since that fateful night. He wandered alone instead, sad, melancholy, but not wanting to die, either.

"You still there?" The female vampire's voice brought him back to the park, to the humid August air, to the parade of fans in the distance. "She captured you?"

"Yes, captured me, made me, then wanted to kill me. I escaped. Alone. That's how I like it."

Her harsh demeanor had disappeared despite his obstinacy. She touched him lightly and held his hand. "There's more."

"A lot more that I don't like to talk about. I've never loved because it was forbidden. And now it's too late. I'm too old to adjust. I don't know how."

"I get it." She clutched his hand harder. "That's why I didn't get a reaction. Take my advice. I lived under the Roman Empire, so I know about longevity." Piotr marveled at how much older she was than even him. "You have to adjust, age to age. Things change, and you have to change, too. And it's not good to try to do it alone." She stood in front of him and smiled, her fangs now gone. She took his face in her hands, leaned over, and kissed him on the forehead. "There's a man out there for you. Find him. Don't give up yet. You're too young."

Piotr watched her walk away, wanting to scream for her to come back but at the same time thankful that his solitude had returned. He wiped the blood tears from his face and waited until he had control of himself to get up. He thought of going back to one of the bars that he had visited, with all of those men looking to hook up. She had wanted him to do that.

But what if he wasn't ready? What if she was wrong, and he couldn't adjust? He started back toward Cleveland Heights and the cemetery he had called home for several months now. He had found a nice crypt across from President Garfield's Monument that served him nicely. A bank clock told him that he had hardly been up an hour, however, and so instead he walked up the hill to Coventry, deciding to go to the coffee shop and watch people while he considered her plea to him.

He entered the narrow store and walked to the counter, where he ordered a café mocha. He hardly needed human food or beverages for survival, but the manuscript of long ago had explained how it would not harm him and helped a vampire blend into a crowd. The packed coffee shop offered precisely what he needed at this moment: humans everywhere to keep him from going crazy in his solitude or losing himself in depression over his loneliness, but at the same time a dull roar of sound that posed little risk of forced interaction.

He grabbed his coffee and turned around, hoping to find a free table or at least a stool where he could sit alone in his introspection. Nothing was available. He glanced at one empty chair but noticed someone at the table across from it. Too late, he realized that the young man sitting there had looked up from his reading.

"You can sit here." The youth, probably in his late teens, smiled and motioned across from him.

Stuck, Piotr accepted the invitation. At least this one was adorable, with curly brown hair that frizzed out and deep dimples. He sat down slowly, unsure of what to say. "Thank you." He wished he could come up with something more clever and inviting. But did he really want a conversation with some stranger?

The youth bit the top of his pen and tilted his head toward Piotr. "Andy." He held out his hand by way of consummating the introduction.

"Piotr." Their hands lingered together. Piotr lost himself for a moment in the big brown eyes that stared back. "What are you reading?" There, he had initiated something. Perhaps this encounter would at least distract him from his misery. He imagined the woman from the park encouraging him to continue.

"A history book. It's not for class. It's for fun. I mean, I read for class, too. I'm a history major. But Case doesn't have any classes in gay history." Andy stopped cold.

"Interesting. I'm afraid I lived through too much of what you study as history to appreciate reading about it."

This made Andy laugh. "You're not that old."

"If you only knew."

"What's that mean?"

"It's a long story. Well, I'm sorry to bother you. I only came for a quick cup of coffee." Andy's face fell. "What?"

"Oh, nothing. I mean, sure. Thanks for the company." Andy flipped a page of his book.

"Did I offend you?" Some force propelled Piotr toward this young man. At any other time, he would have fled at that moment without another word. He had tried to leave, wanted to really, but something kept him in that chair.

"No. Of course not. It's just, well. I don't know you. I better not."

"It's a little late now, isn't it? Why don't you try me? I've heard a lot in my time."

"There you go again, acting like some old dude." Andy had recovered and smiled again.

"Why don't you tell this old dude what's on your mind."

"When did you come out? I mean, how old were you? See, I just did. Recently. Like, last week. I know, like, what the hell have I been doing all this time?" Andy shrugged his shoulders. "I knew, right? Since like, fifth grade. Of course! But saying it is another thing. So I just finally did it. Well, my counselor said I should, you know? Actually, my parents were pretty cool. Handled it better than I expected."

"What else?" Piotr prodded and ignored the question about himself. How had Andy determined that Piotr was gay? "Why are you here tonight?"

"Oh, well." Andy stopped and chuckled, mostly to himself. "*That's* a good question. Stupid I guess. I'm not twenty-one yet. Just turned twenty. So I can't go to the bars with my friends. Actually, I don't really have that many gay friends. More like acquaintances. Anyway, I came here hoping to meet other gay guys. You know? It sucks hanging alone. And I don't know where to go, except the bars I can't get in. Oh, are you even gay? I didn't mean to presume anything."

Piotr smiled across at Andy. "You're nervous. Don't be. Yes, I'm gay." Piotr had never said those words about himself before. It felt wonderful.

"Whew. Good. Oh, I didn't mean that."

"Would you like to go someplace to talk? More private?"

Andy hesitated. "Sure."

"I'm not going to harm you. It's just hot and crowded in here."

Andy packed his book in a bag, stood up, and straightened his shirt. He chugged down the last of his drink and started to leave. "You didn't touch your coffee," he said to Piotr. "Are you just leaving it?"

"I'm in a different mood than when I ordered it."

They walked up the hill, past the public library and toward a residential street. Andy continued his monologue, about how he wanted more friends, about how he was usually very shy, and about nothing in particular. Finally, he stopped beneath a tree and turned toward Piotr.

"Isn't that enough about me? What about you?"

Piotr had no idea what came over him, for he had never engaged in such activity, let alone in public. The only man he had ever had sex with was the member of the council, right after Piotr was made.

Tonight, unseen forces took control of his body as he leaned over and kissed Andy on the lips. He pulled Andy closer. Andy kissed back, pushing his tongue into Piotr's mouth, though his arms remained firmly at his sides. Piotr pushed him back and gazed again into those incredible brown eyes.

"Wow, first kiss." Andy grinned and licked his lips.

"Come here." Piotr pulled Andy into a backyard, behind a small shed concealed by trees. This time, Andy stood on his tiptoes and kissed Piotr first. He tasted of mint and chocolate as Piotr ran his tongue lightly across his teeth, then deep into the back of his throat.

Andy helped Piotr unbutton his own shirt to expose his hairless chest. He was so smooth, so delicious, with his slight build and glowing skin. Piotr trailed down to Andy's belly button, then slowly undid the top button of his shorts. He released Andy and sucked longingly at the slightly small penis in front of him. He heard Andy moan as he ran his hand along the inside of Andy's thigh, around to his firm ass cheek. He felt lightly along Andy's anus, pushing softly with his finger. Andy spread his legs willingly as Piotr pushed in deeper with his index finger.

Overcome with passion, Piotr reached down and unzipped his own pants. He fumbled to release his engorged dick and stroked it rapidly. Then he stood up to get another taste of Andy's mouth.

"I've never done this before." Andy said it matter-of-factly, but a slight apprehension crept into his voice.

"We won't do anything you don't want."

Andy fell to his knees and suddenly engulfed Piotr's penis. Despite a vampire's resistance to pain, Piotr winced slightly as Andy's teeth scraped the top of his head. "Cover your teeth." Andy looked up, then tried again. Whatever he did, it fixed the problem. Piotr slid in and out of Andy's mouth, his passion rising quickly. Just before he came, he pulled Andy away gently and shot all over the ground, his legs convulsing and his knees weakening.

He pulled Andy back to his feet and kissed him again, more fiercely, more deeply than before. Andy seized Piotr's still-hardened cock and held tightly to it as they leaned into one another. Piotr finally pulled away from the kiss and turned Andy around slowly. He licked at Andy's ear, then felt again at his beautiful ass.

With one hand, he reached around and began stroking Andy, and with the other he plunged a finger into Andy's tight ass. He worked it for but seconds when Andy's body tensed and Piotr felt the warm goo slide across his hand.

He held the young boy in his arms for several seconds before turning him around again and kissing.

"Um, I don't know what to say." Andy slowly reached down and pulled up his underwear, then his shorts. "I mean, I guess this is it, huh? This is how it goes?" Piotr dressed himself as Andy continued to chatter away. "That was awesome. Wow. I mean, I always guessed sex with a guy would be the thing, you know? But wow. Oh, well, I heard we aren't really supposed to talk or something. These one-time things are like that, right? Never mind, you don't have to teach me."

Piotr reached over and touched Andy on the shoulder. With his free hand, he ran his fingers through Andy's hair and pulled him into another kiss.

"Give me your phone number." Piotr reached down and handed Andy his bag. Andy fumbled around inside for a pen and receipt from the coffee shop, then wrote his number on it.

"What's this mean?" Andy stared up at Piotr, for the first time seemingly lost for words.

Piotr led Andy back to the sidewalk and toward Coventry. "That I'd like to see you again. Is that okay?" Piotr knew the answer before he got it.

"Yeah, that's great. Wow. I mean, you're hot. Really hot." Andy's face turned bright red in the glow of a nearby streetlight. "I like you. Not that I'm going to be clingy or anything. Unless you want me to be! Shit. I didn't mean that."

Piotr put his arm around Andy and nudged them together. "You're a jittery one. We'll see where this goes. But, for the record, you're amazingly hot yourself." Piotr tapped his finger on Andy's nose.

"Shit." Andy looked at his watch. "I gotta go. I promised my friend I'd help her study for an exam. Sorry. Call me? You promise? I didn't get your number."

"No need. I have yours. Go. I'll call you tomorrow."

Piotr watched Andy race around the corner. He followed as Andy ran down Coventry and turned onto Mayfield Avenue. His butt looked even better as he sprinted away. His backpack flopped all over the place as it dangled from one shoulder.

A wave of excitement coursed through Piotr like he had never experienced, in life or in his subsequent death. He had only heard tales of such infatuation, or in the twentieth century seen what it "looked like" on film. Hollywood had hardly ever satisfied him with anything that it portrayed. Vampires always reveled in their perfect evil or longed to be human again. He had experienced neither. He never thought of himself as demonic, and the mortality and fear of death as a human held no allure. Experiences never ended as perfectly as movies implied, and not everyone found their special someone. Perhaps Andy signaled something new, that just maybe a Hollywood ending could happen for Piotr.

Piotr strolled along the street, turning the corner where he had just seen Andy. The row of apartments no longer appeared sad and lonely to him, but rather alive with people. People partnered. People partying. People in love!

There, it happened again, a pure infatuation that Piotr had never experienced. His head spun. His heart leapt at the possibilities. Exhilaration like never before flooded every sense of Piotr's being. Andy's adorable face appeared again in Piotr's mind, then his gorgeous smile, frizzy hair, and nervous chatter. Finally Piotr remembered the darkened encounter behind the shed, Andy's hairless chest, his skinny arms, and the taste of his penis on his lips.

Piotr wanted to see Andy again, right then and there. Yet he had to wait. It might crush him forever if Andy became a one-night stand and ignored Piotr's calls. Piotr must take it slowly, cautiously, making sure that he and Andy both prepared themselves for every step they took. In fact, he decided to simply call Andy tomorrow without meeting him. Instead they could set a date, for a few days from then. Slow. Piotr had to go slowly to avoid ruining this first chance with love.

Besides, the vampire ethic regulated how quickly one could get into a relationship. He had not read the entire manuscript, given to him by his savior after his making, in a long time but recalled that vampires mated for life. He never paid it much attention, assuming that he was destined to wander alone for eternity. In a chance encounter, Andy had changed that. Piotr struggled to remember what the manuscript had said, something about picking another vampire or human to pair with, but in the case of humans it warned to take things very slowly. It had used an example in which it took several years before the vampire converted a human despite their being in love since they met. Piotr wanted to review that part of the manuscript, since he had ignored it for decades.

Piotr decided to go examine the manuscript right now, hoping it might give some direction as he plotted his courtship of Andy. Crossing Mayfield Road, Piotr glanced around to make sure that no one looked before he jumped the fence surrounding Lake View Cemetery. He sauntered through the tombstones and trees, wanting to whistle but again afraid that someone might notice him. Several yards into the cemetery he turned a corner that led to his crypt and froze.

Two muscular men, in their early twenties, towered over a figure who lay on the ground, motionless and bleeding.

"Fucking faggot." One of the assailants stepped back and ran toward the poor victim, kicking him in the head with the full force of his boot. His partner in crime spit down on the target.

Piotr had encountered such scenes before. The ethic allowed him to dispatch both of these brutes for dinner, thus ridding human society of two less than desirable elements. It especially angered him that they had attacked some poor person simply for being or looking gay.

Piotr snapped a branch off a nearby tree to alert his prey to his presence. One whipped around and saw him standing there. "Fuckin' peeping tom, huh?" His friend, who had bent over the victim with a knife, looked up and smirked.

Before either could move toward him and gain any advantage, Piotr used his vampiric speed to close the distance between them. In a mere second, he stood between the two men and allowed his fangs to descend.

When they jumped to attack, Piotr captured each by the neck and held them at arm's length. The one with the knife lashed at Piotr with it and even cut his arm, but the wound healed immediately. Just as he was about to commence with the rest of his theatrics, Piotr glimpsed the body beneath them.

No. Impossible. His entire body collapsed and he let go of the two men when he recognized the backpack, then the shirt, still only half buttoned from their earlier encounter. Andy lay motionless, his face so bloodied and bruised that Piotr would never have recognized him without the familiar clothing.

Rage welled within every inch of Piotr's being. A rage of protectiveness, of anger at someone attacking the innocent. But even more, a rage that his chance at love, after all these centuries, lay shattered and dead beneath him.

Piotr whipped around and in no time came up behind one of the men, both of whom had raced away when he released his grip. He roared as he got close enough to kill him. Piotr extended both arms in front of him, and in one swift motioned clapped his hands together, the fiend's head exploding with the vampiric force.

The other man, the one with the knife who had kicked Andy in the head, screamed in terror as he turned around and saw his friend's brains all over the pavement, his face nothing more than a deflated balloon. Piotr captured him easily by reaching out and grabbing his face like a bowling ball, two fingers penetrating each eye socket and his thumb ramming into the man's mouth and up into the top of it. With relative ease, Piotr pulled his hand back and ripped off the man's face. He slumped to the ground, where Piotr could only hope he would suffer a slow and painful death.

Piotr hardly stopped to contemplate this vindication, however, as he hurried back to Andy's limp form. He fell to the ground and huddled Andy close to him, ignoring the blood that got everywhere. He swayed back and forth, crying so hard that the blood tears streamed down his face and dripped onto Andy, mingling with the youth's blood.

What vile twist of fate had brought him to this point? What karma or force would finally bring the possibility of companionship to his life, only to strip it away in a few minutes of bitter hatred and prejudice? Was this what Piotr deserved, after years of following some ethic outlined in a manuscript, thrust at him as he ran for his life? Was God so cruel as to punish him for nothing?

The damn book gave no instructions for this situation. Neither had the various vampires he had met along the way. What could he do? How could he possibly go on with immortal life, not only in its continued loneliness, but now the loss of love?

Piotr lifted Andy's crushed skull and smashed it against his own face, wanting desperately to pretend that they lay together, in his crypt after he had brought Andy over to death. He licked a bit of Andy's blood, knowing that it always gave a vampire the complete view of that person's life. Piotr saw nothing but goodness there, a kind heart, a loving son and friend, a scared and lonely gay man trying to find himself in a world that often hated him.

No matter how gruesome, even to him, Piotr kissed Andy. Passionately, sucking in the blood and tasting every bit of this youth whom he had grown to love in less than an hour.

Then it hit him. The blood not only came into his mouth at his sucking, but flowed into it, pumped by Andy's heart. He still lived! Faintly, and not for long, but he lived.

Piotr sucked harder at the blood, pulling every ounce into his stomach until he felt the heart stop, just before it brought death to Andy. Piotr tore at his own wrist, spraying blood all over the ground before he smashed his arm over Andy's mouth and let the blood flow into the weakened body.

Slowly, taking so much time that Piotr feared he had waited too long, Andy sucked at the blood. His muscles tensed on their own finally, as Andy licked and drank and came back to life. Piotr watched as the blood healed Andy. His bones came back together, his face healed, and in minutes Piotr had in his arms the beautiful youth from the coffee shop.

Andy glanced around, bewildered. He sat up, completely healed and now immortal. "Piotr?" he asked. Piotr nodded his head. "What happened? I don't understand. Why do I feel this way?"

"What way?" Piotr stalled for time. Of course he knew what Andy meant.

"Strong. Wait!" Andy whipped his head around in fear. "Where are they? They'll attack me again."

Piotr reached out, yanked Andy back to him, and clutched the young man tightly. "No, they're gone. Dead. Not here."

Andy turned his head to Piotr, his eyes wide open. "What?"

Piotr's heart skipped several beats. He had but moments to explain everything to Andy or risk losing him forever. He could sense the panic rising in Andy, the fear taking over despite the fact he must now sense his immortal power.

Piotr unleashed the entire tale on Andy in one breath, including his love and the attack that he had come upon. "I didn't know what else to do. I couldn't sit here with my power and watch you die. I should have asked your permission, or left it alone. This wasn't mine alone to choose. I know that. I couldn't, though."

"Couldn't what?" Andy had relaxed as Piotr talked, leaning into his chest for support.

"Watch you die." The blood tears trickled down Piotr's face again.

Shocking Piotr, Andy reached up and swiped at the blood, taking a bit on his finger and licking it off. "So you saw my life, as I saw yours?"

Piotr nodded slightly in answer. Then Andy reached up and pulled Piotr into a long and passionate kiss.

The unexpected contact broke Piotr from his worry. The manuscript expressly forbade such a transformation. It dictated that bringing a lover over should take time and care. It warned that the council might get involved and punish those who defied it. But who? And how would they know? As Piotr kissed Andy back and held him so tightly that human bones would break, he cared nothing about these rules. He had had no choice. He only worried about Andy.

The sound of approaching voices shocked Piotr back to reality. "I don't know. Dispatch said the scream came from in here. Probably some damn ghost." A policeman's light flashed across the trees around them.

"Come on." Piotr took Andy's backpack, then reached over and pulled him off the ground. Andy jumped up with little assistance. Piotr had already forgotten he was a vampire, too. He led them quickly through the cemetery and to his chosen crypt. With little effort, he moved the enormous slab of marble and hurried them inside. Piotr closed it quickly behind them.

"Wicked." Andy stood a few inches from Piotr and took in the atmosphere. "Do all vampires live with this luxury? Shit."

Piotr had forgotten how the crypt might appear to anyone else. He had taken the bodies and buried them underneath, then secretly gutted the old room, turning it into a small studio-type apartment for himself. Despite its small size, he had a twin bed, chair, and shelves of books in it. He'd also decorated the walls with artwork and heavy curtains, like a castle back home.

"Actually, this is rather shabby compared to how other—" Piotr choked on the word, not knowing if Andy could yet handle the idea of being a vampire.

"Vampires?" Andy tilted his head at Piotr, then broke into a huge grin.

"You're okay with it? This quickly? You realize you lost your mortal life?"

"I lost it before you got there. Remember? I'd be dead, one way or another. Right?"

"True." Piotr nodded his head sadly. He felt sick for Andy.

"Well, this sure beats the alternative." Andy smiled again. "I mean, who wants to die, right? I suppose I just need to know what it means and all. Like, any rules I have to follow. Or, you know, other stuff."

"Other stuff?"

Andy fidgeted with the tassel of a curtain. "Yeah, stuff like love and stuff. You know, stuff."

"Ah." Piotr walked over and picked Andy up. He carried him to the bed and laid him gently on it. "Stuff like this?" Piotr leaned over and kissed Andy. "Stuff, like the fact that I love you? Already I love you, after one brief encounter?"

Andy had closed his eyes but opened them and stared back at Piotr. "You do?" He smiled again, that giddy, kidlike grin that had enraptured Piotr from the beginning.

"You know I do. You saw it in my blood when you drank it."

"Yeah. You don't have to be lonely anymore, you know. Right? 'Cuz you drank my blood, too, right? It told you things?"

Piotr remembered the visions from Andy's blood. He had lingered on it for a moment at the time. After passing over Andy's life, he saw the feeling of infatuation and longing that had enveloped Andy as he raced around the corner onto Mayfield. Right before the men jumped him and dragged him into the cemetery, Andy had dreamed about a ceremony, wedding the two of them. He had worried that it was but a fantasy that would never come true for him, but refused to stop it.

"We can have the ceremony, if you still want." Piotr climbed onto the bed next to Andy. "I'm not afraid, like you are, or at least were, about how fast this happened. It's right. I know it."

"Me, too. I mean, I was scared until I knew you liked me, too. It just worried me, you know? Like, what if I was some punk kid in love with an older man who just wanted to fuck me for a while or something. But I know now. I know what you wanted, all along. So, like you're here for me, I'm here for you. Cool?"

Piotr laughed. Modern slang still made him giggle. "Cool." He kissed Andy on the tip of his nose. "I have a lot to teach you about being a vampire. And you need to read that manuscript." He pointed to it, sitting near the bed on a table. "I'm afraid we already violated a rule when I made you this quickly. We need to make sure to toe the line now."

"We'll do. Just tell me what to do." Andy traced his hand along Piotr's arms. The passion welled within both of them.

"About those fantasies. Do you care what order we fulfill them in?"

"Huh?" Andy scrunched his brow together but smiled at Piotr, who had moved on top of his love.

"Well, you had a wedding and then—" Piotr still had Old World sensibilities, making it difficult to simply blurt out personal things.

"Consummation?" Andy leaned up and kissed Piotr on the cheek. "Sex? You mean, you want to fuck me?"

Piotr felt his face blush red, which made Andy laugh, a deep, guttural laugh. When he stopped, he pulled Piotr into another kiss, then fumbled to take off his shirt. He sat up and yanked his own off, too.

"Well, you want to? The order doesn't matter to me." Andy had grabbed Piotr by the pants and pulled him back over.

"Want to what?" Piotr played the game, teasing Andy back now.

"Fuck me. Please."

"No." Andy's grin fell, so Piotr leaned in for another kiss. "But I'll make love to you, every night, forever."

Slowly, Piotr probed every inch of Andy's mouth with his tongue, running it along his teeth and feeling the fangs that had descended in Andy's excitement. Not wanting to wait, Piotr yanked his pants off and released his passion, then literally ripped off Andy's shorts.

Piotr cupped Andy's balls, then felt along the thin penis and fondled the tip, rubbing the pre-cum around in his finger. He brought it to his lips and tasted it. Andy scooted down the bed and licked Piotr's chest before stopping at his penis. He sucked hungrily at it, nipping Piotr a couple of times with the tips of his fangs. The pain felt exquisite.

Not wanting to climax, Piotr pulled himself out of Andy's mouth and flipped him onto his stomach. He clutched onto Andy's hairless ass with both hands and squeezed. Andy raised his hips in the air, begging for more. Piotr licked along Andy's crack and drove his tongue into Andy's ass. Andy pushed back, groaning with pleasure. He spat into Andy's anus, then slid on top of his love.

"Make love to me, please." Andy turned his head sideways and licked Piotr's cheek. Then Andy reached his arms behind him and pulled Piotr hard on top of himself, hanging on to Piotr's ass tightly.

Piotr slid in effortlessly. Andy gasped and writhed under Piotr, then strained his neck to pull Piotr into a kiss. Piotr went slowly at first, then moved more and more swiftly. Andy urged him to go faster and harder, until Piotr sensed that his penis had swollen beyond belief, to the point of nearly aching. Spasms convulsed his body and he shot inside Andy, who continued to pump underneath him.

Piotr pulled out then, and flipped Andy over. He dove down and took all of Andy's penis in his mouth. As two of his fingers dug back into Andy's ass, he bobbed up and down until seconds later his lover's cum hit the back of his throat and the salty taste covered his tongue.

Sated, he lay next to Andy and kissed him softly on the cheek. They held each other in silence for several minutes.

"So, when do we gotta go to bed? Is that what you call it?" Andy started playing with Piotr's limp cock, making him hard again.

"I don't think I've ever given it a name before. We must sleep before the sun comes up. Actually, we'll become so tired that we'll just fall asleep."

"How long till then? I can't tell in this coffin."

"A couple of hours or so."

"Cool."

"Why is that cool?"

"Because you're hard again. Can vampires recover that fast and go at it?"

"Let me show you." Piotr wrapped his lover in another warm embrace and kissed deeply.

Out of Light and Into the Night
Wayne Mansfield

The battered old pickup truck rumbled along the dirt track sending a great plume of dust swirling into the night.

"Are you okay to drive?" asked Daniel, resting a hand on his partner's thigh.

"Yeah, it's just been a long night," replied Karl, rubbing Daniel's hand. "Did you have a good birthday?"

Daniel smiled and looked at Karl's silhouette against the moonlight.

"I did," he answered. "Best ever birthday party, thanks to you."

He leaned over and kissed Karl on the side of his face, the bristles tickling his lips.

"I guess if you really wanted to thank me…"

Karl took his hand off Daniel's and undid the zipper on his jeans.

"You're kidding, aren't you?" Daniel said.

Karl snickered in the semi-darkness.

"Nope," he replied. "Feel this, then you'll know I'm not joking."

Karl grabbed Daniel's hand and pressed it against the erection that was jutting out of his open fly.

"Well if I have to." Daniel grinned.

"You have to! You have to!"

He leaned back and settled into the seat while Daniel undid his seat belt. Keeping his eyes on the road ahead, he lifted a hand off the steering wheel to let Daniel get to his cock and when he felt Daniel grab it and guide it into his mouth, the sensitive flesh of his cock head brushing against his lover's lips, he sighed a long, breathy sigh.

"Nice and slow," said Karl softly. "We're nearly home but don't stop till you've finished."

He placed a hand on Daniel's head, pushing it gently down onto his cock. Even after a long day spent mending fences on the small farm they owned and a night of partying, he wasn't too tired to enjoy a bit of oral. His balls had already begun to tighten. And why wouldn't they? Daniel gave the best head jobs he'd ever had. "That mouth should come with a licence," he'd say, only half jokingly.

As he neared climax he was having trouble keeping the truck on the road. Twice he almost veered into the ditch as his body tensed in anticipation of ejaculation. But the near accidents didn't seem to bother Daniel, who kept his hand and mouth steady on his rigid cock.

"Oh yeah," Karl moaned. "Suck that motherfucker and get ready to swallow."

Daniel picked up the pace, his full lips sliding up and down the length of his shaft with ease, sucking it hard as his hand worked the base.

"Here it comes, Danny. Get ready!"

Suddenly there was an almighty bang and the sound of screeching tyres as Karl slammed on the brakes. He lurched forwards, slamming Daniel's head into the bottom of the steering wheel.

"Aw shit!" Daniel cried out. "What the fuck are you doing?"

"We hit something," said Karl. "Or something hit us."

Karl moved his arm so that Daniel could sit up, then reached up and turned the interior light on so Daniel could check himself in the rear vision mirror.

"You okay?"

"That fucking hurt," said Daniel, rubbing the small bump that was growing on the side of his head.

"Shh. Can you hear that?" he asked. "There it is. Listen!"

"I'm trying to, if you'll just shut up and let me."

Daniel cocked his head and looked at Karl. Both of them wore puzzled expressions on their faces.

"It sounds like giant wings flapping," said Karl, searching the sky through the windscreen.

Then something heavy landed on the roof. Daniel gasped. Whatever it was took a step, denting the metal as its foot came down.

"Let's get the fuck out of here," said Karl, nearly flooding the engine in his hurry to get away.

The vehicle skidded forwards, sending a dark shape spilling onto the tray at the back of the truck and bouncing over the edge.

"What was that?" asked Daniel, scanning the road through the back window of the cabin.

"How the hell should I know?" asked Karl as he pressed the accelerator pedal to the floor. "Can you see anything? What was it?"

Daniel wound the window down and leaned out.

"I can't see anything," he yelled back. "There's nothing there."

Karl spun the wheel and steered the truck into the driveway of their farm, and as he did Daniel disappeared out the window.

"Daniel!" he yelled.

He stopped the pickup and leapt out. Adrenaline flooded his veins, sending his heart racing. He raced around to the other side of the truck, tucking his flaccid cock back into his jeans as he went, but there was no trace of his lover. He heard the beating wings again, massive wings, and the sound of Daniel calling his name. He looked up and could just make out a large black shape flying away from him towards the full moon.

"Daniel!" he yelled, cupping his mouth. "Daniel! I'll find you, baby. I'll find—"

A great force hit him from behind, winding him, and as he struggled to get his breath back he was lifted off the ground. He looked down, watching the road and his truck grow smaller and smaller. For a moment he struggled to free himself, but the creature's powerful arms were secure around his torso. With a bit of effort he managed to twist himself around and look upon the face of the creature that held him in its grip. The eyes were black and dead, its nose no more than two folds of skin in the centre of its face, and when the creature grinned at him its long fangs glistened in the moonlight. Vampire! There had been rumours and he had seen pictures. How could it be anything else? Suddenly it became difficult to breathe. The smell of death and decay was strong in his nostrils. He could feel vomit biting at the back of his throat, but he swallowed it down. He had to be strong. For Daniel.

His instinct for survival kicked in and once more he struggled to free himself, yet it was useless. The vampire's arms were like metal bands around him. Even when he tried to swing his legs forwards, trying to work up enough momentum to give the creature a good kick, he failed. The vampire barely noticed his efforts and he'd exhausted himself to the point of giving up the fight.

They soared over farmhouses and patches of forest, over a hamlet and a small river that he recognised as being the river that marked the boundary between counties. The wind was harsh against his face, making his eyes water and drying the back of his throat. He swallowed though the action brought him scant relief; there was no saliva to lubricate his mouth with.

Finally they began to descend. Below them stood an imposing granite mansion which stood on the side of a large, lonely hill and was, for the most part, hidden amongst a grove of ancient oaks. He guessed that they had arrived at their destination.

The breeze from the vampire's wings rustled the leaves as they came in for a landing and Karl's feet dragged along the treetops. Their landing was smooth but the minute the creature let go of him he balled his hands into fists and spun around, taking a swing at his kidnapper. But the vampire was too fast and too strong. As he slammed into the vampire's hand, he jarred his arm and when the vampire's hand closed around his fist he heard his knuckles crack. He cried out as spears of sharp pain shot up his arm.

"Don't be a fool," said the vampire, his words coloured by a thick Eastern European accent. "I could crush your head now and suck out your brain."

"Do it," said Karl defiantly, his eyes fixed on the black eyes of the vampire.

The vampire regarded him through narrowed eyes. Its nostrils, mere pits protected by folds of reddish-pink flesh, flared wide.

"I smell your fear," said the vampire coldly. "Your words are brave but your galloping heart betrays you."

The vampire picked him up by the back of his jacket with one hand and pushed the door to the mansion open with the other. Once inside the giant entrance hall he let go. Karl took a tentative step forwards, his eyes scanning the grandeur of the enormous space. Original works of art hung on every wall and there were small groups of well-padded chairs standing on expensive Persian carpets. Two handsome, well-dressed men sat chatting to Karl's left; both glancing up at him as he took a second step. Another younger man, no older than twenty, walked into the room and draped himself over the railing at the foot of the grand staircase, resting his head on his arms and looking thoroughly bored.

"Ah, Vadim, you have arrived with your prize."

Karl watched as a second winged vampire descended the stairs.

"Yes, Jasper. He is a fine specimen, too. Full of spirit."

In the blink of an eye Jasper was in front of him, sniffing him, inspecting him.

At seven feet Jasper towered over him. His dark brown hair was slicked back over his skull, accentuating his heavy brow. His purple lips were thin and cruel, and the flaps of his nostrils flared as they took in his aroma. Tucked neatly behind him were two massive wings, black and leathery with age. The creature's chest was muscular and looked as though it had been chiselled from white marble, the illusion only broken by a small patch of dark hair which sat in the centre. And through the fabric of his tight black breeches Karl could see the outline of his sizeable cock.

"Hopefully not too spirited," said Jasper with the same Eastern European accent. "We don't want any trouble."

Karl understood the warning but didn't indicate it. He knew he was no match for these creatures of the night. He'd tasted all he wanted to of Vadim's strength, and the second vampire, Jasper, was taller and more solidly built. He'd have to be stupid to take the vampires on.

"What have you done with Daniel?" he asked.

Jasper's thin lips widened into a grin.

"Ah yes, your lover."

"Yes. What have you done with him?"

Jasper walked a circle around him, eyeing him up and down. He cupped a hand over the rounded mound of Karl's hairy butt cheek.

"He's all right for the moment," he replied. "I shouldn't worry too much. You'll be with him presently. Now remove your clothing."

Karl moved his mouth to speak but his vocal cords let him down.

"Yes, now. Do it now. Take them off. All of them."

Jasper stepped back and folded his arms.

Karl looked over his shoulder at Vadim, at his dark eyes which were shadowed by the heavy brow common to both vampires. He swallowed. What choice did he have? Even the others in the room were looking at him now, all waiting to see what he'd do.

He began with his shoes and socks, flicking first one shoe off and then the other before peeling his damp, sweaty socks off. He removed his jacket and let it drop onto the flagstones, and then did the same with his shirt.

He noticed a look of approval flicker on Jasper's face and saw how the vampire's fat cock was growing larger inside the fabric of his breeches.

His fingers fumbled with the buckle of his belt but it was soon undone, the zipper pulled down and his blue jeans removed. He looked again at Jasper, hoping the vampire would indicate that he had gone far enough, but there was no such signal. After a deep breath he hooked his thumbs into the elastic band of his underpants and pulled them down to his ankles before stepping out of them and kicking them away. When he'd finished he stood with his arms stretched out to the sides.

"Here you are," he said, letting his arms drop. "Take a good look!"

Jasper stepped towards him and reached out, taking Karl's cock in his hand.

"I had hoped for something larger, but I guess it will do."

Karl felt his cheeks burn red.

"Take him away," Jasper said, turning his back on Karl and returning up the stairs.

Karl glared at the departing vampire as Vadim prodded and pushed him towards a door at the side of the great stairway. He didn't protest. He knew he was theirs, at least for the time being, but more importantly he didn't want to jeopardise any chance he had of finding Daniel. Only then would he consider his plans for escape. And revenge.

On the other side of the door was a set of stairs that led down into the bowels of the house. They were lit by electric lights which cast no more illumination than was necessary. At the foot of the stairs was a long corridor, the first part of which was flanked by plastered and painted walls, which soon gave way to bare rock. The wooden floor continued into the shadows at the end of the corridor.

"Are we going into the hill?" asked Karl.

"Correct," Vadim replied, pushing him sharply forwards.

They came to a door which Vadim instructed Karl to push open. On the other side was a dimly lit room. The floor was grey flagstone and the walls were solid rock. Set into the wall were hooks from which hung empty and rusting manacles, though not quite all of them were empty. He saw Daniel immediately, on the far side of the room, naked and with his wrists manacled above his head.

"Karl!"

"Daniel!" he yelled as he rushed over and hugged his lover. "What have they done to you?"

"I'm all right," he replied. "You know, just hanging around."

They both laughed out loud though it was more a laugh of relief than of amusement.

"It's so good to see you," said Karl, tightening his arms around Daniel.

"Very touching," said Vadim, "but that's enough. You're making me nauseous."

He wrenched Karl away from Daniel and sent him hurtling into the far wall. In an instant he was there too, lifting Karl up into a set of manacles and securing them around his wrists.

"I'll leave you two alone now," said Vadim. "But I'll be back."

Vadim smiled, his fangs pressing into the flesh of his bottom lip.

Karl didn't watch the vampire leave. His eyes stayed riveted on Daniel, noticing that while he could stand quite comfortably with his feet flat on the floor, Daniel was standing on the balls of his feet.

"Are you okay, baby?" he asked.

"I'm feeling better now. Those things aren't really…"

"Vampires? What else can they be?"

Daniel pondered the question for a few seconds. "But vampires don't really exist, do they? I mean, it's impossible."

"Well, babe, those things are all too real. They have bat wings and fuck ugly faces. That all says 'vampire' to me."

"Then why haven't they drunk our blood? Isn't that what vampires do? Why have they left us hanging around in here?"

Karl laughed. "Steady on, Danny boy. I only just got here myself. I don't know what the hell is happening."

For a long while they chatted, keeping each other company, but then the late hour and the effects of a night on alcohol kicked in and silence descended over them. The endless minutes drifted into hours and finally they managed to fall into a deep sleep, despite the discomfort of being on their feet.

They were awoken the following evening by a commotion at the door to the dungeon. Jasper was the first to enter and behind him a man on a leash. The man's wrists were bound behind his back and he had been hobbled. He was a great wall of hair and muscle, with a thick moustache and a three-day growth. The shadows on his face accentuated the defiant look he wore. His massive uncircumcised cock swung from side to side, slapping against his muscular thighs as he shuffled into the room.

Karl looked at the man but could not feel any sympathy for him. His arms had gone numb and there was a gnawing emptiness in his stomach that reminded him he hadn't eaten for many hours. Even when the man looked at him he could do no more than offer him a pathetic half-smile.

Jasper led the man to the centre of the room so that both Daniel and Karl could easily see this latest acquisition. He removed the leash and pushed the man away from him.

"On your knees," he ordered.

But the man stood his ground, thickly haired legs slightly apart, his eyes staring unblinkingly at Jasper.

Karl looked away. He knew what the vampires were capable of. But curiosity and the lack of anything else to distract him eventually drew his attention back to the man.

Jasper levitated himself into the air and then dropped back to the floor, bringing his fist down hard on the man's chest as he did so. The man collapsed onto his knees, his eyes still locked onto Jasper's and his lips pressed tight.

Jasper smiled. "You will submit!" he said, his voice frosty. "And the longer it takes, the more delicious your blood will taste."

Karl looked across the room at Daniel, whose eyes were wide and riveted on the battle of wills unfolding in front of him.

Jasper regarded the man for a moment, then reached out and punched him in the chest, creating a sound that made Karl wince. The man fell backwards. There was a cracking sound and Karl saw the man grit his teeth. He had fallen onto his hands and had probably fractured a finger or two, or his wrist.

"Hold him down!" Jasper growled.

Karl looked at Daniel and noticed for the first time that his lover was looking back at him. Karl mouthed the words "Who's he talking to?" but before Daniel had a chance to respond Vadim stepped out of the shadows and into the centre of the room. He launched himself into the air and came down hard on the man's chest, pinning him against the cold, hard flagstones of the dungeon floor.

Jasper removed the short chain from the manacles around the

man's feet and replaced it with a longer chain which he then fed through Vadim's legs.

"Off!" he said.

Vadim stepped off and watched as Jasper pulled the man's ankles up to his chest, slipped the chain over the man's head, and secured it to the back of his metal collar with a lock. The man's legs were now pulled back as far as they would go and spread wide so that his furry butthole was fully exposed and vulnerable.

"What do you think?" asked Jasper as the two vampires looked down at the man's arsehole.

"Delicious," Vadim replied, licking his lips.

He leaned down and smacked the pucker with an open hand, making it twitch. The man remained silent, much to the annoyance of the vampires. Vadim lifted his hand up higher and brought it down hammer-hard on the thickly furred sphincter, but still there was no sound from the man. Vadim's frown deepened, the shadows almost hiding his eyes completely.

"This one is strong," he said, looking over his shoulder at Jasper.

"No mind. His blood will taste all the better."

"What shall we do with him?"

Jasper looked across at Daniel and then at Karl. His eyes lingered on Karl for a moment as he thought.

"You can have him," he said finally. "I can't be bothered playing today."

Vadim beamed, his lips curling up and exposing his bright red gums. He put his face to the man's arsehole and sniffed, touching his cock through his breeches as he inhaled the earthy aroma of the man's anus. Then he started licking it, running his dark tongue up and down the puckered skin and moaning with delight.

For a moment Jasper stayed and watched his friend savouring the taste of the man's hairy hole, but he was not a creature interested in simple pleasures and he soon grew bored. He turned and left the room at a pace that blurred him to Karl's eyes.

As Karl watched the vampire sucking and licking the man's arse crack he felt his cock growing hard and when he looked across at Daniel he could see that his lover was similarly turned on by the vampire's lust for the anonymous he-man. The sight of Daniel aroused and of Vadim hungrily licking and tonguing the man's arsehole was driving him wild.

He thrust his hips forwards in frustration, his erect cock stabbing at the air and sending tiny strands of pre-cum flying off the tip of his prick. If only someone would touch it, would help him to blow, but there was no-one, and his hip-thrusting served only to further frustrate him.

Then the man cried out. It seemed strange that he should save any vocalisations until that point. But Karl noticed that the vampire's pale face was smeared with blood. As he leaned away from the man he saw the man's arse was dark with blood and there was more bubbling out through the twin puncture marks in his arse lips. He watched in horror as Vadim returned to the wound, sucking the warm, crimson liquid into his mouth and then throwing his head back to savour the taste of it as it ran down his gullet.

Karl's erection died, just as Daniel's had. He closed his eyes against the scene but he could not close his ears to the agonizing cries of the man, who eventually died in a pool of his own blood. And when he opened his eyes next the vampire had disappeared.

"Do you still find it hard to believe they are vampires?" he asked Daniel, his face a screwed-up mask of disgust.

"They're not going to do that to us, are they?"

Karl shook his head because he couldn't vocalise what he knew was a lie. Not to Daniel.

Neither of them felt like talking. Their arms were numb, their bellies were groaning to be fed, and both were beset by a feeling of great lethargy. They stood hanging from the wall, heads lolling from side to side, resting on one shoulder and then, when the niggling ache in their necks got too much to bear, on the other.

Later that day, or perhaps it was night, Jasper returned with a pair of younger and more handsome vampires flanking him. Each carried a tray of food.

"I expect you're both hungry by now," he said.

Karl and Daniel watched him suspiciously. After what they had seen, they had no reason to trust the vampires.

"Gee, ya think?" quipped Karl sarcastically.

Daniel swallowed hard.

"It's that attitude that will bring you great suffering. You get fed twice a day, so if I were you, I'd show a bit more appreciation. If I was to get annoyed by anything you said, I might take my trays and leave."

Karl pressed his lips together in case any more of his "attitude" found its way out.

"Now put those trays down and get that out of here," said Jasper, gesturing at the body of the man.

The two underlings did as they had been bid, one grabbing the he-man's arms and the other grabbing his feet. Together they hurried out of the room, taking the bloodless corpse with them.

"Now," said Jasper, walking across the room to Daniel, "what do you have for me in exchange for your dinner?"

"I have nothing," Daniel replied. "Look at me. I have nothing."

Jasper smiled and ran a finger down the side of Daniel's face. "Don't be so sure about that."

His index finger traced the outline of Daniel's full lips, pressing on them and pushing past them into his mouth.

"I think today I will settle for a kiss," he said. "But make it a good one, like you mean it."

The vampire leaned down, his lips puckered.

Daniel looked across at Karl, who nodded. He closed his eyes and waited to feel the vampire's lips on his own, and when he did he winced.

"Make it good, my darling," Jasper whispered. "Make me believe you mean it."

Karl watched as Jasper pressed his lips against Daniel's, and felt his cheeks burn as Daniel kissed back. He told himself that Daniel was only thinking of the food that sat cooling on the trays by the door. But when the vampire reached down and took Daniel's growing cock in his hand, he grew agitated. He strained against the manacles and snorted, knowing that escape was impossible but feeling like he needed to do something. He couldn't just stand there passively as Jasper stroked his boyfriend's erect penis. And after Daniel had shot his load, which splattered in a straight line across the flagstones, Karl watched as the vampire freed him, removing the manacles and letting Daniel's arms drop like dead weights against his sides.

"There's a bucket over in that corner should you need to relieve yourself. Go now. I won't watch. Then come and get your food."

Jasper turned and walked across the room to Karl.

"Now I need a little something from you. I wonder what it will be."

Jasper ran his hands over Karl's hairy chest, pausing to pinch his nipples tenderly between his thumb and index finger.

"Your body hair feels rough beneath my palm," he said as his hand moved over Karl's belly and pubic bush.

Karl let the vampire's hand explore his crotch but his eyes were on Daniel as he walked away from the bucket and came towards him to get his dinner.

"Just take the tray and return to the other side of the room," said Jasper without turning to address Daniel directly.

Karl nodded, watching the muscles in his lover's arse tensing and flexing as he walked away from them with his tray of food.

Jasper now had Karl's cock in his hand and was stroking it.

"You have a nice cock," he said. "Not as big as I would have thought on a man of your stature, but pleasant enough."

Karl felt his cock start to harden. In a bid to stop it from growing further he kept his eyes on Daniel, watching his beloved wolf down his dinner, but the vampire's firm hand and steady motion was irresistible. Soon his cock had grown to its full eight inches. He looked down at it as it disappeared inside Jasper's mouth. He hated to admit it but the vampire was good at sucking cock. He could feel his hard prick being taken all the way down the back of the vampire's throat and up again, the vampire keeping his lips firmly around the girth and his tongue flat against the bottom of his shaft.

A small groan escaped his lips and his eyes flashed wide. He looked across at Daniel but it appeared that he hadn't heard it. He was still busy with his dinner, stuffing it into his face like an animal.

Jasper reached between Karl's legs and began to massage the skin around his arsehole with a fingertip.

Karl let his head fall back against the wall and began to thrust forwards into Jasper's mouth, gyrating slowly against the finger that teased his hole with a promise of penetration. Another moan escaped, but this time rather than check to see if Daniel had heard it, he closed his eyes. He could feel his balls tightening as Jasper's mouth slid faster and faster along the length of his cock. Then Jasper pushed his finger into Karl's hairy arsehole, pressing it against his prostate as it disappeared further inside. Karl grunted and filled the vampire's mouth with a flood of creamy jism, which the vampire swallowed down greedily.

Jasper stood up, licking the last traces of cum from his lips.

"I think you well and truly deserve to be fed after that," he said as he reached up and released Karl from his chains. "Remember, if I have any trouble, you will back in those chains faster than you can get hard!"

Karl nodded and walked over to the toilet bucket. He did what he had to, blocking his nose against his lover's waste, then returned to his tray of food.

"I'll leave you now and send someone back for the dishes later."

As the door to their prison closed Karl and Daniel ran to each other and kissed.

"I've missed you," said Karl. "It was torture watching you hanging there, naked, and not to be able to do anything about it."

"It was torture for me too but we can enjoy each other now, at least for the time being."

The two lovers kissed each other hungrily, their warm breath mingling as their lips and tongues slid over each other. Karl wrapped his muscular arms around Daniel and pulled him closer, savouring the feel of his younger lover's smooth, toned body against his more powerful, hairier body. Between them, crushed together, were their erect cocks. Endless ribbons of pre-cum leaked out from both of them, one coating the other until they were slipping over and against each other in a passionate ballet.

Karl's lips sucked on Daniel's bottom lip before moving down his whiskery chin. He bit down gently, scraping his teeth over the bristles that had grown since his last shave the morning before. When Daniel let his head fall back Karl planted a trail of kisses down his throat, sucking his Adam's apple before continuing down to his chest, and his nipple. He took the swollen little teat into his mouth and sucked firmly on it then, holding it between his teeth, he flicked his tongue over the sensitive tip. He heard Daniel moan and bit down just a little harder. Daniel yelped and he smiled to himself.

He continued downwards, hurrying over the smooth, flat stomach and navel to get to the cock that was sticking straight out, demanding to be acknowledged. He grabbed it with his hand and fed the entire length of it into his mouth and down his throat. Now wasn't the time for romantic foreplay. He wanted to feel his lover's cock inside his mouth, to taste it and the juice that was even now welling in the hairy balls that hung down behind it.

As he sucked Daniel's cock down his throat and back again he could smell the stale sweat and piss of the last few hours sticking to his lover's flesh like the scent on an animal. He opened his throat up to Daniel's cock and then reached around and cupped the firm, rounded mounds of his butt. While Daniel's throbbing prick slipped effortlessly in and out of his mouth, his hands massaged his lover's arse cheeks, pulling them apart to expose the lightly haired ring of puckered skin between.

His lips were firm on his lover's cock, his tongue flat, providing a soft carpet for the cock to slide across on its path down his throat. He felt Daniel's hands on his head, pulling him deeper onto his cock. Another moan. The balls that had been slapping against the bottom of his chin were not swinging with such gusto any more. They had tightened, and Karl knew that Daniel was soon going to blow his load.

He spit-lubed a finger and wriggled it against the sphincter muscle, soon gaining access to the warm, moist cavern beyond. He felt Daniel arch his back, pushing his tight hole further onto his finger, and heard him groan as the finger slid all the way in. He continued sucking, the rhythm not being broken, but getting slowly faster. His own cock was twitching and pulsing between his thick, muscular thighs but he would have to take care of that later. He was here to please his lover since he didn't know what would happen to them next in this hellish place.

Karl felt the cock head begin to swell inside his mouth. Daniel's balls had tightened until they were close up to his groin and he could feel Daniel's arse muscles clamping down onto his finger as it gently massaged the pebble-hard prostate.

"Here it comes!" moaned Daniel, breathlessly.

With a long, loud moan Daniel's cock exploded into Karl's mouth. He swallowed hard, taking care not to miss a drop of his lover's sweet nectar. His head was being pulled roughly onto the cock; he could feel it stabbing at the back of his throat. His nostrils flared as he tried to take in oxygen while at the same time keeping his throat open so all that lovely man cream could slide down into his stomach. As Daniel's orgasm neared its end Karl licked the last few drops of pearly jizz from his piss slit, savouring the salty taste of it on his tongue before standing up and passing a small creamy dollop back to him in a passionate kiss.

"Thank you, baby," Daniel whispered. "Now fuck me. I want *your* load."

Karl leaned back and took Daniel's face between his hands. He looked into Daniel's large, brown eyes and smiled.

"I love you," he said.

"I love you too," Daniel replied, turning around and bracing himself against the wall.

Karl spat onto his hand and rubbed the glob of saliva over his cock, mixing it with the pre-cum that was still dribbling out. He pulled Daniel's arse cheeks apart. The hole was a mid-pink colour, and tight. He knelt down and sniffed it, drawing the earthy, musty aroma into his nostrils. The tip of his nose tickled as he leaned in closer to more fully enjoy the strong man-smell that lingered there. The tip of his tongue made contact with the sensitive flesh and Daniel shuddered. Pulling the arse cheeks open even wider, Karl looked at the hole, slightly open and a deep red at the centre. He kissed it then pushed his tongue through the tight ring of muscle. His lover let out a long, slow sigh.

He licked and sucked at the arse lips, sometimes poking the hole and sometimes pushing through to the other side. As he tongued the juicy rosebud, he introduced his finger, licking around it and managing to push a second finger inside. He began to finger-fuck his lover, gently massaging his hole until it relaxed enough for him to stand up and slowly guide his pulsing prick inside.

"How's that, babe?" he asked, whispering into Daniel's ear and giving it a little lick.

"Ah, that's it. Fuck me," Daniel replied. "Seed my arse."

Karl, who had been grinding his hips gently against his lover as he spoke, grabbed Daniel's hips and began thrusting. His low-hanging balls swung back, slapping against his groin as he pumped his lover's hole. He loved the feeling of balls slapping against him and spread his feet a little farther apart so his ball sac could swing more freely.

As he began to pound Daniel's hole, to really open up and give it to him, he watched his cock sliding in and out; the sight of his glistening shaft, of Daniel's arse hairs being dragged back and forth along it and of his pubic hair against the rounded mounds of Daniel's butt sent bolts of electricity sparking and buzzing throughout his body. He closed his eyes for a moment to savour the sensation and became aware of the smell of their lovemaking, richer and sharper than the scent between his lover's arse cheeks a few moments before.

He also realised that he had started to sweat. He could feel it slithering down his temples and over his chest. He opened his eyes and wiped his forehead with the back of his forearm. He could feel his balls tightening. He readjusted his hands on Daniel's hips and closed his eyes once again. Letting his head fall back slightly, he slammed his hips against Daniel's arse, hard and fast like a jackhammer.

"Baby, I'm gonna come," he announced suddenly.

"Yeah, do it," replied Daniel. "Seed my hole. Seed it."

Daniel's voice and the visual of his seed flowing into his lover's arsehole sent him over the edge. He cried out as the first jet of sperm gushed into Daniel's hole and pulled him back onto his cock as jet after jet erupted deep inside him, splashing against his bowels in a warm wave.

When he had finished ejaculating Karl fell forwards, puffing and panting, onto Daniel.

"It feels so good to have your cock inside me," said Daniel, "to know that your seed is inside me. I'll keep it there for as long as I can, and if they separate us again at least I will have part of you with me."

Karl kissed the back of Daniel's neck, tender pecks that tingled.

"Very sweet," said a voice from behind them.

They both looked over their shoulder to see Jasper standing on the top step by the door. Karl pulled his cock out of Daniel's arse and turned around. He noticed the vampire's eyes immediately drop to it.

"Impressive," said Jasper. "Of course, if you two are just going to fuck down here like animals then we'll have to keep you restrained."

With a wave of the vampire's hand Karl was pulled across the room by a powerful force and sent smashing into the wall.

"You bastard!" shouted Daniel.

A cold smile bloomed on Jasper's face. "Young love. So nauseatingly sweet."

Then suddenly the top step was empty and Jasper was across the other side of the room. In an instant he had Daniel back in manacles.

"You're still a bastard!" snarled Daniel defiantly, although the small crack in his voice betrayed him. Karl had always been the strong one, the protector.

He was rewarded for his false bravado with a stinging slap.

"I will not tolerate insolence!" Jasper growled.

Karl launched into a run.

"I'll fucking kill you!" he said, forgetting the vampire's strength in a moment of rage.

Jasper smirked and lifted a hand, sending Karl slamming once again into the wall.

Daniel felt his eyes water. He kicked out with his feet, connecting with Jasper once before the vampire moved out of range.

Jasper glowered at him.

"You will regret doing that," he spat.

Turning, he flew across the room and soon had Karl back in manacles.

"You would be wise to think before you act," he said, brushing his hands over Karl's muscular chest. "There are others here who think of you only as food. It is only because of me that you and you lover are still drawing breath."

He pressed his lips against Karl's nipple, sucking on it a couple of times as his hand found Karl's slippery, flaccid cock and started playing with it.

"Oh, it feels so good," he whispered. "That strength and power! That life! That blood pumping through it."

For despite himself Karl was getting hard. As Jasper moved from one nipple to the other he could feel himself growing in the vampire's hand. He closed his eyes and thought of other things, anything that would stop the flow of blood to his cock. Yet still it grew.

It was only a noise at the door that stopped Jasper from proceeding.

He spun around. "Vadim! What are you doing down here?"

Vadim stepped forwards. "I could ask you the same."

Karl opened his eyes and noticed that Vadim was looking at him, at his cock. He also noticed Jasper stepping to one side, blocking Vadim's view of his erection.

"I've come to get the dinner dishes," Jasper snapped. "And you?"

Vadim took the three steps one at a time.

"Dinner dishes? That's a little menial for you, isn't it? Why didn't you just send one of the underlings?"

Jasper frowned. "You forget your place!" he growled. "I am clan leader. I answer to no one."

Vadim snorted.

"And since you are so concerned that I should be clearing dinner plates, you can clear them."

The two vampires glared at each other for a moment, then Jasper pushed past Vadim, looking over his shoulder at him as he left the room.

For a moment Vadim didn't move. He stood on the spot, his head cocked slightly to one side, listening. When he was sure Jasper had gone he walked up to Karl.

"I see Jasper has wasted no time in getting to know you," he said, taking Karl's cock in his hand. "I can smell him all over your deflating manhood. Did he suck it?"

Karl stared straight ahead, ignoring the question.

"Did he suck it like this?"

Vadim took Karl's cock and held it while his lips slipped over the head and along its length. For a moment he just held it in his mouth before he began sucking it. His lips were thin and offered little protection against the long fangs.

Karl grimaced as his cock was raked by the tips of the vampire's teeth. He screwed his nose up, thinking about his cock being inside the vampire's mouth. He was amazed his cock could grow against such odds, but he could feel it thickening against the back of the vampire's throat.

"You're wasting your time," said Karl. "I just blew."

The vampire didn't respond but kept sucking. Karl could feel Vadim's tongue sliding like a serpent over his shaft. And then Vadim grabbed his balls and started massaging them, producing a fresh river of pre-cum that oozed out of the slit in his cockhead. Vadim's mouth turned into a vacuum, sucking hard at the clear gel that was leaking out, several times getting a little too enthusiastic and nicking the skin.

It was the tickling sensation at his balls that finally did it, that and the constant sucking. Against his will he blew a third, smaller load into Vadim's hungry mouth.

Vadim looked up at him, grinning and licking his lips.

"Jasper may be clan leader, but I got the nectar," he said. "And if he ever finds out, I will kill the boy."

Karl stared straight through him. His lips remained together, though the small movement at the top of his jaw belied his calm exterior.

The boy? Why did everyone refer to Daniel as the boy? He was thirty-three, only two years younger than he was. Daniel was slender and had smaller features, it was true. It was also true that his own muscles and body hair made him look more manly, perhaps older, but neither of them were boys. But one thing was for sure, if either Jasper or Vadim touched a hair on Daniel's head, they would pay dearly for it.

Over the following days and weeks both Vadim and Jasper took every opportunity to drain Karl of his cum, both uttering threats against Daniel's life if he told one about the other. Meal times were supervised, if not by Jasper or Vadim then by one of the underlings, younger and less powerful vampires who didn't appear to have wings and could therefore wear a full set of clothes.

"You have cast a spell over me," Jasper whispered into his ear. "I have to have you."

"One day you will be mine and mine alone," whispered Vadim.

Karl ignored both of them, keeping his eyes either closed while they violated his body, or directed at Daniel, whose touch he craved more than food or water. It pained him to see the look on Daniel's face as he endured the sight of the vampires taking what they wanted from him.

"What can I do?" he asked once when they were alone.

"I know you can't do anything," Daniel replied. "I just wish it was me tasting your lips and sucking your cock. I miss you so much. It's torture being stuck over here in the shadows."

The words were like darts piercing his heart, but as Daniel had said himself, he couldn't do anything about it.

One day Karl woke up and saw that Daniel was still asleep. In the semi-light and silence of their underground prison he stared at his lover and realised that Daniel had become someone he almost didn't recognise. Tears welled in his eyes as he looked upon the withered features of his lover; he had turned to skin and bone. His ribs were showing and his skin hung like dough from his arms. There were dark rings around his once beautiful chocolate brown eyes and his breathing had become loud and raspy.

"What have they done to you?" he sobbed quietly to himself.

And when the door was flung open and Jasper walked in with the pitiful portion of food that was to be their breakfast, Daniel still didn't stir.

"There's something wrong with Daniel!" Karl cried out. "You have to take him down. Get him to a hospital!"

Jasper put the tray of food down and walked towards the limp body hanging against the wall.

"Ah yes," he said. "This one is not long for the world."

Jasper lifted Daniel's chin with a finger, producing nothing but a low groan from him.

"What are you doing, you bastard!" Karl ranted. "Get him down. Get him to a doctor!"

Tears stung his eyes and twin rivers of snot ran from his nostrils. His cheeks burned from crying and yelling, and the nauseous feeling in his stomach was growing stronger.

"Help him, you bastard! Help him…"

Jasper looked across at Karl and again at Daniel, then in a flash he was at Daniel's neck. His fangs pierced the loose skin easily, though finding the artery was more difficult. He punctured many smaller blood vessels, creating a bloody mess around the wound before finding what he was looking for. As Karl's wails and cries filled the room, he drank thirstily, gulping down the fresh blood of a dying man.

"You dirty fucking animal!" Karl spat, his insults tasting of tears. "You cocksucking bastard! I'll fucking get you for this. I'll make you fucking pay!"

His words were nothing to the vampire. He watched helplessly as Jasper drank until the life force drained out of Daniel, turning the blood bitter and repelling the creature from taking any more.

"Bastard!" he screamed. "You fucking bastard!"

Vadim appeared at the door, a blur that materialised seemingly from out of nowhere.

"What's all this shouting?" he demanded.

He looked across the room and had no trouble seeing Jasper emerging from the shadows, his lips and chin bloodied. A smile bloomed on his lips.

"I see you have had the boy. Well, if that is the case then I shall have this one."

He flew at Karl, fangs exposed, claws extended. The look in Vadim's eyes would ordinarily have terrified him, but for the moment he didn't care what happened to him. If they killed him, he would join Daniel in some afterlife and then he would be happy. In this world, with these creatures and without Daniel, he could never be happy. Let them take his blood if that was what they wanted.

"That is not how it works!" growled Jasper, landing between Karl and Vadim. "You forget your place."

"Which is interesting, considering how often you keep reminding me of it," Vadim retorted.

Jasper backhanded Vadim across the room. But they were equal in strength and power. Both were ancient. Both had been created by the original vampires, so long ago in antiquity that they had forgotten their parents.

Vadim sprang to his feet, launched himself into the air, and struck Jasper feet first, sending him crashing into the wall. They moved with preternatural speed and Vadim had no sooner landed than he was upon Jasper, pounding him with his fists before gripping the clan leader's head between his hands and smashing it into the stone wall.

Karl watched horrified, his tears slowing to a dribble, his face cooling as his mind was, for a moment, taken off the death of his beloved Daniel.

Jasper brought a foot up from behind and kicked Vadim with enough power to dislodge him. He was dizzy from Vadim's assault but freshly fuelled by Daniel's blood. He leapt to his feet, grabbed Vadim by the jacket, and rammed him against the wall with such a force that splinters of rock showered the floor. He pulled the groaning vampire back from the rock before slamming him once more into it. Again and again he used Vadim as a battering ram, creating a larger indentation in the granite with each impact. Finally, he felt Vadim give up the struggle and let the defeated vampire fall to the floor.

As he turned to leave the room he glared at Karl.

"That is why I am clan leader. And that is why he needs constant reminding!"

Karl let himself go limp. His wrists were red raw from the friction of the metal manacles against his bare skin. Every time he put any kind of pressure on them, they smarted. But now he didn't care. The throbbing pain of his wrists was nothing compared to the pain in his soul. He stared at Daniel's body and let the tears fall once again, though this time they fell in silence.

So consumed by his loss was he that he didn't notice Vadim struggling to his feet. Nor did he notice the look in Vadim's eyes as the creature stalked towards him. The first thing he noticed was the vampire's hands on him, one hand on his shoulder and the other pulling his head to one side so that his neck was stretched taut. A glint of light on enamel and then a white hot pain as two fangs pierced his skin.

He cried out but his pain was of no consequence to the vampire who was feasting on the fresh blood pouring into his mouth. As Vadim drank at his neck, swallowing great gulps of blood, he noticed how light-headed he had begun to feel. His heart was racing, and for the first time since his capture he began to think about dying. The vampire had been about to attack him only minutes earlier, but only now as the creature was sucking the very life out of him did he think about his mortality. Suddenly he felt frightened and alone, like a child lost at the fair. If he'd had the strength, he would have struggled, for even though he knew he would soon be joining Daniel there was a part of his spirit that refused to go easily.

But then something peculiar happened. Vadim started regurgitating the blood back into the wound, feeding it back into Karl's system, though now it contained the virus that swarmed in his own body.

At first Karl's body was racked with pain. His muscles began to spasm and cramp, but as the virus took hold, mutating and multiplying inside him, he began to feel invincible. He felt a new strength returning to his body, energising and reinvigorating him.

Vadim lifted his head and wiped his mouth on the palm of his hand.

"Remember who did this for you," he said smiling. "Remember it is I, Vadim de Bourneville, who has won the prize."

And as his lips parted Karl could see how his blood had stained the vampire's teeth and gums.

"What do you mean?" he asked.

But the vampire's only response was a guttural laugh.

"Just remember," he repeated before fleeing the room in a blur of light and shadow.

Karl brought a hand to the wound in his neck and was surprised to feel that the blood had already clotted, forming a scab. He felt his newfound strength surging through his body, tingling and tickling as it spread. His arms, which had previously been numb, were now pulsing with energy. Even his cock had grown to full mast and the shadows that had obscured his ability to see anything clearly seemed to hide no more secrets. He could see Daniel's body as clearly as if the sunlight itself was bathing him in its glorious light.

The door to the dungeon opened and took Karl's mind off the changes that were still going on within his body.

"I have had enough of games and petty jealousies," said Jasper. "The time for that has ended."

Jasper flew at Karl, pulling his head towards him, simultaneously stretching the far side of his neck taut and hiding the wounds Vadim had left behind on the side closest to him. Without hesitation he sank his fangs into Karl's neck, puncturing the artery and sucking the crimson liquid down his throat, not once suspecting that his rival had been there just minutes before.

Again Karl felt light-headed. The room seemed to spin around him. He was at the centre of a maelstrom, and as Jasper drank at his throat the light and shadows became grotesque faces that leered at him from some other dimension. Throbbing. Pounding. His heart beat so fast that he was sure it would tear itself free from the ligaments that held it in place.

But as Jasper began to feed the blood back into him, adding his strain of the vampire virus to that which Vadim had already deposited, he felt his head pulse with a screaming pain. One virus battled the other, merging to become something else, something much more powerful. As the roar in his ears grew to a deafening level he lost consciousness, leaving Jasper to finish the transformation before stealing back along the corridor to join the rest of his clan upstairs. Undetected.

Karl regained consciousness some hours later, his eyes immediately detecting something moving in the corner. A rat. As he watched it, the rodent stopped and stuck its twitching snout into the air, sniffing. It let out a squeak of alarm and scurried off as fast as its legs would carry it. Karl snarled and wrenched his hands free of the rusty iron manacles. For a moment he stared at the marks on his wrists but wasted no time thinking about things that were not important. He was free, and in his soul he knew that he had greatly changed.

He walked over to where Daniel's body lay. Rigor mortis had begun to set in and the pale body was now quite rigid and beginning to smell; the sickly sweet smell of death. Yet to Karl his beloved was still as beautiful as he had ever been. He lifted Daniel's head up and pressed his lips against the pale purple lips he had kissed a thousand times before when they were fuller and pinker with life.

"Good-bye, baby," he whispered, but this time there were no tears. He had moved on from tears. Now there was only hatred and anger.

The door to the dungeon presented no problem. He was able to easily rip it from its hinges, flinging the object of wood and iron over his shoulder. He walked along the corridor he had walked with Daniel many days before, climbed the stairs, and pushed the door at the top open with no regard for what might be waiting for him on the other side. He stepped out onto the carpeted floor, noticing how fresh the air smelt away from his stale prison cell. He took a deep breath and walked past the staircase and into the great entrance hall. A quick scan of the room told him that he was alone.

The large front door had been securely bolted against the world, but it took no effort at all to pull each bolt back, despite their size and weight. He flung the door open and at first the sunlight on his face was a welcome sensation. He smiled despite himself, lifting his face to its rays. There was still just enough human left in him to tolerate that small kiss of sunshine, but his joy did not last for long. The mutant vampire virus was still at work on the organs and systems of his body. The warmth of the sun began to burn and he noticed steam coming off his face. He slammed the door shut and patted his face with his hand. His skin felt hot and had just started to melt. But his first thought was not of his handsome face, but of Jasper and Vadim. His lip curled like a snarling dog's when he thought of them, and he wasted no more time before flying up the stairs to where he suspected the vampires slept.

It was difficult to know what time it was. The vampires lived only by the constraints of daylight and night. The windows had all been boarded up so there was no clue from outside. But one thing was for sure, the sun was out, and if what he'd heard about vampires was true, they would all be resting now.

He stole along the corridor, taking care not to make the slightest noise, though he knew from experience that if the vampires were awake they would soon sense him the way they seemed to always know what had been going on in the dungeon. He opened one door after another, observing that the vampires slept not in coffins, as was the popular myth, but in great four-posted beds; a habit left over from a time when they had been human.

But how was he going to exact his revenge on them? Could he simply smash a window and let the sunshine pour in to do its work? That would work for one of them, but the howls of pain and the noise of the commotion that followed would draw the others. Then a thought occurred to him. He need not get rid of the entire clan, just Jasper and Vadim. They were the ones he wanted to destroy. They were the only ones that had to suffer for what had happened to Daniel. The others he would subdue. He might even decide to stay and become clan leader. There were so many things to think about, but he would ignore them all except for thoughts relating to avenging Daniel's death.

As he made his way down the corridor, past paintings of ancestors, some dead and some forever trapped in a limbo between life and death, he noticed a coat of arms at the end of the hall. Beneath it, one crossed over the other, was a sword and an axe. It seemed fortuitous that he should find such objects when his very thoughts were of destroying the two vampires who had destroyed his lover. He flew to the end of the corridor, colliding gently with the wall; his powers were not yet fully under his control. The sound was no more than a dull thud but he took the time to stop and listen for signs of anyone stirring, hearing nothing but sounds of sleep coming from within the upstairs rooms. Safe in that knowledge, he reached up and unhooked first the axe and then the sword.

He opened the door closest to him, pushing it ajar just enough for him to see inside. The space beyond was dark but for the sliver of light that filtered in around him. Still it was enough for him to see that hanging upside down from a rail attached the ceiling, in the manner of the ancestors, was his first victim, Vadim. His great wings were wrapped around him so that only his pale head was visible. His feet were great claws that gripped the metal rod, locked on by a temporary paralysis that was triggered by the sleeping mechanism in his brain.

Karl crept up to the sleeping vampire and with one swing of the axe had his head off, sending it flying across the room where it hit the skirting board with a crack. Vadim's body began to convulse and the great wings flapped frantically, but the claws of the vampire's feet stayed clamped to the rail so that the body swung back and forth in a frenzied swinging motion. Streamers of blood splattered the floorboards and wallpapered walls.

Wasting no time, Karl ran across the hallway to the other bedroom which he suspected was Jasper's. He burst into the room just as Jasper, awoken by the commotion in the other room, was unfurling his wings. He leapt at the clan leader, both hands swinging, but Jasper was too fast. As Karl took another swing, the vampire kicked the axe out of his hand with a force that spun him around on the spot. The vampire then levitated and swooped down, tearing three lines across the width of Karl's face with his yellowed claws.

"You bastard!" he snarled. "I'll kill you if it's the last thing I do."

Karl staggered back against the door, which he slammed shut and locked. It was only a thought but he wondered why the vampire didn't keep it locked. Yet he had no time to ponder such trivialities. What did he care? He was grateful the vampire had been so careless. Jasper launched himself at Karl, though this time he was ready for him, swinging the mighty sword and slicing a great hole in the sensitive membrane of the vampire's wing.

But the battle had not been won yet. Karl bounded across the bed, landing with bent knees and ready for another assault.

"You'll pay for this!" growled Jasper, fingering the split in his wing before running at Karl with claws extended and fangs bared and gleaming.

Karl stood fast. Even when the vampire lowered his head, ready to ram Karl into the wall, he stood fast. It wasn't until he could smell Jasper's foul breath that he stepped to the side, brought the sword down on Jasper's neck, and severed his head from his torso. The head bounced into a corner, where it spun for a while and then settled, while his body smashed through the thin wooden boards at the window, through the glass and out into the bright light of day where it disintegrated into a ball of flame before it reached the ground below.

Still, neither death brought Karl the feelings of satisfaction or elation he'd been anticipating. The deaths of Vadim and Jasper would not bring Daniel back. He was alone now; more alone than ever before. He could never go back to his family, nor see his friends again. He was a creature of the night now. He could only move in darkness, forever exiled from the warmth of the sun and of family.

The other vampires, who had been awakened by the noise, were banging and clawing at the door. A fist came through the thick wood and a beady black eye peered through, followed by a scream as a beam of daylight found it. More screams followed as other vampires peered through into the light-filled room to learn what had transpired in their leader's sleeping quarters.

Karl unlocked the door and stepped out into the corridor. The throng awaiting him scratched and bit at him, a welcome he had fully expected.

"Wait!" he shouted, his voice deep and commanding.

He darted into Vadim's room, retrieved the head, and marched back out again holding the dripping body part high.

"This is Vadim. The rest of him lies in there," he said, gesturing with his head. "Jasper has been destroyed." He tossed the head through the open door of Jasper's room where it landed and burst into flames. He pulled the door shut after him. "I have destroyed your leaders, so I suggest that if you want to keep your heads, you listen to me."

The snarls and growls slowly died away.

"I have no love for you, in fact you disgust me. But as I have lost all that I love and have nowhere else to go, I am prepared to make my home here."

"And what makes you think that we won't kill you in your sleep?" asked a handsome young vampire.

Karl lifted up a hand, fingers clawed, and immediately the man gripped his throat. As Karl brought his fingers together, the young vampire gasped and scratched at his throat to remove something that wasn't there.

"Before your clan leader and his second died they gave me a powerful gift, one which I could use to destroy any or all of you. Don't test me, for I promise that you shall lose. Further to this power, I have with me hatred. I will not tolerate the slightest disrespect from any one of you, for it will please me too much to end your misery."

He could not say where the words were coming from. They poured from him like water over a cliff edge. In truth he didn't know exactly what powers he had, though it was true he had powers he didn't yet know about. Every now and again he became aware of something else he could do, be it hear the dull noise of his clan's thoughts or smell the blood as something living meandered by outside in the daylight.

He released the young vampire from his psychic grip.

"What's your name?" he asked.

"Samuel," replied the vampire, rubbing his reddened throat.

"Samuel, why don't you show me to your room? The night is still a few hours away and I am tired."

Samuel escorted Karl into a room two doors down as the others melted back to their chambers.

"Now, Samuel, before we go to sleep how about you come over here and show me how well you can suck my cock. There could be benefits for you if you do it well enough."

Samuel, realising that he had the opportunity for something great, took Karl's cock and kissed the fleshy cockhead. His tongue circled the glans once, twice, and then he took the entire organ into his mouth.

Karl closed his eyes. There was a vague memory of someone else doing this, someone he used to care about, but his thoughts were cloudy and it could have all just been a dream.

The Morning After
Lawrence Schimel

The best sex I've ever had in my life has always been with men in the few hours after their having been bitten by a vampire, and this morning was no exception.

Luckily for my sex life, Stefano, my current boyfriend, works as a cater-waiter specializing in only the most elite vampiric soirées. He's a toothsome morsel if I say so myself. His job consists of walking around the party dressed in a tiny black thong and large black boots, his oiled body gleaming in the candlelight to show off his chiseled musculature. He doesn't carry a tray. When a guest wishes a drink, Stefano tilts his head to one side or the other and bares his neck.

When he's working, Stefano always carries with him a list, which serves two purposes: on the one hand, it is the record of how much he'll get paid for that night, depending on how many clients he's served. But most importantly, it's a historical record as well, since he began this job; a second drink by the same vampire is far more expensive than a first. And a third is, of course, forbidden, lest he lose his humanity and cross over to the undead side.

That morning when he came to the salon, he was still human, and his human urges were raging out of control.

"Ciao, bello," Efraim said, coquettish as ever, when Stefano burst through the front door with its sign, as was always the case at dawn, turned to CLOSED.

Efraim is my lazy assistant, and any excuse to not work, like flirting with my boyfriend, is a welcome one for him.

"Caro, what are you doing here?" I called to my beloved, although I could guess. "I thought you were meeting me at the house."

"I couldn't wait," Stefano said, sexual need making his voice even lower and huskier.

I didn't even need to look over at Efraim to know he was blushing as Stefano continued moving toward me. I loved how my boyfriend inspired such lust and envy in most everyone, and also how quaintly faithful he was with regard to sex.

"You can go, Efraim," I called out as Stefano grabbed me and pulled me toward the inner sanctum of the salon. "I'll finish sweeping up. Lock the doors on your way out."

Efraim would dawdle, I knew, trying to hear what was going on behind the curtain. Not that I cared much, I've always been quite an exhibitionist, which is partly how I gained my current prominence, but I also think it's best to maintain the proper owner-employee relationship, and it's one thing for him to hear me recount my sexual exploits with Stefano (or whomever) as I'm styling some vamp, and quite another to hear me squeal like a stuck pig while Stefano and I are in flagrante delicto.

Still, I try to support promising young gay men and help give them a leg up in this world, so I tolerated Efraim, even though he was such a lousy hairdresser I often wondered if he might not be straight (not even bisexual). It didn't hurt that he had a cute butt and a pixie-ish sort of face that was easy on the eyes.

Stefano pulled me with him behind the curtain, not out of any prurience on his part, but because that's where the best chair for him to fuck me in was situated. In the state he was in, Stefano would've done me on the ground in the middle of the public square if that's where we were.

Being bitten by a vampire seems to do this to men.

I don't know what it is, whether it's the closeness to death, or undeath, that makes the body strive so for life and joy and pleasure, to banish the darkness that came so dangerously close. And sex has all these procreative aspects, even when diverted to homosexual ends, as in the case at hand; that doesn't stop semen from being potent and indicative of potential, symbol of life itself.

I wonder sometimes if the being penetrated, that utter vulnerability, translates into a desire to penetrate in turn.

I've never asked whether women who are bitten are also horny immediately thereafter. Just not interested, I'm afraid. But one of these days, I'd ask Sophie to find out for me. She might even know already. I wouldn't put it past her to have tried it herself.

I'd never myself been bitten. Perhaps I'm too close to the process of helping create their glamour for it to do anything for me—kind of how I imagine gynecologists must feel about the naked female form. But maybe those're just my prejudices again.

On the other hand, I've never met a gay gynecologist, so perhaps behind the clinical detachment is a sated sexual obsessive. Who knows, maybe some men channel their S&M urges into certain arenas to make themselves productive, tax-paying members of society by becoming proctologists instead of spending their lives standing in front of a sling, sticking their fist up strangers' assholes.

I've always had a better time in a sling than the proctologist's office, but that's another matter.

In my case, I'm a hairdresser, which is an eminently respectable profession for an effete homosexual such as myself, in addition to making me a socially productive member of society. I cater to an exclusively undead clientele, a small detail responsible for my transformation from a bookish science geek into my current position of social prominence, not to mention a high tax bracket. My career began innocently one day in high school biology class, when we learned that hair and nails continue to grow even after death. It seemed quite obvious to me that this meant that vampires, additionally afflicted by their not casting a reflection in mirrors, would need to turn to someone else to keep themselves immaculately groomed.

Thus, Antoinne's All-Night Salon was born, and was literally an overnight success.

Okay, okay, the fact that my best friend from grade school was also the society columnist for the twilight edition of the paper didn't hurt, as Sophie's quick to point out whenever she feels slighted by me or wants to blackmail me into performing some favor or another. Sophie knows me from back when I was plain old Tony Horrowitz before my current debonair reincarnation as Antoinne van Gelder, and is always threatening to reveal that little detail—among many other of my peccadilloes—in her column, whenever she's trying to get me under her thumb.

We all know they're just idle threats, but I play along with her, just in case one day she has PMS or something and decides she's serious about trying to take me down a peg or forty.

Not that I think anything could hurt my reputation at this point. A little scandal might even improve it. After all, it's hard for the journalists to think of new excuses to keep writing about me and my fabulous life.

Stefano spun me around and I fell into his massive arms. I love how I feel like a waif when he holds me like this. Although he wasn't so much holding as groping, his tongue seeking mine as he struggled to get under my smock and pull down my pants. I wiggled an arm loose from his embrace to give him a helping hand, although it didn't matter if he popped a button or five, since that's what the houseboy was for. Well, one of the things, anyway.

Even after having been repeatedly drained of blood all night by customers, he still had plenty left over, if his pulsing erection was anything to judge by. After all the fumbling to get my clothes off me, his own had proved no problem; in the blink of an eye, they were gone, almost as if by magic. No matter, foreplay has its time and place, but this morning wasn't going to be one of them. This was about raw sexual need, and my body was responding in kind.

Still locked in a kiss that left us half gasping for a single breath that we passed back and forth between us, Stefano gently bent me backward, like dancers in a tango, until my shoulders rested against the warm leather of the salon's best chair. A moment later, still without releasing my lips from his own, as if my tongue were the anchor that kept him rooted to his humanity, he'd swept my feet out from under me, lifting me up by the knees so that my ass was exposed. As he leaned over my body, Stefano pumped the pedestal with one foot, raising the chair and my body until my ass was perfectly aligned with his waiting cock.

That's one of the great things about fucking in salon chairs; they're height-adjustable. It's like being able to personalize a sling. Except that instead of cold rubber and chains, the chair Stefano had thrown me onto was fully padded and warm. Just because I like things a little rough doesn't mean I don't also enjoy my creature comforts.

One of the creature comforts I do need, though, is lubricant, and without even needing to open my eyes (I am a romantic at heart and close my eyes when I am kissed) I reached out behind me for a tube of hair gel. As the head of Stefano's cock pressed its way against my asshole, I quickly squirted some onto my hands and reached down to slick his organ before it tore into me of its own accord. And a moment later, that's exactly what it did, sliding inexorably deeper inside of me as I exhaled into his mouth, as if I needed to empty my lungs to make space in my torso for such large firmness.

In the state he was in, there was no way I could've stopped things to have him put on a condom, but it didn't matter. We didn't use them between us.

As part of his job, Stefano's regularly having blood tests done. The agency he works for prides itself on only offerings its clients the choicest waiters or waitresses, by blood type as well as physical attractiveness. I always suspected that part of all the blood work was to be able to offer samplers to prospective clients.

At last, our kiss came to a breathless end as the rhythm of Stefano's cock sliding into me began to pick up speed. I opened my eyes to look up at him, his lips looking almost bruised they were so full after sucking face for so long, his dark eyes staring at me with such longing and desire it made me catch my breath again. What had I done to deserve this? I asked myself for what must've the millionth's time. And I surrendered myself up to our congress, letting him take from me whatever pleasure and solace he needed, however he needed it.

I didn't know how many clients he'd served tonight, although he bore marks on both sides of his neck. I reached out to caress the scabs, and Stefano pounded into me with renewed vigor, as if my touching those bite marks unleashed some hormone within him.

There were days (we rarely had sex at night, since we both worked then) when we could spend hours fucking without stop, a give-and-take of pleasure. But this morning's sex was of a different sort, a higher-pitched intensity, forceful and abrupt. I didn't even touch my own dick, reaching up instead to pinch one of Stefano's nipples, or to again touch one of the bite marks.

And moments later, Stefano was leaning over me, his mouth searching for mine, and as we kissed he suddenly began to come. We were locked together like that for what seemed an infinite moment, as if I were breathing life into him with each breath while he filled me with spurt after spurt of his seed, with sexual energy.

As our mouths broke apart, to let us catch our breath, even though his cock was still sunk deep up my ass, still hard even after he'd come, I tasted salt, and seeing the crimson stain on his lips, realized I'd bit my lip, or he had, or we both had. My glance dropped to the marks along his neck, then back to the smudge on his lips, and I smiled at the irony, as he began to shift inside me again, building up to begin fucking again, but in control now that the edge was taken off, fully human, and his hands dropped to my own cock to make sure he gave me pleasure at the same time as he took his own.

Possession: A Priest's Tale
Max Reynolds

*P*ossession. It is a common enough word. We use it all the time for things, do we not? Yet almost no one thinks about what it means to be possessed, because we think of the term only in its twenty-first-century connotation. The first listing in the dictionary: "the act of having and controlling property."

There are, of course, other definitions. Definitions that revert back to the fourteenth-century Latin origins of the word. Those are the ones I am talking about. Such as "domination by something (as an evil spirit, a passion or an idea)" or "a psychological state in which an individual's normal state is replaced by another."

I'm not sure exactly when it was that I became possessed by Raul Garcia, when my "normal state" was replaced by his extra-normal one, when I became dominated by him and his passion and—I still can hardly bear to say it—evil spirit, for ours is not the world of the benign vampire, but once I was, there was no turning back. I was owned, taken over. I would do whatever it was he asked of me. There was nothing too intimate, too lurid, too *outré*. I was possessed by my love for him, by the intensity of the heat between us, by the passion of sharing everything with him—from my very blood to my now-damned soul.

So when he pushed me against the wall at Carville, his hand gripping my cock through my cassock, when he jerked my arm up over my head and bit deeply through the thin fabric of my surplice, tearing the sheer white fabric, when he bit beyond the sacred cloth and into the vein beneath, I could have only one response. I could only acquiesce. I could only become whatever it was he was, whatever it was he wanted me to be. I was, then, no longer possessed by God but by Garcia. I had ceased to be a priest and had become Garcia's—this vampire's—acolyte.

❖

No one ever fully describes the taste of blood. It is often referred to as metallic, which it is—a biting, coppery flavor. But no one ever talks about the texture or the savoring of blood. I have wondered over the years—and this comes of being far too studious a creature, I suppose—why it is that no vampire has written of the total allure of blood to…us.

It still galls me to include myself among them. I don't think of myself as a vampire, still, despite having been one now for—well, the number of years does not matter, not really. I still look like a young man in his late twenties, and who is to say I am not? After all, one can now become quite worldly at a very young age. Not like it was when I was actually a youth. All that has really changed for me is the century in which I presently live. And of course, my companions.

But back to blood, my new holy water. As a boy, one tastes blood early. There are the schoolyard fights, the blood in the back of the throat as the just-right punch hits a lip or a nose. As men we become accustomed to blood early. I suppose women do as well, although for different reasons, but since women were never a part of my life, my mother having died in childbirth, God rest her soul, and my father having died soon after in the war and thus never remarried, I never really knew women. My uncle raised me and he preferred his women kept many and frequent and separate in a small private hotel in the Vieux Carré, or as it's known now, the French Quarter. I entered the priesthood early, and in between there were other men who schooled me, not women. I never had a need for women. My needs were all, God forgive me, met by men.

And so blood never fazed me. One slices a finger chopping wood or runs a nail through one's foot or is grazed by a bullet while hunting—these things happen and we men survive them. Men are brutes—we seem to like ourselves best that way. I have not seen that when we exclude women we become more refined, but rather more ourselves—and so blood is part of who we are. Because despite intellect, we are simply not that far from the cave and our most animal natures.

Yet we are not all vampires, clearly. But for those of us to whom blood is more than just the thing that pumps through our veins—for those vampires among us—blood is an aphrodisiac, it has a mesmerizing effect on us. The scent of it is intoxicating—we can smell it from yards away, begin to imagine the taste as one does when meat is cooking in a kitchen nearby. Blood has its own aroma. It isn't a scent that most people find provocative or enticing, but I have come to yearn for it, to savor all aspects of it. And to associate it with him, with Garcia and with the way he awakened my senses even more than my formerly quite profligate ways had already done.

Blood is thick in the mouth, not thin as those who have never tasted it describe it. It is not like the juice that runs off a too-rare steak. Rather it is viscous—more like the roux we make down here in Louisiana, thickened, like a gravy.

Perhaps these food similes repulse you—I'm sorry for that. That is, of course, a nuance of sensibility. We each choose the foods we find sublime and the tastes we prefer to savor. Mine was once simply men—not their blood, but that other liquid, which it seemed I could not get enough of at one time. Now those things are one and the same: the men and the blood. Because that is the vampire spirit, is it not: all blood and sensuality and the dark steaminess of the night in which they commingle?

I cannot talk about blood or men without talking about him, of course, without talking about Garcia. Because it was my blood that beat for him first.

I don't remember exactly when I began to long for the visits from Raul Garcia. I would sit by the window in the vestry behind the little chapel, my books open before me, and look out over what was once described upon one's admission as "the lush and bucolic grounds of Carville, isolated discreetly beyond sugarcane fields and a veritable forest of live oaks." That nineteenth-century-flourish in description was apt. The grounds were indeed bucolic and lush. And the place was certainly discreetly isolated.

What was really meant, the subtext behind the flourish, was that if you did not have a horse, a carriage, or later, a car, the sanatorium was far from the highway and still farther—twenty miles or more—from the city, which meant no one could just wander off, whether they were voluntarily committed like myself, or involuntarily so, as were the majority of the inmates.

But then I had never had any intention of wandering off—at least not before I met Garcia. When I settled in at Carville, I expected it to be for what would remain of my life. It was both a dedication and a penance. I thought I was renouncing all that had so inevitably led me there and in so doing would somehow mitigate all that I had done which I should not have done.

But my commitment was before I knew that I could have another life, a different life, a life beyond death, the life Garcia opened up for me just as he had opened up my vein on that evening as we walked in portentous silence to my rooms behind the chapel. Garcia was to be my savior, as I was once to be the savior of those I served at Carville. The distinction was, Garcia was indeed a savior and I, I was just a handsome young man new to the priesthood who had given himself over like Father Damien to the lepers of which we each knew ourselves to be one.

Before Garcia, it was St. Damien I had begun to venerate. Like me, he had come to care for the lepers in his youth. I doubt, however, that Damien shared my other youthful predilections. Nevertheless, I would pray fervently to him for guidance as I wandered the corridors at Carville. In his story I saw my own fate—he was not yet fifty when the disease killed him. I had become resigned and wondered if he had as well. I had re-dedicated myself as much as I could, attempting always to quell my desires and focus on the healing of souls as I was bidden to do. The service was no penance. I had always been drawn to service. My uncle told me that my mother, his sister, had been one to give of herself as well, and so I presumed it was something of her in me, my call to service. But the other—the pain of repressing my desires—that was something else again. That was, as they say, hell.

Garcia changed all of it: the service, the yearning, the repression. Sundered it all. But then that is the way with vampires, that is the way with that sort of battle between this world and the others, dark and light, that swirl around us.

My story begins so long ago. Not longer ago than Garcia's, of course: he was what he is before I was born, but longer ago than one would imagine, given that I still appear to be a man of about thirty.

Which story should I tell you first? My own or that of Garcia? My own or that of Carville? Or can I even separate these interwoven tales now, inextricably bound as they all are?

Carville is the nexus, of course. And so it is with Carville that I shall begin. Carville—that is what we all called it, the sanatorium, the leprosarium, although Carville is actually the town, nestled in an almost continual bank of fog near the Mississippi River between Baton Rouge and New Orleans. When I first arrived at Carville, it was called the Louisiana Leper Home, if you can imagine. It is difficult to believe that such a name could have done anything but strike fear in the hearts of those who were sent there or even those who came, as did I, to help and succor those poor souls relegated to the life-in-death there.

And yet, every attempt was made to embrace those who lived at Carville. The Daughters of Charity did the bulk of the care for the inmates—Louisiana was, after all, a Catholic place, and lepers were scourged doubly through biblical invective. I found the Sisters to be kind and nurturing, however: there was never reproach in their mien.

Shortly before I came to Carville, it was a time of transition. The National Public Health Service would soon take over the running of the place (this would be how Garcia found his way there, to me) and a secondary research facility would be opening nearby. Somehow I found little difference between "Louisiana Leper Home" and "National Leprosarium," but the government appeared to think the more clinical title to be less alarming. It was not. Nevertheless, the credo remained the same: Carville was to be "a place of refuge, not reproach; a place of treatment and research, not detention." That none who entered could leave put the lie to that last bit, but good intentions were still inherent in that motto.

Carville is a sumptuously beautiful place, although I never visited anywhere in Louisiana that I didn't find almost heartbreakingly beautiful. Louisiana had my heart even before Garcia did—and in as firm, compelling and eternal a grasp. Raul Garcia was as breathtakingly handsome as Carville was breathtakingly lush and he would possess me just as surely as that place had done. And—although I had no way of knowing until it was far, far too late—Garcia was as corrupted and decayed and degenerate as the disease out of which Carville was created.

But as was true of what infected all of us who lived there, no one could detect that rot at first. No one could see it. It spread, just below the surface of everything until one day it erupted—small and unremarkable at first. A tiny pink blush on the earlobe or a rosy spot on the inner thigh. And then…

There were several elements to my possession. First, there was

Carville and why I was there. Then there was Garcia and how he found me. And then there was the degeneracy that followed—because that is what we called it then, although there are other names for it now. Just as there are other names for what we were at Carville. But underneath, underneath it is all the same. When death stalks you, no amount of literary flourish can alter the facts as they are. Death will win. Death—like desire—is immutable and transcendent.

I came to Carville as a shape shifter. No, I did not turn into a bat or wolf as the moon rose over the fog-dense fields, although I would have loved to roam there as the animal I felt I was.

Rather, I came to Carville in the guise of a redeemer, but I was nothing more than a charlatan, a poseur, a plain and simple liar and cheat. I might as well have been a snake oil salesman who knew his product to be nothing more than lamp or cooking oil. The magic I brought was faux to its core. As I had become faux at my own core. If I promised redemption, then I knew it to be a false promise and myself a false prophet. I came to Carville for one reason—to escape.

Was I a rogue? I was not. I was a newly ordained priest, Thomas Desmarais, from an old, if small, New Orleans family. While still a novitiate, I had traveled abroad to traverse the paths of those saints before me—Aquinas, for whom I was named, and so many others. And it was there in those hallowed and havoc-ridden lands that I discovered the biblical scourge that brought me, surreptitiously, inevitably, to Carville.

I arrived there under the guise of spiritual advisor to the Daughters of Charity who tended to the poor souls who had been brought there by coal barge or shrouded carriage in the darkest of nights, shunned by their families and communities and seeking solace in the desicated beauty of Carville. I was to give succor to those who felt betrayed by God. And yet God and I had parted several times before I ever reached that haunting place. My tight collar and vestiture proclaimed what I was. But just as Garcia did not arrive at Carville disguised as a bat, my own *habillement* could easily have made one think I was something other than what I was.

As I recount, it is a beautiful and solitary land of its own, Carville. It isn't as isolated as Father Damien's Molokai outpost, to be sure, but it is still a secret place. The long winding roadway that leads through the low, flat fields runs studded with live oaks that encircle and appear to hold each other at dusk as the fog begins to seep in. At the end of the road, right before one enters Carville proper, one old, gnarled, leafless oak stands like a portent to what lies beyond. Its stubs of limbs are both grotesque and fantastical.

An ominous welcome for us, the denizens of Carville, the slowly dying, those cast out from society at all its levels, high and low.

The old Indian Camp Plantation House is where they first brought them, the lepers, back in 1894. It had been a sugar plantation—stalks of cane still stand, unbidden, even now. It was a dark place then—or so I have heard. I arrived somewhat later and Garcia, later still. The building is all historical perfection now—big and white as plantation houses in the Old South were meant to be, with black shutters and a delicate black iron grillwork along the balconied and balustraded front.

It seems small to me now, but then it was—despite its decrepitude—impossibly grand in the way that every plantation was, even so soon after that war.

No one who lived there knew how it was they came to be there. Men and women—none knew how the scourge had come to touch them and only them, singular as they always were in their families or communities. The taint of leprosy never left—it's still there to this day, despite science and renaming and our knowledge that some are prone to the disease and others not. There is no sin in being a leper—just lack of fortune, bad luck, a grim deal of the cards. But then, as now, we shudder at the thought. No one comes before us ringing a bell and calling out "unclean, unclean," with the sumptuary zeal of the Middle Ages. No one needs to. Exile has been imposed by language alone: *Leper.* There is no worse word, still.

There is no romance in *leper*—only horror. Not as there is in *vampire*, which evokes both a frisson of fear as well as one of sensual excitement. I would learn that from Garcia when he chose me for his own. I would learn that I could transcend one naming by embracing another. And yet death is death, is it not? Disease and decay are all one, are they not? Had I run a stake through the heart of Garcia as he slept, I would have seen the onset of a decay so swift, it would make a leper cringe in abject revulsion. Not that I could, of course, betray Garcia in that way. After all, he had saved me from a dread fate by offering another. And with what he offered came him—and at the time, that was all I could envision, all I wanted. I was, for all my worldliness, still a youth, after all. And being possessed by Garcia, I felt then, was akin to being possessed by God, blasphemous a statement as that is. Garcia, after all, had become my god. It was he, not my true Savior, who had given me back my life. For I was already dead when he found me at Carville. And now I am something else entirely.

❖

Was it in Egypt that I caught the dread disease? Or Jerusalem—that most holy of cities where I walked the Stations of the Cross and knelt where Christ had knelt? Was it at Damascus, where Paul had been struck with the lightning of salvation and redemption? Or was it on the sun-drenched beach at Crete where I lay one night with a young man my own age as we discussed divergent theologies until the tide swelled and we ran naked into the surf and then, as we rubbed ourselves dry on the moon-struck beach, found ourselves entangled in the very thing I had fled Louisiana to escape?

I remember that encounter in Crete as if it were yesterday, of course. I have so much time for memory now. An eternity, in fact.

The young man's name was Nikolos, but it might as well have been Thanatos, because he brought me death. Not like Garcia would later, but without knowing.

We had met at a café late one afternoon. I had expected to take myself off to vespers, but never managed to leave. The climate imbued me with inertia. The heat of the sun, the impossibly bright white light of that part of the world, the pale blue shadows that were cast under the awnings that spread over our little cloth-covered table—it all held a crisp sensuality. We struck up a conversation over that thick coffee and *tiropita*, a flaky *beignet*-style pastry filled with a soft cheese. He had ordered these and fed me a bit, ordering me to "taste, taste" in his thickly accented English, and I had. The pastry was salty-sweet—savory and delicious. Later I would taste him on the night beach, savoring his saltiness—the ocean on his skin as well as his own brininess. I still did not know how to describe these degenerate dalliances, but I would have to say that he, too, was delectable. I could not get enough of him, his body hard and wet against mine on the silken sand and his cock pulsing against mine until we both... But I had not wanted to stray again like that. I had pledged myself to God and had every intention of maintaining that pledge. But the heat and the light followed by the cool dark on the beach—it all led me inevitably to take him, devour him, descend into the most lustful of places with him.

I had felt not the least regret. Rather I had felt a wave's rush of longing for more and more of him. It was this very desire—and its damnation—that I had fled. And yet Nikolos led me back to that abyss and I went willingly, aching for the scent and taste and feel of him as a starving man does for bread, a thirsting man does for water. It was on that beach that I began to realize my calling might not be to God, but to some Other. I wish I could plead ignorance of my actions—claim to have been led and seduced and not to have known what it was I was doing. I could not even plead drunkenness, for we had but a few sips of a ghastly drink, retsina, which left me neither drunk nor desirous. That was all Nikolos. Nikolos and my burning cock.

It was Nikolos's black hair and even blacker eyes that lured me. The scent that came off him was of the sea and leaves and something I could not quite discern. He grabbed me when we ran out of the surf and I stiffened despite the chill of the water. I won't deny I ached to have his mouth on my cock and his hands caressing my buttocks. Is it any wonder then that this latter thing would happen within minutes and that I would be unable to restrain myself from paroxysmic orgasm? One that I wished to repeat as soon as I had sated him as well?

We had lain on that beach for hours, Nikolos and I, and I had drunk as deeply of him as I could. And as I did, without remorse, knew that I was indeed damned.

All of this, I now know, was in preparation for Garcia. I was being made into a creature ready to accept the dark vampire from Mexico with his ruff of black hair and his strong laborer's hands. Garcia was, when we met, an artist. He had in fact come to Carville to do paintings of the place for the government's museum, and to give the remaining inmates the treat of someone who was neither doctor nor scientist yet fully, wholly interested in them. Garcia had been trained by the great Diego Rivera—but he had the tall, muscular build of the laboring class he had been born into. I was equally attracted to both the men that he was. And also to, I must acknowledge, the darker being he held at bay to all but me in our days at Carville.

Yes, Nikolos was one of those who prepared me for Garcia. Without Nikolos I would never have gone to Carville and never have met the man who brought me into the realm I inhabit today. Without Nikolos I would never have understood that passion—like the Abyss—has no real depth of ending, it just goes on and on, into infinity.

Did Nikolos know he carried the disease when we lay together, drinking each other in? I doubt it. He was far from a malevolent sort. And in fact, I could have intuited it, had my focus been more on my surroundings and less on my companion and the urges he stoked in me. But for that, my companion would have had to have been a less handsome, less virile, less willing partner in debauchery and drawn my thoughts more toward the spiritual than to the viscerally corporeal. Instead we spent my week in Crete dazed with the days' white heat and besotted by the very different heat that came with each subsequent night.

Nikolos told me—another novitiate, he was—that he was beginning to train to work at Spinalonga, the leper colony on Crete. He spoke passionately of St. Damien and the work he had done. Somehow Nikolos had managed to separate our debauchery from his spiritual calling. Or he saw it all as one and the same—his body as a temple, as God's temple, and all the actions performed by it a form of worship. Thus his tending of the lepers was no different from his tending of my pulsing cock. He believed in giving of himself. And so he did for the entirety of my visit, leaving me with memories that would heat me up on nights I spent alone after I left him and Crete behind.

❖

No one knew why I had left Louisiana to travel abroad, but I knew. There was a man—a man who was as much like Garcia would later be as I had known up to that time. A dark, truly unholy man with unholy desires who had discovered me in St. Louis Cathedral one evening kneeling at the *Prie Dieu* before vespers. He had invited me back to his home for dinner. What had transpired after a meal of fish and rice and a wine I had never drunk before had made me question my faith and myself.

I had stood looking out on the bayou—for he had lived in St. John's Parish and the bayou loomed in the near dark before the long, unshuttered windows. I held my wineglass and contemplated the encroaching night and inhaled the sumptuousness of the wine and the leftover aromas of the meal.

When he came up behind me, his arm draped lightly over my shoulders. I felt an inexplicable and alarming frisson run down my spine and into my cock. I would like to say that I fought him, that he did not take me easily or readily. But that would be one more lie like the ones I told when I went to Carville.

As a boy I had felt this frisson again and again, but I had satisfied it solitarily and always felt ashamed after, washing my hands again and again, promising myself I would never touch myself with desire in future, saying a prayer or two or more. But it was a vain promise that I could never maintain. Desire is immutable, I have discovered. It must be sated one way or another. I had hoped to sublimate my base desires into love of God and pursuit of all that was holy and decent. I would surround myself with good works and I would wash away the uncleanness with which I felt I had debased myself.

Or so I thought. But desire might not come from evil, always. Or so I am starting to convince myself. Certainly Nikolos believed this—I was keenly aware that he felt none of the shame and guilt I had come to associate with sensual desire before I met him. Desire may be God's way of making us feel alive and in harmony with him at a deep and impenetrable—yes, that is the appropriate word—level.

This is not what Garcia would say. For he is, to be sure, from that other side, the dark one. Although I still cannot bring myself to think of him as evil, even after all he has done and all he has told me.

I have steeled myself against that dark side—or so I say. I have tried to keep myself from succumbing to it, except that Garcia is there, and how can I not want to be with him wherever he is? These are the things all men have wrestled with as long as there has been desire and heat and the elusive promise of immortality—be it in Heaven with God or elsewhere.

My own struggles began with that man at the Cathedral. I will not reveal his name, even now. Yet it was he who brought me to this ultimate place. He was the first one, the one to show me what desire fulfilled really was. He wanted to show me even more, but I was not yet ready. I'm not sure I was even ready when Garcia took me over and made me what I am now—vampire.

But then, then I knew nothing of the world but books and my own conflicted desire. Why had I let this man lure me back to his home? What had I told myself? I had told myself that he was older and cultured and I was young and in need of mentoring. And over dinner it had indeed seemed like a lesson—in food, in wine, in conversation, in literature—he quoted liberally from books I had barely skimmed and I considered myself a budding scholar. He had told me about his trips abroad. We had discussed Aquinas and Augustine and the flaws of men attempting to be saintly when they were merely men. He had grown discursive over Augustine, lingering over Augustine's life of degeneracy and sin, barely touching on his conversion. But I was rapt. I might as easily have been a schoolgirl, I was so attentive to his every discourse. But of course he was handsome and virile, and his trim beard and well-cut suit merely accentuated the body beneath. As he talked of Augustine, I felt myself wondering, shamelessly, given where we had met, what lay beneath the morning coat he wore, and where the buttons on his trousers would lead. I shook myself from that reverie, however, and took a long—perhaps too long—draft of the wine and stood, a bit unsteadily.

I had gone to the window and he had come up behind me. I had held fast to my glass as his arms encircled my waist and then his strong right hand traveled down onto my already stiffened cock. As I said, I should have resisted. But I never thought to. I wanted it—what he offered—and clearly he knew this. He had stalked me like prey, I realized. I wanted it and he sensed it. Just as I had wanted the dinner and the talk and the excitation of my intellect, I wanted this: I wanted his hands on me. I wanted to feel his flesh against mine. I wanted to feel the pulse of him against me, and soon I would.

We left the window. He led me to his bedroom and lay me on the bed. He took time undressing me—a fetishist's time, I would think later. The slow unbuttoning of my shirt, the opening of my pants, the exposing of my cock—it all happened slowly. Deliberately, maddeningly and exquisitely and torturously slowly. I ached for him to touch me, to touch me fully, to release me from the intensity of my desire.

The mosquito net billowed over us. I was naked. Soon, so was he. He slid his fingers into my mouth and told me to suck. Then he held his own prick in his hand and pushed my mouth toward it. The shock of what I was about to do nearly caused me to release onto his crisp linen sheets. I reached for myself, but he took me instead, his hand so strong on my cock that I felt briefly faint. It wasn't painful—it was blissful. It was everything I felt I had yearned for as a youth and now, finally as a man, could have. Like a child who waits for the first glass of wine or the first bedtime after dark. The deliciousness was overwhelming. When the release came, I knew it would be life-altering. I wondered, fleetingly, if I should leave before these things happened. But I could not. And yet I knew that I was crossing a threshold from which I could never return. What's more, I knew I would not wish to.

He tasted salty and thick and it was like nothing I had ever experienced before. The sound he made was deeply masculine and I wondered briefly if I was too much of a boy still for this man who was so much a man. So refined and degenerate all at once. I wanted to please him. I wanted him to desire me the way I desired him at that moment. I wanted to be the best at whatever it was we were doing. I wanted to excel—to lick and suck and stroke until I broke the barrier between all he had experienced and all I had not.

When he was near to it I took my mouth away from his prick and lay myself across him, my thighs pressing against his. His cock was pulsing in my hand and I thought that the milky fluid that had for weeks built up within me would squirt out unbidden, my excitement was so intense. He grabbed my hand hard and jerked it on his cock, his other hand gripping my buttock so hard I felt blood come, but didn't care. The hot jet spurted over my hand and he relaxed briefly underneath me.

He kept me there the whole long night: We slept and woke and spent each other again and again until I was certain we could not do more. As dawn broke, I knew I would need to leave, go home and hope no explanations were required to my uncle, with whom I had lived these past years. He too was known to spend a night away from home and I had learned never to ask where. But while I presumed my uncle to be entertaining himself at one of the local brothels on St. Charles, I was engaging in something far less common—or so I believed.

The man and I spent several months in similar pursuits as those of that first night. I would go to meet him at the Vieux Carré in a private dining room of his choosing. We would share wine and food and he would sharpen my wit and intellect as he honed my desire. Then we would return to his house and the servants would have retired and

I would be hastened to his bedroom for the same slow disrobing, the same veneration of my cock, the same long nights beneath the mosquito netting. He had expanded his and my repertoire to include other intimacies, each more exotic and, I cannot deny, enthralling than the last.

Then after a night of particular intensity with him, I left. Once I had met Garcia I understood that my mentor was something more, something other than mere degenerate. I realized that he—the patience of centuries behind him—had been grooming me for months to be a companion. A companion in another world than this. For he was also, I understood that night, vampire.

We lay, spent, on his bed. I could never seem to get enough of him and had blurted this out in a moment of deepest passion. I wanted ever more—more tutelage in both the intellectual and sensual arts that he was teaching me. I wanted to be part of him. I had no words to explain it, which may have been my youth or my inexperience or both. But he understood. And he chose then to explain what more there could be.

"What if I could offer you eternal life?" he asked with the soft forcefulness that had first lured me to his bed. "What if I could offer you this and more forever?"

I was caught off guard. What did he mean—eternal life? That was the purview of God, not of man. What hubris was this? I must have shuddered.

"It's a heady thought, I know." His deep voice rushed over me, exciting me all over again. I reached for him and he took my wrist, hard, and brought it to his lips.

His teeth were in my vein before I could protest, but he stopped there. He did not go the extra step as Garcia would later. Instead he merely licked at the blood as he had licked at my thighs and more.

I could not respond—had no words to respond. What was this strangeness? He had taken me with some force before, but not without my acquiescence, and each time he had known just how far he could take us both and never went past that point. But this—I watched my blood drip onto the linens and for the first time realized that this man had a power over me that was, perhaps, dangerous.

I did not pull my arm away. Rather, I let him hold on to me as one does not yank one's leg from a bear trap but instead plans an escape, despite the fear and pain.

"Only God can offer us eternal life." I finally spoke, my voice holding none of the fear I felt. "You have offered me a different life than the one I had—but I am still intent on being the priest I have trained to be. Surely you know this?"

We lay for a while in silence. He released my arm and I saw that the bleeding had—surprisingly—ceased. There was a small wound where he had bitten into my flesh.

"I had hoped for more from you," he said, with some finality, as if whatever I had forgone meant the end of what had been between us.

"I have tried to give you all I have," I responded, my voice choked despite my best efforts, suddenly as fearful of losing him as I had been moments earlier of losing my life.

"There is more than that to give, and I won't pretend I don't want it," he said then. I had no response. I didn't know what it was he was asking of me, only that I was certain it meant crossing a boundary from which—unlike our nights together thus far—I could not return.

I turned onto my stomach, away from him but hoping he would lure me back. Instead he lowered himself onto me and took me a final time. I was still mesmerized by him and his abilities as a lover and I opened myself to him in the hope that he would see that he should not cast me aside because I would not do whatever dark thing it was he still wanted.

I left before dawn—I knew he needed me to leave and that only a woman would linger and debase herself with some level of pleading to be kept on. I would not do that. I could not. But I ached to stay and I gazed at him a long while as I dressed. His nakedness was all I wanted—the strength his body exuded even in sleep. But I knew to the core of my being that I could not allow my desire to supersede my self, my soul. And I was in danger of losing that self—I saw that now.

My studies and these extracurricular excursions with my philosopher mentor had become far too at odds with each other over the past few months. As I left him for what I knew to be the final time, I found my desire not in the least slackened, but awakened and stirred. Far from being chastened and sent back to my divinity studies as I should have been, instead I had left his house a few hours before dawn and found myself on the streets wondering if there were others like us and if what I had learned with him could be translated to another—sans the bloodletting. I wandered the streets for an hour or so, looking at men who seemed aimless in the narrow alleyways—what were they seeking? Some looked at me with what I now knew to be desire, but I chose to ignore them. It seemed enough to know they were there and that I had access to them if I needed them.

I had taken myself home then and while I should have gone directly to sleep or at the very least to prayer, instead I debauched myself, who should have been already spent from the hours with my mentor. As I touched myself, images of his body were in the forefront of my mind, but commingled with the sensation of his biting into my flesh and my blood flowing into his mouth. I tried to imagine other men then, men my own age as well as men older, men strong and powerful and… That was when I knew I had to flee New Orleans or lose myself forever to this demimonde I had uncovered. Instead of seeking God, I would be searching, ever searching, for men like myself or neophytes as I myself had been a few short months ago. I wanted to be neither teacher nor student. I wanted to re-dedicate myself to celibacy and set myself anew on the path I had initially staked out for myself.

But that is when I discovered Nikolos and after him, Garcia. Now I am possessed as I had never been by my own puny desires, nor even by my mentor and his burgeoning ones. Now I live in and for the night and when I cannot slake my darker thirsts, I ache in ways I can only think of as damnable. And in fact I wonder if I am forever damned. Garcia says I am not—not yet. But then he is my downfall, he is the one who has taken me to the brink of this darkness and he is the one who has made it possible for me to live beyond the disease, beyond mere mortality. He says he can free me at any time, but I do not believe him and I think that if he does—if he runs a stake through my heart or cuts off my head as I sleep, there will be no redemption, although possibly no hell either. Just the blackness of the eternal abyss.

And yet I never could have said no to him. No one has ever done so, I think. Garcia has that much power, his desire is that enveloping, he is that incalculably charismatic. Who would have believed that the tales I had heard as a child were true, anyway? Who would have thought that there were indeed beings who traversed this world who had come from another? Who would have thought that men could drink each other in so many different ways?

Which story should I tell you now? The one where I contracted the disease that led me to Carville or the one where I became what I am now—vampire?

No one really knows when they first learn of lepers. The term itself has become a commonplace, a moniker for any despised individual or group. It is almost archetypal, this term. And yet there are real people, real lepers, who die the slow and awful death the disease brings them.

As I said, I was not sure how I acquired it—the leprosy. But I believe it was from Nikolos. And if it came from my dalliances with him, so be it. For those were remarkable and I would not have chosen otherwise. He brought me to a new and different level of my desire. We were equals on those nights in Crete—I was not his protégé, nor he mine. And our discourse traversed theology as well the sensual. We lay entangled and spent and he would talk of Damien and Molokai and I would talk of Aquinas. In that regard we were both novitiates to a religion of our own making—we were Catholic and also degenerate. Except with Nikolos I never felt a degenerate as I had with my mentor. Instead I felt alive, as if this were the better part of myself.

I think sometimes I should have stayed in Crete, stayed with the young man who brought me back to life from the brink of my soul's death. For leaving my mentor had left me adrift and devastated and wondering if I should have stayed and let him take me wherever it was he thought we could go. But Nikolos had opened other avenues to me. Alas, he was pledged to Spinalonga and nurturing the souls of the poor lepers there where he had already been doing spiritual duty. And so we parted—not as I had done with my mentor, but as friends, as companions, as two men who had shared something lasting. We assured each other we would write, but I knew enough by then to know that was a promise never to be kept.

When did I discover that Nikolos had infected me? I am unsure. It was nearly a year before I returned to Louisiana after traveling on from Crete. There were other men—not nameless, nor faceless, but fleeting. A night here, a stolen afternoon there. I was always amazed at how many men stood in the doorways of holy places with their hats over their cocks, waiting for another man to ask them to walk down the Via Dolorosa or some other darker, less public place.

It had become clear to me that I could not break myself of the habit of other men, the habit of an almost daily debauchery with them or lying in my room, wherever I was, thinking of them as I debauched myself.

And so I returned home. One night on the voyage back I had spent time with a member of the captain's table who had led me off to have an aperitif and to quaff something equally heady port side. As I buttoned up my trousers I noticed a small pink spot on my thigh that I knew should not be there.

A family friend confirmed the diagnosis upon my return to Louisiana. It was then I determined to head to Carville, to take the place of the priest retiring—uninfected. My status was never disclosed—even my uncle was unaware. I had thought to write to Nikolos, but presumed it was he from whom I had contracted the dread disease.

Two full years passed at Carville before Garcia arrived one day with a veritable caravan of things with which to do his work. If I said I was not smitten immediately, I would be lying. He was everything my mentor had been and more, and I had never managed to quell that desire that only men can fulfill for each other.

I knew right away that he wanted me as well, despite the disease which had not yet spread beyond that small spot on my thigh—and thanks to Garcia, never would.

There is no lack of certainty in how I became what I am now: vampire. Although from a metaphoric perspective, it could be said I was merely waiting to be crossed over. I was certainly preying upon innocents long before Garcia sank his teeth deep into my thigh, draining my femoral artery as he stroked my cock.

It's not always the neck, you know. It's not always a young, female virgin lying demurely on a bed, sleeping the sleep of innocence while the vile and be-fanged Nosferatu beats through her open window on the wings of a shape-shifted bat.

Garcia arrived at Carville at dusk one day in a wholly different guise: as artist and also as tutor to the unfortunate. He had come, as I noted, at the request of the government to paint the leper home in all its fading magnificence before it changed to a wholly different place than it had been in the years I had spent there.

There were a few days of pretense, of course. We were introduced by the director and I was asked to acquaint him with all of Carville. You see, even the staff did not know of my condition, so I was among the elite of the place. Only I knew I did not really have carte blanche to leave.

How to describe Raul Garcia? He was what was called in those days a man's man—an irony that bears noting. He was tall and well-built and his skin was a bronze hue because of his Mexican origins and his hair and eyes were deeply black. He exuded an air of confidence and also of sensuality. I noted the nuns would blush when he was about. That charisma was not lost on anyone.

But it was men Garcia preferred, and he told me as much a mere three days after his arrival. We were walking at dusk—he was never around much in the day, saying that he'd never acquired an ability to tolerate the heat, despite his birthright. We had gone through the arbor of live oaks and were coming round the old charnel house, long since abandoned. The air was thick with the late-day heat and we both had a film of sweat on us. I suggested we stop and sit on a nearby bench as the moon rose and then go back to the main building.

He did not speak for a time. Nor did I. Then he said, with shocking bluntness, "I haven't been with a man since well before I left New York. I suppose that could be called a confession, *padre*."

The comment had the requisite effect, which no doubt he had already calculated. My cassock strained at the crotch. He looked squarely at me there and for a moment I was certain he would reach out to touch me. There can be no question that I hoped he would.

But instead he stood and spoke, his accent somewhat thicker with what I presumed to be a desire of his own, for my eyes strayed as well and saw him hard against his trousers.

"I am glad to see that I have not shocked you, *padre*. That is good to know. As no doubt I will be revealing other aspects of myself to you during my visit that others might find"—he waved his hand in the still air—"unsettling."

I heard him outside my room later that night. I could hear his breathing outside my door and wondered why he didn't just come in, for I had been thinking of him rather than immersing myself in prayer. I had been yearning for him to come and confess more to me, reveal whatever else it was he had suggested needed revelation. But he left without even knocking.

It was the thirteenth day after his arrival that he finally took me.

One might say he courted me prior to that day. We talked a great deal in those early days—I imagine that he wanted to be certain that I would acquiesce and also that I would want to be taken over, to leave the life I had and become part of his. No doubt he also wanted to know if I would be a worthy companion.

When I had traveled abroad, the places I could always be assured of finding like-minded men seeking the pleasures I could no longer live without had been churches and other holy sites. I had often wondered how they could stand so near to God and pleasure themselves openly while waiting for a similarly inclined companion. And yet this was almost *de rigeur*. The hat over the exposed cock thrust through the unbuttoned trousers, the sussurations that could have been mumbled prayers as easily as they could have been obscenities meant to excite and tease and lure. I had found it as surprising as it was tantalizing.

And so it was with Garcia, then. He sought out the priest, the one creature at Carville most likely to fend him off, holding up his crucifix and sending him screaming away.

Except, of course, I never ran, never held up any religious artifact to ward him off. Rather with each passing day, each moment I spent nurturing our growing friendship—if that is what it was—I was opening myself more and more to him. Until one evening I told him about Nikolos. And then, temptation girding me onward, about my mentor. And about the blood.

That was to be the night when Garcia and I would become one, companions in the semi-afterlife that is where we vampires inhabit the world. No longer fully living, yet decidedly not dead.

My mentor had taught me well about how to exploit the tension of repressed desire. Throughout our dinners together I would be hot with the anticipation of what was to follow. Yet he would keep me at the table, sometimes stroking my trousered thigh beneath, even when the servants were about, and I would have to control myself as he watched me. He wanted to see the tension build in me, for that is what built it in him. And so I played the same game with Garcia—and found in him an appreciative respondent.

Each evening at dusk we would walk together, sometimes in silence but most often sharing tales of our previous lives, the life before we met.

Garcia looked to be a man of about forty. He was quite tall—more than six feet—and he was, as we said then, darkly handsome. We did not speak of such things as sensuality and virility in those days, but he was both sensual and virile and he exuded a palpable sexuality that was almost unseemly. It was only his casual air and his—I thought—pretense of not knowing he had this affect on others (for women were lured by him as well) that made it possible to even be in his presence.

Yet I was mesmerized by him and needed to be with him as much as he and my own work would allow. He was a cultured, well-traveled, and educated man, of course. An intellectual as well as a political vanguard, although we did not speak of politics much at Carville. His work, his paintings, were, even to the unschooled eye, remarkable. He had followed what would later become known as a neo-realist stance with his work. The sketches and preliminary *gouaches* that he did in his first days at Carville were stunning. They had both an epic quality and a tragic one, which imbued them with poignancy, but not sentimentality. I was in awe of his skill and talent.

I'm not sure what it was that Garcia was taken by in me. He was not shallow enough to have been merely attracted by my looks, although I knew I was handsome and false modesty in that regard would be a lie. And I had told enough of those.

I knew Garcia liked the look of me, of course. He'd actually said so in a strangely offhand manner when he had said one evening at Carville that I was far too attractive a man to have devoted myself to celibacy. To which I had blurted, unthinking, that I hadn't always.

"Ah, women," he had noted, nodding. Then I had said simply, looking directly at him with a boldness that shocked even me, "No. Not women."

Garcia had raised an eyebrow and murmured something in Spanish, an idiomatic phrase I did not know, but which I presumed to be sexual in nature. It was then that our mutual attraction became apparent to us both and the game of sexual tension, repression, and ultimately, release, began in earnest between us.

I wonder if I would have run from Garcia had I known what he was then. I have pondered this over and over and can come to no honest conclusion. We were what we were: I an irrepressible sodomite and he a blood-lusting vampire. It would be impossible for either of us to change such entrenched identities. Surely I had tried to change mine and had been wholly unsuccessful. And once one has been turned to the lust for blood, one cannot switch off those desires. They are more than just mere wanting, they are need. Blood is more than sensuality incarnate—it is sustenance.

Each night Garcia and I had our walks around the grounds. This went on every evening for the first week. Then Garcia told me he needed to paint at that time, but I could either come by the rooms he had engaged as his studio and sleeping quarters or we could meet for a late supper and conversation in the refectory.

I had chosen supper at first. But on the thirteenth day I decided to go by his studio. He had previously shown me sketches which he had carried in a case on our walks. Now I saw the paintings—large, almost gigantic, canvases. Four different ones, each of them in varying stages of progress, which hardly seemed possible given he had been at Carville barely a fortnight. Tacked to boards near each canvas were sketches, an abundance of them. Some were of the haunting place itself, others of the denizens in various stages of their illness. There was a poignancy to Garcia's interpretation that imbued me with respect for him. He had portrayed this place of horror as somehow ordinary—a world within a world where the creatures who lived here were as vital as in the world we knew outside this place. He had featured them engaged in normal daily tasks or in pensive contemplation. He had taken them from the realm of the reviled and resituated them as something other than the lepers that they were. There was no voyeuristic content here, only respect.

I was impressed by his work and told him so. I said he had humanized these women and men and that he saw them as I did—as merely people who had been dealt a grim hand not of their own choosing. I told him this was what I was attempting to do also, with my work at Carville. But that my work would leave no legacy of the lepers, while his would.

He had put down the brush with which he was painting and had turned to me, a look I could not discern on his face. At first I thought he was going to reach for me, as he had raised his arm and started to stretch it toward me. But then he turned back to the canvas. Yet I could tell he was holding something back. I simply did not know what it was.

Had I crossed some unknown or unknowable line with Garcia with what I had said? Our conversations to this point had veered away from Carville, from why I was there or even why he was. We had spoken very personally at points, as when I told him I had not always been a celibate priest. Somehow this current exchange—or rather my acknowledgments of how closely aligned I felt myself to be to the denizens of Carville, the lepers of which I was one but about which Garcia had no way of knowing—had taken us to a different level of intimacy.

I was overwhelmed then with desire for him, to touch him. As I watched the sinews of his back move beneath his linen shirt as he painted, I wanted to trace them with my fingers, my tongue. The desire was so intense that I knew I must leave or my celibacy would be at an end and who knew what scandal might ensue, even in this godforsaken place.

Garcia sensed the uptick in my pulse, the rush of blood. I saw his muscles tighten involuntarily. This time he did not turn when he put down his brush, but he spoke, his voice very low and deep, rich with the same tone that my former mentor would have when we were in his bed and he was directing me to accomplish some new and previously unmentionable act.

"We shall speak again, *padre*." Garcia said this with a note of something I could not quite elicit. I knew I had been dismissed, but I knew just as succinctly that he would come to my room that night as he had before. The dismissal was temporary and more, I believed, to think and to decide what it was he wanted from me rather than to cast me out of his studio. This time, I felt sure, when Garcia arrived at my door, he would not hover and leave, but would come inside. And once there, stay.

I murmured a farewell and walked to the door.

"We shall see each other soon, *padre. Biselo espera para verle.*"

Did he know I understood what he said to me, that he could not wait to see me? Or did he think I was completely ignorant of his words, if not his tone?

"*Espero que sí,*" I responded. *I hope so.* Now there would be no doubt. I left the studio and walked toward my own quarters.

How long did it take before he was behind me, before he had me up against the wall in the semi-dark of what was now late evening, the gas-lit sconce flickering above us? How long before my cock was in his hand, his mouth was on mine and then his teeth were in my vein? How long before that first bite led us to my rooms and a night in which he drained me of everything and I gave myself over to him? How long before I was possessed by Garcia?

I warned him about the spot on my thigh. Unlike Nikolos, who must have been unaware of his lethal infection, I was not unaware. Garcia laughed a small, wry laugh and told me that there was nothing I could do to him. Rather it was he who was taking great license with me and I needed to know that once I crossed over—once he took me fully—I could not come back. The brink would have been passed once we had tasted each other's blood and I had acquiesced to being his companion.

Yet warnings aside, acquiesce I did. How long had I restrained myself from my most degenerate desires? It had been nearly four years since I had come to Carville. There had been a few brief encounters in the Vieux Carré when I had visited my uncle in that first year. After that I had been too concerned with passing on the disease. I kept myself at Carville, not even visiting my uncle, and I kept to myself as well. The rosy spot that was the mark of my disease had gotten somewhat larger but had not spread elsewhere. I knew the disease moved slowly in some—that had been the case with Father Damien. But I could not risk damning some other soul to my same hell.

That night Garcia said it would all be gone. I would never become *that*—leper—because now I would be *this*—vampire. How could I resist such a gift? How could I resist this man, this artist of the canvas and the flesh who promised immortality?

I knew I would, in the end, be damned. Can there be a worse crime than the apostasy of choosing man over God? And yet I chose and would choose again. For I was, from the day he arrived at Carville, possessed by Garcia. He was in my blood long before we actually shared blood.

In the years since, I have heard both men and women say that they would give their lives for someone, or that this person is "in their blood." But really, can anyone know this without actually being asked to give their life, without actually sharing their blood? No, one cannot. And not everyone is ready for the test, ready to choose possession, ready to give one's very soul to be the blood beat to someone else.

I know because I had not been ready the first time. My mentor—I still call him this because he primed me for everything: for my search abroad, for Nikolos, for Carville, for Garcia—my mentor had tried to take me to this same place, but although I wanted to stay with him, I was not prepared to give my life for him.

There are those—I am among them, I think, still—who view what I am as degenerate and damned. And yet I cannot, I would not divest myself of this life I lead with Garcia. I saw more than a charismatic and desirable man when he arrived at Carville. There was something inimitable in him that drew me from that first day when the nun had brought him round to me. And then that day, the end of the first fortnight, when I saw his work, his art. Then I knew that he had a soul still and that despite the dark road he had been brought to by another, he was still as much human as he was vampire.

❖

That is my story, the tale of the leper priest turned vampire. Is it a cautionary tale? I cannot say, because at every caution I kept going forward, never looking back, never choosing to stop.

Am I still a priest? They say once a priest, always a priest, so yes, I am still a priest. I even still wear the vestiture, although I cannot be said to belong to any particular order as my age—or lack of aging—prevents me from being in any one place for too extended a period of time. But I still serve the sick and the poor as I have always done. I just serve them differently now. And with my companion, Garcia.

Quite a bit of time has passed since Carville. Decades, but not yet a full century. Garcia and I left there together when his work was complete. There is a portrait of me among the denizens there, a paean he felt compelled to paint as part of his homage to the work that was done there.

I realized soon after our first night together—the first of the nights in which he would turn me into what he was—that what had caused him, finally, to choose me was my commentary on his paintings. He told me that I saw inside him, that there was more than darkness, that there was still that shimmer of humanity that he tried to keep alight.

And so we have been together for these many years, traveling, working, and, as we must, killing. We took no one at Carville. None were well enough to be crossed over without living an eternity of horror. I had thought about Nikolos, but decided it was best for him to end his days as the Damien of Spinalonga, as I presume he did, eventually, and go on to his own manner of sainthood.

As for my mentor, I have no doubt that at some point our paths will cross again. There are not that many of us, really, despite the literature to the contrary. It is a surprisingly small group, given the six billion people out there from whom one can feed upon. Most, I have found, are not like us: They kill and have done with their prey with little thought to the humanity involved. I would not say we are better than they, of course, for we do still kill. But we choose our prey with care and in the parts of the world where we are more savior than savage.

At times I think that I should end this spree we are on, Garcia and I. That I should take his life as he sleeps and then sit in the bright sun until I am nothing but ash. But I cannot. That is the thing about possession. I am his, and in as much as he trusts me not to expose him or kill him, he is mine as well.

Garcia has said to me again and again, *"Nada dura eternamente."* Nothing lasts forever. I always say the same thing in response: *"Te amaré por siempre."* I will be yours forever.

And I shall be. Because Garcia is in my blood, forever.

WILLING
XAN WEST

I slam him against the wall. Bring out my knife. Whisper words across his skin, the steel teasing, tempting. Kick his legs apart. The blade ripping through his shirt, tormenting, aching to slice him open. Up close breathing on his neck, teeth almost breaking skin. Step back slapping, leaving a handprint on his cheek. My knife at his throat. My hand covering his mouth. My eyes on his. Feeding on his helplessness. Feeding on his fear. A slow smile creeping across my face as I begin. My fist driving into his pecs. My gloved hand slapping his face. His nipple twisted between my fingers, hot under my teeth. Turned over, face against the exposed brick of the wall. My fist on his back, methodical. My boot ramming into his ass. My open hand menacing him with slaps. My cock throbbing hard as I press into him and bite down on his shoulder, holding back, yet feeding on his pain. I ride with him as I pull out my tools, laying into his back…until I am ready to thrust the pain home with my quirt. Driving welts into his back, we will soar together, gliding on his pain, his helplessness, my power, our pleasure. And when we are done flying, he will be on the floor at my feet, tongue wrapped around my boot.

It will do. The beast inside me calls for flesh, for pain. He is demanding and relentless and I barely keep him in check. It's better if they choose it. Want it. It adds a certain something that is indescribable and yet has become necessary to the meal. So I keep him sated with sadism, feeding on fear and pain and sex and helplessness. Once, I was waiting for the willing. That illusive willing boy I might call my own. I no longer hope for him. He does not exist.

Now I find boys at the Lure. Boys like this one, who want to open themselves to my tools. But sometimes that is not enough to take the edge off. Sometimes it just stokes the hunger. When the urge for blood becomes incontrollable I return to Gomorrah, looking for those hungry eyes, the pulse in a boy's throat that shows he wants it. It's hard to keep a straight face here, amidst the pretenders, the elitist pseudo vampires, the Stand and Model version of SM, the Sanguinarium, the followers of the Black Veil. So it's a last resort, this feast of image and fantasy. When the beast must feed and pain is not enough.

I stride to a shadowed corner and watch for food. The rhythm of the music brings a booming to my brain as my eyes slide along the flesh exposed, watching for that look, that swiftly beating pulse in his throat.

Whispers begin as I am glimpsed by the regulars, and I know all it will take is a crook of my head and a smoldering gaze. It's too easy here. I am not seen. I am simply a fantasy come true, made all the more fantastic by my refusal to be showy in dress or demeanor. A growl of disgust rolls through me. I choose my meat, a tall broad-shouldered goth boy with long black hair and a carefully trimmed beard. I draw him to me, and lead him out to the alley. He thinks this is a quick fuck and drops to his knees. My hand grips him by that delicious hair and yanks him up, tossing him against the wall. I want to savor this meal. He needs to last.

I pull out my blade and show it to him. His eyes widen and he whispers, "My safeword is chocolate." I am surprised. Most who frequent the fetish scene know nothing about real BDSM. That these are the first words out of his mouth shows that there may be more to this boy than I thought. I stand still, watching him. He is older than I had first surmised, at least twenty-four. The little leather he wears is well kept, his belt clearly conditioned and his boots cared for by a loving hand. He is motionless, knees slightly bent, shoulders back, offering me his chest. His pulse is not rapid, but his eyes eat up the knife and his lips are slightly parted, as if all he wanted was to take my blade down his throat.

His brown eyes stay fixed on the knife as I move toward him. I tease his lip with the tip of it and then speak softly.

"How black do you flag?"

His eyes stay on the blade. He swallows.

"Very black, on the right, Sir."

"Is there anything I need to know?"

"I am healthy and strong. My limits are animals, children, suspension, and humiliation, Sir."

"And blood, hmm?" I am teasing. I know the answer. It is why I found him here, and not at the Lure.

"Oh please, Sir. I would gladly offer my blood."

"Why?"

He takes a deep breath, closes his eyes a moment, and then opens them. The pulse in his throat starts racing, but his voice is calm and matter-of-fact. I tease my blade against his neck.

"I have been watching you a long time, Sir. I have seen how you play. I see the beast inside you. I know what is missing. Those boys at the Lure don't know how to give you what you really need. They don't see that they are barely feeding your craving, and not touching your hunger. The boys here don't see you. They just see their own fantasy. They are simply food. I am strong, Sir. Strong enough for you. I can be yours. My blood, my flesh, my sex, my service. Yours to take however you choose, for as long as you want. To slake your hunger. I would be honored, Sir."

I take a deep breath, stunned, studying him. This boy who would offer what I never really thought was possible. He has surprised me again. That alone shows this boy is more than a meal. He just might be able to be all that he has offered.

I almost leave him there. I am ready to walk away. Fear creeps along my spine. With the centuries I have lived and the things I have seen, this boy is what scares me. There is nothing more terrifying than hope. I rake my eyes over him. He is standing quietly. He looks like he could stand in that position for hours. He has said his piece; he is content to wait for my response. Oh, he is more than food, this one. What a gift to offer a vampire. Can I refuse this offering when it's laid out before me? I step back, looking him over, and decide.

I breathe in possibility, watching the pulse in his throat. My senses heighten further as I focus my hunger on him, noticing the minute changes in breath, scenting him.

I want to see him tremble. I want to smell his fear. I want to devour his pain, without holding back. Forget this public arena. If there is even a possibility that I might truly let go and move with the beast inside my skin, his growl on my lips and his claws grasping prey, I know exactly where I need to take this boy.

I put the knife away, pull the black handkerchief from his back pocket, and wrap it around his head, covering his eyes. He cannot see the way to where we are going. He has not earned that much trust. I grip him by the back of the neck and lead him to my bike. When I start the engine, its growl answers me, echoing off the walls of the alley. I take the long way, through twists and turns of the back streets, enjoying the wind on my face and the purr of the bike.

We are here. I ease him off the bike and lead him by the neck down the stairs into the lower level of the brownstone. It is a large soundproof room. There are no windows. It is one big tomb. Every detail is designed for my pleasure, down to the exposed brick wall installed for the simple gratification of slamming meat against it. This room is where I sleep, and where I take my prey when I want privacy. Private play means I let my hair down and roam free, claws unsheathed. I leave him in the doorway and ready myself, breathing deep and freeing my hair. I strip off my shirt so I can feel it brush my lower back. It is my vanity, and I have worn it long for centuries, no matter the current fashion.

I keep him blindfolded and throw him against the wall. There is a ritual about it, beginning with a wall and a knife. It communicates the road we are on. He is trapped, nowhere to run. He is pressed against the wall and going to take any impact into his body, through it to the wall, and back again, driven in a second time. He is facing danger, sharp edges. He could be torn open. He is pressed against something rough and hard. He is still. I am moving. He cannot see what's coming. My knife breaks the unspoken rules of knife play and goes to places that feel forbidden and fraught with more danger than expected. And my knife shows my need. You can hear it in my breathing, feel it surge through my body. It travels the air in electric bursts of energy.

I play with it, toying with him, ramping my need up through his fear. I slap his face with the large blade. I run it along the top of his eye, just under the blindfold, teasing it against his eyelid, so he knows just how easy it would be to burst the eyeball. I fuck him with it, thrusting the tip under his jaw, not breaking skin, just teasing my cock to hardness at the thought of thrusting it deep. His breath is catching as I draw his lower lip down and slide the blade along it. My mouth swoops in out of nowhere and bites down on that lip, just barely breaking skin. This is a test of my control, as I slowly lick the fruit I have exposed and growl deep in my throat. He is hypnotically delicious, his blood electric in a way that is familiar and yet surprising. I grip his throat in my hand, constricting his breath, watching his face, his mouth. It is true. He has surprised me again. I tuck my new knowledge and my surprise away, knowing that I can do my worst. Folks always said that his kind make good boys for us. Perhaps I will be able to test that tonight. I release his throat and watch him breath deeply. I grip his hair and tilt his head back.

"Keep your mouth open and still."

I start to tease it in, watching the large black blade slide into his throat. I exhale loudly.

He is motionless for me, breath held, taking my knife. My cock jumps at the sight as I start to fuck his throat. Mine. This incredible wave of possessiveness roars through me as I thrust into him. And I want to see his eyes. I tear through the blindfold with my teeth, the blade still lodged in his throat, and meet his gaze. His eyes are shimmering, large, and full...full of what? I thrust in deeper, watching his pupils dilate with...is that joy? I can feel his heart race, see him struggle as he realizes he needs to breathe. He must exercise perfect control, and not move his mouth or throat as he exhales and takes his first breath. Fear fills him. Not because he is afraid of the knife. Because he knows that it would displease me to draw blood when I don't intend to, and his whole being is focused on pleasing me. He works to do it perfectly, and contentment washes over his face as he succeeds. I thrust deeper in appreciation, picturing his throat muscles working to avoid contact with the blade. Oh, this will be fun. I slide out of his throat.

I want my claws on his chest, now. I want to rip him open, expose him to my gaze, my teeth, my hunger. I want his blood on every tool in my possession. Now. I want to feast on him. I can feel the beast roll through my body.

Not yet. I want more pain to draw it out. I want to see if it's true. I want to know he can take my worst and still want more. I want to see his strength. That is worth delaying my feed. And postponing it will only make it sweeter.

I breathe deeply, focusing my senses as I walk slowly in front of him, inspecting him from every angle. He straightens his posture, easing into a position he can hold. I move close and grip his shirt, tearing it swiftly from his chest and tossing it onto the floor. That's what I want first. I throw my shoulder into the body slam, and feel the electricity of our skins' contact. I trace my fingertips along the horizontal scars on his chest, and then grip his nipples, twisting. I am so close, I cannot resist sinking my teeth in and teasing myself. I bite deeply, barely avoiding breaking skin. Building connection. Making my cock throb. Drawing out my beast. I lift up and bite down, feeling his body shift with the pain, laying my mark on him. I claim him like this, first. Begin how you wish to proceed. With fear and pain and teeth and sex all rolled together. I can feel the blood pulsing just at the surface, calling me. I bite down hard and thrust my cock against him. My low growl mixes with the slow soft moan that escapes his lips. I lift my head to meet his eyes, and see that he has begun to fly.

I step back and begin my dance around him. Heaving my fist into his chest. My boot into his thigh. My open hand slamming down onto his pecs. I move rapidly, layering and shifting, gliding around him. Thrusting pain into him in unpredictable gusts of movement. Upping the ante. Ramming my boot into his cock, grinding the heel in and watching his eyes. He is twirling high in the air, lips parted, offering himself to me. His eyes entreat me to use him. And I do, exercising minute control, I coil into him, watching as he floats. This is just the beginning. I constrict his breath, cover his mouth and nose and thrust my teeth into his shoulder, feeling his heart against my tongue.

I lead him to the table and tell him to remove what he must to give me access to his ass. He takes off his pants and socks, folding them neatly and stacking them on top of his boots in the corner. He is wearing a simple leather jock. I order him face-down onto the table. He is quivering. Mine, I think. And catch myself. I watch him, building on his fear, and remove my touch. There is only the knife sliding along him, forcing him to remain still. There is only the knife, as silence lays on him like a blanket. I step away, moving quietly, and leave him alone. We will see how much he needs connection, how much fear I can build. We will see, I think slowly to myself, how much distance I can tolerate.

My play is usually about connection. About driving myself inside. About opening someone up to my gaze. My tools are up close and personal. Play is my source of connection, and I usually hurl into it, deep and hard. I don't want to show myself yet. This must be done slowly. I want to see what he can do. I want to wait, before I commit myself to what I have already thought. I will come to that on my terms, in my time.

I collect my favorite canes, needing air between us. Needing that sound that whips through the air and blasts into flesh. Needing controlled, careful cruelty. Canes are a special love of mine. It takes a lot for me to risk thin sticks of wood, easily broken to form deadly weapons. Canes are about my risk, too. Their simple existence menaces. Their joy is unmatchable.

I line up my weapons on a nearby table, carefully. Thinking ahead, I select another item and place it on the table softly. I am ready.

I step back, allowing the necessary distance, and begin from stillness. I place my stripes precisely, just slow enough for him to get the full ripping effect of the bite. I lay lines of piercing sting, not holding back my strokes, saturating him with an invasive assault. There is nothing like the sound of a cane mutilating air, and he shivers at it. I can feel the fear rising off him like steam and breathe it in as my due. I am unforgiving. It will never end. I can loom over him, layering slashes on skin, for eternity. I am breathing deeply. This is meditative. And I realize though there is air and space between us, I am attuned to his breathing. My cock swells at the almost imperceptible sounds he makes. We are connected. There is no breaking that. I know that he could be halfway across the country and I would feel the pulse of his blood. I smile at the thought, accepting it. I am ready. Ready to rend his skin with my teeth and tools. To break him open and take a good long taste. To unleash the beast roaming in my skin.

I feel an incredible calm at the roaring in my blood. A new calm. I can fully be who I am in this room, with this man. He is strong enough. And I trust him enough to risk. I pick up my belt and begin.

There are few tools I have a deeper connection with. I have had this belt since the nineteenth century, and cared for it well. It is a part of me. An extension of my cock and my will. Nothing brings out my beast like my belt. Which is why I keep it at home and only use it on prey I am going to devour. Until now.

I explain this to him, watching him tremble.

"Please use me, Sir," is all he says.

Mine. Possessiveness washes over me. I double the belt and start slamming him with it, the welts rising rapidly. Vision begins to blur. This is all about sound and movement. My body senses where to strike. My blows hammer him into the table. I can feel a growl building in my throat as his scent shifts. My cock swells as I hurl the belt into his back in rapid crashing surges.

"Mine," I growl. "Mine to hurt. Mine to use. Mine to feed on. Mine."

The possessiveness rises in me, a tsunami cresting and breaking over him as I blast the belt into his back, rending his skin. Welts form on top of welts, and break the surface. He is moaning as I howl, the beast fully in my skin and oh so hungry. I lay the belt across the back of his neck and crouch on the table above him, eyes focused on the gashes opening his back to me. I drop on top of him, rubbing my chest into the blood on his back.

I breathe the scent of him in and growl happily, "Mine."

I free my cock, swollen to bursting, and shed my pants. I will savor the first real taste. Right now, it's enough to smell it and feel it against my skin, and know there is more for the taking. I rub it onto my cock, stroking it in as I close my eyes. I want inside, now. Want to rend him open. Thrust myself into him, bloody and hard. I want to tear his back open with claws and teeth, and feast.

I describe this to him, and he moans his consent.

"Please, Sir," he says softly. "Please."

He is all want and need and craving, and where his hunger meets mine we will crest. Mine. The word fills me, taking me over.

I thrust into him, my cock smeared in his blood, ramming into his ass for my pleasure. He is so open for me, so willing. His groans are loud and true as I fuck him, rubbing my face in the blood on his back. I grip his hips, and stop, embedded in him. I can feel my claws extend right before I slash into his back, ripping him open. The blood flows freely and I bathe my chest in it, bellowing as I hurl my cock into him. I wrap the belt around his neck, constricting his breath, my cock pounding him into the table, and I bite. Mulled wine. Spicy. Sweet. Tangy. I drink him down, savoring each gulp, thrusting steadily. I release his neck, hear his gasping breaths, and bite harder, feeding.

"Please, Sir," he manages in a throaty whisper.

I lift my head. "Please what, boy?"

This is the first time I have called him boy, and he whimpers at the sound of it.

"Please, Sir. Please may I come, Sir?"

I thrust into him hard and feel his ass grab me.

"Mine. You are my boy. Mine to fuck. Mine to slash open. Mine to devour. Mine to mark. Mine to command. You may come when I sink my teeth into you again, boy. I want to hear it. Tell me you are mine, and then you may come."

I drive my cock into him, reaming him deeply, and rub my chest against his bloody back. I reach around to grab his cock, gripping it tightly and stroking it in quick bursts. I plunge my teeth into his shoulder. Gnawing him open. Snarling as I drink. My dick pumping into him.

"I am yours, Sir. I offer myself freely for your use. I am so glad to be yours, Sir."

I explode into him, storms crashing in huge tidal waves. Drinking and coming. Releasing myself and drawing him in. His ass clenches around me in spasms as he bursts, his body bucking and shuddering. I continue to feed. When his body calms, I am sated, and I ease myself out of him slowly. I take my time licking his wounds closed, savoring the taste of him. I pull him up into my arms, smiling.

"Now let's see that cock of yours, boy."

His eyes go wide, he looks down and he starts trembling again. I lift his chin to meet his eyes, and then trace the scars on his chest lightly with my tongue. I lift my head to stare into his eyes again, and slowly unzip the jock, revealing a large black silicone cock. I pump it hard, stroking it against him, where I know he is enlarged by testosterone.

"Did you think I didn't know, boy? After all the centuries I've lived, did you think I did not learn how to read people?"

I grin into his eyes.

"You are my boy. And I am proud to claim you as mine."

I gather him to me, holding him tight, and start imagining possibilities.

Beauty, Blood-Deep
Shephard Summers

Tourist season: a banquet of choices. Hiroshi looked forward to the influx of Americans in particular because they reminded him of the United States, where he'd grown up. But mostly he was tired of the same old blood coursing sluggishly through Kyoto's ample arteries, and welcomed any change.

He exited the train and walked up the hill through quaint old streets lined with restaurants and shops that, not unlike him, waited to take advantage of visitors. And which, like Kyoto overall, seemed too familiar to Hiroshi's tired eyes. He jumped out of the way of a young cyclist just in time, glared at the boy, then passed under the massive Bengal-orange torii gate that spanned the narrow street, hurrying to reach the mystical Fushimi Inari Shrine of Ten Thousand Gates before the start of sunset. The smell of incense grew stronger as he got closer.

Darting down a side path through a gray neighborhood no tourist ever noticed, he found his secret entrance into the mountain sanctuary. Sullen clouds covered the sky. He smiled; the overcast would also keep the tourists from crowding the trail. He jumped a rickety fence and climbed between two of the ubiquitous large fox statues, the Kitsune guardians seeming to grin at him as if they understood his intentions.

Emerging from the back of an alcove crowded with prayer flags and statuettes, Hiroshi stepped carefully around stacks of miniature orange torii gates and followed a worn cement pathway up the long hill arching to the right, walking quickly but casually. He passed several altars and alcoves, all decked with guardians, flowery tributes, lions, foxes, and stone markers. Multitudes of vertical red and white prayer banners waved him along his path as the wind picked up. He would soon be under the quiet cover of the mountain forest.

His bones ached with anticipation. Tonight would be a good night.

It was Tuesday, and the tourist guidebooks recommended this early-evening stroll; it rarely let him down.

The trees became more numerous, his climb more arduous. Two young girls and a businessman carrying a briefcase passed him on the path and he avoided eye contact, walking briskly toward the top and his favorite little side path surrounded by stone guardians.

Descending the uneven carved steps, Hiroshi positioned himself out of the sight-line of those on the main path above. He leaned against a stone wall that flanked the steps near a small ramshackle building, breathing deeply to calm his anxiety.

Movement caught his eye, and he turned to see a small cat perched above him on the flat slab of the wall. She came forward, recognizing him. "Miyu," he said, recognizing her markings. The brindled cat stretched and came closer. The mountain was populated by feral cats, any of whom were exceptional ice-breakers and conversation-starters. He petted her twice and touched noses with her, then reached into his pocket to pull out the dried fish she was waiting for, and smiled as she ate it gratefully.

Noise on the pathway above shattered his moment with Miyu. He leaned nonchalantly against the stone wall, one knee propped up, striking his best seductive pose. A young couple passed by, holding hands, paying no attention to him. And soon after, a group of young boys. The boys regarded him with snickering and exaggerated eyebrows, as if they understood some joke of which he was a part. He looked to Miyu, who sat patiently on the stone slab, cleaning her face with one paw. He petted her again. "You understand me," he said, mostly for his own comfort.

"Hello? I'm sorry, do you speak English?"

Caught off guard, Hiroshi jumped, but his eyes landed on exactly what he'd been waiting for: a tall blond man, most likely American. Hiroshi composed himself. "Yes, I speak English. I grew up in San Francisco."

"Oh, thank God, because my Japanese is a bit rusty."

Hiroshi looked the man up and down, not caring if he noticed the scrutiny. Straight nose, large eyes, small ears and square jaw, and a generally relaxed demeanor. He wore tight jeans and boots; his shirt had not weathered the humidity very well. Judging by the way the clothes hung, this man was in great shape. Hiroshi felt his hunger stirring. A man in great shape sent all the right signals, like two magnets that attract and repel at the same time.

"Are you trying to find your way out?" he asked.

"Oh, uh…no. I was trying to go all the way to the top, but I seem to be going downhill now. I must have taken the wrong path. I've been walking up and down for about an hour, and I'm all turned around."

Perfect. "Well, why don't I walk you up to the right path? It's not too far."

"Oh, are you sure? I wouldn't want to bother you."

"I'm happy to," Hiroshi said, adding a short and submissive bow. Americans seemed to like that.

"Is that your cat?"

"Oh, no. But I've known Miyu since she was a kitten." Hiroshi flashed him a smile and let his eyes linger. The stranger didn't look away, just smiled back. Another good sign. "Would you like to pet her?"

"Oh sure, I love cats." The man trotted down the stone steps to Hiroshi and the heavy slab.

Hiroshi's luck was holding. All signs seemed to point to gay. An openly gay American meant less challenge. The man stepped timidly forward and reached out to pet Miyu. As he got closer, his eyes met Hiroshi's, and Hiroshi looked down, feigning shyness. The hiss that came from Miyu startled both of them.

"I guess she doesn't like me."

"It's okay. She's wild, feral. Sometimes she's not in a very friendly mood." He watched Miyu jump into the underbrush, then turned back to the American. "I might be a little wild too, but I'm always friendly."

The man raised his eyebrows in mock surprise, then grinned slowly. "Thanks for the…warning."

Hiroshi brushed by the man and walked up the stone steps to the main trail. He glanced at the sky as the sun tried to break through the clouds. "This way."

Hiroshi's pulse raced as the man followed him. He avoided eye contact to hide the hunger in his eyes, feigning more shyness. "So where are you from?"

"Everywhere. I love to travel. I'm a bit of a wanderer. But I'm sure you can tell I'm American. I've spent a lot of time in San Francisco, actually."

"Oh, what area?" Hiroshi hoped he would take the bait.

"All over, really. Mission Dolores, Sunset, Nob Hill, Richmond, Noe Valley, The Castro."

Signal received. "So you're all alone in Japan? Just wandering around?"

"Yeah, for now."

Hiroshi smiled to himself. The American noticed.

"You're smiling?"

"Well, I would never have guessed you didn't have a boy…or girlfriend or whatever. I mean, you're quite handsome. How can you meet someone if you're constantly traveling around?"

"I meet lots of people. I met you, didn't I?"

Charming as well. Inari was truly the god of prosperity. A yellow tabby cat darted across their path into the bushes, and Hiroshi slowed, then stepped over a fallen limb and glanced back. "Careful."

The man tripped on the fallen limb anyway, and Hiroshi reached out to steady him.

"Thanks."

"Do you like Kyoto?"

"So far, yes. I love history and old places. I love college towns— so much youth and energy."

Trees arched completely over the uphill path now, and the air was alive with chirping forest spirits, like a sound blanket of anticipation. "My name is Hiroshi. You haven't told me your name yet."

"Josh."

"Wow, very American."

"It's short for Joshua—family name."

"Ah, Joshua. I like older names."

"No one calls me Joshua—it's too old-fashioned. My mother always called me that, though."

Hiroshi's senses buzzed and tingled as he closed on their destination. "Is she no longer alive?"

"No. My family was murdered. I'm an orphan, more or less."

"Oh my God, I'm so sorry."

"There are some distant cousins maybe, but no real family left. It was in San Francisco."

"I walked right into that one. I'm so sorry."

"No, it's okay. I don't mind talking about them. It helps me remember them. I was very young. I...I have to work to remember sometimes."

Hiroshi steered the subject back. "So what are you really doing out here in this mountain forest all alone, with dusk approaching?"

"Well, the guidebooks said it's a great time to visit the shrine and see the ten thousand torii gates—not as many people, more private."

Bull's-eye. Hiroshi took a left turn. "The torii gates are impressive, aren't they? But there are actually more than ten thousand. They are considered taxable donations, so the monks won't reveal exactly how many there are. But it's closer to twenty thousand, probably more."

"Donations. That's why I see so many smaller ones stacked in rows and piled up in corners of the shrines?"

"Yes."

"And the black writing going up and down one side of the gates?"

"That identifies who donated it, so their prosperity can be read by all."

"Ah. So anyone can do that?"

"Sure. A donation is a donation. Mostly businesses, but anyone who wants prosperity."

"I like that. What about the foxes I keep seeing?"

"The Kitsune are guardians, messengers. Legend says they're mischievous forest spirits that can possess or bewitch a human by entering your body through your fingernails. Most people think they're creepy," Hiroshi said as they passed a rather large, glowering fox sculpture, "but I kinda like them."

"Doesn't the park—I mean sanctuary—close soon?"

Hiroshi looked at the fading sunlight filtering through the dense tree cover, then back at Josh. "Yes, but I know my way around. If you'd like to see a beautiful sunset, I know a great place. No one will care."

"I'd like that."

An old woman passed them on the path as they entered the orange tunnel of torii gates. She eyed them with great suspicion. Hiroshi nodded respectfully, but she just stared at him.

A cat sprang from between two of the black bases of the torii, crossing their path and startling them both. "They seem to be everywhere," Josh noted.

"Yes, the monks and noodle shop owners look after them. They can be skittish until they get to know you."

The torii tunnel spilled into a small clearing with a lake, almost a pond, railed off in brilliant orange to protect onlookers. Tall trees hemmed the clearing, amplifying the sounds of insects and birds around them.

"This is one of the prettiest spots, though there are so many on the mountain." Hiroshi turned to witness Josh's reaction to the lake and found him within a foot of his face. "Oh."

Without warning Josh moved in, strong arms snaking around Hiroshi's middle, pulling him close. He kissed Hiroshi with surprising hunger and passion, lips exploring and savoring Hiroshi's. Hiroshi pushed gently away, looking around for the monks or caretakers.

"Maybe you know a more private spot?" Josh asked, reflecting back his hunger.

"Yes," Hiroshi said, grinning. He led Josh back the way they'd come, taking a sharp right down a shadowy path, then descending a short incline to a small stream. The sound of its water rushed them along through yet another towering torii tunnel, each ten-foot-tall orange and black arch no more than a foot apart. The tunnel of arches swallowed them up, its smooth wooden poles glowing tangerine in the twilight. Wooden beam steps carried them to a forked pathway with the giant orange gates splitting off in two directions. Hiroshi chose the left tunnel, and his breathing rose along with the path.

They came to a gap in the gates where a small, uncluttered forest path cut away from the main trail. He smiled at Josh and ascended the dirt path. At the top he stopped in a nice secluded area and turned—to see no sign of Josh. Confused, he spun around to find Josh grinning mischievously in front of him.

"Enough small talk, I'm not waiting any longer," Josh said. His large hands pulled Hiroshi in tight to kiss his jawline and neck. Their lips soon found each other and hands began exploring soft flesh. Hiroshi could feel hormones coursing through his body, and he let his lips wander along the man's cheek and neck. He breathed deeply the welcome scent and felt his lips caress supple skin, overcome with desire.

Josh made a small sound of surprise and pulled back when Hiroshi let his teeth graze Josh's neck. "Did you try to bite me?" he said with a big grin. Hiroshi returned more a leer than a grin. Josh pulled him close and kissed him full on the lips, the only sound the unison of their breathing.

Josh moved to explore his neck with his nose and lips, then Hiroshi felt a sudden small but sharp pain. "Ouch, not so hard," Hiroshi said, breaking away. He looked into Josh's eyes, saw his pupils, dilated and shining, penetrating the gloom of the dying day.

Josh parted his lips, revealing the point of one tooth stained with a single drop of blood. Hiroshi felt his neck with one hand and felt a warm wetness that sent a pang of panic through him. "You really bit me," he managed through his confusion. "I was just being playful." He tried to pull away, but Josh's strength held fast. Josh parted his lips wider to reveal the full size of his incisors. "Uh, you're kinda freaking me out. I'd appreciate it if you'd let me go."

"Is that what you really want?" Josh said, his voice low and frightening.

"Yes, let me go," Hiroshi demanded. He felt the vise release him, and he straightened his shirt before touching his wet neck again. "You really bit me. I…I don't think this is going to work out for me."

"I agree," Josh said, taking a step closer.

"Look, I liked you, but I'm not into this whole creepy *Twilight* thing, okay?" Hiroshi started to walk down the dirt path toward the torii tunnel, fighting panic as he thought about just how much bigger and stronger Josh was. His senses were on hyper alert, sure that Josh was following, so he quickened his pace to get to the bottom of the dirt path.

He turned tentatively, but no Josh. He turned back to find Josh standing tall and still, blocking his way. "Look Josh, I'm sure you're a nice guy, you could have any guy you wanted—why put on this whole freak show act?"

Josh's face remained stony, his boyish looks now marred by the slashing shadows cast by tree branches. A thin smile told Hiroshi the man had had this confrontation before. He pointed. "I'm going *that* way, to a shrine just a couple hundred feet from here. There are caretakers there," he lied.

Hiroshi pushed past Josh and entered the torii tunnel, his heart thundering in his chest, his legs wobbling a bit more than he expected. At any moment the man could grab him and that would be the end of his struggling. He walked uphill through the glowing orange tunnel, the twinkling lights in the distance quickening his pace. He heard no footsteps but his own. In fact, he heard no usual night sounds at all. He jogged the last few paces through the torii tunnel until the path opened up to a set of small buildings and shrines. In the middle of the clearing was an offering area with many paper prayers tied in the shape of little white fox heads.

His breathing was heavy as the last bit of light faded toward indigo. The dim glow of abandoned work lights offered little comfort. He looked back at the torii tunnel, but saw no sign of Josh. Three torii tunnels led from the clearing; he had to choose one and get out of the forest.

The hair on the back of his neck stood straight up, but before he could react, strong hands shoved him to the ground. When he rolled and his eyes oriented, Josh was on top of him, his eyes blazing with a terrifying hunger. He was shirtless, his breath labored and frightening. Hiroshi screamed twice, but the weight of the man's body on top of his muffled his voice. He shivered as Josh's cold hands begin to explore his body.

The man leaned in close. "You are *beautiful*, Hiroshi."

"Please, please let me go! Please, I'll do anything, just let me go, I'll give you money!"

The man kissed Hiroshi's neck and Hiroshi screamed, anticipating the feel of sharp teeth again, but the man pulled up. "This can be enjoyable. You don't have to die for me to feed."

"Feed?" Hiroshi managed. His stomach turned and fear seized his chest and throat. One of the man's hands slid under the fabric of his pants to the vulnerable soft part below his belly button and Hiroshi cried out, but the man's lips silenced him. Hiroshi's mind stabbed at him with the guilt of dozens of one-night stands, as if this was his final punishment for leading such an empty life, for not heeding warnings. "Please, just don't kill me, please," he managed, his voice soaked in fear.

The man leaned back so Hiroshi could see his eyes. "I'm not going to kill you, Hiroshi. I just want what you have."

"My blood?"

"More than that." The man lowered himself again and this time bit into Hiroshi's neck.

Hiroshi screamed at the piercing pain. The pain soon ebbed, replaced by a numbness that spread like ink over paper. He wanted to cry, but his body and eyes felt dry. He could barely move. The man's mouth sucked noisily at his neck. Hiroshi's focus shifted from the numbness in his body to the movement of the man's hand unzipping his pants. He gasped as he felt the man grab him.

Hiroshi's resistance faded with the last light of day. As his eyesight blurred, the stars in the sky became sequins sparkling on an azure dress, and a lightness of being swept through his body. He rode wave after wave of pleasure as the man's hand ravaged him, all the while with his lips and teeth clamped to Hiroshi's neck. He felt his own arms reach for the man's bare shoulders as he crested the final wave. The man continued to suck at his neck as Hiroshi tried to cry out, but the intensity choked off the sound, and his body crashed into shudders of pleasure.

Exhausted, Hiroshi lay helplessly on the ground, the man still on top of him. He felt another small bite and then Josh gently lifted himself off him. Hiroshi's face must have registered the shock of seeing Josh's bloodstained lips, because he wiped his mouth self-consciously, then smiled. It was an oddly beautiful smile now, daggered teeth and all, and his eyes beamed victory.

Hiroshi's heart felt light, his mind clean and clear, though bewildered. "Am I bleeding to death?" he asked calmly.

Josh smiled at him. "No, you're not bleeding at all."

Hiroshi was too weak to touch his own neck. "Are you...am I...?"

"No, you're not a vampire," Josh answered.

"Why do I...I can't...I didn't..."

"The best painkiller in the world," Josh said, raking his tongue across the sharp point of one incisor. His blue eyes reflected the night sky, dark pools against his pale skin. Hiroshi marveled at his ability to see beauty in such a savage man. Josh reached out and ran his hand gently through Hiroshi's black hair.

The euphoric feeling began to ebb like water from the beach, replaced by pangs of anxiety. "How old are you?" Hiroshi asked, his voice cracking.

"Why do you ask?"

"Just tell me."

"I'm a hundred sixteen. Well, I'll be a hundred seventeen next week. I think."

"You'll be a hundred seventeen *years* old?"

"I was alive before that, for twenty-two years." His beautiful brow furrowed. "Or maybe it was twenty-six. I can't remember anymore."

Hiroshi looked into the playful, almost childlike eyes staring down at him. His body was haloed by a hundred pinpoints in the night sky and he almost looked like an angel. Hiroshi sighed. "You look twenty-five." The sounds of the mountain began filtering back into his ears.

"Thank you." Josh laughed, and his eyes crinkled seductively. He got up off of Hiroshi.

Embarrassment and shame and confusion nagged at Hiroshi as his hands fumbled with the zipper on his pants, his arms searching for the energy to move in normal ways. Josh didn't take his eyes off of him. Hiroshi sat up, propping himself on one hand as he reached up to touch his neck. He felt two tiny dry holes. Josh laughed gently.

The skin all over his body tightened as the mantle of life took hold of him. He felt the ache return to his heart. "I want you to make me a vampire."

"What?" Josh's face twisted quizzically.

"I want to be a vampire. I don't want this emptiness anymore! I'm tired of the pain."

"That pain…is life, Hiroshi. And you should be grateful for it."

"I left San Francisco hoping to find a different life here in Japan, but instead I found only the same pain. I can't take it anymore, Josh. I'm so tired." Josh said nothing. "Please help me…Joshua?"

Josh started at the name. He reached out and pulled Hiroshi to his feet with almost no effort. "Hiroshi, you mistake the absence of pain for happiness. They're not the same," Josh sighed as he propped Hiroshi against a little fence.

"Why didn't you kill me?"

"Why would I need to?"

"So you're not like the vampires in movies and books?"

"Are you just like the gay men you see in movies and books?"

Hiroshi didn't know how to answer. "I…rarely see myself in movies or books at all."

"Then why would you think I'd be just like the vampires you see there? People in movies and books aren't real."

"I didn't think vampires were real. But I don't care about real, I just wish I was beautiful, like you."

Josh sighed, and his eyes darkened. "It's always the same with you gay men." He straightened his back and came toward Hiroshi, who flinched unconsciously. Josh put his hands on Hiroshi's cheeks and spoke softly, gently. "Hiroshi, you *are* beautiful already. You're the real thing, you are flesh and blood and life personified, not some glossy page in a magazine."

"But would you say that if I was thirty-five?"

Josh frowned.

"I've heard it all before, ya know," Hiroshi continued. "People saying gay men are vain, and we worship youth and we don't have to be this way, but you don't live in our world, you don't know what it's like."

"I don't know what it's like to *what*? To live my life on the fringe, to be the target of prejudice, to be ostracized and misunderstood, to have to hide who I am, to be ashamed of my secret, or know that there are people out there who think my secret is ugly and an abomination? Not to mention fear of too much sun. It's really hard on the skin. That last part is a joke," Josh added when Hiroshi remained silent.

Hiroshi didn't laugh. "But you won't age. You stay beautiful, you can have anything you want."

"No, Hiroshi, not anything. Not life. I can't have a *life*. A life full of ups and downs, surprises, sorrows and joys. A life full of loss and heartache, of triumph and defeat. My days and nights are endlessly the same, endlessly empty."

Hiroshi found the strength to stand and move away from the vampire, his own frustration fueling his limbs. "My life is empty. I may as well be a vampire. I'm on a treadmill, looking at no future. You're not gay, you wouldn't understand!" he said, turning away to hide his anger.

Josh's strong hands gripped his shoulders and shoved him hard against the nearby torii gate. "I'm so tired of your kind thinking they know everything about what it's like to be a vampire. You make assumptions about what a vampire is and isn't, but you have no fucking clue. You just assume you know. I can assure you, contrary to mythology, that I'm quite *alive*. And I may live forever, I don't know. But even if I don't live forever, I have no life—so it will *feel* like forever."

Hiroshi stared deeply into Josh's pained face. "Please. Please Joshua, make me a vampire! Please…" His voice cracked and trailed off with the last ounce of his hope.

The vampire breathed heavily. Hiroshi watched tension spreading from his temples to strain the tendons in his neck. His breath grew cold, issuing from his mouth like vapor. Then he hissed and his eyes grew black and narrow, and the cold spread to his hands, pinning Hiroshi in place with fingers of ice. Hiroshi's heart beat faster as the cold seized him. He felt his body react instinctively, trying to avoid the advancing cold.

Josh growled deep in his throat and moved in very slowly. Hiroshi could feel his cool breath on his nose and cheeks. Just as second thoughts found a voice inside Hiroshi's head, Josh lunged forward and sank his teeth into Hiroshi's neck. Hiroshi shuddered and heard a rattle of pain escape his mouth. Then Josh turned his teeth, and Hiroshi cried out in pain. Nausea swept over him and his eyes blurred. The stars became pinpoints, then flickered out as his world grew black.

Panic gripped him and he tried to speak. The blackness suffocated him until he dropped like a deadweight, limp in Josh's arms. He sank deeper, tumbling like Alice through the rabbit hole into an empty chasm. He felt a deep loneliness collide with the infinite passage of time. Gone was the intake and exhalation of life. Gone was any sense of rhythm by which time could be measured. His soul yearned for the breath of life, the passage of time, the end of infinity and sameness. And then a surge of breath spiked through his chest with a jolt, and he felt Josh's teeth release him. The ground disappeared from under his feet and he realized he was being carried.

He came to, the memory fresh and bleak and threatening to steal his breath again. He felt moisture gathering in the corners of his eyes as the wind buffeted his face. Stars glistened in the night sky once again, and he realized he was lying down on something cold and hard.

Josh's stony face appeared above him, looking down without any sign of feeling at all. "Remember this feeling. Remember what you asked of me. And know now why I denied you," Josh said in a low and gentle voice. "It's always the same. Those who have choices take them for granted. Those of us who don't…well. Hiroshi, you can lead whatever life you want if you simply stop perpetuating *this* one.

I cannot choose my life's path, but I can choose to spare yours. That's my choice."

Hiroshi held the frail piece of rice paper tightly as the wind tried to pry it from him. He passed under the last orange and black torii gate and emerged from the fiery tunnel into the serenity of the clearing. He had not been back since that night, and he returned today with trepidation and the smallest hope.

The irises were blooming again, dotting the perimeter with purple as the sun sparkled across the calm lake. He looked at the piece of paper, reading the directions carefully. Knowing who sent the note, but not how it had found him, he counted four posts from the right, and saw lashed to it with a scarlet ribbon a knee-high torii gate, shiny and new, its coat of paint gleaming to shame the sunshine. He read the vertical writing down its poles: on the left side *Hiroshi Yoshida*, his name in shiny black letters. And on the right, dark as the blackest ink, the words *Choose* and *Remember*.

SEX ON THE BEACH
F. A. POLLARD

As he sat by himself, Daniel popped the top on his third beer and took a swallow. The ocean was so much better at night, the crash of the waves, the moonlight glimmering in a band across the black water, the absence of crowds.

Senior class trip, Azalea Beach, South Carolina. Daniel snorted. He should be at a party right now. He ought to be getting drunk with his buddies. He was supposed to be having sex. That was the point of spring break. But Daniel was alone, as usual. An outsider. An exile. Timid. Frail. Socially lacking.

He never should have let Elliott convince him to come. Elliott who, an hour ago, had thrown Daniel out of their hotel room after somehow managing to score a blind-drunk college sophomore who would most certainly kick herself in the morning when she woke up, hungover, in Elliott's bed.

Daniel drank his beer, smoothed a bit of sand off his towel, and stared out at the shimmering water. The later it got, the fewer people remained. Mostly couples walking at the edge of the surf, holding hands, often carrying flashlights, pale yellow beams that swept back and forth.

About twenty yards down the beach, someone else sat in the dry sand above the boundary of high tide. Daniel could see the shape silhouetted in the backlight of the hotels lining the shore but couldn't make out any details.

It was nice to think that there was someone else as alone as he was.

Throughout high school, Daniel had been interested in various boys. Mostly jocks who insisted they were straight and publicly gave him, at best, a sneering glance, or at worst, a beating. No one Daniel wanted ever wanted him. Not for long, anyway. No longer than a few sweaty minutes in an empty locker room or a clumsy half hour behind the bleachers on the field.

Daniel was fair, slender and small-boned, not really feminine but certainly not masculine. He liked how he looked, imagined himself pretty and unusual. No one seemed to share his opinion, however, at least no one he had met in the course of his eighteen years. In the past several months, Daniel had fallen in with a few other outcasts who didn't fit anywhere else, and he planned to follow fellow-pariah Elliott to Concord University in the fall.

Daniel was an only child whose drunken mother had drowned in the bathtub when he was four. His father was a verbally abusive man who liked to fall asleep with a six-pack in front of the TV. College was a chance to get away, made possible by a lottery scholarship Daniel had qualified for. He was set to room with Elliott who was, sadly, Daniel's best friend. They tolerated one another, but as Elliott filled out in his masculinity, Daniel grew more fragile and pale and insubstantial. Blurry around the edges in a way that made Daniel more comfortable in isolation and less a part of anyone else around him.

Shit, he was depressing himself.

Daniel finished his beer and looked down to wrest another can from the plastic webbing that bound them. When he raised his head, someone was standing over him.

"Oh," Daniel said, looking up the tight, ripped jeans to a body-hugging black T-shirt and a gorgeous guy gazing down.

"May I?" he said as he sat next to Daniel on the towel.

"Sure." The floodlights from the hotel behind them illuminated the guy's glossy black hair. He was almost the same size as Daniel but with a defined, well-built body noticeable beneath his snug clothing.

Leaning back, Daniel saw that the person who had sat on the beach was gone.

"You've been watching me." The guy smiled a wide, lazy smile and squinted his eyes at Daniel.

The beers had given Daniel a considerable buzz, eliminating the nervousness he would otherwise have felt in the presence of someone so good-looking, but he was sober enough to recognize that his new acquaintance was high on something.

"You want a beer?" Daniel said, holding up his two unopened cans.

The guy shook his head, then raised a graceful hand to brush his bangs out of his eyes, tuck a strand of hair behind his ear.

"Are you down here on spring break, too?" Daniel asked.

"No."

"Then you're from around here?"

"No." The guy laughed softly and looked out at the ocean.

His black hair hung long and thick down his back, and he had the loveliest skin Daniel had ever seen, flawless and lustrous, the color of champagne. His face was delicately featured. Yet a long, sinewy neck met shoulders that looked strong and arms that were lean and muscled just enough. He had drawn up his knees to his chest and sat hugging them. With a jolt of lust, Daniel admired the flexed bicep that was close enough to lick.

"You like watching me," the guy whispered, lips curving up into another luscious smile.

A rush of heat flooded Daniel's face, so he put his nearly forgotten beer to his mouth and drank in hard swallows.

When the can was empty, he crushed it and said, "My name's Daniel."

"Nikolos. With a k-o-l-o-s. Call me Nik."

"Okay, Nik." Daniel tried to think of something else to say, something clever and disarming. But he wasn't drunk enough to be either one.

Nik pulled his long hair into a ponytail. Then he stretched, extending his arms straight above his head, and unfolded gracefully to lie on his back, apparently unconcerned that the lower half of his body was in the sand.

Daniel looked down at him, leaned a little too far, and nearly took a header into the guy's face.

"Careful." Laughing, Nik caught him with both hands on Daniel's shoulders.

Fingers firm, grip sure, eyes darker than the night. Daniel gazed down into those eyes, hypnotized, giddy, and felt himself falling again, swallowed up by sweet black magic.

"Are you okay?"

Daniel blinked stupidly and straightened up. "Yeah. I guess I'm a little drunk."

An uncomfortable silence fell, so Daniel detached another can and said, "Sure you don't want a beer? I've got two more."

"I don't drink…beer." Nik smiled and his teeth glinted against the blush of his lips. "Well, maybe a taste," he said.

Then Nik pushed up on one arm and kissed Daniel on the mouth. The kiss was soft and brief and stunning. The beer can almost slipped out of Daniel's hand. He felt hot and tingly all over.

Nik twisted around so he could lie on the length of the towel.

Daniel sat frozen, staring out at the water, unsure of what to do. Until feathery fingers brushed across his arm and Nik said, low and insistent, "Come here."

The command thrilled Daniel. He tossed his can aside and rolled onto his hands and knees.

Nik gazed up at him, pupils huge and dilated by whatever drug he was on. He smiled and reached to lock his arms around Daniel, drawing him down, fusing their mouths together. He opened Daniel's lips with his tongue and licked up into him. Nik's skin was cool but Daniel was burning up, as electric fire spread through him, curling his toes and making the hair on the back of his neck stand on end.

Clutching Daniel, Nik pulled their chests together, and in one swift movement, flipped them over. Nik's tight, powerful body was on top of Daniel's now, straddling him, pinning him firmly.

A pang of fear struck Daniel as he realized they weren't exactly concealed with all the artificial lighting. "What if somebody sees?"

"Nobody cares," Nik said, smiling wider, teeth insanely pointed, and flicked his tongue in the corner of his mouth.

Cool fingers stroked up under Daniel's shirt, quelling his apprehension, as Nik kissed him again, mouth open and running with saliva. Nik tasted faintly of licorice, sweet and fragrant, refreshing as summer rain. Daniel trailed his hands across the smooth hardness of Nik's shoulders, pressed down into his back, tangled up into his hair.

Nik sucked on Daniel's lips, then moved to kiss his jaw, suck his ear, lick his neck.

"I want to eat you up," Nik whispered, sliding fingers across Daniel's belly, deftly unfastening his pants. "I want to drink you down." Slipping a hand into his underwear. "I want to suck you off."

Daniel jerked with pleasure at Nik's touch. Then Nik bit hard into his throat, and Daniel's arousal exploded away into a blinding flash of pain as everything turned cold and dark and numb.

❖

Sunlight sparkled on the water as Daniel came to. Head throbbing, he sat up and groaned, wondering why the hell he had been sleeping on the beach. Blinking at the blinding glare, he realized that he must have passed out. Daniel remembered a hot guy striking up a conversation with him last night but couldn't recall anything else. Except drinking almost an entire six-pack of beer by himself.

Daniel rubbed his face, dislodging a crust of sand on his cheek, and tried to get to his feet. His stomach flipped with all the moving around and the waves made him want to throw up. He closed his eyes, but blackness spun in his head, so he opened them again. Breathing deeply, he sat very still for several minutes, watching a lifeguard unfold umbrellas to plant them in a line of reserved chairs. The man was edging closer, so to avoid a possible hassle, Daniel forced himself to stand, and walked slowly back to his hotel.

❖

Coffee and food settled his stomach; thankfully, he only had a splitting headache not a full-blown hangover. After a shower, Daniel spent the rest of the afternoon walking the beach, wondering whether… whatshisname…Nik, that was it. Wondering whether Nik would acknowledge Daniel if they ran into one another. Because Daniel had the feeling that they had hit it off, and he was hoping, probably in vain, that they could maybe hook up before Daniel had to go back home.

The sun started to go down, and as Daniel searched, speculation turned to need, and hope bloomed into longing. Bits and pieces of the night before flickered in Daniel's memory. The way Nik had approached him. The way Nik had caught him when he started to fall. The way Nik had—had Nik kissed him? With a rush, Daniel thought he remembered Nik brushing his lips, soft and enticing, right before Daniel had stupidly passed out.

The moon rose, and in the glare of the hotels Daniel saw someone walking toward him. It had to be Nik. A gust of excitement filled Daniel, his heartbeat quickened, and he grinned, surprised at how happy he felt.

"You came back," Nik said. His eyebrows knitted together and indecipherable emotion moved across his face.

"Of course I did."

The look puzzled Daniel. Uncertainty brought nervousness. Nervousness led to fear. And all Daniel's insecurities swooped in. Daniel had been drunk. Nik hadn't kissed him. It was all drunken fantasy.

No one Daniel wanted ever wanted him.

"I mean, you know, I like to sit out here and watch the ocean."

Nik's eyes went flat as he nodded and continued walking.

"Wait." A mad hope filled Daniel and he caught Nik's arm, stepping around to block his path. "I wanted to see you again."

Nik frowned.

Daniel's heart leapt in his throat. Going for broke, he said, "I want to be with you." Then he lost all his words and dropped his head as fear choked him.

Nik put his fingers beneath Daniel's chin and gently lifted his face. Their bodies were so close, and the fragrance of licorice grazed Daniel. Nik's fingers slid up the edge of Daniel's jaw, stroked the side of his neck, as Nik's other hand rose to touch his cheek. Nik traced Daniel's lips with his thumb as his gaze swept across him, settled on his mouth.

Heart pounding, Daniel looked into the midnight of Nik's eyes and felt himself diminish, absorbed into Nik, consumed by Nik.

Reeling, Daniel sighed as Nik leaned in and kissed him.

That mouth, so sweet, so familiar, stealing his breath and taking his strength, making his knees go weak. They had kissed before. Daniel remembered. And this felt like coming home, this felt like love and family and finally belonging.

As their lips parted, Daniel whispered, "Let me stay with you."

Smiling, Nik took his hand and pulled him along the beach, south past the pier to the shadows of the park that closed at nightfall. Away from any people, where there was no manmade illumination, only the faint glow of the moon.

The shadow of Nik dropped gracefully and pulled Daniel down on top of him. Daniel caught himself, palms and knees landing on a blanket or a towel, something soft and free of sand. Nik's hands ran up

Daniel's sides, curled around his back, tugging his shirt out of his pants. Fingers slipped under the fabric and drifted across Daniel's flesh.

The need and longing built within him as Nik awakened every nerve, every inch of his body. Gripping the edge, Nik pulled Daniel's shirt over his head, and he ducked, lifting one arm, then the other to allow it. Arousal throbbed through Daniel. His brief experiences with sex had been nothing like this, never this powerful, never this deeply felt.

Nik was breathing hard. The trail of his fingers caused tiny shivers along Daniel's skin. A shudder ran though him, making his arms tremble as they held his weight above Nik. Hands explored Daniel's ribs, traced his spine, then tracked to the small of his back where a palm pushed gently down. Their hips met and Daniel felt the strength of Nik's arousal, the hardness that Nik pushed against him. Heat surged through Daniel, a flame that began in his groin and spread outward, through his legs, up his torso, into his arms that he could not stop from shaking. Daniel's need was so intense that it scared him. He wanted it so much that it paralyzed him, the fear that the act would come and go and all of this would be lost. Daniel hovered on the brink, wishing that he could stop time and remain on this edge forever, feeling wanted and needed, belonging here in Nik's arms, with Nik craving him and never letting go.

Moving again, Nik cupped his butt, kneading into the muscle there. Nik's breath came fast and short, and the sweet perfume of licorice engulfed Daniel as Nik began to move beneath him, rubbing his pelvis up into Daniel. His body answered, grinding down into Nik.

His hand came around between them, and Nik worked open the button of Daniel's pants, then caught the tab of the zipper and pulled it down. As they moved together, Nik slid his fingers along Daniel's belly, found the band of his underwear, and slipped under to search his heat.

Daniel gasped as Nik's cool fingers curled around him, hard and slick with arousal. Panting with every stroke, Nik ran his other hand to Daniel's shoulder and drew him down, collapsing Daniel's arms and crushing their chests together.

Their mouths connected, and Nik's tongue thrust up into Daniel, moaning with the kiss, then sucking Daniel's tongue deep into him as he nudged their bodies over, throwing his weight to roll on top of Daniel.

Skilled fingers took Daniel higher, to the brink of orgasm as Nik kissed along his cheek and jaw, nipping his ear, then gliding to his neck. Nik lingered there, gently gripping the flesh in his teeth and drawing a suction that Daniel, vaguely in the back of his mind, knew would leave a mark. Shuddering, Nik drifted lower, licking along the line of Daniel's collarbone, flicking his tongue against Daniel's nipple before taking it into his mouth and sucking.

Delight burst from Daniel's throat, a wordless sound as pleasure surged within him.

Nik laughed softly. Then his mouth slipped down Daniel's stomach and abdomen to engulf him, swallowing him up. Succulent lips and a nimble tongue that lapped and curled and swirled around, doing things Daniel had never imagined. It was more than he could stand. Everything coiled within Daniel and he grabbed Nik's head, tangling his fingers in that thick hair, finding the rhythm they had shared and thrusting up into Nik. Daniel cried out as the orgasm came hard, exploding out of him and into Nik. And Nik sucked deeply, somehow making the climax last and last.

Daniel trembled, mind returning from delirium, and realized that he was completely naked. Nik had removed Daniel's pants and was softly kissing his pelvic bone.

"You're so sweet," Nik murmured. "So rich."

Then he slid up and kissed Daniel's mouth.

The exhilarating flavor of Nik mingled with the heady taste of Daniel's own pleasure. With a rush of desire, Daniel sucked on Nik's tongue, making Nik moan. Daniel drank him in, wanting something of Nik, swallowing his saliva, his essence, joining their fluids inside him.

Kissing Nik deeply so that the moment would never end. Yet the bliss dwindled and sadness filled Daniel.

"Please," he whispered, as Nik kissed his neck again. "Please don't leave me."

"I must." Nik had the lobe of Daniel's ear in his teeth.

"No," Daniel said. "You can take me. Take me with you."

"I can't."

"I'm so lonely. So alone. You're the only one who has ever wanted me." Daniel realized he was crying; he took Nik's face in his hands and pulled his mouth back up to kiss his lips. "Please, let me stay with you." Daniel was begging now. Somehow, his entire life had fallen away and

nothing seemed more important than convincing Nik to let him stay.
"Please. I'll do anything."

"It's too dangerous," Nik said.

"I don't care."

"You could die."

"Then let me die like this, in your arms, touching you, loving
you."

He struggled with Nik's shirt, feeling the passion rise in him again,
wanting more, wanting to bind Nik to him somehow. Daniel fought
with the buttons, but couldn't make his hands work, so he gave up and
yanked the shirt over Nik's head.

Daniel reached down to unfasten Nik's pants, fumbled with the
belt buckle, twisted at the button, tugged desperately at the zipper. Nik
stopped kissing him to help. Then Daniel felt the sleekness of Nik's
naked body, pressing his weight along Daniel, sliding against him as he
licked into his mouth. Daniel ran his hands against the smooth flesh of
his butt and squeezed.

Their breathing quickened. Their bodies shared a movement again,
matching cadence.

Daniel trailed his fingers down Nik's side, and Nik raised his hips
to encourage Daniel to slide his hand between them. A sharp breath
greeted Daniel's touch and Nik arched his back, pushing against him,
stiff and uncut. The silky skin rolled up and down, up and down,
growing slippery in Daniel's grip.

Moving faster, Nik panted into Daniel's mouth, abandoning the
kiss to focus on Daniel's stroke.

"I love you," Daniel sighed. He was incredibly turned on yet
couldn't deny the ache that filled him, the need not to lose Nik again.
Daniel's mind could make no sense of the words, but his heart had
taken over. "Nik, I love you."

"You only think you love me," Nik said. His voice was rough with
arousal, but his manner changed. His body slowed and his mouth moved
gently all over Daniel, licking his neck, tickling the sensitive skin of
his inner elbow, lifting his hand to nibble at the soft flesh between his
thumb and index finger, kissing the hollow of his throat.

Curling his arms around Nik's neck, Daniel tangled his legs with
Nik's, weaving them together, clinging to him.

Nik inhaled deeply, breathing Daniel in as if he were life-giving air, taking long tastes of his flesh as if it were a delicacy, stroking his fingers along Daniel's skin as if he were a joy to touch. Nik softened and slowed and he kissed Daniel with unexpected tenderness. Their mouths joined and their tongues met and a new luxurious rhythm moved their bodies. A tempo not merely of sex, but of need and seduction and adoration. Nik was about to make love to him.

"Daniel, Daniel," Nik murmured. Then he nibbled and sucked again at Daniel's throat.

The thick rapture of the moment and the warm velvet of being loved drove away all rationale from Daniel's mind. He arched his neck and put his hand on the back of Nik's head, pulling him harder against him and moaned, "Yes, Nikky, yes. Drink me. Devour me."

Nik stopped, lips trembling against Daniel's throat. Nik moved to kiss him and Daniel felt sharp teeth, tasted blood—his own blood on Nik's tongue, and swallowed it.

Then Nik's mouth was on his throat again, biting hard, demanding and insistent and consuming. It felt as if a hot needle were being drawn out of Daniel. The sensation flared, but Nik shifted his hips, spreading Daniel's thighs and shoving them up. The fire in Daniel's neck was replaced by the push of Nik entering him. Prepared and eager, Daniel opened to receive him as Nik thrust all the way in, then out, then in again. Losing himself to Nik, Daniel felt reality grow distant. Everything melted into a feeling of completion, as though they were a single body climbing toward orgasm.

Dizzy and light-headed, Daniel watched stars swim in the blackness behind his eyes. For a long time, he floated in the euphoria of love, nestled in kisses, swooning in affection, drowning in the depths of Nik's need for him. Knowing that he had found the one place where he truly, finally, had always belonged, Daniel whispered, "Take me, Nikky. Make me yours."

Somewhere, from far away, Daniel felt Nik caress his face. Daniel kissed Nik's palm and found it wet. He licked at it as Nik moved his arm, guiding his wrist to Daniel's lips where his tongue met the open wound.

Nik was giving himself to Daniel, offering him his blood. When it trickled into his mouth, he almost gagged. It was sticky and so much stronger than the flavor of his own blood he had gotten from Nik's tongue, heavier and syrupy and metallic. But Daniel sealed his lips over the gash, pushing away his nausea, and drew, swallowing before he could taste it.

Nik groaned in his arms, making a guttural sound of ecstasy that Daniel wanted to hear again. He sucked hard, and Nik groaned and writhed on top of him, grinding his hips against Daniel, digging his fingers into his flesh, gripping him tightly as the movements became quick and strong.

The blood flowed down Daniel's throat like lava, blazing a path through him. His head cleared and all the sensations blurring around him snapped into sharp focus. His vision returned and the night seemed not so dark. The pain wasn't pain at all, but rather an intense pleasure. Nik was naked above him, muscles rippling, chest covered in a sheen of sweat, head thrown back as he vigorously pounded into him. One sinewy arm beside them on the ground for support, the other across Daniel's body, leading up to Daniel's mouth where Nik's wrist was securely anchored in his teeth. Their bodies locked together as Nik drove into him and Daniel rocked upward to deepen each rapturous thrust.

A desperate sound reached Daniel's ears and he realized he was making it, a needy cry of bliss from somewhere low in his throat that found its way out around the blood, as he felt a thin line dribble down his chin.

Then gasping with abandon, Nik bent forward to find Daniel's neck and sank his teeth into him, biting with a force that would have been agony had Daniel not been already primed with the ecstasy of Nik's blood.

Clutching Nik's head hard against him with one hand, Daniel gripped Nik's wrist with the other and gnawed into it. As deeply as Nik drank, Daniel matched him, feeling oblivion close in then recede, close in then recede, like waves crashing on the shore. He listened to the moist sounds of sucking as they joined and became one blood. Nik moaned with pleasure, and Daniel took satisfaction in having such power over his desire.

Then Daniel felt the climax rise within him. Nik was thrusting faster, sucking hard. And Daniel felt the need build and grow until he could stand it no more.

Daniel's heartbeat throbbed in his ears, pounded with the strength of two hearts together, hammering in his head, rushing through his veins.

The orgasm exploded out of him. Stars burst into brilliance as Daniel came. Nik cried out against his neck, shaking, and Daniel felt his final plunge deep within him as Daniel's pleasure rushed on. White-hot, blinding rapture pulled Daniel into a bottomless river of blood.

And his humanity disappeared.

Lost forever in an endless swirl of mind-blowing, memory-obliterating ecstasy.

FIVE GAY VAMPIRE SHOWS THAT WERE NEVER GREENLIT
STEVE BERMAN

1. For MTV

> ANNOUNCER
>
> Tonight, on the finale of *Goth Band Guerillas*, the lead singers of the three remaining bands—Evensong, Ichor Drunk, and Varney—must spend the night in a hotel room rumored to be where Sid Vicious slashed his wrists over Nancy. Will Mr. Abaiser (Evensong) continue to diva out over being denied a threesome with Carey Black (Varney) and the androgynous Dram (Ichor Drunk)? And when Carey and Dram decide to "sleepwalk" their way into a blood bank heist to promote their new duet, will the security guards dare watch the high jinks on the closed circuit television? Rated TV-14 for D, L, and S.

INT. *GOTH BAND GUERILLAS* CONFESSIONAL - NIGHT

MR. ABAISER speaks into the camera.

> MR. ABAISER
>
> Posers. Bloody posers, that's what they are. And pairin' up? I mean, nobody just has twosomes anymore.

INT. BLOOD BANK FREEZER VAULT - NIGHT

CAREY and DRAM rip open a bag of blood and splash each other's bare chests.

CAREY
That better be something rare. Bombay at least.

DRAM
Trust me. It's Kidd. Now start licking.

CAREY
If I find out it's O neg, you're gonna be bent over the rail, bitch.

2. For Wilde! Network

New to the Wilde! Network: *WeHo Bloodlines*, the series that takes a bite out of steamy nightcrawlers of West Hollywood's hottest clubs. Think barebacking and bumps of Tina are the worst things facing the gym rats and vapid twinks? Think again. When Stoker and his gang of thirsty vampires decide to prowl the alleys and dance floors, no neck is safe. Zach Nefro sizzles as the centuries-old Stoker whose lust (and bloodlust) never are fulfilled. Former porn star Brick Haüs also stars as Timothy van Helsing, the last descendent of a family of vampire hunters. Can Timothy deny his growing ardor for Stoker? Will Stoker drain WeHo dry before moving on to P-town?

EXT. WHITE SWALLOW BAR - NIGHT

TIMOTHY VAN HELSING lingers outside the bar door. He's smoking cigarettes.

TIMOTHY (VOICE-OVER)
Hunting bloodsuckers at the clubs is never easy. Hiding a stake when you're supposed to wear tight clothes…all the cologne overpowering garlic…Great-grandpa never had these problems.

INT. STOKER'S BASEMENT APARTMENT

STOKER and his latest TRICK/VICTIM open the french doors leading to the bedroom. Shot of luxurious-looking bed.

TRICK/VICTIM
Wow. Are those silk sheets?

STOKER
Satin. And a dangerously high thread count.

TRICK/VICTIM
Do you have any poppers? Or Ambien? I can't fall asleep after fucking without Ambien.

STOKER
Trust me. You'll sleep like the dead after I'm finished with you.

3. **For Bravo**

Cast Blog for *Casket Charette:* Repp Beir

As a native Trentonian I am so damn proud to share my candid thoughts regarding *Casket Charette.*

While New Jersey might be known more for its official devil than its vital role in the Funeral Industry as the lead supplier of formaldehyde, Trenton is a bustling city with a nightlife that attracts goth kids from as far away as Philadelphia.

The series follows thirteen of us—YUMs, young urban morticians—while exploring the Trenton social scene. Having to live in a funeral home during the thirty days of shooting will be exhausting. One of the reasons I enrolled in mortuary school was to avoid people (the other reason was because I enjoyed painting the faces of my mother and father while they slept). So while we might all seem likeable on the surface, no one really cares about each other—we all doing this to win that trip to the Carpathian Mountains and $100,000. So, there will be drama.

I hope to breathe new life into casket design. I'm thinking glass. Enough wood. That's so Old World. Stained glass. Mosaic glass. For Jews, bits of the wineglass they stomp when they get married. Tinted glass for the goths, so if they do vamp out after dropping, they won't worry about the sun. Glass. It's about *seeing* the real you buried.

4. For The N.

Night Shift: Ned Mack is looking for summer work in the sleepy town of Carmilla, California. But few places are willing to hire a morbid, all-in-black boy who doodles dead high school jocks with Xs for eyes. Then, while urban exploring the local haunted house with friends, Ned meets Carmilla's newest occupants, the Karnsteins, a vampire family. The Karnsteins are desperate to find a human they can trust to watch over them as they sleep, so Ned is offered the job. Of course, Ned's preacher father doesn't like his son working late hours. And what happens when the Karnsteins' teenage son, Edward, develops a crush on a "breather"? Ned never knew growing up alive could ever be so crazy.

EXT. STREET RUNNING THROUGH CARMILLA - NIGHT

NED and EDWARD walking.

> EDWARD
> So is he like a fire-and-brimstone sort of dad?

> NED
> Sometimes. I wish he'd take up a more interesting religion.
> Like snake handling. Or voodoo.

[Insert laugh track]

EDWARD

Then he'd catch you playing with dolls.

NED

He already has. I was ten.

[Insert laugh track]

EDWARD

My dad keeps on trying to set me up with this succubus. I mean, she's okay. Snappy dresser. Jewish, too. He doesn't understand that I like—

NED

Blood?

EDWARD

Duh. I was going to say boys.

[Insert laugh track]

Ned and Edward kiss.

5. For Comedy Central

Don't Be Batty

Pilot Episode Summary
A stowaway aboard a Caribbean cruise ship, Bastian is a Jamaican vampire who keeps trying to seduce the male guests. Effeminate, Bastian has the world's worst gaydar, and lisps inappropriate remarks to honeymooning hunks. He finally meets the one other gay man aboard ship, but on their "date night" the guy turns out to be a Klansman and the romantic dinner by candlelight is actually a portable burning cross in his stateroom, which scares Bastian off.

Trivia/Allusions

The cruise ship is named the *Demeter*, which was the ship Dracula arrived on.

Quotes

Never saw the ocean before. My wife and I are from Oklahoma.
—Husband

Oooh, I just love a redneck. Though I have to watch nibbling around your beard.—Bastian waving aside Husband's Wife.

Sir, are you a passenger?—Cabin Steward
I'm the night watchman.—Bastian
[As a whisper] *I like the night life and watching for men.*—Bastian

CONTRIBUTORS

JOSEPH BANETH ALLEN grew up in Camp Lejeune, North Carolina. His non-fiction has been published in *OMNI*, *Popular Science*, *Final Frontier*, *Astronomy*, *Florida Living*, *Dog Fancy*, *Pet Life*, *eBay Magazine*, and many others. He now lives in Jacksonville, Florida, where he continues to write fiction and non-fiction.

STEVE BERMAN's combination of gay sensibility and the fantastical has earned him finalist nods for the Andre Norton Award, the Gaylactic Spectrum Awards, and the Lambda Literary Awards. His boy-meets-ghost novel, *Vintage*, made the Rainbow List of recommended queer-themed titles by the American Library Association. Recent sales include a lesbian retelling of Swan Lake for *The Beastly Bride: Tales of the Animal People* (Viking) and another gay vampire story for the forthcoming young adult anthology *Teeth* (HarperCollins).

'NATHAN BURGOINE lives in Ottawa, Canada, with his husband Daniel. His work appears in *Fool For Love*, *I Like It Like That*, *I Do 2*, and *Tented*. You can find him online at n8an.livejournal.com. He promises not to bite.

S.A. GARCIA can never decide between red or white. Nor can the always pondering life's mysteries S.A. decide between creating visual art or word art. Back in the misty past S.A.'s teachers waged war over those diverse skills until it felt easier to succumb and create both. S.A. spins the talents in between cooking, drinking, sitting before the computer far more than healthy, and growing legal herbs and oddly named flowers. Good thing S.A.'s eternal partner is a successful visual arts/photography professor. Their hungry house bunnies appreciate one steady artistic income paying for the baby carrots, parsley, and kale.

TODD GREGORY is the author of the novels *Every Frat Boy Wants It* and *What Every Frat Boy Wants*. His anthology *Rough Trade* was a finalist for the Lambda Literary Award for Best Gay Erotica of 2009. His novella "Blood on the Moon" was published in the anthology *Midnight Hungers*, and he is currently working on a novel, *A Vampire's Heart*, which continues the story. "Bloodletting" is the first chapter of that novel.

Winner of the 2008 Seattle Erotic Arts Festival's short story competition, JAY LYGON has published over fifty short stories in anthologies such as *Inside Him*, *Gods and Myths*, *Bonded*, *Toy Box: Floggers*, *Toy Box: Quiches*, and *Torqued Tales*. His novels *Chaos Magic*, *Love Runes*, and *Personal Demons* (Torquere Press) have been praised as "Magical realism, unlike any other BDSM novel ever written." Jay lives in Los Angeles, on the 405 freeway. Visit Jay at www.JayLygonWrites.com.

JEFF MANN's books include two collections of poetry, *Bones Washed with Wine* and *On the Tongue*; a book of personal essays, *Edge: Travels of an Appalachian Leather Bear*; a novella, "Devoured," included in *Masters of Midnight: Erotic Tales of the Vampire*; a collection of poetry and memoir, *Loving Mountains, Loving Men*; and a volume of short fiction, *A History of Barbed Wire*, winner of a Lambda Literary Award. He teaches creative writing at Virginia Tech in Blacksburg, Virginia.

WAYNE MANSFIELD was born and raised in rural Western Australia. He left home at seventeen to attend university in the state capital, Perth. Since graduating he has been published many times, both in print and online, in the U.S., the U.K., and Australia. Most notably, his story "Highway Patrol" (Eternal Press) has been a best seller. He also has many stories published with Torquere Press, Damnation Books and StarBooks Press. Find out more and check out his blog containing a full history of publishing credits at waynemansfieldwrites.weebly.com.

F. A. POLLARD (fa.pollard@live.com) has had stories published in over a dozen magazines and anthologies, including *The Ultimate*

Zombie, *Chilled To The Bone*, and *The Year's Best Horror Stories: XXII*. Most recently, "Game Boyz" appeared in the anthology *Boy Crazy: Coming Out Erotica*, edited by Richard Labonté. Current projects include a speculative-fiction novel entitled *Shattered Mirrors*.

MAX REYNOLDS is the pseudonym of a well-known East Coast writer and journalist. Reynolds writes extensively in both the mainstream and queer press, with a focus on national politics and sexual politics. Reynolds's gay erotica has appeared in *His Underwear: An Erotic Anthology*, *Frat Boys*, *BloodLust: Erotic Vampire Tales*, *Rough Trade*, *A View to a Thrill*, and *Men of Mystery*, among others. "Possession: A Priest's Tale" is one in a series of stories featuring Reynolds's vampire protagonist Raul Garcia. Reynolds's forthcoming novel, *At the Blue House*, also stars Raul Garcia.

JEFFREY A. RICKER lives in St. Louis with his partner and two dogs. His writing has appeared in the anthologies *Paws and Reflect* and *Fool for Love: New Gay Fiction*. He is working on a novel and dislikes referring to himself in the third person. Follow his blog at jeffreyricker.wordpress.com.

ROB ROSEN, author of the novels *Sparkle: The Queerest Book You'll Ever Love* and the Lambda Literary Award–nominated *Divas Las Vegas*, has had short stories featured in more than 100 anthologies, most notably the erotic collections: *Best Gay Romance* (2007, 2008, 2009, & 2010), *Ride Me Cowboy*, *Surfer Boys*, *Truckers*, *Frat Sex 2*, and *Ultimate Gay Erotica* (2008 & 2009); and the speculative collections: *Southern Comfort*, *Hell's Hangmen: Horror in the Old West*, *Our Shadows Speak*, *Damned in Dixie: Southern Horror*, *Twisted Fayrie Tales*, *Don't Turn the Lights On*, *Bloody October*, and *Black Box*. Please visit him at www.therobrosen.com.

LAWRENCE SCHIMEL has published over 100 books as author or anthologist, including *The Drag Queen of Elfland* (Circlet), *The Future is Queer* (Arsenal Pulp), *Things Invisible to See: Lesbian and Gay Tales of Magic Realism* (Circlet), *Two Boys in Love* (Seventh Window), and *Fairy Tales for Writers* (A Midsummer

Night's Press). He has twice won the Lambda Literary Award, for *First Person Queer* (Arsenal Pulp) and *PoMoSexuals* (Cleis), and has also won the Spectrum, the Independent Publisher Book Award, the Rhysling, and other awards. He lives in Madrid, Spain, where he works as a Spanish->English translator.

DAMIAN SERBU lives in Chicago with his partner of seventeen years, where their two dogs are firmly in control of the household. After earning a Ph.D. in history, he now teaches at the collegiate level. His love for vampires—and all things horrific—fused together with his academic training to inspire his first novel, *The Vampire's Angel*, which is set during the French Revolution. A childhood nightmare led to his second novel, *Secrets in the Attic*. Come visit him at www.DamianSerbu.com!

NATHAN SIMS's short fiction has appeared in the anthologies *Blood Fruit* and *Queer Gothic*, both from QueeredFiction. It can also be found in the July 2010 issue of *Collective Fallout Magazine* and online at Velvet Mafia: Dangerous Queer Fiction. He lives with his partner across the street from Washington, DC.

KYLE STONE first appeared as the author of the scorching SM/SF erotic adventure novels *The Initiation of PB500* and *The Citadel*, which have been labeled "cult classics." Four other novels and several short story collections soon followed. Stone's short stories have appeared in many gay magazines and anthologies.

SHEPHARD SUMMERS is a writer living in Southern California, sharing his life with his husband, three quirky cats, and a great group of friends—all providing endless inspiration. When not writing, he indulges his other passions, theatre and travel. His favorite quote: "You have to pick up the mantle. Whatever your mantle is in life, whatever you've been dealt, you have to pick it up and wear it well. Be your authentic self; that's the toughest thing to do."—Jim Carrey.

Born in '53 in New Haven, Connecticut, CHARLES TAUTVID left in '73 for the Air Force, spending time in Thailand, England, and

Omaha, Nebraska, where in a men's bar he discovered his true nature. Leaving the USAF, he resided in San Francisco and stood in that candlelight vigil mourning the slain Harvey Milk. In '89, he moved to Manhattan. Joining the GLBV, he published their monthly newsletter. From New York, he migrated to Ft Lauderdale, Florida, where he works as a programmer and writes in his spare time.

DAVEM VERNE has never spent the night in a Medieval Celtic oratory, but his love of Irishmen and Irish history inspired him to write "The Celtic Confessional." Since 1995, he has devoted his pen to erotic literature and the revelation of physical desire on paper. His stories have lent themselves to fanciful journeys in time and around the world, secret adventures in the college dorm, and wild obsessions with neighborhood men. Mr. Verne's stories have been printed in numerous anthologies including *Fratsex*, *Dorm Porn*, and *Boy Crazy*. He is pleased to finally take a bite out of the Vampire genre.

XAN WEST is the pseudonym of an NYC BDSM/sex educator and writer. "Willing" was previously published in *Leathermen*. Xan's story "First Time Since," won honorable mention for the 2008 National Leather Association's John Preston Short Fiction Award. Xan's erotica can be found in *Best SM Erotica* Volumes 2 & 3, *Hurts So Good*, *Love at First Sting*, *Leathermen*, *Men on the Edge*, *Backdraft*, *Frenzy*, *Best Gay Erotica 2009*, *DADDIES*, *Pleasure Bound*, *SexTime*, *Cruising for Bad Boys*, and *Biker Boys*. Xan also wrote the introduction to *Wired Hard 4*. Xan wants to hear from you, and can be reached at Xan_West@yahoo.com.

Books Available From Bold Strokes Books

Head Trip by D.L. Line. Shelby Hutchinson, a young computer professional, can't wait to take a virtual trip. She soon learns that chasing spies through Cold War Europe might be a great adventure, but nothing is ever as easy as it seems—especially love. (978-1-60282-187-3)

Desire by Starlight by Radclyffe. The only thing that might possibly save romance author Jenna Hardy from dying of boredom during a summer of forced R&R is a dalliance with Gardiner Davis, the local vet—even if Gard is as unimpressed with Jenna's charms as she appears to be with Jenna's fame. (978-1-60282-188-0)

River Walker by Cate Culpepper. Grady Wrenn, a cultural anthropologist, and Elena Montalvo, a spiritual healer, must find a way to end the River Walker's murderous vendetta—and overcome a maze of cultural barriers to find each other. (978-1-60282-189-7)

Blood Sacraments, edited by Todd Gregory. In these tales of the gay vampire, some of today's top erotic writers explore the duality of blood lust coupled with passion and sensuality. (978-1-60282-190-3)

Mesmerized by David-Matthew Barnes. Through her close friendship with Brodie and Lance, Serena Albright learns about the many forms of love and finds comfort for the grief and guilt she feels over the brutal death of her older brother, the victim of a hate crime. (978-1-60282-191-0)

Whatever Gods May Be by Sophia Kell Hagin. Army sniper Jamie Gwynmorgan expects to fight hard for her country and her future. What she never expects is to find love. (978-1-60282-183-5)

nevermore by Nell Stark and Trinity Tam. In this sequel to *everafter*, Vampire Valentine Darrow and Were Alexa Newland confront a mysterious disease that ravages the shifter population of New York City. (978-1-60282-184-2)

Playing the Player by Lea Santos. Grace Obregon is beautiful, vulnerable, and exactly the kind of woman Madeira Pacias usually avoids, but when Madeira rescues Grace from a traffic accident, escape is impossible. (978-1-60282-185-9)

Midnight Whispers: The Blake Danzig Chronicles by Curtis Christopher Comer. Paranormal investigator Blake Danzig, star of the syndicated show *Haunted California* and owner of Danzig Paranormal Investigations, has been able to see and talk to the dead since he was a small boy, but when he gets too close to a psychotic spirit, all hell breaks loose. (978-1-60282-186-6)

The Long Way Home by Rachel Spangler. They say you can't go home again, but Raine St. James doesn't know why anyone would want to. When she is forced to accept a job in the town she's been publicly bashing for the last decade, she has to face down old hurts and the woman she left behind. (978-1-60282-178-1)

Water Mark by J.M. Redmann. PI Micky Knight's professional and personal lives are torn asunder by Katrina and its aftermath. She needs to solve a murder and recapture the woman she lost—while struggling to simply survive in a world gone mad. (978-1-60282-179-8)

Picture Imperfect by Lea Santos. Young love doesn't always stand the test of time, but Deanne is determined to get her marriage to childhood sweetheart Paloma back on the road to happily ever after, by way of Memory Lane—and Lover's Lane. (978-1-60282-180-4)

The Perfect Family by Kathryn Shay. A mother and her gay son stand hand in hand as the storms of change engulf their perfect family and the life they knew. (978-1-60282-181-1)

Raven Mask by Winter Pennington. Preternatural Private Investigator (and closeted werewolf) Kassandra Lyall needs to solve a murder and protect her Vampire lover Lenorre, Countess Vampire of Oklahoma—all while fending off the advances of the local werewolf alpha female. (978-1-60282-182-8)

The Devil be Damned by Ali Vali. The fourth book in the best-selling Cain Casey Devil series. (978-1-60282-159-0)